COPPERHEAD COVE

To my big brother, Rog, and the Holler Gang in Burkesville, KY.
You were my inspiration and spirit during the writing of this novel.
R.I.P., Rog.

ALSO BY RON PARHAM

Molly's Moon

COPPERHEAD COVE

RON PARHAM

P
Pen-L Publishing
Fayetteville, AR
Pen-L.com

PROLOGUE

It was a different world than when he was young, the days when you could whack somebody and get away with it, even gain the envy and respect of the other wise guys, maybe even move up in the chain of command. But now? Hell no. Organized crime was underground, invisible—corporate, for God's sake. Anthony "Two Toes" Tonelli paced back and forth, mumbling to himself, occasionally slamming the wall with his open palm. He glared out the window of his sixty-second floor office overlooking Michigan Avenue.

All those empty suits down there, they don't give a damn about us anymore. They don't even think we exist. Television, movies, books, they all make fun of us now, write us off as a bunch of cafones, an embarrassment.

He stared out at the Chicago skyline, hands laced behind his back, then turned around and paced back to the other side of his well-appointed office. He was a top corporate lawyer, a respected pillar of the Chicago community, a donor to many charities, but in his heart and soul he was the Don of the Southside Family. He was the boss, the capo.

Tonelli looked at his reflection in the floor to ceiling window. He brushed his thinning, graying hair back and smiled. He saw a large man who filled out his double-breasted suit but carried it well. His smile turned to a frown as he peered down at Michigan Avenue again.

I'll show those jamooks that we're still around, still able to take care of our business, and put the fear back in all those empty suits down there in the street.

He had to do something, but what could he do in today's world that wouldn't bring the wrath of the FBI down on his head? The friggin' feds had no respect for them anymore, just a minor inconvenience in a world of terrorism. Wise guys were ancient history, little ants for the FBI to crush under their shoes. He pressed the button on his phone.

"Maria, tell Frankie to come up to my office."

"Yes, Mr. Tonelli," his secretary said, smacking her gum into the phone. "He may be at lunch."

"Just get him. And Maria, what's the date?"

"The day or the date?" she said, smacking on her gum again.

"The date, goddammit!" *I'm gonna shove that gum up her ass one of these days.*

"Well, it's May twentieth. Do you want the day or date?"

Tonelli punched the button to end the call. *I'm surrounded by morons.*

Tonelli began pacing again, his mind racing from one idea to the next. Goddammit! He was a crime boss, he had obligations. He had to make examples when someone crossed him, had to keep their respect, goddammit!

"Mr. Tonelli, Frankie's on the line."

Tonelli punched the lit button. "Frankie, where the hell are you?"

"I'm at lunch, boss. I didn't think you needed me for a while."

"Well, get your ass back up here. Five minutes." Tonelli slammed the phone down.

He began pacing and mumbling, waiting for the young punk to show up. He was just about to call his secretary when her voice came over the phone.

"Mr. Tonelli, Frankie's here."

Tonelli pushed the button. "Get his ass in here!"

Frankie Farmer walked into Tonelli's office, smelling of garlic, using his sleeve to wipe marinara sauce from his chin.

"What's up, boss?" he said, picking his teeth with a toothpick.

"Get that goddamned toothpick out of your mouth, you peasant!"

"What? Oh, sorry boss. What's up?"

Tonelli stared at his son-in-law, his blond hair and blue eyes and skinny ass a constant irritant. What his daughter saw in this loser he'd never understand. *And where did he get that Podunk name of Farmer? How can I get any respect when my only daughter is married to someone named Farmer? Goddammit!*

"What's up? I'll tell you what's up, you friggin' imbecile. You remember that bozo coach from Podunk U? The one that YOU said you convinced to shave points last March? You remember him?"

"Podunk U?" Frankie said, scratching his head. "Oh," he laughed, "you mean Midwestern University. That's funny, boss."

Tonelli stared at him. *I should shoot this bonehead right now, right here.*

"Did your mother drop you on your head when you were a baby?" Tonelli said, towering over the younger man.

"Uh, I don't think so," Frankie said, looking up nervously. "'Course, I was a little baby, so can't really remember."

"Shut up! Shut the fuck up!" Tonelli rubbed his graying temples and closed his eyes.

Frankie stepped back. "Okay, boss."

"What was the guy's name?"

"The guy? Oh, yeah. Williams," Frankie said. "Jerry Joe Williams. Why?"

Tonelli opened his eyes and glared at the young wannabe thug. "Because he didn't do what he said he was gonna do, and he took our money . . . my money!"

"Well, boss, I hate to differ with you, but—"

"You hate to differ with me? Is that what you just said?" Tonelli's eyes were blazing.

"Uh, well, yeah, 'cause he did bench his best player in the final period against St. Johns."

"And why did he do that?" Tonelli said, taking a step toward Frankie.

"Well, I guess because he fouled out." Frankie took a step backward, wiping sweat from his forehead.

"Exactly, he fouled out. Did the coach tell him to foul out?"

"I don't know, maybe," Frankie said. "Anyway, the guy couldn't score anymore, so—"

"Shut up! The coach didn't do what he told us he would do. You know why? The kid that replaced his star player scored twenty points in the fourth quarter! They covered the spread because some dipshit second stringer wanted to be a star. Where was the goddamned coach?"

"Hmm. Never thought about that."

"You know how much we lost on that one game? That one game that we thought we had in the bag, that we paid that idiot coach fifty large to make sure they didn't cover the spread?"

Frankie shrugged his shoulders.

"I dunno, boss."

Tonelli walked up to Frankie and put his face an inch from his.

"A million, that's how much. We lost a million fucking bucks because one Podunk coach from Podunk wherever couldn't get a Podunk second stringer out of the game." Tonelli stepped back. "What should we do about that, Frankie?"

Frankie put his finger under his collar, pulled it out, and blew out a deep breath.

"I guess we have to talk to him and get our money back?"

Tonelli stared at him, finally throwing his arms up in the air.

"Our money? My money, you friggin' . . . . Talk to him?" His face was deep red, the veins in his neck sticking out like twigs on a branch. "We don't talk to him," Tonelli said, putting his index finger on Frankie's temple. "We pop him! Bada bing, bada boom."

Frankie's eyes bulged. "We . . . we don't do that anymore . . . do we?"

Tonelli calmed down and looked toward his office door.

"C'mere, you little prick," he said, barely audible.

Frankie walked slowly toward his boss, the fear palpable in his eyes.

Tonelli grabbed him by his tie and pulled him close, putting his mouth next to Frankie's ear.

"We ice him and send a message to every other asshole out there that we won't be fucked with."

Frankie gulped some air, his face getting red as the tie tightened around his neck.

"And you're going to arrange it, you and Augie."

"Augie Stellato?" Frankie said, his eyes bulging again. "I thought he was dead." He gasped.

Tonelli let loose of Frankie's tie.

"No, he's not dead, you jamook. He's just been . . . in hibernation. I'll have him here tomorrow."

"But why me, boss?" Frankie said, rubbing his throat. "I ain't never killed anybody."

"Augie will whack him, but I want you to watch and learn. And be my eyes. Capisci?"

"Okay, boss. Uh, Capeesh."

Tonelli held his ears. "And find out where that Podunk coach is going to be in the next two weeks. We'll ice him when he's alone somewhere."

Frankie swallowed again and began backing out of the office. "Uh, okay."

"One more thing," Tonelli said. "This doesn't get out to anyone, and I mean anyone, and that includes my daughter. Understand?"

He gulped air. "Yeah, boss, er, Dad."

Tonelli tensed as he picked up a stapler and threw it at Frankie's head as the young punk ran out the door, the stapler shattering into tiny pieces against the wall.

"I'm not your dad, you friggin' moron!"

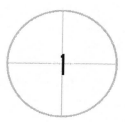

The two brothers sat motionless in the cherry-red bass boat, staring at their respective fishing lines like hawks circling the landscape for their next meal. The water was as still as mirrored glass, with no ripples or abstractions, reflecting the setting sun overhead. The silence was broken only by the occasional song of a bird. They watched their lines on the surface, waiting for a slight dip or movement. The weighted hooks, with tube jig lures, were somewhere close to the bottom where the smallmouth liked to feed.

The stillness was suddenly broken by the whir of a fishing line as something grabbed a hook and ran.

"Got one," Bo Paxton said, jerking his fiberglass rod upwards and back in one smooth motion. "Good sized sucker, too."

Bo fought the fish with an ease and confidence that came with experience. Ethan Paxton watched his older brother with envy and a little bit of annoyance. This was the fifth smallmouth of the day for Bo, and Ethan had only a single, tiny bluegill to show for his efforts.

"Way to go, big brother," he said, with a hint of sarcasm. "You think the bass know I'm from the city? They want nothing to do with me today."

Bo laughed as he reeled the fish in effortlessly, stretching the net out to capture it. He held it up over his head, smiling broadly as only Bo could.

"Good four-pounder, little brother," he said, admiring his catch.

Ethan looked at him with the admiration one would give a professional athlete or world-class musician, witnessing a true professional at work.

"I thought you threw everything back under five pounds," he said, grinning. "Save some for the rest of us, bro."

Bo laughed the way someone would who loved what he did for a living. He was a fishing guide on a lake with a six-hundred-mile shoreline that straddled Kentucky and Tennessee, and he got paid for doing what most men did for relaxation.

"It's your last day, little brother," Bo said, taking the hook out of the bass's mouth and tossing the fish back into the lake. "We can't go home until you land one."

"You gave me a bad rod or something," Ethan said. "Lend me your rod, maybe the fish will think I'm you."

Bo reared his head back and laughed.

"You know how many times I've heard that from my clients? It ain't the pole, son, it's the man on the business end of it that counts." He threw a live cricket at his brother. "Here, use this guy. They like crickets."

Ethan ducked the flying insect and watched it hop on the bottom of the boat.

"You tell me this after we've been out here all day? Where was this information when we first cast out this morning?"

"Well, hell, little brother, I can't do everything for you. Watch and learn, son. Watch and learn."

Ethan put the cricket on his lure and shook his head as Bo cast his line back into the smooth water of Quail Hollow Lake. He enjoyed sitting back and watching his brother, getting more enjoyment out of that than the fishing itself. Bo had such an ease about him, a carefree spirit that Ethan had long admired. He'd been staying with his brother on his little farm in the southern hills of Kentucky for three days, taking a break from business meetings in the Midwest. He had to drive two hundred miles the next day, and he cringed at the thought. Chicago last week, Memphis this week.

"Well, Ethan, you can at least crack me another beer," Bo said. "You're good at that, son."

"Screw you, asshole," he said as he cracked another Pabst Blue Ribbon and handed it to his brother.

Bo laughed the hearty laugh of someone that was content with his life. Ethan envied him for his simple life, his enjoyment of the little things. Ethan had been working in the high-tech world for almost twenty years, traveling the globe and racking up thousands of flight miles. He loved coming to Kentucky just to decompress and clear his mind of the stresses and demands of his job. He suddenly felt empty and sad when he thought about leaving the next morning.

"Sure hate to leave tomorrow, Bo," Ethan said as he made a decent cast into the smooth water.

"I keep tellin' you, little brother, tell them to take that job and shove it. Move back here with me and Kathy and the kids. Hell, with the money you've made you could buy half of Crockett County."

"Yeah, I wish it was that simple, Bo. I've got a son in college, a daughter in private school who'll be going to college in a few months, and a half-million-dollar house to pay for. I can't just say adios and move to the country."

"Well, that's what I did fifteen years ago, and I'm as happy as a pig in slop. Ain't got much money, but son, I've got a hell of a lot more."

Ethan nodded. His brother was the happiest, most secure, and content person he knew. Bo had his own little corner of the world here on Quail Hollow Lake and didn't have a care. He had bills and expenses just like everyone, but he never worried about them like most of the civilized world. Ethan looked at his forty-eight-year-old brother, four years older than himself, sitting there waiting for the next smallmouth bass to hit his line. He loved his brother and his family and respected Bo for chucking it all and moving to this remote, rural area. Bo had been a mover and a shaker himself when he was in his twenties but decided early on that he didn't want that kind of life, so he left California with his wife and two small children, found an eighty-acre plot of land close to the lake, and settled down. Kind of like the Beverly Hillbillies in reverse. Ethan always admired his brother for what he did and thought many times of taking him up on his offer.

"When are we going to head back in, Bo?"

"You gettin' restless, little brother? Anxious to get back to the grind?"

Ethan shook his head. "No, but I have to make a couple of calls tonight. Work stuff. Believe me, I don't want to leave, but it'd be nice if I had a smallmouth to show for being out here all day."

Just then, Ethan felt a tug on his line. He held his six-foot rod in one hand and lifted the six-pound test line with his other, feeling the tension, just as his brother had taught him.

"Gently, son, gently," Bo said. "Don't wanna scare him off."

Ethan waited, feeling the tension on the line grow. When it went taut, he jerked his rod upwards. The line whistled out of the reel as the fish began its run.

"Holy crap, Bo. It's a big one."

"Well, bring her in, son. Don't talk about it, just do it."

Ethan pulled on the rod and frantically spun the reel, the smallmouth putting up a fight. He pulled the fish closer and closer, each time setting the hook a little deeper. After several minutes of fighting the fish, he was exhausted. Suddenly, it quit struggling. He began reeling it in and then looked down into the clear, green water and saw the most beautiful smallmouth bass he had ever seen. Bo put the net into the water and brought the fish up in one swift motion.

"Holy crap!" Ethan said. "How big is it, Bo?

Bo was grinning from ear to ear. "I think you just landed the biggest of the day, little brother. You got a seven pounder for sure."

Ethan laughed as he held the wriggling fish up over his head with one hand.

"Hold it up while I get a picture of this," Bo said, grabbing his little disposable camera. "May be the only one you ever catch, little brother."

Ethan grinned broadly as his older brother snapped the picture.

"Way to go, son. Now we can go home." Bo took the hook out of the bass's mouth and put it in the live well with three other smaller fish. "And we're having this baby for dinner tonight."

Ethan grinned as widely as his mouth would stretch. He felt the glow of success. As Bo pulled the anchor up and started the motor, Ethan gazed at the quiet cove.

"What's the name of this cove, again?"

"I call it Copperhead Cove," Bo said. "I've been coming here for over ten years. It's my own private spot. I never bring clients here. This is for me and my family. Hardly anyone else knows about it."

As the boat sped out onto the main part of the lake, Ethan looked behind him at the idyllic cove. It was formed in a semi-circle and was isolated from the main lake by big pines and cottonwoods that towered over the cove, keeping it hidden from the average tourist or boater. Ethan hadn't seen another boat in the cove all day.

"Love this place, Bo. Why'd you name it Copperhead Cove?"

Bo pulled his right pant leg up and showed his brother healed-over bite marks.

"That's why. A mean, old copperhead clipped me while I was pulling my pontoon boat up on the shore a few years back. That sucker wanted to bite me again, but I jumped into the boat before he could sink his fangs in me. Thank God I had a snakebite kit with me. I injected the anti-venom serum in my leg and took off for the dock. I was a sick puppy for a few days."

Ethan stared at the two red welts on his brother's leg.

"Damn, Bo. Glad you didn't tell me that earlier. What would happen if you didn't have the anti-venom serum?"

"Just be sick as a dog for a while. Throbbing pain, nausea, stuff like that. Copperheads have some serious stuff in their fangs, but unless they bite you more than once it's usually not fatal. If you make 'em real mad and don't get away, they'll clip you three or four times. That's when it's fatal. Every fishing guide on the lake carries a kit with him, and if they don't they're playing Russian roulette out here."

Ethan narrowed his eyes as he glanced back at the cove, looking at it a little differently now. Bo looked at his brother.

"The cottonmouth is the one that scares the crap outta me. Those suckers pack a wallop."

"You have those around here, too?"

"Oh, yeah. Some folks call 'em water moccasins. They stay in the marshy stuff, like in creeks, rivers, sometimes in coves like Copperhead Cove. Never been bitten by one 'cause one bite will put you down."

"Damn," Ethan said. "Such a beautiful little cove, but so dangerous."

"Yeah, well, I don't go on the shore much anymore, especially in the cove. An old dog learns his lessons well. I just stay out on the water and play with the smallmouth at the bottom. That's good enough for ol' Bo."

They traveled in silence for a while, the hot June sun warming them and the wind whipping at their faces while they sped down the middle of the huge lake. Finally, Ethan broke the silence, having to yell over the outboard motor.

"How's the guide business going? You making any money?"

Bo grinned at his brother, who was sitting in the back of the boat, hat off, the wind whipping his salt and pepper hair.

"Guess who I'm taking out in a couple days?"

Ethan looked at his brother. "Who?"

"You're a big sports fan, right?"

"Yeah."

"You follow college basketball?"

"Yeah."

"You heard of Sonny Daye, coach at Southern Tennessee?"

"Hell, yeah. They won the NCAA championship this year," Ethan said. "No way! You're taking Sonny Daye out?"

Bo had a big grin on his face. "Yep. And another big-time coach from somewhere in Iowa or Indiana, can't remember which."

Ethan stared at his brother.

"I'll be goddamned, Bo. What's the other coach's name?"

"Williams, I think. He made the final four and lost against Sonny Daye's team."

Ethan nodded. "Yeah, Jerry Joe Williams, coach at Midwestern, in Iowa."

"That's him. And the best part is they're paying me double my usual fee," Bo said proudly. "It's going to be a big payday for ol' Bo."

Ethan grinned at his brother.

"I'll be goddamned."

The two brothers rode the rest of the way in silence, the sun almost down and the beer having its effect.

———————————— |┼┼┼ ——— ┼┼┼| ————————————

Bo picked at his plate, getting every last piece of the fish from the bones.

"That was a mighty nice bass you caught, Ethan. Best eatin' we've had yet this summer."

Ethan had finished his meal and was sitting back in his deck chair, looking out at the peaceful surroundings of his brother's farm. Bo had built a redwood deck just off of the kitchen, and that's where they spent every summer evening until the sun went behind the hills. Ethan especially enjoyed the small pond that his brother had dug and supplied with fish, frogs, and other wildlife. At dusk, the wildlife was active around the little pond, with ducks quacking and diving for fish, bullfrogs belching, and the occasional rabbit or furry critter wandering up from the creek.

"I love it here, Bo. I really do," Ethan said, leaning back, his arms behind his head. "Sure beats sitting on an airplane for fourteen hours at a time and fighting with security and immigration lines."

Bo looked over at his brother, a contented smile on his face, along with barbeque sauce in his beard.

"Well, you know you can chuck it all whenever you want to and move back here. Hell, I'll clear off some land over there by the pond, and we'll build you a little shack. You can fish from your porch."

Ethan smiled at this. He'd dreamed of doing just that many times while crossing the Pacific or Atlantic oceans. He was forty-four years old, his children almost grown and on their own.

"It's real tempting, Bo. Once Molly goes off to college I might think about it a little more seriously. I do love it here."

"Speaking of Molly," Bo said between bites and licking his fingers, "how's she doin'? Did she get over that deal she went through a couple years ago?"

Ethan's smile faded as he thought about the nightmare of 9/11, when Molly was kidnapped by a crazed Mexican sex-trafficker. She had made it out thanks to his good friend Jake Delgado and lots of help from some ex-San Diego cops. Molly was sixteen when 9/11 happened, and it had taken her nearly a year to get over the nightmares. Now she was a beautiful seventeen, almost eighteen-year-old, in her final year at Santa Elena Academy in California, and due to graduate in a week.

"It took a long time," Ethan said. "She had nightmares almost every night for quite a while. But, like everything, they eventually faded away. She has a boyfriend." He frowned at that part. "But he's a good kid, a football player, nice family." He looked up at the trees surrounding the hollow. "She got a scholarship to UC San Diego, so I'll be an empty-nester in the fall."

Bo was staring at him. "That was hell on you, too, wasn't it? I mean, being in Europe and not able to get home, then finding out your little girl is kidnapped." Bo shook his head. "Hell of a deal."

Ethan continued to look up at the pines on the crest of the hollow.

"Two good things came out of it," he said, not looking at Bo. "My renewed friendship with Jake Delgado is strong. We talk about once a month. And Vicki."

Bo looked at him, his eyes softening.

"How's that going, her being in Mexico and all?"

Ethan lowered his head and looked at Bo.

"Well, guess I might as well tell you now." Ethan took a deep breath and blew it out. "We're getting married in September."

Bo straightened up as a grin filled his face.

"No shit? Ha! Congratulations, son, that's great news," he said. "Hey, mother, come out here. Got some news!"

Ethan grinned broadly as he waited for Kathy Paxton to step out to the deck. She was a handsome woman, big-boned but attractive, with flaming-red hair and an easy smile. She was the perfect mate for his brother. Kathy came out, wiping her hands with a dish towel.

"What's all the racket out here, you two?"

Bo was beside himself.

"Remember that gorgeous Mexican gal that Ethan brought out here last summer, the one he met in Mexico when, uh, well, you remember."

"Victoria? Sure, she was so nice, and she couldn't keep her eyes off of Ethan," Kathy said, smiling at her brother-in-law. "Why, what's—"

"They're gettin' hitched!" Bo said, unable to wait.

Kathy's mouth fell open, and a scream escaped that sent the ducks on the pond flying and quacking toward the trees.

"Ethan!" she yelled as she ran to him and gave him a big, long, bear hug. "Congratulations."

Bo, grinning like a boy at Christmas, just watched as his wife and little brother did a little dance on the deck.

"Son, I didn't think you'd ever take that step again. I mean, when Connie died . . . . "

"Bo, knock it off," Kathy said, frowning at her exuberant husband. "Your brother's getting married, nothing else matters."

Bo nodded at his wife of twenty-five years.

"Sorry," he said, like a scolded child. "But I'm just so damn happy for you, son!" His grin was back in a flash.

Ethan couldn't get the smile off his face as Bo and Kathy Paxton took turns hugging and jostling him. He had proposed to Victoria Calderon two weeks before, when she flew into Los Angeles on a charter trip. They had seen each other sporadically since the ordeal of 9/11, and Ethan had wondered if they would ever have a chance to build their relationship. As a charter pilot in Mexico, she was almost always gone and hardly ever had time off. His travel and work schedule kept him flying all over the world, so it was a miracle that they both had three days free at the same time in May. They spent the entire three days on Catalina Island and rarely ever left their hotel room. When they finally emerged, they were engaged.

Bo popped open three Pabst Blue Ribbons and handed one to Kathy and one to Ethan.

"A toast to my little brother, who I thought would remain a bachelor forever. You hooked a good woman, son, and now you'll be able to skin her and—"

"Bo!" Kathy said, frowning again. "She's not a fish, for crying out loud."

"Ah, hell, woman, I was just using one of them, whatcha call, analogies. Ethan got me, right?"

Ethan was laughing so hard he couldn't speak. Bo broke out laughing, slapping his knee, and then Kathy smiled, chuckled, then laughed until she had tears in her eyes. Garth and Brooks, Bo's hunting dogs, looked up at the crazy humans, cocking their heads and whimpering. The ducks flew off the pond again, heading for a quieter environment. Finally, Bo got himself under control.

"What about Charlie and Molly? You tell them yet?

Ethan quit laughing, the smile fading from his face.

"No, not yet. Charlie's taking finals at UCLA this week, and Molly is . . . . "

Kathy grabbed Ethan's hand. "You think Molly will be upset because of, well, her mom and what happened in Mexico?"

Ethan's mood turned serious.

"She's not over her mom's death yet. The ordeal in Mexico riled things up inside of her, and she's been struggling with Connie's death, with her birth mom, and the lady she met in Mexico." Ethan pursed his lips. "I just didn't want to upset her right now, you know?"

"Does she like Victoria?" Kathy said.

"Oh, yeah, she loves her," Ethan replied. "But they haven't seen much of her since the . . . kidnapping, what with Vicki's schedule and living in Mexico . . . you know."

Bo walked over and clapped his brother on the shoulder.

"You need to trust her feelings. You shouldn't hide it from her or Charlie. They deserve to know."

Ethan looked at his brother and nodded.

"You're right. I'll tell them this weekend when I get home from Memphis. Thanks, you guys."

Bo slapped Ethan's shoulder again. "Now, let's party! My little brother is gettin' married!"

The ducks never came back that evening.

The next morning, Ethan got up early, showered and shaved, then tiptoed down the steep stairs and out of the house. His head was pounding from too many Pabst Blue Ribbons the night before, but he and his brother had had a great time. Kathy had given up before the first case of PBR was finished. He'd decided to let Bo sleep in and slip out quietly. Ethan hated goodbyes anyway. He opened the door to the deck and pushed it closed as gently as possible. The sun was barely peeking over the hills, the hollow slowly coming awake.

"Got the coffee brewin', little brother."

Ethan looked out on the deck, and there was Bo, sipping on his coffee and petting Garth. *I should have known I couldn't make it up before him.*

"Damn, Bo, I thought you'd be sleeping till noon today the way you pounded those PBR's last night."

"Well, I gotta admit, I feel some little fellas hammering nails in my head this morning, but I wasn't gonna let you sneak out without saying goodbye," he said. "I know you too well, son."

Ethan sighed and pulled out a chair on the deck and sat down. The coffee pot was on the table in front of him, along with his favorite coffee cup.

"Never could get up before you, Bo, but I thought I had a chance this morning."

Bo smiled, took a drink of the strong coffee, and gazed out over his domain.

"Sure is pretty, ain't it?"

Ethan looked out at the pond, the early morning steam rising into the air, and a couple of ducks waddling around.

"That it is, brother. You've made a nice life for yourself back here."

Bo just nodded, taking another swig of coffee.

"You ever miss California?"

"Not once in fifteen years. You can have all the traffic and yuppies and noise. I couldn't do it again, not in this lifetime."

Ethan smiled, having heard the same thing from Bo for years.

"Well, maybe someday I'll join you back here." He gazed out at the tree-covered hollow, which they called "hollers" in Kentucky. He had an ache in his heart, knowing he was going back to the grind of meetings and deadlines and airplanes. He gulped his coffee down and stood up. "I've got to get on the road, Bo. I have meetings in Memphis this afternoon."

Bo just shook his head.

"Don't know how you do it, Ethan. But it's your choice. When you're ready, that plot of land next to the pond will be here waitin' for ya."

Ethan smiled and started walking toward his rental car. He had a four-hour drive ahead of him and an afternoon full of meetings. His shoulders sagged as he threw his suitcase into the trunk of the Buick LeSabre. He looked back and saw Bo slowly walking toward him, Garth at his side.

"Say hey to Charlie and Molly for me," he said. "Tell 'em I'm looking forward to them coming back again this summer. I got a houseboat reserved so we can park it in a quiet little cove for a couple days."

"Not Copperhead Cove," Ethan said, smiling.

"No, that's for fishing only. No swimming, camping, or exploring. We don't wanna run into the mean son-of-a-bitch that clipped me."

"I don't think they can make it this summer," Ethan replied. "Charlie is twenty-one now, heading into his senior year at UCLA, and may be doing some clerking for an attorney this summer. Molly's got a job for the summer, saving up for college in the fall."

"Ah, hell," Bo said, a grimace on his face. "Hope they don't forget about Uncle Bo."

"No chance. They'll be back someday." Ethan wiped a tear away. "Things change, Bo, that's the one thing we can count on."

"Well, goodbye, little brother," Bo said. "It's been fun, as always."

"Have fun with old Sonny Daye and Jerry Joe tomorrow," he said, hugging his brother and slapping his back. "Take some pictures and send 'em to me, will you?"

"Ah, hell, you know me and cameras. If it don't have a hook on it, I can't use it."

Ethan clapped his brother on the shoulder and climbed into his rented Buick.

"I love you, Bo."

"Love you, too, little brother," Bo said, wiping a tear away. "Drive safe. See you in July."

Ethan started the engine and backed out of the driveway. As he put it in drive, he waved to Bo, who was standing next to Garth, petting him behind the ears. He drove down the long, gravel driveway and made a sharp right turn next to the pond. He looked in his rearview mirror and saw Bo standing in the same spot, watching him, Garth still sitting at his side. The little farm disappeared from view as he crossed over the creek and onto the road that would take him back to civilization.

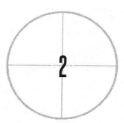

2

Frankie Farmer and Augustus "Augie" Stellato pulled out of the rent-a-car lot in a Cadillac Deville and began the eight-hour drive to southern Kentucky. Frankie wound through the early morning rush-hour traffic in downtown Chicago, finally getting out of the city around nine o'clock. They took Interstate 65 south, toward Indianapolis and points south.

Augie Stellato was a big man, much older than Frankie by at least thirty years. He was bald, with a snow-white goatee, and lines in his tanned face that made Frankie think of an ancient redwood. His arms were as big as Frankie's thigh. He'd been retired from the "business" for fifteen years, living on the South Side of Chicago with his common-law wife, Florence. He attended a few Cubs games, but for the most part kept to himself.

"So Augie," Frankie said, glancing nervously at the big man in the passenger seat, "what've you been doing for the past fifteen years?" Polite conversation.

"Fuck you, asshole. Just drive." Augie's voice was low, raspy, with a strong Italian accent.

"I just thought, since—"

"Fugetaboutit. Drive. Don't talk."

Frankie gripped the steering wheel with both hands, looking straight ahead. *Damn, how'd I get saddled with this prick? It's going to be a long couple of days.*

"Hey, kid," Augie said, not looking at him, "how'd a pretty white boy like you get hooked up with Two Toes?"

Frankie blinked, deciding if he should answer.

"Two Toes? Who's that?"

Augie turned and stared at him.

"Your boss, you friggin' jamook. Tony 'Two Toes' Tonelli. You never heard that before?"

"Uh, no. Why 'Two Toes'? Did he have an accident or . . . ?"

Augie reared his watermelon-sized head back and laughed.

"Hell, kid, you are somethin'. Wait till I tell your boss. He'll either laugh his ass off or shoot your ass." Augie laughed again. "Tony Tonelli, smart guy, think about it. Both names start with 'To'–'Two Toes,' get it?"

Frankie laughed nervously. "Oh, yeah." *Ha ha, you caveman asshole.*

"So, how'd you get hooked up with him?" Augie said, staring at Frankie.

"I dated his daughter in college."

"No shit? I remember her. I bet she was a nice piece of ass."

Frankie cleared his throat. "Well, uh, she's my wife now."

"No shit. Is she a good piece of ass?"

Frankie turned and looked at Augie. He smiled weakly and turned his gaze back to the interstate.

"Yeah, I bet she's a good piece of ass," Augie said, closing his eyes, a smile on his face.

They drove in complete silence, except for Augie's snoring, for the next three hours until they hit the outskirts of Indianapolis.

"I'm hungry," Augie said, rubbing his eyes. "There's a place just south of the airport called The Rawhide. Good steaks."

Frankie did a double take, glancing back and forth from Augie to the highway.

"Uh, okay, where is—"

"South of the airport."

Frankie nodded and pulled out his cell phone and dialed information. "The Rawhide, uh, south of the Indianapolis airport," he said into the phone.

Frankie listened to the voice on the phone, nodding his head several times.

"Okay, thanks," he said, closing the phone.

"Be there in half an hour," he said, listening to Augie snore again. *What the hell?*

After lunch, and after Augie had polished off a porterhouse steak that would feed a small Asian country, they got back into the rented Cadillac and continued the drive south. Frankie listened to Augie's concert of farting and belching for several miles before he spoke.

"How long have you and Tony been working together?" He thought maybe the big man would be in a better mood with his stomach full.

"Just drive," Augie said, leaning back and closing his eyes.

Frankie headed south on Interstate 65, crossing over the bridge and into Louisville around three o'clock. Augie was snoring again, which was a nice change from the farting and belching. *What the hell am I doing here? I have this Neanderthal next to me that thinks intelligent conversation is a belch, followed by a fart. What the hell?*

They drove further south into the bowels of Kentucky, passing the "Abe Lincoln cabin" sign, and headed for Bowling Green. The landscape got greener and rockier. Frankie began seeing lots of high rock bluffs. *Pretty country. Too bad we have to whack somebody when we get there.*

"Hey, kid, you never answered me," Augie said, sitting up and belching again.

"What . . . what was that?"

"Your wife, is she a nice piece of ass?"

Frankie glanced at Augie.

"Okay, that's enough! Goddammit, I'm not gonna take this shit anymore. She's my wife, for crying out loud!"

Augie turned his head and looked at the outraged man. He tilted his head back and laughed so loud Frankie thought he'd blow the roof off the Cadillac.

"Good for you, kid," Augie said, laughing and punching Frankie's shoulder. "I was startin' to think you were a little pussy. Nice to see you have some balls."

Frankie's eyes were bulging, his face beet red.

"What?"

"Hey, kid. We need to talk about what's going to happen when we get to this Podunk lake. This coach is going to go fishing tomorrow, right?" Augie was staring at Frankie.

"Yeah. He's going out at six o'clock tomorrow morning with another basketball coach," Frankie said. "They hired a fishing guide out of Silver Creek Resort. Some guy named Bo."

"Bo," Augie said. "Figures. Some country yahoo that thinks he knows what he's doin'."

"Uh, my source says that this guy is the best fishing guide in Kentucky. Really knows his stuff."

Augie took his right hand and shook it up and down, like he was masturbating.

"Yeah, okay. Anyway, we follow this yahoo and the two Podunk coaches, and hit 'em when nobody's around. Capisci?"

Frankie's eyes grew wide as he looked at Augie.

"No, no, we can't hit all of 'em. The other coach is famous. He just won the NCAA tournament."

"Well, looks like he'll go out a winner then."

"What?" Frankie screamed, his voice two octaves higher. "The boss said Williams. He wanted Williams dead. We can't whack a famous coach. And the fishing guide? No."

"The yahoo fishing guide will be fish food, along with the two Podunk coaches."

Frankie pounded on the steering wheel.

"I'm calling the boss. He never said anything about whacking—"

"He told me he wanted everyone dead. You callin' me a liar?" Augie said, his voice low and menacing.

Frankie looked frantically at the giant man next to him.

"No, I'm not calling you a liar, but why kill innocent—"

Augie laughed loudly. "Innocent? Nobody in this fucked-up world is innocent, you naïve little bastard. We get rid of all witnesses. They just disappear. Capisci?"

Frankie stared at the road, his eyes as big as saucers. He glanced at Augie, sweat dripping down his face. *What had the boss gotten him into?*

"Okay. Where we staying tonight?" Augie said.

Frankie fished in his shirt pocket and pulled out a slip of paper.

"The Ridge Motel, in Crockett."

"Okay, wake me up when we get to the Ridge Motel," Augie said, smiling and punching the air with another fart.

3

Ethan stared with glassy eyes at the man in the front of the room, not listening to a word he was saying. His mind was on Copperhead Cove, on his brother's farm and the little pond. He'd arrived in Memphis the previous afternoon and was pushed right into meeting after meeting, with a business dinner thrown in. By the time his head hit the pillow that night at the Peabody Hotel, he was gone. Today had been round after round of meetings, but they were finally wrapping up. He was looking forward to getting back to the Peabody and having a glass of wine in the Corner Bar. Maybe even a cigar, since this was one of the few places in the U.S. where you could still fire up a stogie.

He thought about tomorrow and how excited his brother must be, taking Sonny Daye out on the lake for a day of fishing and telling stories. He couldn't wait to call Bo tomorrow night to see how it all went. A smile creased Ethan's face as he thought of his brother telling Sonny Daye and Jerry Joe Williams how to fish. *It's not the pole, son, it's the man on the business end of the pole that counts.* Ethan chuckled to himself.

"Ethan?" the man in the front of the room said. "Can you answer that?"

Jolted out of his daydream, Ethan said, "What? Sorry, Patrick, I didn't hear you," and looked sheepishly around the room.

"His mind's on that pretty charter pilot he spent the weekend with," Vinnie, the general manager of the Memphis office and Ethan's friend of ten years, said. Ethan laughed along with everyone else.

"Can you repeat the question, Patrick?"

"We're talking about the packaging out of China. Too many ocean containers are arriving with moisture damage. What can we do about that?"

Ethan cleared his throat.

"I'll look into it with our forwarders and get some answers and some options. I'll call China tonight and find out what's going on. Get back to you tomorrow."

"Okay. We'll take it up again tomorrow morning," Patrick said. "It's five thirty, so let's call it a day and meet again tomorrow morning at eight thirty, same place."

Ethan sat still until everyone had gathered their laptops and material and left the room. Only Vinnie was left in the room.

"Hey, Vinnie, you got a second?" Ethan said.

"Sure, buddy, what's up, other than your job if you don't quit daydreaming in these meetings?"

They both laughed. "Hey, you're a big basketball fan, right? I mean college, not pro."

"Yeah, both. Why do you ask?"

"Well, you know that Southern Tennessee won the NCAA championship in April, right?"

"Hell, yeah, big news around these parts. South Tenn, as we call 'em, is just east of here about a hundred miles. Sonny Daye could run for governor right now and win in a landslide."

Ethan smiled at this. "Funny you should mention him. Guess who my brother is taking out on a guide trip tomorrow morning?"

"No way. Sonny Daye?"

Ethan laughed. "Vinnie, you're a poet."

Vinnie laughed at his unintentional rhyme. "You serious, he's gonna be with Sonny Daye all day on Quail Hollow?"

Ethan nodded, grinning broadly. "And another coach that made the Final Four, from Midwestern. You heard of Jerry Joe Williams?"

Vinnie's smile eroded when he heard the name. "Yeah, he's been in the news the past week or so. Not good news, either."

Ethan sat up straight, staring at his friend. "What kind of news? I've been out of touch for about a week or so, just too damn bushed to watch the news at night."

"Jerry Joe Williams is being investigated for point shaving. Rumor has it he intentionally kept the score down on a few games so Midwestern wouldn't beat the spread."

Ethan's eyes grew wide. "Oh, shit. Who's investigating?"

"Midwestern is in Iowa, so right now it's just an Iowa and an NCAA issue. But last thing I read was that the FBI might get involved."

Ethan looked down at the long, wooden conference table. "You think I should warn my brother? I mean, usually where there's smoke, there's fire, right? And I remember the big points shaving scandal twenty years or so ago, but it was Boston College then. And the mob was involved." He felt a queasiness when he said this.

Ethan could see Vinnie thinking. He'd hate to ruin his brother's big day tomorrow, but . . . .

"I wouldn't tell him," Vinnie said. "From what I've read, the investigation is just starting so it'll take a long time before anything happens, if it happens at all. I wouldn't ruin Bo's day by saying anything."

Ethan nodded. "Yeah, I agree. Let him bask in the moment."

"Any chance that Bo will know anything about it?"

Ethan laughed. "Bo? Hell, if it doesn't happen on Quail Hollow Lake or on his farm, he won't know anything about anything. He's buried in his own world, and it sure doesn't include newspapers or news programs—unless NASCAR is involved."

They both laughed, slapping the big table.

"You want to grab some dinner tonight? I have something going with the wife, but I can cancel it," Vinnie said. "There's a new barbeque place close to the Peabody."

"No, thanks, Vinnie. I'm beat and I can't eat barbeque again tonight. I think I'll just go back to the Peabody and hang out in the Corner Bar for a while. Sip on some wine, smoke a stogie, and listen to some music."

"Got it. Maybe tomorrow night?"

"Yeah, tomorrow night would work great. I can call Bo during dinner to get the scoop on his big day . . . with Daye."

The two friends stood up, laughing. They walked out of the conference room with their arms around each other's shoulder.

Ethan sipped his chardonnay at a small table just off the bar. He had a good view of the stage where a young woman was playing the piano and singing softly. Cigar smoke rose up from the ashtray in small, gray swirls, the aroma filling his nostrils. He'd arrived at the Corner Bar in the Peabody Hotel around six thirty after dropping off his laptop and briefcase in his room. The Peabody was the oldest hotel in Memphis and the center of action in the city. The Corner Bar was a respite from the noise of Beale Street, the Elvis impersonators, and blues bars. It was a quiet place to unwind, with most of the clientele in business attire.

He took a drag on his cigar, blew the smoke out, and smiled contentedly. *This makes it worthwhile, these small, quiet moments alone. Something Bo would appreciate.* He thought of Bo, how excited he must be tonight, getting his boat and gear ready for two famous coaches. Ethan thought again about telling him about Jerry Joe Williams, but decided against it. He didn't want to spoil it for his brother and, besides, what could happen out on a huge lake in the middle of nowhere? *Wish I was gonna be out there with him instead of stuck in a hot, boring conference room tomorrow.*

The music stopped, so Ethan picked up his cell phone and dialed his brother's number, hoping he'd be home and not at the lake. Bo didn't own a cell phone, so if he wasn't home Ethan wasn't talking to him.

"Hello?" Ethan heard Kathy's voice.

"Hi, Kathy. It's Ethan."

"Ethan! Hey, how you doin' down there in Elvis country?"

"Just sipping on a glass of wine and smoking a cigar. Exciting, huh?"

"Whatever floats your boat, as Bo would say. You wanna talk to him? He's excited as a little puppy with his first bone."

Ethan smiled at Kathy's remark.

"Sure. Thanks, Kath."

She handed the phone to Bo.

"Hey, little brother! You ready to come back up here already?"

"Hell, yeah, but no can do quite yet," Ethan said, laughing. "Kathy said you're pretty excited about tomorrow."

"Nah, just another day on the lake, son," Bo lied. "They're just people, like you and me."

Ethan chuckled. "Don't bullshit a bullshitter, Bo. You know you'll love taking those two guys out tomorrow. You got the gear all shined up and pretty?"

"Never could fool you, little brother. Yeah, I'm all ready for the big show. Got the gear all cleaned up, the boat shining, and two cases of Budweiser cooling in two coolers."

"Budweiser? Thought you were a Pabst Blue Ribbon man?"

"I am, but I ain't drinkin' tomorrow. Never do when I'm guidin'. They asked for Bud and two bottles of Jack Daniel's."

Ethan's smile faded.

"Uh oh, they plan on fishing or getting drunk?"

"Probably a little of both. Most folks like their beer, but I have to keep it under control. It's not like when you and I go out on the lake. I'll have a few beers 'cause I'm not workin', but when I have clients in my boat I gotta be careful."

"Especially two high profile clients like Sonny Daye and Jerry Joe Williams. Pretty big names right now."

"Yeah, well, like I always say, they put their pants on one leg at a time, just like you and me."

Ethan struggled with telling Bo about Jerry Joe Williams but bit his lip. *Maybe tomorrow night, after the big day is over.*

"What are you up to, big shot?" Bo said. "You out to some fancy dinner, or you slummin' it with greasy barbeque?"

"Neither. I'm holed up in a quiet little bar in the Peabody Hotel, drinking chardonnay and smoking a stogie. Life is good."

"Ahhh, you and your chardonnay. Give me a PBR any day. But the stogie sounds good. I might fire one up tomorrow night, after I get rid of the two big-shot coaches."

"Call me on my cell phone when you get home. I want to hear all about it."

"You sure you have time for me, son? What with all the corporate bullshit you have to deal with?"

Ethan laughed. "Just call me, asshole. Have a great day tomorrow, and stay away from Copperhead Cove."

"No Copperhead Cove for these guys. I'll take 'em to some spots where if they don't catch a smallmouth they don't know nothing about fishin'."

"Kiss Kathy for me, and make sure you give me a call tomorrow night. Any time after seven."

"Okay, little brother. Talk to ya."

"Later, Bo."

Ethan hit the end button on his cell. His cigar was out, so he picked it up and lit it, drawing in the smoke until he saw bright orange on the end. He blew the smoke out and closed his eyes, knowing he had to call his office in China soon. But right now he was going to enjoy his wine and his cigar. His thoughts drifted to the tranquil water on Copperhead Cove.

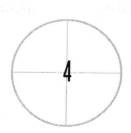

4

Frankie pulled into Crockett, Kentucky, and thought he'd stepped back in time. *We're in friggin' Mayberry RFD. Andy Griffith has to be around somewhere.* Maria's instructions said to check in at the Riverside Motel on Main Street. He drove a block and saw it on his left. He pulled into the full parking lot and glanced over at Augie, who was snoring, as always. *I'll let the human fart machine sleep.*

Frankie got out of the Cadillac, which stood out like a sore thumb in the parking lot full of pickups and old Chevys and Fords. He walked into the lobby, hearing the tinkle of a bell, and sauntered up to the desk. A young, plump girl with an acne problem looked up.

"Hey, sir, what can I do ya for?"

Frankie looked at her and smiled.

"I have a reservation at the Ridge Motel. Is this it?"

The girl laughed.

"No, silly. The Ridge is up there," she said, pointing out the window.

Frankie bent over and looked out the window.

"Across the street?"

She laughed again, louder this time.

"No, up on the Ridge. The Ridge Motel, hello!" she said, mocking him.

Frankie looked at her like she was an alien.

"Why can't I stay here at the, uh, Riverside Motel."

"Oh, we're all booked up for graduation week. Y'all here for the graduation?"

"What graduation?"

She laughed again.

"The hiiigh school," she said, drawing out the high school.

Damn, I wish she was the one we were gonna whack.

"Oh, no, not here for the graduation. Why can't I check in at the Ridge?"

She laughed again.

"You're not from around here, are ya? We own the Ridge. I mean, I don't own it, the owner owns it." She giggled. "Well, you know what I mean. Anyway," she said, laughing at herself, "folks have to check in here 'cause there ain't nobody up there to check you in."

Frankie cocked his head, trying to understand.

"What do you mean, there's nobody up there?" If she laughed again he was going to coldcock her.

"Well, there ain't nobody up there. I don't know how else to say it." She held her hands on her plump hips and sighed.

"Let me get this straight," he said, closing his eyes and concentrating. "I'm booked into a motel that doesn't have an office, or maids, or anything?"

"Well, we're the office for it, and our maids do the cleanin' for it."

Frankie's head sagged.

"So I guess it's stupid to ask if there's room service." He knew the answer but just wanted to see what lame-ass answer she'd give him.

She giggled. "Room service?" She leaned back and laughed so hard Frankie thought she was going to pee herself. "Y'all ain't from here, for sure. This is Kentucky. Southern Kentucky. You ain't findin' no room service around here."

Frankie rubbed his forehead, trying to find a reason not to whack her right then.

"Okay . . . what's your name?"

"Jamie May. What's yours?"

"Uh," he hesitated, looking out the window at the parking lot. "Ford," he said.

"Like the car?"

He rubbed his forehead again.

"Yes! Like the fucking car! Can I get a room with two beds at the fucking Ridge Motel, Jamie May, so I can get out of this fucking looney bin?"

She didn't laugh. She cleared her throat and pulled out a registration card.

"Fill this out, Mr. FORD, and you can be on your way." She emphasized Ford a little too much.

Frankie filled out the form with a fake name, Festus Ford or some shit, and slid it back to Jamie.

"I'm sorry, Jamie May. I've been driving for ten hours and I'm tired. I just want a nice, quiet room, that's all."

"Fine, Mr. FORD. Can I have a credit card, please?" She said this very formally, without a smile, let alone a laugh.

"I'll pay cash. How much is it?"

"Well, we need a credit card anyway."

"I'm not giving you a fucking credit card. How much is the room?"

"The room is forty dollars, plus tax, but I need a—"

"Here's a hundred, Jamie May. I want the room for two nights. The change is all yours, okay?"

"Well, I'm supposed to get a credit card . . . . "

He reached back into his wallet.

"Here's an extra forty bucks, just for you. You can take your boyfriend out to KFC tonight."

Jamie May looked around, as if there was anyone around, and took the two twenties and the hundred.

"Okay, Mr. Ford," she said, handing him the key. "You're in room twelve, at the end of the building. Have a nice stay."

"Jamie May?" Frankie said, leaning in.

"Yeah?"

"How the hell do I get to the Ridge Motel?" he shouted, his eyes bulging.

Jamie May stepped back, her lips beginning to pull up into a smirk as she pulled out a handwritten mimeographed map with directions.

"Y'all have a nice day, Mr. FORD." She waddled away and disappeared into a room behind the reception counter.

What the hell?

Frankie got into the Cadillac and stared straight ahead for several minutes, trying to figure out what just happened.

"What room are we in?" Augie said, belching twice and picking his nose.

Frankie looked at the man, shook his head, and pulled out of the parking lot.

"We're in room twelve, and shut the fuck up!"

Frankie stopped at the only stoplight in town and looked at the map. It was seven thirty and the sun was setting in the west, making it hard to read. He turned on the overhead light and peered at the handwritten map. He turned it around and looked at it from a different angle. *This makes no goddamn sense!* Seeing a gas station on his right, he pulled in and got out of the car.

"What the hell you doin'?" Augie said through the window.

"Shut the hell up."

Frankie walked into the office of the greasy station. A young man with a big silver cap with an orange "T" on it was sitting behind a counter eating something that Frankie couldn't identify.

"Hey, kid, can you help me out?"

The kid licked his fingers and stared up at Frankie.

"What do y'all need?"

What? "I need directions to the Ridge Motel."

The kid chuckled and pointed out the window, the same direction that Jamie May had pointed.

"I know it's on the ridge, you little . . . " Frankie took a deep breath. "How do I get there from here?"

The kid licked his fingers again, wiping them on his shirt.

"Y'all know Crockett?"

"No. Never been here before."

The kid sucked air between his teeth, making a whistling sound.

"Y'all go down to the stop sign yonder, take a left until ya get to the Rite-Aid, then take another left on Ridge Road and follow it to the end."

"How far is it from here?"

"Hell, I don't know."

Frankie nodded his head. *Another candidate for a whack job.*

"Where can we get some dinner?"

"There's Joe's Ribs and Taters next to the Rite-Aid," the kid said. "Just finished off a slab myself." He showed the greasy bag to Frankie. "Finger lickin' good."

"Joe's Ribs and what?" Frankie said.

"Taters." The kid looked at Frankie like he was from Mars. "Ain't you never heard of taters, mister?"

"Are you trying to say 'potatoes'?" Frankie said, his eyes starting to bug out.

"Yeah, them things."

Frankie shook his head and walked out of the shabby station, wiping his hands on his pants even though he hadn't touched anything. He climbed into the Cadillac, started it up, and squealed out of the gas station, never once looking at Augie. He heard a fart, so knew he was in the car.

Frankie passed Joe's Ribs and Taters, saw the Rite-Aid next to it, and took the next left. There was no street sign, so he assumed it was Ridge Road. He drove up a winding road, wide enough for two cars if one of the cars was in the ditch. After several hairpin turns, he glanced at Augie, who was staring at him, his eyes in squint mode.

"What? We're goin' to the motel," Frankie said.

"I thought we were just AT the motel," Augie said.

"We're not staying at THAT motel, we're staying at . . . this motel, up here, somewhere."

They drove what seemed to be five miles, but it actually was just a mile. The road finally reached the top of the ridge, and they saw the motel. The parking lot was empty. Augie looked at Frankie again.

"What the fuck is this?"

"Home for two days," Frankie said, not daring to look at the big man. *I can't believe I told him to shut the fuck up.*

Frankie peered out the window until he saw "12" on one of the rooms, the last room on the first floor. What looked like a jungle was on the other side.

"Here we are, room twelve," he said, pulling into the parking space, glancing at Augie nervously.

Augie was sitting still, staring at the run-down motel. Frankie could hear the man's sweat popping out of his pours. *Oh shit, why did I tell him to shut the fuck up?*

"I ain't stayin' here, you jamook," Augie said. "This is a friggin' dump, and there ain't nobody else around." He turned and glared at Frankie. "Where the hell is everybody?"

Frankie gulped and tried to remain confident.

"It's the only place they had available. It's graduation week."

Augie continued to stare at him, so Frankie got out of the car and walked up to the door to room twelve. He put the key in the door and nothing happened. He glanced back at Augie, who was sitting quietly, glaring at him. *At least I found a way to stop the belching and farting.* He tried the key again, wiggling it in the lock. The door suddenly opened. Frankie turned and smiled at Augie, then walked into the musty, dark room. He turned on the light and just about had a heart attack on the spot. There was only one double bed. He quickly closed the door and grinned at Augie.

"Looks like they made a mistake," Frankie said. "There's, uh, only one . . . ." He stopped when he saw Augie slowly getting out of the car.

Augie stood and stretched, lifting his leg long enough to let out a balloon of gas that evidently had been kept under wraps for miles. He walked up to room twelve, opened the door, looked inside, and turned slowly to Frankie.

"Where's your room?"

Frankie nodded, looking around the dilapidated motel. He walked up to room eleven and tried the door. It was locked. He smiled at Augie, then tried the key to room twelve, just on the off-chance . . . it opened. The key opened both rooms. *What the hell?* Frankie opened the door and looked inside. Same musty smell, same double bed.

"This is my room," he said, walking to the Cadillac and opening the trunk.

He pulled out Augie's bag and a long case that he knew held the rifle. He handed them both to Augie, glancing nervously at the big man. He then got his single overnight bag and slammed the trunk.

"Uh, we can get some dinner down at Joe's Ribs and, uh, Taters," he said.

"What the hell did you just say?"

"They don't have room service here. Matter of fact, they don't have anything here, except us, so we have to go back down the road to get some dinner."

"No, the name of the place, what did you call it?" Augie had a menacing look on his face.

Oh God, I'm gonna die tonight. "Joe's Ribs and," Frankie cleared his throat, "taters."

Augie stared at him and then cracked a huge grin.

"My kinda place! Let's get the hell down there."

What the hell?

5

At five o'clock on Wednesday morning, Bo loaded his fishing gear, two ice chests of Budweiser and a sack with two bottles of Jack Daniel's, paper cups, and some sandwiches and chips into his old Ford Explorer. It was still dark outside, the sun still an hour or so away from making an appearance. He walked back to the door and entered the kitchen where Kathy was stirring up some hash and potatoes. Bo walked up behind her, put his hands on her ample hips, and looked over her shoulder.

"Smells mighty good, mother." He kissed her on the cheek as she slapped his hand away and giggled. "But I don't have much time."

"Sit your hillybilly butt down. You're eatin' this," Kathy said, carrying the skillet over and scooping a huge portion onto Bo's plate. "You ain't goin' out there on that hot lake with two drinkers without a full belly."

Bo grinned at his wife.

"Okay, baby. You win, as always."

Bo dug into the hash and taters like he hadn't eaten in two days. Kathy threw two fried eggs on top of the pile and a piece of toast beside it. Bo mixed the eggs in with the hash and taters and scooped it into his mouth.

"Hmm. Hmm. Good," he said. "You make the best hash and taters in Crockett County, mother."

Kathy stood over him and smiled. She took his filthy cap off his head and ran her fingers through his hair.

"You ain't gonna wear this greasy old thing today, are you, Bo?"

Bo barely looked up from his scooping.

"That's my fishin' hat, woman. What else am I gonna wear when I go fishin'?"

Kathy walked over and picked out an orange cap with a letter "T" on the front, the University of Tennessee logo.

"Show them yahoos that you're a Volunteer fan. Wear the "T" today."

Bo took a break from filling his face and looked up at her.

"That might piss 'em off, 'specially Sonny Daye. He's coach at Southern Tennessee. They hate the Volunteers."

"Too bad. You're a Vols fan, so show 'em."

Bo laughed as he stood up, rubbing his stomach.

"Mother's always right," he said, grabbing the orange cap and putting it on. When Kathy took his plate to the sink, he stuck his fishin' cap in his back pocket. *But not today.*

"Gotta go, Kath. Them boys will be at the dock at six, and I want my boat packed up and ready to go."

Kathy turned and smiled at her husband.

"Look at you, excited as a dog with a rabbit in his mouth." She walked up to him and kissed him on the lips. "Good luck, Bo Paxton. Bring some smallmouth back with you tonight. I'll have the PBR waitin' for ya." She reached around and grabbed his fishin' cap. "And you can go one day without this filthy thing," she said, grinning.

Bo grabbed for the cap, but Kathy was too fast for him. *Ah, hell.* He slapped her on the rear end and walked to his truck. He opened the door and looked back. Kathy was walking up to him. She took the orange cap off his head and replaced it with his fishin' cap.

"It ain't you without this old thing on. Have fun today, Bo."

He grinned and gave her a quick peck on the lips.

"Now we're ready. Later, babe."

Bo climbed into the blue Explorer and slowly pulled out onto the gravel driveway. Halfway down the drive, he looked back and waved to his wife.

"It's gonna be a Sonny Daye," he yelled, grinning.

Bo had made the drive to Silver Creek dock so many times he could do it in his sleep. It was about a mile down a couple of country roads. Then when he got close to the lake it took a sharp decline, right down to the lake shore. He had his favorite parking place close to the dock, and at that time of the morning didn't have to fight for it. He parked his Explorer and began to unload his stuff out of the back. It was still dark, but the lights around the dock were on.

He carried the first cooler of Bud the fifty feet to his boat. He'd docked his bass boat right next to the resort store the night before and gassed it up. He had to walk down a long gangway from the parking lot to the dock store, which was on pilings and surrounded by water. He put the cooler into the back of the boat and returned for the next one. In ten minutes he was all loaded up and ready to go. He looked at his waterproof watch. Five forty-five. *I got fifteen minutes to grab a cup of coffee.*

Bo walked into the resort store, which was open only for fishing guides at that hour. He sauntered back to the kitchen and smelled the coffee brewing in the big, silver percolator.

"Mornin' Bo," said a heavyset woman, cutting up potatoes in the corner. "Big day for you, huh?"

Bo laughed. "Is that a joke, Milly?"

The woman thought for a second, then burst out laughing.

"I just got my own joke." She laughed again. "With a name like Daye, guess you could make all sorts of jokes."

Bo poured himself a steaming cup of coffee in a silver mug. He looked out into the restaurant and saw two men who were also fishing guides, sitting at a table, sipping on coffee. He walked up to them and sat down.

"Mornin', gents," Bo said.

"Mornin', Bo," said a silver-haired man with a blue cap with the letter "K" on it. "You gonna talk to us little peons?" He said this with a laugh.

"Yeah, you and your big-shot clients," said the man next to him, a younger man with a full, brown beard, no cap.

Bo smiled and took a sip of his coffee.

"Well, this one time, but I can't let anyone see me with you two hillbillies." He knew the two men had their own clients, but Daye and Williams were the big deal of the summer.

"Who you got today, Slammer," Bo said, looking at the silver-haired man.

"Ah, some guys from Cincinnati. The usual city folk."

Bo nodded. "How about you, Ronnie?"

The younger man shook his head.

"The assholes canceled on me at the last minute. I'm goin' out with Slammer to help him with his group."

"They give you a deposit?" Bo said.

"Yeah, and they ain't gettin' it back," the bearded man said. "Called me last night and said one of 'em had to work. Lame-ass excuse."

Bo shook his head. He'd had last-minute cancellations before, and they screwed up his whole day. He hoped that didn't happen today.

"When is Sonny Daye gettin' here?" Slammer said.

"Six, but I bet they don't get here till seven," Bo said. "These yahoos are used to people waitin' for 'em."

A commotion from the front of the restaurant made them turn to look. Two men dressed in brand-new, store-bought fishing vests and caps with hooks on them stood there looking around.

"Anybody know where we can find Bo Paxton?" one of the men yelled. He had gray hair and had the air of a big shot. *Sonny Daye.*

Bo raised his hand. "I'm Bo Paxton, gents. Be right with ya."

Bo drained his coffee cup and looked at the two men at the table.

"Here we go. Wish me luck, fellas."

"Keep 'em sober, Bo," Slammer said.

"Get your money up front," said Ronnie.

Bo smiled, turned, and walked down the hallway toward Sonny Daye and Jerry Joe Williams.

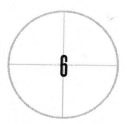

Frankie hadn't slept a wink all night, hearing squeaks and weird sounds every few seconds. He actually was comforted by Augie's snoring in the next room. At least he knew that there was another person close by, assuming that Augie was an actual person. Frankie got up a few times during the night to look outside, to see if anyone had "checked in" to Motel Hell. The parking lot was empty, except for the Cadillac. It gave him the creeps and made him think about the Bates Motel in "Psycho" and the Overlook Hotel in the freaky Stephen King novel "The Shining." He finally decided to give up and took a shower around forty thirty in the morning. He sat in his room until five, afraid to wake up the caveman next door.

It was still pitch dark outside when he knocked on room twelve at exactly five o'clock, not knowing what to expect. *Please don't let him kill me.* A sliver of a moon was the only thing lighting the parking lot. He knocked again and stepped away from the door, in case Augie decided to shoot first and ask questions later. He saw the door open slowly. *Oh shit!* Augie poked his head out, looked around, and said, "Be out in a second."

Frankie blew a huge amount of air out of his lungs. He started to walk around the parking lot but retreated to the Cadillac when he heard rustling in the brush next to Augie's room. *What the hell are those noises?* Finally, at five thirty, Augie opened his door.

"Let's get this shit over with," Augie said, walking out of his room to the Cadillac, carrying the long case.

Frankie got in the driver's seat and started up the engine. Augie was staring straight ahead, as if in a trance. They pulled out of the parking lot and started down the steep hill. It was so dark Frankie couldn't see the turns until he was on top of them. He almost ran off the road several times. Augie kept staring straight ahead, scaring the shit out of Frankie. *Fart, belch, or do something. Let me know you're human.*

When they finally got to the bottom of the hill, Frankie blew out another breath, glancing at Augie to see his reaction. Nothing. He turned right and headed for the town. He'd studied the map of the area and knew that they had to drive through Crockett and hit Highway 495 on the east end of town. The burg was deserted as they drove through, except for a pickup or two that were either coming home from a long night out or leaving home for a long day at work. Frankie decided to risk it.

"You sleep okay, Augie?" He winced when the words came out.

Augie stared straight ahead.

"Okay," he said.

They drove in silence on Highway 495 until they came to a sign that said "Quail Hollow Lake." Frankie turned left and drove down the country road toward what he assumed was their destination. About ten minutes later they reached the top of a steep grade and began driving downhill. With no lights other than his headlights, Frankie began to panic.

"Jesus Christ, this is one steep hill," he said, trying to sound nonchalant. It didn't work. Augie finally turned toward him.

"When you get to the bottom of the hill, turn off your lights."

What the hell? Turn off my lights? With a big lake right in front of us?

"Augie, I can't turn off my lights until I know where we are." He tried to say this as calmly as he could, but it came out as a whine.

As soon as they reached the bottom of the hill, Augie reached over and turned off the headlights. Frankie was driving solely by the moonlight, leaning forward and opening his eyes as far as he could, staring into the blackness. He saw a small opening on his right and drove into it.

"Good job," Augie said. "We walk from here."

Frankie put his head on the steering wheel until he got his breathing under control. *What the hell?*

Augie got out of the car and walked to the rear, waiting for Frankie to open the truck. Frankie, seeing the hulk of a man standing in his rear view mirror, popped the trunk with a button on the dash. Augie got the rifle case and closed the trunk.

"Let's go."

Frankie followed the big man down the road until they came to the Silver Creek parking lot. They saw lights in the building next to the dock and kept walking along the shore. *Where the hell are we going?*

Augie walked to a boat anchored on the shore about one hundred feet from the dock, seeming to know exactly where he was going, even in the darkness. *How come no one told me about the damn boat?* Augie put his rifle case in the boat and got in.

"Push us off," he said.

What? We never talked about this.

Frankie grabbed the rope that was tied around a stump and threw it into the boat, pushing off with all his strength. The boat slowly drifted out into the lake. Frankie jumped in after standing in a foot of water. He tried to make as little noise as possible, knowing that the Hulk would shoot his ass if he drew any attention. They drifted out into the lake, the lights of the resort on their left. Frankie looked at his watch. It was exactly six o'clock. The sun was just barely starting to peek over the horizon.

"Row," Augie said.

What? With what?

"Paddles are on the bottom," Augie said, staring at the lights at the dock.

Frankie found a paddle and began rowing silently through the water, out toward the main lake. The sun was beginning to shed some light on the lake, enough to guide them out of the "no wave" area. Frankie looked behind them and saw three men climbing into a boat next to the dock.

"They're coming," he said to Augie.

"Stay close to the shore until they get past us."

Frankie looked behind him and saw the outboard motor. He had never operated one so looked at Augie.

"Uh, Augie, I've never been in a boat before. How do we start this thing?"

"I'll do it when the time is right. Just row and keep to the shore."

Frankie kept stroking slowly, trying to keep the boat as close to the shore as possible. He looked behind them and saw the boat with the three men leaving the dock. He heard the low rumble of an outboard motor, laughter, and the sound of a sleek boat cutting slowly through the water.

"Paddle over to the shore and stop under that tree up there," Augie said.

Frankie did as he was told, and they sat under the low-hanging branches of a cottonwood and waited for the three men to pass.

"Get down low in the boat," Augie said, lowering himself, binoculars in his hand.

Frankie bent down so that he was even with the side of the boat. He kept his eyes on the oncoming boat, which was almost to the buoys that marked the "no wave" zone. Frankie and Augie were just past the line, in the dark shadows. The sun was peeking over the hills, showering shards of sunlight onto the lake.

As the three men reached the buoys, Frankie raised his head and peeked. The boat was only thirty yards from them. He heard the men talking, and he recognized the brown hair and beard of Jerry Joe Williams. The other man had gray hair. Must be Sonny Daye. The fishing guide was in the front of the boat, steering them through the "no wave" zone. He had on a baseball cap and was looking straight ahead, oblivious to the two men behind him or the boat sitting in the shadows of the cottonwood.

"That's them," Frankie whispered.

Augie put his binoculars on the side of the boat and peered at the passing craft. Apparently satisfied that it was the target, he lowered them and sat still. Once the red boat was fifty yards past and picking up speed, Augie motioned for Frankie to move to the front.

Augie sat in the back and pulled the cord on the outboard motor. It fired up immediately, the water making gurgling sounds as they sat motionless for several seconds.

"Take the binoculars and follow them. Don't let that red boat out of your sight," Augie said.

Frankie grabbed the binoculars and put them up to his eyes as Augie slowly maneuvered the boat out of the shadows and into the middle of the lake. Frankie adjusted the lens until he could focus on the speeding boat up ahead, which was going fast and creating quite a wake behind it. Augie reached cruising speed and kept them a hundred yards behind the red boat.

"Here, put this on," he said, handing a brimmed fishing hat to Frankie. "Have to look like a fisherman." Frankie put it on, looking back at Augie. He had a blue baseball cap on with a silver letter "K" in front. They were both dressed in khaki pants and polo shirts. Just two city folks, out for a day on the lake.

Frankie looked down at his feet and noticed a cardboard box, a cooler, and a metal suitcase in the front of the boat. He opened the cooler and saw two six-packs of Old Style beer, a few bottles of water, and a salami roll. *Figures, he brought the cheap stuff.* He opened the box and saw chips, bread, and several cans of Vienna sausage. *Ugh.* He started to open the metal suitcase but heard a grunt behind him. He turned and looked at Augie, who was shaking his head. *What the hell's in THAT thing? And how the hell did they get into the boat? Someone else is here, working with Augie.* Frankie turned his attention back to the red boat, his heart beating a little faster.

The red bass boat stayed in the middle of the lake for fifteen minutes, cruising at about fifteen miles per hour. There were several other boats on the lake at that early hour, probably other fishermen. Augie kept his hundred yard distance as Frankie watched through the binoculars. He noticed the two men in back drinking something from cans, but the guide was focusing on his driving and staring forward. Frankie screwed up his courage and turned toward Augie.

"Where are we gonna do this?"

Augie didn't look at him, just kept his eyes on the red boat. The long rifle case was lying next to him.

"Leave that to me. Just keep your eyes on 'em. If they start to slow down, let me know."

Frankie nodded and turned back around. He hadn't heard one fart or belch all morning, a pleasant change from yesterday. His stomach was churning, knowing that three people were going to die that day, and he would be an accomplice. *What is in that box?*

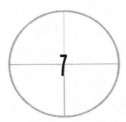

7

After twenty minutes on the lake, Bo spotted one of his favorite fishing spots off to the left, in a rocky cove close to the Kentucky/Tennessee border. He cut back on the motor and drifted slowly toward the isolated cove, checking to see if there were any other boats or houseboats. Seeing nothing, he guided his boat in and cut the power close to a rock outcropping. Large pines shielded the spot from the morning sun. This was his usual starting-off point with clients. He'd work his way back to the dock and hit a few more spots along the way.

He turned around and looked at the two men in the back of the boat. He noticed four empty beer cans on the deck of the boat and another in each man's hand.

"Okay, gents, here we are," he said, as he threw down the anchor. "Why don't you get your gear ready, and I'll get your bait."

"All right!" Jerry Joe Williams said loudly. He took a final swig of his Budweiser and tossed it on the deck next to the others.

Bo grabbed a plastic bag from his stash and tossed it to Williams.

"Throw all your empties in this," he said, not smiling. "You guys might wanna slow down if you wanna catch anything, let alone make it to the end of the day."

Sonny Daye picked up the empties and threw them into the plastic bag.

"Just excited to be out here, Bob," he said.

"It's Bo," Williams said, laughing. "Sorry, Bo. We're here to fish, so let's get crackin.'"

Bo grabbed their rods, both with tube jig lures attached.

"No problem. Just want you fellas to have a good day."

He handed the rods back to the men and watched how they handled their gear. Daye seemed to have a casual knowledge of how to handle a rod and reel, but Williams fumbled with his line, getting it caught in his vest. When Bo decided he was a complete novice, he walked back and helped him unhook himself.

"You fellas ever been bass fishing?" he asked.

Daye nodded. "A few times, down south around Chattanooga," he said. "Couple years ago, though, so I might need some pointers."

"That's what I'm here for," Bo said, smiling at the silver-haired man. "How about you?" he said to Williams.

"Never fished for bass," Williams said, "but fishing is fishing though, right?"

Bo glanced up at him.

"Not really. Bass are smart, and they're tough to hook. You gotta hit 'em at exactly the right moment, or they'll be gone. Tough to reel in, too."

Bo watched as Sonny Daye got a nice cast out by the rocks. *Not bad. He knows what he's doin'.*

Then Williams reached back with his rod, and his line got caught in the trees behind him.

It's gonna be a long-ass day.

"Can you get that out for me, Bo?" Williams said, as he popped another Budweiser.

Daye and Williams laughed and chugged another Bud. Bo was used to dealing with guys like this, guys that would rather drink than fish. All he could do was make sure they didn't fall in and drown. Other than that, they were grown men.

"Just yank it. It'll come out," he said to Williams.

He watched the man jerk his rod several times, but the line didn't move from the tree limbs. Bo grabbed the rod and flicked his wrist, the line freeing from the trees and falling in the water.

"How'd you do that?" Williams said.

"Lots of practice, son."

Yeah, it's going to be a long, long day for ol' Bo.

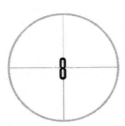

Frankie looked up and saw the sun straight overhead. High noon. It was getting hot, and he was getting hungry. They had followed the red bass boat to three spots along the lake, staying at least one hundred yards behind them. At the third spot, Augie had slowly chugged past the small inlet where the red boat was anchored. He glanced at the location and saw another boat anchored further down so continued past, trying to not look conspicuous.

"They have to be alone, isolated," Augie said. "Can't have any witnesses."

Frankie stared at Augie, still trying to figure out how they were going to pull this off. *Maybe there are grenades in the mystery suitcase. We'll blow 'em out of the water.* This sent a chill up his spine. *Too noisy.* His mind raced as he thought about killing three people in cold blood. *How the hell did I get into this mess? And why did the boss send me?* That thought brought a whole new set of questions to his rattled mind. *Why me? I've never killed any-body . . . don't even know how to.*

"Let's eat while they're back there in the inlet," Augie said as he guided the boat to a small cove just past where the red boat was anchored. "Make me a salami sandwich."

Now I know why they sent me . . . to make fucking sandwiches for the caveman. Frankie grabbed some bread, cut up some salami with a butter knife conveniently left in the box, and slapped it in between the bread.

"You want mustard, mayonnaise . . . ?

"Yeah."

Frankie was waiting for the rest of the answer, but got none. *Tough shit, there ain't any.*

"You want chips?"

"Yeah."

Great talking to ya, Augie. Frankie put the sandwich together, threw some chips onto the paper plate and handed it to Augie.

"Beer," Augie said.

Frankie nodded. *Of course, the rot gut stuff. Watered-down piss.* He handed Augie an Old Style beer and then made himself a salami sandwich, no chips, no beer. He took a bottle of water instead. They sat in the little cove for close to forty-five minutes before they heard an outboard motor rev up in the inlet behind them.

Augie threw his beer in the water, belched, and lifted his ass to let a silent fart slip out.

Christ, he can control his farts. He isn't human.

"Get ready to move," Augie said. "Turn your head when they pass, like you're looking up at the hills or something."

Frankie looked behind them and saw the red boat rounding the bend. He turned his head to the trees behind the cove until the sound of the outboard motor passed. He glanced out to the lake and didn't see anything.

"Looks good to go," he said to Augie.

Augie pulled the cord and the outboard started up. They pulled out of the cove and into the main body of the lake. Augie had his binoculars and searched for the red boat.

"Ah, shit," he said. "I don't see 'em."

Frankie suddenly had hope. *Maybe we lost 'em. C'mon, fishing guide, find your secret hideaway, wherever it is, and stay there.*

Suddenly, the red boat zipped out of a cove right in front of the two men, a mere twenty yards ahead of them. The driver of the boat saw them and waved.

"Shit," Augie said again. "Wave back."

Frankie waved, throwing in a fake smile.

Augie slowed down and let the red boat get far ahead of them. Frankie saw a sign on the shore that said "Welcome to Tennessee." He looked for some kind of line in the water, but saw nothing. He started to ask Augie how they knew when they crossed a state line, but decided against it. *He already thinks I'm a friggin' idiot.*

The red boat suddenly took a turn to the right and headed for the far shore. Up to that point they had been on the eastern shore of the lake, but now were headed for the western shore. Augie didn't turn right away, but waited until the red boat was across the lake and headed back in the direction of Silver Creek dock. He looked through his binoculars, following the boat from a distance. Finally, he turned the rudder right and headed for the western shore.

"You think they're headed back?" Frankie said.

"Nope, just headed for another spot." Augie looked at Frankie. "We gotta do it soon, before they get too close to the dock."

Frankie swallowed and looked at the western shore. *Get the hell to the dock now, you poor schmucks.*

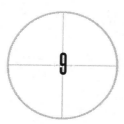

9

Bo anchored at a spot on the western shore that had never let him down. His clients, no matter how pathetic or drunk they might be, always landed at least one smallmouth bass there. It was his favorite spot other than Copperhead Cove, which was off limits to clients. He called this cove "Cottonwood Cove" because of all the cottonwoods lining the shore. It wasn't as pretty or as isolated as Copperhead Cove, but it had the right elements for catching a smallmouth.

Bo looked at the two men, who were getting sloppy now. They'd finished off one case of Budweiser already, and it was only one thirty. Sonny Daye was still somewhat in control of himself and had caught a couple of bluegill, but Williams was slurring his words and wasn't even attempting to fish anymore. *What the hell you doin' out here, you drunk SOB?*

"Hey, Bo, you want a shot of JD?" Williams said, holding up a bottle of Jack Daniel's. He almost fell overboard backward when he stood up.

"Sit down, sir," Bo said sternly. "There's still waves out here, and you can go overboard pretty damn easy." Bo looked at Sonny Daye for some help.

"He's right, JJ. Sit the hell down," Daye said, smiling at Bo.

Williams sat down and spilled a quarter of the Jack Daniel's as he did so. "Hokay," he said, "but do you want a shot, B . . . Bo?"

Bo stared at the pathetic mess.

"I don't drink while I'm guidin'," he said. "We still have four hours, so I think you guys should slow down on the booze a little . . . if you want to catch a smallmouth anyway."

Sonny Daye smiled at Bo again, his eyes red and his complexion somewhat ruddy. He was feeling the effects of half a case of beer, but he wanted to fish.

"This a good spot, Bob?"

Bo shook his head. "It's Bo, and yeah, this is one of the best spots this side of the lake. Afternoon sun is shaded by the cottonwoods, so the water doesn't get as hot. Smallmouth like the cooler water. That's why they stay to the bottom during the day."

"Cool, then let's do some fishin'," Daye said. "Put that JD down, JJ, and do some fishin'."

Bo grabbed Daye's rod and put a live cricket on the hook.

"New bait. See if they like it here."

"Wazat?" Williams slurred. "A fuckin' cricket?"

Bo shook his head. "Yeah, let's see if they go for it today. I've had good luck with 'em here."

Daye stood up, which worried the hell out of Bo, and threw a perfect cast toward the rocks near the shore. Bo watched him slowly reel the line in, feeling the tension in the line with his index finger on his right hand. *Even drunk, he's pretty damn good.*

"Might wanna sit down, Sonny. Don't want the NCAA champion coach falling overboard," Bo said, his first reference to the man's profession. "And nice cast, by the way." *A little positive reinforcement might keep him from that bottle of JD.*

Daye smiled, sitting down.

"Thanks, Bo. Didn't know if you knew who I was or not." He reeled his line in, checked the bait, and sent out another perfect cast, looking at Bo for approval.

Bo smiled and nodded. Then he looked at Williams, who was slumped down in the boat, snoring. *Good place for him until he sobers up.*

Bo decided to throw his own line out while Williams was passed out, taking advantage of the peace and quiet. He put a live cricket on his hook and threw his line out past the rock outcrop, into a shadowy spot close to some fallen tree limbs. He looked over at Daye and saw him yawning. *This trip might be winding down.*

Bo watched his line and Daye's, hoping that a smallmouth would jump on Daye's hook. Nothing was happening. Maybe it was too hot. The fish needed more seclusion from the sun. Bo grabbed his water bottle and took a swig, looking out at the main part of the lake. He saw a small outboard passing by the mouth of the cove. He'd seen the same boat earlier, on the eastern shore. Probably just coincidence, but it made him wonder. The two guys in the boat didn't look like locals, and they didn't seem to be doing any fishing. Bo watched them as they passed by, the smaller man in front glancing in his direction, then turning away quickly. *Strange.*

"My brother's a big sports fan," Bo said, looking at Daye. "He was pretty damn excited when I told him I was takin' you and," he looked down at the man, now lying on the bottom of the boat, "him out today."

Daye laughed. "I've been getting a lot of that lately, 'specially in Tennessee," he said. "Glad to see I'm liked in Kentucky, too."

Bo, always honest to a fault, laughed.

"No, son, we're either Vols fans or Kentucky fans 'round here, and my brother's from California. Just saying, pretty cool havin' a famous coach in my boat, no matter where you're from."

Daye laughed as he pulled his line in and held the hook.

"Think I'll try a night crawler, Bo. They ain't bitin' on this cricket."

Bo pulled a night crawler from his bucket and slid it onto Daye's hook.

"Maybe they're into worms today."

Daye cast out and stared at Williams, snoring on the bottom of the boat.

"I know he doesn't look like much right now," he said, nodding toward Williams, "but JJ's a pretty damn good coach, too. He went to the final four this year. 'Course, I beat him in the semis, but he had a pretty damn good team."

Bo nodded. "Didn't hear too much about him. Where'd he coach again?"

"Midwestern, up in Iowa. They had a powerhouse earlier in the year, just blowin' teams away by fifteen, twenty points every night. They struggled later in the season, still winning, but not by as much. Just ran out of gas, I guess."

Bo looked at Williams, then at Daye.

"Well, it ain't how you start, it's how you finish, right?"

He looked down at Williams. *That pretty much sums you up, pal.*

Daye bent his head back and laughed.

"That's right, Bo. You sound like a pretty bright fella."

"I feel dumb as shit right now, until you land a smallmouth."

Bo looked at his watch. Three o'clock. He glanced out at his line, which hadn't twitched in over an hour, and looked at Daye's. Same thing. A thought entered his head that he tried to shake. *Copperhead Cove.* Bo hesitated, then started to reel his line in.

"What's say we head on over to another cove I know. It has much cooler water, and I can almost guarantee you'll land a smallmouth there."

Daye nodded and began reeling his line in.

"Sounds good to me. Nothing much happening here."

Bo looked down again at the snoring Williams.

"We'll let him sleep it off until we get over there. It's about twenty minutes north, back toward the dock."

Bo raised the anchor and started up the outboard motor. They slowly slipped out of Cottonwood Cove, headed for Bo's private place. *What the hell. He's a famous coach and a nice guy.*

10

The red bass boat had been sitting in a small cove surrounded by Cottonwood trees for over an hour. Frankie and Augie had passed it twice from a distance and didn't see any other boats around. They turned around for a third pass, just to make sure. Frankie felt certain that no one on the boat had seen them, as they were concentrating on the fishing. On the second pass, Frankie only saw two men. He wondered where the third was.

As they approached the mouth of the cove for the third time, Frankie was nervous. As they passed, he glanced at the red boat and saw the fishing guide looking at them. He quickly looked away. *Shit, he saw us. I knew we were pressing our luck.*

"I think he saw us," Frankie said. "And I only saw two men."

Augie grunted. "I have to take a piss," he said, after finishing his third beer. He headed close to the shore and pulled the front of the boat up onto a small sandy beach. They were about eighty yards from the mouth of the cove where the men were fishing.

"Get out and pull the boat up and tie it off," Augie said, moving past Frankie and jumping out of the boat. He headed for the trees in a hurry.

Frankie jumped out and pulled the small boat up onto the little beach. He tied the line to a small tree several feet from the water. He looked around and saw nothing but pines and cottonwoods. He peered out over the lake, looking for any movement on the water. He thought about getting in the boat and taking off, leaving Augie stranded, but there were two problems with that idea. One, he didn't know how to operate the damn boat, and two, he'd be on Augie's hit list, the next one to get whacked. Oh yeah, and a third problem. He was a friggin' coward.

Frankie looked at the unopened metal suitcase in the boat and thought about looking inside. He glanced back and didn't see Augie. But the third problem entered his mind again. He was a friggin' coward. Suddenly, he heard a motor on the lake, getting closer. *Oh, damn, it's them. They're gonna see us.* He ducked down behind the boat but thought that would look even stranger, so turned and walked up into the woods, hiding behind a stand of cottonwoods. He saw Augie out of the corner of his eye and waved to him to stop, pointing to the lake.

The red bass boat came around the bend and headed their way, only twenty feet or so from the shore. The fishing guide was driving, as usual, and the silver-haired man was sitting in the back. The third man was nowhere to be seen. *What the hell happened to him? Did they whack him? If so, great, let's go home.*

Frankie didn't know if the men in the boat could see him, but he'd bet anything they could see Augie, the human redwood tree. He stared at the boat as it passed. The fishing guide was looking in their direction. He continued to look until they disappeared around the next bend. Frankie didn't know if he'd seen them or not, but he had to have seen the boat. Augie began walking toward the boat.

"Let's go," he said.

Frankie untied the knot, threw the rope into the boat, and climbed in. He knew what was coming next: the moment he'd been dreading since they left Chicago.

11

Bo heard a moan behind him, so he turned around. Jerry Joe Williams was starting to come to life. He was still lying on the bottom of the boat, but his head was up, looking around. *Ten to one he goes for another beer.* As Bo turned back around, he heard the pop of a beer can. *What a putz.* Glancing to his left, he saw a small boat tied up on a small beach. It looked like the same boat that he had seen twice before. Looking up into the cottonwoods, he saw a skinny man standing behind a tree. *What the hell is he doing?* Then he saw another man, a huge man with a blue cap on, standing still, staring out at them. Bo passed them by, staring at the strange sight until he rounded the bend. *Something is really wrong with that scene.*

He heard Williams and Daye talking behind him, then heard another pop of a beer can. Looking around, the two men were sitting next to each other, gulping down another Bud. Williams had his other hand on the bottle of Jack Daniel's. *That stupid sonofabitch.*

Bo decided to let 'em drink and enjoy themselves. If they started getting sloppy at Copperhead Cove he'd make a beeline back to the dock, get his money, and say "adios" to the two famous coaches. He liked Sonny Daye, but he didn't take to JJ one little bit.

Bo slowed the boat as they came to the mouth of Copperhead Cove. He didn't see any other boats, but they could be hidden inside the cove. He looked behind him and decided to go for it. He turned the boat to the left and entered the cove, heading for his favorite spot just inside the semi-circle—the same place he and Ethan had fished just a few days before.

As Bo maneuvered the boat into the cove, he pulled up to an area with some fallen trees, mostly under water, with one big one lying just over the shoreline, its branches dipping into the green water. Just past the big tree, he shut the motor down and threw his anchor in the water. They were ten feet from the shoreline, but the water was fairly deep underneath them.

"Here we are, gentlemen, our last stop of the day." He turned and saw both men throwing back a shot of Jack Daniel's. "You guys want to fish or drink?"

"Fish," Daye said. "I want a smallmouth, something to show for being out here all day."

Williams belched and poured himself another shot.

"Think I'll sit this one out."

Bo looked at Daye, who shrugged his shoulders as if to say "oh well."

"Okay, Sonny, looks like it's you and me and the smallmouth. Let's get baited up." Bo threw Sonny a cricket and put another one on his own hook.

"Why we trying these crickets again?" Daye said. "They didn't work in the last place."

"They'll work here," Bo said, smiling. "I almost guarantee it."

"Hey," Williams said. "Bo." He belched again. "You're a good guy. Sure you don't wanna shot of JD?"

Bo picked up his rod and cast out close to the fallen trees, knowing that the smallmouth liked the shady shallows under the trees.

"Yep, I'm sure."

"That a good spot to cast?" Daye said.

"Sure is, just past that big tree, where the fallen trees are in the water. Nice and shady. The smallmouth like it there."

Bo watched Daye cast out close to his line. *A little too close there, Sonny.* Bo looked down at this watch. It was four forty-four and the sun was just above the top of the ridge to the west. They had about half an hour before they had to start heading back to the dock.

"We got about half an hour, Sonny, and then we have to head back."

Sonny nodded as he watched his line, feeling it for any tension. Bo could see in his face he wanted to catch a smallmouth badly. *C'mon, give him one damn fish.*

Bo heard a shout and saw Sonny pulling up on his rod.

"I got one, Bo!"

Bo put his rod down and walked back to Sonny, grabbing his net.

"Did you hook it? You still got tension?"

"Yeah."

Then Bo heard the sweet sound of a whirring fishing line as the smallmouth began his run.

"Snap it, Sonny! Now!"

Sonny snapped his rod up and back, the six-foot rod bending, more line escaping from the reel.

"I got him!" Sonny yelled.

"Good job. Now start reeling him in. They're fighters, so he's gonna make you earn it," Bo said, grinning. "Just keep the line comin' in. I'll snag him when he gets close."

Sonny was pulling and reeling, pulling and reeling. Bo saw the sweat pop out on his forehead.

"You're doin' great, Sonny. Keep him comin'."

Williams sat next to Sonny, staring at the scene.

"Way to go," he belched, "Sonny."

Bo bent over the side and saw the fish wiggling about a foot from the boat.

"Bring him in a little closer, Sonny."

When the fish was just under him, Bo reached out with the net and brought it up in one smooth motion. He held the net up so Sonny could see it.

"Mighty nice smallmouth, Sonny," Bo said. "I'd say about a five or six pounder. Good sized fish."

Sonny gave a whoop and did a fist pump in the air.

"Hot damn!"

"Hot damn," Williams said. "Good . . . good job, Sonny."

At the same moment, Bo saw movement on his left out of the corner of his eye. He glanced over and saw the small boat entering the cove, with the two men he had seen earlier staring in his direction, the big one sitting in the back. The boat moved to the other end of the cove, about forty yards away. Bo kept staring at them, the hair on his neck standing up. A cold shudder passed through him as he saw the big man lift something from the boat bottom. It wasn't a fishing rod.

"Sit down, Sonny. Now!" Bo said, as he started the outboard and began pulling the anchor up.

"What the . . . ?" Sonny said, staring at Bo.

Bo stared at the big man in the boat, who now had a scoped rifle pointed at them.

"Get down!" Bo said, as the first shot shattered the silence of the cove, echoing off the trees.

Jerry Joe Williams sat stone still, eyes wide open, a bullet hole in his temple. Bo watched in horror as he fell backward, hitting what was left of his head on the side of the boat with a dull thud.

Within seconds a second shot rang out, and Bo saw Sonny Daye grab his throat with both hands, blood spurting out between his fingers. Bo didn't wait to see what happened next, flipping backward as the third shot rang out. Bo felt the bullet slice through his leg as he tumbled into the green water. He grimaced in pain, holding his calf, and knew he had to start swimming. Still underwater, he headed for the fallen trees where he had cast so many lines over the years.

His head was pounding as he swam under the big tree that hung out over the cove. He saw the fallen trees ahead and pumped his arms as fast as he could, his bloodied leg dragging behind him. He reached the trees, swam to the other side, and came up for a breath, hoping they couldn't see him. He heard the sound of a motor but didn't know if it was his boat or the other one. He looked around through the brush and knew that his only chance was to get lost in the fallen trees. He took a deep breath and headed for the bottom, his left leg oozing blood into the green water, a smallmouth bass darting out of his way.

12

Frankie held his ears and watched in horror as Augie fired the first shot. He saw the man he knew as Jerry Joe Williams fall backward into the red boat. Augie ejected the shell and fired again, hitting the silver-haired man in the neck. Frankie saw the man clutch at his throat and fall forward. He held his breath as he stared at the fishing guide, who fell backward over the side of the boat, his legs rising in the air. Augie fired again, and Frankie saw blood fly from the fishing guide's leg.

Augie put the rifle in the bottom of the boat and scrambled back to the motor. He gave it some gas and pointed the boat toward the carnage on the other side of the cove. The red boat was floating in a circle, still anchored to the bottom of the lake, the motor running.

"Holy shit," Frankie said, as they approached the spinning boat.

"Grab the boat, climb in, and shut off the damn motor," Augie said.

Frankie looked at him, terror is his eyes.

"What?"

"Get in the fucking boat, now."

Frankie reached out and grabbed the spinning boat, clambering over the side, spilling into it. He felt something soft underneath him and looked in horror as Sonny Daye stared back at him with lifeless eyes, his throat a mass of torn flesh and blood.

"Holy Mother of God," he yelled, lifting his hands from the pool of blood on the bottom of the boat, wiping them on his pants. He scrambled to the front of the boat and hit the only switch he could find. The outboard motor shut down, and the boat slowly stopped spinning. He glanced at the back of the boat and saw Jerry Joe Williams lying twisted on the bottom in a pool of his own blood, half his face blown off, bits of flesh and bone lying everywhere.

What the hell am I doing here?

Augie guided his boat to the shore, ran it up on a narrow, rocky beach, and shut the motor off. Frankie watched him grab his rifle and climb out of the boat.

"Get the fuck out of the boat, you fucking jamook," Augie said.

Frankie looked at ten feet of water between him and the shore.

"Get over here, now!"

Frankie slipped over the side of the red boat and dog paddled to the shore, scrambling up the rocky beach.

"We have to find the guide. If he's still alive, he won't be for long," Augie said. "Look for blood in the water."

Frankie looked in the direction of the fallen trees. He walked the other way.

Augie stared at him, shook his head, and began walking toward the big tree hanging out over the water. Frankie watched him as he climbed over the big tree and approached the grove of fallen trees.

"Over here," Augie yelled. "I see blood."

Frankie wanted to run up the forested hill and disappear, but he knew he'd get a bullet in his back if he did, so he walked slowly toward Augie, peering over the big tree.

"Get your ass over that tree," Augie said. "I need you to swim down under the trees and see if you can find the body."

Frankie froze. "What? I'm not going down there."

Augie slowly pointed the rifle at him.

Frankie climbed over the big tree and scrambled down to the water. He saw the blood, which formed a dark pool in the green water.

"Follow the blood," Augie said. "Now."

Frankie stepped into the cold water and, using his hands against the fallen trees, walked as far as he could before putting his head under the water. He saw trees and limbs beneath the surface and knew the guide was somewhere underneath them. He raised his head out of the water, wiping blood and water from his face.

"I didn't see any—"

"Get your scrawny ass down there or you're next," Augie said, pointing the rifle at him.

Frankie took a deep breath and dove beneath the water.

13

Bo held on to a small tree, hidden by some bushes, and watched the scene on the shore. He knew the blood would give him away, so he surfaced and swam to an area about ten feet to the left of the fallen trees. Watching the other boat cross the cove, he took his shirt off and tied it around his leg just above the wound, to use as a tourniquet to stop the flow of blood from his calf. He looked down and saw that the circle in the water was not as dark.

He stared through the bushes as the big man got out of the boat and walked onto the rocky beach of Copperhead Cove. He watched as the second man, the blond, skinny one, swam ashore and shook the water off, like a scared dog. He stared at the man with the rifle and knew right away that he was a professional killer. The way he had put down Daye and Williams, he had to be. He also knew it was just a matter of time before they found him, so he tried to lower himself into the murky water as far as possible.

He watched as the terrified skinny man dove into the water, the big man watching from the shore, aiming his rifle, ready to shoot whatever came up. A minute later the skinny man rose out of the water, wiping his face and gasping for breath. The skinny man swam back to the shore and fell in front of the big man.

Suddenly, Bo heard a vibrating sound to his right. He'd heard that sound before, when the old copperhead had bit him years ago. He slowly turned his head and stared into the face of an angry snake, only two feet away. But it was too large for a copperhead, and it had a triangular head and a dark body. He froze in terror when he realized what it was—a cottonmouth. They were fierce and aggressive and had venom twice as deadly as a copperhead. The cottonmouth was a rattlesnake that could swim. The snake was on the shore right next to the water, coiled and shaking its tail in the weeds, causing the vibrating sound.

Bo stared at the snake, trying to remain as still as he could. He had nowhere to go and couldn't scream for help. He was screwed. He glanced over at the men on the shore and saw the big man looking his way. He must have heard the vibrating. Bo shifted his eyes between the cottonmouth and the big man, trying to decide which predator was the most dangerous. He couldn't decide, so remained still. He knew if the cottonmouth opened its jaws wide to show its fangs and snow-white mouth, it meant it was about to strike. So far, it was just vibrating its tail. If it opened its mouth, he was a goner. He glanced to the left and saw the big man getting closer, looking at the brush next to the water.

Bo slid deeper into the water, trying not to disturb the surface, just his eyes showing. It didn't work. The big man locked onto Bo's eyes and smiled.

"Hello, fishing guide," the man said, staring down at Bo. "Goodbye, fishing guide."

He raised the rifle and pointed it at Bo's head. Bo glanced to his right and saw a glimpse of the white mouth and fangs, but the cottonmouth wasn't facing him, it was facing the big man. The man took one more step toward Bo, his left foot just inches from the deadly snake. The cottonmouth struck with lightning speed, hitting the big man's calf. The man screamed and reached for his leg, dropping his rifle. The cottonmouth recoiled, ready to strike again. The man dropped to his knees, holding his leg. The cottonmouth struck, this time sinking its fangs into the man's bare arm. The man yelled at the top of his lungs as he bent down, his head near the ground. The snake recoiled and struck yet again, this time in the neck, near the jugular vein.

No sound came out of the man as he raised up, staring down at Bo, who was just a few feet below him. He slowly collapsed forward, landing only inches from Bo's face, his head in the murky water, twitching and making gurgling sounds. Bo turned to face the cottonmouth, and all he saw was a white mouth and fangs, this time facing directly at him. Bo pushed off of the shore with his good leg, out into the green water, terror rising up in his throat. He finally took a breath as he watched the cottonmouth close its jaws and retreat, evidently satisfied that the threat was gone.

Bo floated in the green, murky water, staring at the big man, who was still jerking and gurgling. He looked up in horror as he saw the skinny man, the rifle in his hands, pointed at him. The game was over. Bo waited for the shot that would end his life, but it never came. Instead, he watched in amazement as the skinny man put his foot on the big man's head and pushed it further into the muddy water. The big man began to flail his arms, but the snake venom was paralyzing his nervous system, making him unable to fight. Bo watched the flailing stop, and then the bubbles stopped. He was dead.

Bo glanced to the right to see if the cottonmouth was still around, but didn't see it. The skinny man had gotten lucky. Bo looked up into the eyes of the terrified man, who was shaking from head to toe, and held his breath as the man took a step toward him, the rifle pointed at his head. But the man's finger wasn't on the trigger, it was holding the butt. He was offering him a lift out of the water.

Bo stared at the strange-looking man, trying to decide if he was offering help or if it was a trick. He decided to take a chance, reaching out and grabbing the barrel tightly. The skinny man began pulling him in closer to the shore. When Bo was close enough, the man reached down and grabbed his arm and pulled him up onto the rocky bank.

Bo was breathing heavily, holding his left leg. He glanced around nervously, looking for the cottonmouth.

"Thanks, but we have to get out of here," he said, coughing up water. "Snakes everywhere." He glanced up at the skinny man, who was now shifting his horrified eyes around. "You gotta help me up," Bo said. "I can't walk."

The skinny man put his arms under Bo's armpits and lifted him to a standing position. Bo grimaced in pain as the man put his arm around him and began walking toward the boat. He glanced back, afraid of what he might see, but saw only tree limbs and brush. When they reached the big fallen tree, they stopped. Bo knew he couldn't climb over, so he lowered himself and, like a marine in basic training, slid under it on his back, head first. He dragged his useless left leg, pushing with his right. It was a tight squeeze, but he made it. The skinny man climbed over the tree and picked him up. They reached the boat, where he helped Bo over the side. Once Bo was safely in the boat, the skinny man glanced back at the dead man in the water.

"I . . . I have to make sure he's dead . . . and isn't found," he said, looking at Bo. "I'll be right back."

"Watch where you step," Bo said, grimacing in pain. "That cottonmouth is still around."

Bo watched him climb over the big fallen tree and slowly walk back to where the big man was lying face down in the water. Then Bo looked down and saw the rifle lying right next to him. He picked it up and checked the chamber, seeing one round in it. He waited until the skinny man came back several minutes later.

"He's dead," the skinny man said. When he looked at Bo, he stopped cold. Bo had the rifle pointed at him.

"Who are you?" Bo said. "And why shouldn't I blow your brains out?"

The skinny man began shaking again.

"I'm Frankie . . . Frankie Farmer. I wanted no part of this," he said pointing to the red boat where two men lay dead. "I . . . I saved you."

"Who do you work for? Him?" Bo said, pointing to the dead man. He was starting to shake from the pain and loss of blood.

Frankie's eyes were bulging, and the sweat was rolling off his forehead. "I work for the people that wanted those guys over there dead."

Bo glanced at his boat.

"Why? What'd they do?"

Frankie stared at Bo.

"They fixed some games—basketball games—and made the wrong enemies."

Now Bo's eyes opened wide.

"They shaved points?" he said. "Even Daye?"

Frankie shook his head. "Don't know about him, but the other one did, a lot, and he screwed up."

Bo digested this information.

"The big guy was the shooter. What did you do?"

Frankie shrugged his shoulders.

"I made sandwiches."

"What?"

"I don't know what I was here for. I'm married to the boss's daughter, and he hates my guts. I guess he wanted to get rid of me, too."

If Bo wasn't in so much pain, he'd laugh at the bizarre situation he was in.

"So the big guy was gonna kill you, too, when the three of us were dead?"

Frankie nodded. "I think so. That's the only reason my boss sent me out here. To get rid of me."

Bo stared at the man, not knowing whether to believe him or not, but he had helped him out of the lake when he could have just shot him and left him for dead.

"I have to get to a doctor," Bo said. "Can you drive a boat?"

"Fuck no. I've never been in one before today."

Bo stopped to think, glancing at his red bass boat and then at the small gray fishing boat he was sitting in, with the small outboard. They could get to the dock much faster in his boat, but it had two dead bodies in it. He glanced at his watch. It was five thirty.

"Okay, the bass boat is anchored, so isn't going anywhere. We can lay some blankets over the two . . . dead men, so the birds don't pick them apart." *I can't believe what I'm saying.* "I need to get to a hospital before I bleed to death and before shock sets in. I'll have to help you drive the boat." Bo lowered the rifle. "Get in, Frankie. You just became my new best friend."

Frankie's shoulders sagged as the fear and adrenaline escaped.

"Thanks, Bo," he said as he climbed into the boat.

"How'd you know my name? I didn't tell you my name," Bo said.

"I did some research on you in Chicago, when I found out you'd be the fishing guide for . . . them."

Bo glared at him.

"So you knew the big guy was going to kill me, too?"

Frankie nodded.

"I didn't want to kill you or Sonny Daye, or even Williams." Frankie looked at Bo. "You and Daye were collateral damage, just like I would've been if that . . . that snake wouldn't have saved our asses."

"You're from Chicago? Sounds like the mob," Bo said. "Are you with the mob?"

Frankie swallowed hard. "Yes."

Bo pointed the rifle at Frankie again. He felt faint from the loss of blood and all the activity and possible infection from the murky water.

"Throw a couple of blankets on those guys, and let's get out of here," he said, blinking his eyes.

"You okay, Bo?"

Bo tried to focus on Frankie, but the image became blurry. He began to rock backward, dropping the rifle. The last thing he saw was Frankie picking up the rifle and pointing it at him. Then everything turned black.

14

Holy Mother of God! Frankie watched Bo slump down into the boat, passed out cold. He grabbed the rifle as soon as Bo dropped it, with no intention of using it. *I can't let him go into shock, he has to drive the boat!* Frankie slapped the fishing guide on the cheek, with no response. *C'mon, Bo, wake up, dammit.* He slapped him again, harder. Nothing.

Frankie looked around and thought about the mess he was in. The red bass boat with two dead men in it, another man sinking to the bottom of the lake with snake venom in him. And him, saddled with the only man who could identify him as an accomplice to murder, and the only man who could get them out of here, passed out cold.

Frankie bent over and felt Bo's neck for a pulse and let out a big sigh when he found one. He sat back and thought for a moment, looking around the cove to make sure they were alone. *Think, Frankie.*

Okay, no one knows who he was except the fishing guide, lying in his boat unconscious. He'd given a fake name and fake license plate number to the ditzy clerk when he checked into Motel Hell. He had one more night paid for, so knew he had a place for tonight at least. What about the mess here in this cove? What the hell does he do with the two dead bodies? He could leave them for someone to find, as Bo had said. Both of them with a bullet hole in their heads? All hell will break loose if that happens. What if he makes them disappear, like it never happened? Then he'd have only the mob after him, if they even knew he was still alive. *I've got to disappear, just like Augie and the coaches . . . but not at the bottom of the lake. But what to do with the fishing guide?*

He looked at his watch. It was five forty-five. The sun would be down within an hour, an hour-and-a-half at the most. He looked past Bo and stared at the metal suitcase. Maybe there was something inside that he could use. He scrambled over Bo and grabbed it. He pulled the two buttons on each side and the top popped free.

He looked around the cove for a few seconds, making sure he was still alone. *Do I want to know what's in there?* He opened the top and checked out the contents. *What the hell?* He took out a shovel, the kind with a collapsible handle. His eyes grew wide when he saw the hacksaw. *What the hell was that for?* He shuddered at the thought of Augie with the hacksaw in his hands. *Holy crap, he was going to saw them up, maybe saw me up!*

He moved the hacksaw and peered inside at a portable drill with a big bit, causing a shudder to go through his body. He saw four bungee cords in the original plastic bags, having no clue what they were for, but it was the last item underneath everything else that sent a shiver down his spine. It was a .357 Magnum handgun and a box of shells. *Who was that for?* His eyes grew wider. *That was for me! Augie was going to make me fish food, just like the two dead men.*

Frankie sat back, looking up at the sun, which was just beginning to set behind the hills. He had an hour to do whatever he was going to do and get the hell out of there. Or he could stay here with the two dead men, the dying fishing guide, the man-eating snakes on the shore, and half a salami, a couple of beers, and a bag of chips. He decided against the second idea.

He looked at the portable drill, scratching his head. What was that damn thing for? He glanced at the red boat and back at the drill. Then it hit him. Augie was going to sink the red boat to the bottom of the lake, probably with the two, make that three—*Holy crap!*—make it four men inside, secured to the boat with the bungee cords. How about the saw? A grotesque thought entered his head. Augie was going to saw their hands off to get rid of the fingerprints, and the shovel was to bury the hands. No clues, no witnesses, no murders. Augie had thought of everything, except one—a poisonous, pissed-off snake. *Take that, you belching, farting, caveman son-of-a-bitch.*

Frankie looked at Bo again, moving his head around, slapping him, trying to get him to wake up. He'd never killed anybody and didn't want to start now. *Augie didn't count because he was mostly dead already. Bo had called me his new best friend, but he also was the only person that could identify me, that knew what happened in the cove.* On the other hand, Bo knew that Augie was the killer, not him. But he also knew that Frankie was an accomplice.

Frankie then knew what he had to do. He got out of the boat and pushed it off the sandy shore, climbing back in when it was fully in the water. He grabbed the oar and paddled out to the red boat. He tied the two boats together, grabbed the drill and the bungee cords, and climbed into the red boat. He held his nose as the smell of two dead bodies hit him. *Holy crap, what a mess. Blood and brains everywhere.*

Frankie wrapped two bungee cords around Sonny Daye, holding his head away from the man, and secured the ends to hooks on either side of the boat. Daye's eyes were wide open, freaking him out, so he reached down and closed them. *He didn't deserve to die, dammit.* Jerry Joe Williams, who had half his head blown off, was messier. When they were both secured tightly, he threw everything that wasn't attached into the smaller boat, including the unopened bottle of Jack Daniel's and the second case of Budweiser. *I'll need these tonight.* He also found a medicine kit in the red boat, which had an antibiotic vial and a needle. He'd use that on Bo when he had the chance.

Satisfied that there was nothing left that wasn't secured, he grabbed the drill. After looking around one more time, he turned it on, the drill coming to life, placed the bit on the bottom of the boat, and pressed down as hard as he could. The half-inch drill bit cut through the fiberglass and through the sheet metal until he saw water beginning to seep into the boat. He did the same thing in four different places until the bottom of the boat was completely under an inch of water. He watched the water slap against Sonny Daye and Jerry Joe Williams, causing more blood and flesh to float to the surface. He hung his head over the side, losing his salami lunch. *What the hell am I doing?*

Frankie climbed into the smaller boat, untied it from the red boat, and paddled backward, away from the sinking bass boat. He sat motionless, watching it slowly sink into the green water. The water gurgled when the boat was totally submerged, then it was gone. Frankie sat for another ten minutes to make sure nothing came floating up to the surface. When he was satisfied that everything was buried in the green water forever, he slapped

Bo one more time, just for the hell of it, then looked at the outboard motor. *Augie made it look easy, so just do what Augie did.*

He dragged Bo to the front of the boat, gently laying him down on the metal bottom. Then he went back to the rear and grabbed the rope attached to the outboard motor and pulled with all his might. The motor spun, but didn't start. He pulled the rope again, and still nothing happened. *What the hell?* He looked at the motor and saw the on/off switch. *You friggin' jamook.* He turned the switch to on and pulled the rope again. This time the motor came to life, gurgling in the green lake water.

He looked at the motor again and saw the lever. One side said reverse, the other side said forward. It was sitting in idle, so he moved it to forward and grabbed the rudder stick. The boat began to move forward, inch by inch. *How the hell do I make it go faster? I'll get to the dock by next Tuesday at this rate.*

Frankie stared at the motor again, looking for something that said "Go Fast" or "Zoom." Then it hit him. *Just like my old Harley when I was in college, the rudder handle is the throttle.* He twisted his wrist slightly to the right, and the boat began moving faster. Frankie cracked a small smile, so proud of himself. *I'm driving a damn boat.* He maneuvered out into the middle of the cove, away from the shore, and glanced back at the area where the red boat had disappeared. The water was smooth and still, nothing popping up to disturb the surface. He gunned the throttle and roared past the area where Augie had been bitten. *Who's the jamook now, you friggin' animal?* He left the deadly cove and entered the main body of the lake, looking around to see if anyone had seen him. Seeing no one, he began the journey back to the Silver Creek Resort dock. The sun was starting to set, casting shadows on the lake.

Frankie guided the small fishing boat the six miles to the Silver Creek Resort area, taking about fifteen minutes. He glanced at his watch again. Six o'clock. He stopped and idled before entering the "no wave" zone. He peered at the dock and saw lots of people walking around and several boats tied up to the dock. *I can't go down there, not with the fishing guide passed out in the boat.* He looked around and saw a small private dock to his left, with two boats tied up. There was an empty slip on the outside of the small dock, so he headed for it. The sunlight was just about gone, leaving just the twilight to illuminate the lake. He was far enough away from the dock to go unnoticed, if he was quiet. He guided the small boat into the slip, bouncing off the sides several times, and shut the motor down. He looked around to see if anyone was around, but saw no movement. A cabin was thirty yards away, but it was dark, no lights on inside.

What am I going to do with Bo? He looked at the man slumped on the bottom of the boat, reaching over to check his pulse. It was still beating. He looked around again and then remembered the medicine kit with the antibiotics. He pulled it out, loaded the needle, and injected it into Bo's leg, hoping it would stem any infection. He knew he had to get Bo and the equipment to his Cadillac. It seemed like days ago that he had parked it along the road in the darkness, but it was actually just that morning.

Frankie climbed out of the boat, tied it to the slip, and walked quickly off the dock and to dry land. *Hallelujah!* He followed the shoreline around a bend of trees and saw a walking path to the resort parking lot. He remembered walking past the lot in the darkness that morning. There were only a couple of cars then, but it was three-quarters full now. He saw several people carrying coolers and fishing gear to their cars, so he waited until they passed then walked briskly through the parking lot, up the hill, and spotted the silver Cadillac DeVille off to his left, sitting exactly where he had left it along the shoulder of the road. There were several other cars parked in front and behind. Frankie dug the keys out of his pocket, unlocked the door, and got in.

He drove down past the parking lot and continued up the road, hoping there would be an opening to the dock where he had left Bo. He saw it off to his left and pulled into the small boat launch area next to the dock. He looked around to make sure he was alone and walked quickly to the boat. He grabbed Bo by the underarms and lifted him out of the boat. Bo groaned, but remained unconscious. *At least he's still alive.*

Frankie dragged the fishing guide up the short hill to the car, opened the rear passenger door, and pulled him in, laying him on the back seat. He felt for a pulse again and breathed easier when he found one. He then went back to the boat and retrieved everything else and carried it to the car, putting it in the trunk. He went back to the boat with a beach towel and wiped down the sides and everything that he had touched. When he was finished, he stood on the small dock and stared at the boat.

This is going to cause a lot of questions if I leave it here. He walked back to the car and opened the trunk, getting the drill out of the metal suitcase.

He walked back to the boat, climbed in, and after glancing around began drilling holes in the bottom, every few seconds popping up to look around. It was easier than the bass boat, just sheet metal to drill through. After four or five holes, he saw water quickly seeping into the bottom of the boat. He climbed out, untied the line, and pushed it out from the slip, the boat floating five or six feet from the dock before it stopped, half submerged.

Frankie walked back to the Cadillac and watched the small boat disappear in the murky, green water. He figured they might find it eventually, but he would be long gone.

He climbed into the Cadillac, backed out onto the road, and headed back across the parking lot. He drove up the steep hill that had freaked him out earlier that morning. The sunlight was virtually gone when he reached the crest of the hill and kept going, remembering that it was about a ten minute drive to the highway. Once he saw the sign for Highway 495, he started to breathe a little easier. *Now all I have to do is decide what to do with old Bo in the back seat.*

Frankie turned right and drove down Highway 495 to the outskirts of Crockett, turning left onto Main Street. He passed the Riverside Motel, the parking lot still full of cars for graduation week. He passed the gas station where he'd found out about Joe's Ribs and Taters and came to the stop sign. He turned left, just as he did the night before, and passed Joe's and Rite-Aid, and turned left on the next road, the one that would take him to the Ridge Motel.

As he reached the crest of the hill, he stopped to see if there were any cars in the parking lot. His heart skipped a beat when he saw an old Chevrolet Impala in front of room twelve. *What the hell? Did they find me already?*

He pulled the Cadillac onto the side of the road, hidden behind some bushes, got out, and walked around the edge of the parking lot. He was in the woods across from room twelve, peering through the darkness, panicking, when he saw a light on in the room. *Was it the cops? Or worse, had Tonelli sent someone down already?*

Frankie waited in the woods for five minutes, hearing noises all around him. He remembered the snake that had killed Augie and began looking around the ground at his feet, listening for any movement or vibration. He peered into the woods and saw several beady eyes looking back at him. *What the hell?*

Just then, the door to room twelve opened and a heavy-set woman walked out, holding a mop and some cleaning supplies. She put them in her trunk, got into the dumpy Chevy, started it up, and drove out of the parking lot.

It was the maid! Frankie waited several seconds to make sure she drove down the hill, then walked back to get the Cadillac, glancing back at the forest, still shaking. He parked the Caddy on the side of the building, next to room twelve, out of sight. He quickly walked up to the door of room twelve and put his key in, wiggling it as before. When it opened, he turned the light on and stuck his head inside. The bed was made and everything seemed to be in order. He walked quickly to the bathroom, noticing Augie's toothbrush and razor lying on the sink. Looking in the closet, he saw one pair of slacks and a polo shirt. *His traveling attire while he drove back to Chicago in the Cadillac to report the unfortunate deaths of the two Podunk coaches, the yahoo fishing guide, and poor Frankie Farmer, who fell overboard in the mayhem and drowned.*

Frankie collected the clothes, toothbrush, and razor, and looked around for anything else that would identify Augie. Satisfied that he had everything, he threw them into a plastic bag he had pulled from the trashcan and took them to the car, throwing them into the trunk. *So much for Augie Stellato, the belch and fart machine. May he burn in hell.*

Frankie then walked next door to room eleven and tried the key to room twelve again. With a little wiggling, it opened once again. He turned on the light and looked around. The bed was unmade, his dirty towels still on the bathroom floor, and his toiletries and clothes still intact. No one knew he had slept here the night before. *Perfect.*

Frankie walked outside and opened the back door to the Cadillac, pulling Bo out and carrying him into room eleven. He laid him on the bed, checking his pulse again. He noticed the wound on his left calf was turning an ugly shade of purple. He walked back to the trunk, brought everything into the room, and shut the door. He bent down at the waist, putting his hands on his knees, breathing deeply. He walked to the window, looked outside, and turned off the light. *Now what, you jamook?*

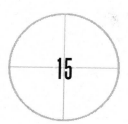

15

Ethan was at dinner at a barbeque restaurant next to the Peabody Hotel with Vinnie when Kathy called.

"Hello," he said, putting his glass of chardonnay on the table.

"Ethan, it's Kathy."

"Hey, sis. How was Bo's big day?" he said, grinning and nodding at Vinnie.

"He hasn't come home yet, and I'm startin' to get worried," she said. "He never stays on the lake after dark."

Ethan glanced at his watch.

"It's only eight o'clock, Kath. He's probably having a beer with the coaches or his buddies."

"He'd call me if he was gonna be late, Ethan. He's never failed to call me."

Ethan sat back and took a drink of his wine.

"Have you talked to anyone at the resort?"

"Yes, I talked with Slammer Perkins, another fishin' guide. He saw Bo this morning when he took the two coaches out but hasn't seen him since."

"Is his boat back at the dock?"

He heard silence on the other end.

"No, and that's why I'm callin' you. He hasn't returned to the dock yet."

Ethan sat up in his chair, suddenly worried. He heard the tone of Kathy's voice, one which he had never heard in fifteen years. Not panic, but serious worry.

"How about anyone else at the dock? They see him or his boat?"

"JB is down there now, checking around."

JB was the acronym for Bo Junior, Bo and Kathy's twenty-four-year-old son. They switched the letters around because Bo didn't want his son to grow up with the nick name of "BJ," for obvious reasons, so he grew up being known as Junior Bo, shortened to JB.

"Has he ever kept clients out past sundown?" Ethan said.

"Only once, but that was years ago during a thunder and lightning storm. He had to get off the lake for an hour or so, but it's a clear sky up here today."

Ethan wasn't sure what to say to Kathy to make her feel better, so he decided to play comforter.

"I'm sure everything's okay, Kathy. Bo's been on that lake thousands of times and knows it better than anyone around."

"But he never—never—keeps a client out late, especially if they've been drinkin'," she said. "He loaded two cases of beer and two bottles of Jack Daniel's in his truck this morning. Ethan, I'm worried sick."

Ethan closed his eyes and rubbed his forehead. He didn't know what to say to his sister-in-law.

"Ethan, are you there?"

"Yeah, Kath, sorry. I was just thinking. Do you want me to drive up tomorrow morning?" he said, looking at Vinnie.

"I hate to ask you . . . . "

"No problem, Kath. I can start out early and be up there by noon."

"Thank you, Ethan. I'll call you if he shows up tonight, so you don't have to make the trip." Her voice cracked when she said this.

"Kath, can you give me a call later tonight to let me know what JB found out?"

"Okay, I will. Thanks, Ethan."

Ethan put his cell phone on the table and looked up at Vinnie, who was staring at him, a grim look on his face.

"Bo didn't come home tonight," he said. "His wife is worried, obviously."

"It's only eight o'clock," Vinnie said. "Still pretty early."

"Not according to Kathy. She said Bo never comes home after sundown without calling, and . . . . "

"And what?"

"And he packed a lot of booze in his truck this morning, so evidently Sonny Daye and Williams were planning on drinking a lot."

"Is that unusual?" Vinnie said. "It sounds like the typical city folks going out for a day on the lake."

"I don't know, Vinnie." Ethan stared at his friend, then finished off his glass of wine. "You okay if I drive up there in the morning and shine off the meetings tomorrow?"

Vinnie nodded. "You don't even have to ask, buddy. Do what you have to do."

Ethan smiled weakly and ordered another glass of wine. Then he remembered what Vinnie had told him the day before.

"Vinnie, you said something yesterday about Jerry Joe Williams being investigated for point shaving," Ethan said, suddenly very worried. "Have you heard anything more?"

"No, just that there's an ongoing investigation. Why?"

Ethan looked down at the table and then back up at Vinnie.

"What if he pissed off the wrong people?"

"What do you mean? What people?"

Ethan cleared his throat, his mind working furiously.

"If you're shaving points, you have to be working with someone that will make money from it, right?"

Vinnie leaned in.

"Yeah?"

"What if Williams was involved with the wrong people . . . like the mob?"

Vinnie sat up straight.

"C'mon, Ethan. The mob? Are they still around?"

Ethan stared at this friend.

"I don't know, but what if they are and Williams was hooked up with them in some way? And let's say he screwed up, and the mob lost money."

Vinnie's eyes grew big.

"Holy shit, Ethan."

Ethan nodded as he rubbed his eyes. *My thoughts exactly.*

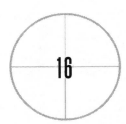

16

"What the hell do you mean they disappeared?" Tony Tonelli shouted. "How do they disappear, goddammit?"

The man standing in front of Tonelli was Tito Barboza, who had worked for Tonelli for ten years and knew the man's temper. It was nine o'clock on Wednesday evening.

"I'm just sayin', boss, Augie never checked in tonight, and the boat never showed up."

Tonelli started pacing, walking from one end of his office to the other. His mind was racing, trying to digest this new information.

"What about that idiot, Frankie? Anyone hear from him?"

"Nope."

"The idiots we hired to get the boat and supplies for Augie, are they still down at that Podunk lake?" Tonelli said, trying to remain calm.

"Yeah, they're the ones that called," Barboza said.

"Well, have 'em check around." Tonelli began pacing faster, slapping the walls every other minute. "Goddammit, how could they screw this up? Augie's never failed me—never!"

Barboza scrunched his shoulders.

"I dunno, boss."

Tonelli kept pacing.

"Something happened. They must've run into trouble. Maybe they got lost on that Podunk lake. Is it a big lake?"

"Pretty big, yeah."

Tonelli's phone rang.

"Hello?"

"Daddy?"

"Hi, Bunny," he said to his daughter. *Damn, she's gonna ask me about Frankie.*

"Dad, Frankie hasn't called, and I'm getting worried. Have you heard from him?"

Tonelli didn't want to get into it right now, so he lied.

"Yeah, they're in a motel down in Kentucky. I guess Frankie must've lost his cell phone on the lake or something."

"Daddy, is he okay?"

"Oh, sure, baby," he said, glancing at Barboza. "He'll be home tomorrow afternoon. Don't worry, okay?"

"Okay, Daddy, but call me if you hear from him."

"All right, Sweet Pea. Good night."

Tonelli hung up the phone. He knew his daughter would never see her husband again, if Augie had done what he was told, anyway. But now Tonelli wasn't sure about anything.

"We need to get someone down there and start checking things out," Tonelli said, pacing again.

Barboza shrugged his shoulders again.

"Who you want on this, boss?"

Tonelli rubbed his forehead. He stopped pacing and looked out the window.

"Put the Jew on it."

"Goldberg? Hell, boss, he's been retired for years. I don't even know where to find—"

"Find him! Get Goldberg, goddammit!"

Barboza nodded and slowly walked to the door. He turned and looked at Tonelli.

"Boss, you think Augie might've, uh, turned?"

Tonelli stared at Barboza, his eyes blazing.

"Augie would never turn against me. Get the hell out of here, and find Goldberg."

Barboza nodded and opened the door.

"Barboza."

"Yeah, boss?"

"Get Fanelli, too."

Barboza stared at Tonelli.

"Geez, boss, isn't this a little small-time for Fanelli?"

"I want both of 'em in my office tomorrow morning at eight o'clock."

"Okay, boss, but I don't know where—"

"What the hell do I pay you for, you friggin' imbecile?" Tonelli picked up his brand new stapler and heaved it at the door. "Get Goldberg and Fanelli!"

17

Frankie sat next to the bed and wiped the wounded man's forehead with a cold, wet washcloth, trying to get his temperature down. He'd tried to clean and bandage the leg as best he could with gauze and tape from the first aid kit, but the bullet had gone clean through his calf. The man had lost a lot of blood and would need a doctor soon. He sat back in the chair and closed his eyes, the exhaustion finally catching up with him. *I just want to sleep and forget this damn nightmare.*

My cell phone! Frankie sat upright with a start. Augie had told him to turn it off when they first got out of the car that morning because he didn't want the damn thing ringing while they were on the lake. Frankie had turned it off and put it in the glove compartment of the Cadillac.

He ran to the window and peeked outside. Not seeing any other cars, he opened the door slowly. He looked around at the creepy sight of the empty parking lot, like something from a bad horror movie. He stared at the dense woods on the other side of the lot as he walked to the Cadillac, hearing noises and seeing little eyes peering at him. When he reached the Cadillac, he stopped again and looked around, listening for any noise. He opened the passenger door, then the glove compartment. He felt something cold and metallic. A glance revealed a snub-nosed revolver, but no cell phone. *Augie must have taken the cell phone and put the gun inside.* Frankie hit the dash board when he realized his cell phone was probably at the bottom of the lake. He decided to leave the revolver in case he might need it later. He had the .357 Magnum in the room.

He closed the glove box and car door and walked quickly back to room eleven, peering at the empty parking lot before closing the door. He walked in the darkness to the cheap desk chair and sat with his head in his hands. Glancing up, he saw the bottle of Jack Daniel's on the desk. *What the hell.* He opened it and poured some into a dirty glass from the bathroom, chugging it in one gulp. It burned on the way down, but it felt so good. He poured another glass, sat down in the chair, and stared at the man in the bed, who was still lying motionless. *If I don't get him to a doctor, he's gonna die.*

Frankie chugged the JD and poured another glass, then turned his chair so it faced the door. He took the .357 out of the metal suitcase, loaded six cartridges, and set it on the desk. He sipped the JD, feeling the heat warm his throat. He thought about his wife, Bunny, who would be calling her dad, his boss, every half-hour. Poor Bunny. He laughed when he thought of her name. *Bunny Farmer.* No wonder Tonelli hated him, having a daughter with a name like that. Frankie laughed again and then clamped his hand over his mouth. He giggled silently, taking another sip of JD. *Bunny Farmer.*

Frankie chugged the rest of the JD in his glass and leaned back in the chair. *I'm so tired, so tired.* He closed his eyes and thought about little bunnies running around, a farmer with a pitchfork chasing them. *Bunny Farmer.* He smiled and was about to nod off when he sat straight upright. He listened, leaning toward the door. *Squeak.* Someone or something was outside the door. He grabbed the Magnum and sat staring at the door. *Squeak.*

Frankie slowly stood up and took a step toward the door, the gun in his right hand. He took another step and heard it again. *Squeak.* He stood between the door and the window, afraid to look outside. *What if it's Augie? He didn't die! Or he did die and his ghost has come back to finish the job.*

Frankie listened for the squeak. When he didn't hear anything he bent down, took the corner of the curtain, and looked outside. He didn't see anything in the parking lot. He glanced to his right, toward the corner of the building, and didn't see anything. *What the hell?*

Squeak.

Holy shit, it's right outside! He closed the curtain and sat down, holding the Magnum with both hands. *Holy Mother of God!* Then he heard a scratch at the door. *A scratch?*

Frankie stood up and reached for the door knob. Holding the gun in his right hand, he slowly opened it a crack, saw nothing, and then opened it wider. He looked down and saw two eyes staring up at him, surrounded by black patches. The raccoon hissed, showing his teeth, and ran off across the parking lot. Frankie fell backward, slamming into the desk. His heart was beating a mile a minute. He slammed the door, sweat pouring from his forehead. *Holy Mother of God, what next?*

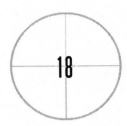

18

Ethan was on his laptop computer in his room at the Peabody Hotel when his cell phone rang. The readout said "Bo," which sent a charge through his body.

"Bo?" he said into the phone.

"No, it's Kathy."

"Oh, hi, Kathy." His shoulders slumped. "I have your number programmed into my cell phone, and it reads out 'Bo.'" He heard crying on the other end. "Kathy, talk to me."

"JB came back from the lake and said no one has seen or heard from Bo or the two coaches."

Ethan looked at his watch. Eleven fifteen. *Damn!*

"And he hasn't called?" Ethan knew the answer but had to ask.

"No."

Ethan put his elbows on the desk and leaned his head on his hand, rubbing his eyes.

"Ethan, I'm scared. Really scared," Kathy said, sniffling.

"I know, Kathy. Is anyone out looking for him on the lake?"

She blew her nose.

"Some other fishing guides are out there right now, checking most of Bo's favorite spots. There's about seven or eight out with spotlights. They've been on the lake for over two hours now."

"Okay, that's good," Ethan said. "If he's out there, they should find him."

"Unless . . . unless he fell overboard. It's a big lake, Ethan."

"Okay, Kathy. I'm leaving at first light and should be up there before noon tomorrow. Will you be home or at the lake?"

"I'll be here, just in case someone calls or he comes home."

"How about JB?"

"He's taking the pontoon boat out first thing in the morning, to check Bo's private spots."

"Like Copperhead Cove?"

"Yeah, and a few others."

"What time is he going out in the morning?"

"He wants to be on the lake when the sun comes up, so around six."

"Hold on, Kathy."

Ethan put the phone down and thought for a few seconds. If he left Memphis by midnight, he could be in Crockett by four thirty and could join JB in his search. He'd have to drive all night, but he wanted to be there.

"Kathy, tell JB to wait for me. I'm going to drive up tonight and should be there around four thirty."

"Oh, Ethan, that means you have to drive all night," Kathy said.

"I know, but I want to go out with JB to look for Bo. Tell him I'll be at the farm at four thirty and not to leave for the lake until I get there."

"Okay, Ethan," she said, sniffling again. "Thank you. Drive safe."

"See you in a few hours," he said and hung up.

He stared at his laptop for several seconds and decided to send Vinnie an email, letting him know what he was doing. Then he turned it off, closed it, and packed it into his laptop bag. He threw his clothes into his suitcase, went to the bathroom and threw water on his face, gave the room a once over, and walked out. *It's gonna be a long night, a longer day, and I hope to God I'm having a PBR with my brother when the sun goes down tomorrow night.*

19

The bottle of Jack Daniel's was nearly empty when Frankie realized he hadn't eaten anything since his salami sandwich at lunch, and he threw that back up on the lake. He looked at his watch, but the numbers were fuzzy from the Jack Daniel's. He closed one eye and focused, seeing the big hand and little hand next to each other on the twelve. *Midnight.* His stomach began to growl, so he reached for the salami, tore off a piece, and began chewing.

He heard a moan from the bed and saw movement. He squinted through the darkness and saw Bo raising his head. *Damn, that's all I need.* He walked to the side of the bed, dragging his chair with him. He sat down with his face close to Bo's.

"Hey, you awake?" Frankie whispered, glancing at the window.

Bo groaned again, louder this time. He opened his eyes slightly and blinked.

"Where am I?" Bo said, his voice weak and hoarse.

Frankie put his finger to his lips. "Shhh. You have to be quiet. We're in a motel room."

Bo opened his eyes wide and peered in the direction of Frankie.

"Who're you?"

Frankie glanced at the door, leaning in closer.

"I'm the guy that saved your ass on the lake."

Bo blinked and looked around.

"Why's it so dark in here?"

Frankie shook his head. *How much do I tell him?*

"Because I don't want anybody to know where we are."

Bo squinted through the darkness at Frankie.

"What time is it?"

"Midnight."

Bo shook his head and rubbed his eyes.

"How long've I been out?"

"Six hours, give or take."

Bo pushed himself up, groaning in pain.

"Ah, hell, my leg."

"You need to lie still," Frankie said, glancing from Bo to the window. "You've lost a lot of blood."

Bo put his hand on his left calf.

"Who bandaged me up?"

"I did."

"I haven't been to a doctor?"

"No."

"Why not?"

Frankie sat back in the chair.

"Because I can't take you to a doctor just yet. Maybe tomorrow."

Bo squinted again, searching for the man in the darkness.

"I could be dead by tomorrow."

Frankie remained silent. *That's a possibility.*

"You got anything for the pain?" Bo said, closing his eyes.

"Some aspirin, that's about all. I injected you with an antibiotic while we were on the lake, to help with the infection."

"I need something for the pain, dammit."

Frankie pursed his lips.

"You like Jack Daniel's?"

"Give it to me," Bo said through clenched teeth.

Frankie stood up and walked to the desk, glancing nervously at the window. He poured half a glass of JD and walked back to the bed.

"Here, sip this."

Bo took the glass and gulped it down.

"More."

Frankie shook his head as he brought the bottle over and poured another half glass.

Bo gulped it down, a little slower this time.

"More," he said, coughing.

"You'd better take it easy there, Bo. You don't have much blood flowing through your veins right now."

"More, dammit."

Frankie poured another half glass.

"That's it, no more."

"Screw you," Bo said after swallowing the whiskey.

"No, I mean there's no more. It's all gone."

Bo stared through the darkness at Frankie.

"You drank this whole bottle?"

"Uh, pretty much, except for what you just inhaled."

"Well, thanks for saving me some."

"How's the pain?" Frankie said.

Bo belched loudly.

"Shhhh! Goddammit, Bo."

"Sorr– sorry," Bo said, putting his hand to his mouth. "I thi–think I'm drunk already."

Jesus, the man must not have any blood in his system. It's all whiskey.

"Why don't you try to get some sleep . . . " Frankie said, his voice trailing off when he heard Bo snoring.

You'd better snore quietly, fishing guide, or you're getting a pillow over your face. Frankie stared at the window, looking for any movement. He slumped in the chair, listening to Bo saw logs. His eyelids began to feel heavy as he watched the window, his head beginning to nod. *This is going to be the longest night . . . .*

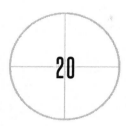

20

After checking out of the Peabody Hotel and calling the rental car company to tell them that he was keeping the Buick for another few days, Ethan drove through downtown Memphis, past Beale Street, which was still lit up and rocking, and headed for the highway. Once on the interstate, he pointed the Buick toward Nashville, put it on cruise control, and then called his children in California.

"Molly, it's Dad," he said, recognizing his daughter's voice.

"Hi, Dad," she said. "Why are you up so late?"

Ethan smiled, knowing that his daughter would know exactly what time it was in Memphis.

"I'm driving to Uncle Bo's," he said, waiting for the questions.

"What? I thought you were there last weekend?"

He grimaced. *How much do I tell her?*

"Yeah, I was, Princess, but I have to go back."

"Why? What's wrong? Is Uncle Bo okay?"

Ethan struggled with how much to tell his daughter, who had been through such an ordeal less than two years ago. He decided to lie, to protect her.

"Oh, he's fine, no problem." He shook his head. "He's taking a couple of famous people out on his boat, and he asked me if I wanted to tag along." He cringed when he said this, knowing how smart his daughter was and how well she read him.

"Why would you care about that, Dad? Why aren't you coming home?"

Ethan shook his head, realizing he could never get anything past Molly and, since the ordeal in Mexico, never thought about trying, until now.

"Listen, Princess," he said, rubbing his forehead while thinking about what to say. "Uncle Bo's in trouble, and I'm going up there to help him and Kathy." There, he said it.

"Dad! What's going on? What kind of trouble? Is he hurt? Did he have an accident—"

"Molly. Hold on. I'll explain, but don't interrupt me, okay?"

Silence. "Okay."

"Uncle Bo took some people out on his boat today and never returned. He's missing, Molly."

Silence again.

"Moll, you there?"

"Daddy, tell me what happened, and don't sugar coat it."

He loved it when she called him Daddy, but the last time was the day after the horrific ordeal in Mexico.

"The two men he took out on the guided trip may have been in trouble with . . . with some bad people, and Uncle Bo may have got caught up in that."

Silence again. Ethan wished he was there so he could hold his seventeen-year-old daughter.

"Molly, you okay?"

He heard sniffles.

"Daddy, I want to come back there, to help Aunt Kathy."

"No!" he said, a little too emphatically. "No, Princess. Not right now. Maybe later."

"Why? Dad, are you in danger? Is Aunt Kathy in danger?"

Ethan rubbed his eyes. *It never gets any easier.*

"I don't know, Moll. I just don't know what's going on, but I need to find out before you or Charlie fly back here. Do you understand, Princess?"

He heard her crying. He waited until he heard her sniffle.

"Okay, Dad. Will you call me as soon as you know something?"

"You know I will, Princess. Will you call Charlie and let him know? I know he has finals next week, so I don't want him to worry."

"I can't lie to him, Dad."

"I know you can't, Princess, but just don't say anything that will upset him right now. Please."

"Okay."

"Thank you, Moll. I love you, sweetheart."

"I love you too, Daddy. Call me."

"I will, Princess. Bye."

Ethan hit the end button and tossed the phone on the passenger seat. He stared at the highway ahead, his mind racing from his present predicament to memories of two years ago, to the days after the 9/11 tragedy. How he was stuck in Europe because of the closure of America's airports, and of the horrific phone call he'd received on the night of 9/11 from his son. *Dad, Molly's been kidnapped.* He'd relived the nightmare over and over in his mind in the twenty-one months since it happened. How he had hired a broken-down private investigator to find his daughter, and how he'd flown on a charter cargo flight from Amsterdam to Mexico City, met Vicki, the Mexican charter pilot who had helped him get to Tijuana, and how he had fallen in love with her, the woman he would marry in three months.

Ethan fought back tears as he looked out of his car window and saw the moon hanging in the dark sky. It was a quarter moon, what he and Molly called a toenail moon. The image brought back more memories of those dark days of September, 2001.

"Jake, I need you to find my daughter," he had said to Jake Delgado, an old friend from his military days.

"But I drink, a lot," Jake had told him.

Ethan had worried about his choice and about whether he would ever see his daughter alive again after a maniacal gang leader kidnapped her, her two friends, and their teacher from a convoy of returning students from a home-building mission trip in Baja California, Mexico. He remembered his six-thousand-mile odyssey from Europe to Tijuana, Mexico, culminating in a climactic confrontation with the Mexican gang leader at the Tijuana border crossing, with Jake Delgado risking his life to save Molly and the other girls.

He remembered staring up at the quarter moon on the balcony of the San Diego hospital, a day after the ordeal, Molly standing next to him, hooked up to an IV.

"That's Molly's moon," he had said to his daughter, as the tension and fear had finally subsided. He remembered everyone inside the hospital room that night, including Jake Delgado, his son Charlie, who had a shattered leg from a car bomb explosion, and Victoria Calderon, the woman he had fallen in love with on the trek from Europe to Mexico, his future wife.

Now, here he was in the middle of the night, almost two years since his daughter's ordeal, and he was heading toward another unknown situation, this one involving his older brother, who, like Molly twenty-one months earlier, could be alive and well, or could be injured, or even dead. A shiver ran up Ethan's spine as he stared at the white line of the interstate.

21

The Kentucky countryside was invisible in the blackness of the night as Ethan turned off Highway 495 and onto the road that led to his brother's farm. Even though he couldn't see anything on his right or left, Ethan knew the road well from so many visits over the years. He knew it was two miles from the 495 turnoff to Bo's dirt gravel road, which would lead him down a steep hill to his brother's farm.

Ethan looked for the small church on the right side of the road, knowing the entrance to his brother's lane was directly across from it. His heart began to beat faster as he thought about what was in store for him that day. He was sleepy from four hours of driving, but a cup of Kathy's strong coffee would wake him up.

He saw the church in his headlights and slowed down to make the left turn onto Paxton's Road, which Bo had named years earlier. He drove in total darkness, except for his headlights, down the narrow country lane, past a dilapidated barn, and over a small bridge. He turned a corner and saw the lights of the Paxton house in the distance. He glanced at his watch. Four twenty-two in the morning.

Ethan pulled onto the gravel driveway that led up to the house. Bo's two hunting dogs, Garth and Brooks, began barking, alerting everyone in the house that someone was coming. A young man walked out of the house holding a piece of toast and watched Ethan as he parked the Buick and got out, Garth and Brooks sniffing his leg, as they always did.

"Morning, JB," Ethan said as he walked up to the house.

"Hey, Uncle Ethan," JB answered. "Not quite mornin' yet."

Ethan smiled. JB reminded him of Bo in so many ways.

"Good point. Good to see you again."

"C'mon in and grab some breakfast before we head out."

Ethan walked into the warm, well-lit kitchen, seeing Kathy at the stove.

"Hi Kath," he said, dropping his overnight bag.

Kathy wiped her hands and walked quickly to him, hugging him tightly, not saying a word.

"Any word yet?" Ethan said, looking at her red, blotchy eyes.

"No, nothing," Kathy said. "The men didn't find anything last night, and they searched for hours."

"They checked every fishin' spot that dad ever took a client to," JB said. "They didn't find anything, 'course it was at night."

"How about Copperhead Cove?" Ethan said.

"They don't know about the cove," JB answered. "That's where we're headed first thing this mornin'."

Ethan nodded as Kathy led him to a stool at the kitchen counter where a plate of scrambled eggs, hash, and bacon were sitting, a cup of steaming black coffee next to it.

"Eat, Ethan. It's gonna be a long day," Kathy said, choking, putting her hands to her face.

"What's wrong, Kath?" Ethan said, resting his hand on her shoulder.

"I said the same thing to Bo yesterday mornin', about this same time." She began softly crying.

JB walked over and held his mother.

"Go ahead and eat, Uncle Ethan. We gotta go in a few minutes."

Ethan turned and started shoveling the food into his mouth. His mind was racing, as it had been all night. *What would they find today? Would it lead to a happy ending or a tragic ending?*

He drank the cup of black coffee, washing down the eggs and hash, and wiped his mouth.

"Could I take a cup of coffee with me?" he said, looking at JB and Kathy.

"Got a thermos already in the truck," JB said. "We'd better hit the road."

Ethan stood up and hugged Kathy, who had stopped crying.

"You have my cell phone number, in case you hear anything while we're on the lake."

She nodded, wiping her tears. Ethan turned and saw JB opening the door.
"We'll find him, Kath. Be strong."

Kathy hugged him again.

"Thank you, Ethan. Bo loves you so much."

Ethan nodded, smiled, and walked outside to the waiting pickup truck. He hopped into the passenger seat as JB put it in reverse and backed out onto the gravel driveway.

"You ready for this, JB?" Ethan said, glancing at the twenty-four-year-old. JB was the spitting image of his dad, except for Bo's salt and pepper beard. JB was clean shaven, taller than Bo, and skinnier, but his mannerisms, his quiet confidence, and his country way of speaking were identical to Ethan's older brother.

"Yeah. You must be tired, Uncle Ethan."

"Probably not any more than you are. I'm sure you didn't get much sleep last night."

JB nodded his head.

"Yep. Me and mom sat up talking most of the night. She's a mess."

Ethan nodded.

"I could tell by her eyes that she hadn't slept much. It's a tough deal, son."

It was still dark outside as the blue F-150 pulled out onto the country road that would lead to Quail Hollow Lake. Ethan glanced at his watch again. Ten minutes after five.

"What time does the sun come up?" Ethan said, watching the road.

"'Bout six," JB said. "It'll take twenty minutes to get the pontoon boat gassed up and ready, and you can have a cup of coffee in the restaurant while I'm doin' that."

"You need any help?"

"No, go on in and relax until we push off. They'll be some fishin' guides in there, gettin' coffee'd up."

JB talked just like Bo, forcing a smile on Ethan's face. He was a smart kid, but the southern Kentucky drawl made him sound like just another hillbilly. Ethan had always made fun of his brother's drawl, but after coming back to Kentucky for so many summers he'd grown fond of it.

"You know, your dad's a tough, smart man," Ethan said. "Chances are good he's okay." Ethan said this more to convince himself than his young nephew.

JB nodded.

"Yep."

They rode in silence until they pulled into the Silver Creek Resort parking lot. Three other cars were in the lot as JB parked the pickup. One of them was Bo's blue Explorer and one was a white Mercedes.

"You know the way to the kitchen," JB said, grabbing a cooler from the pickup bed.

"Yep." Ethan said, smiling, glancing at the white Mercedes.

He walked across the swinging gangway to the dock and the restaurant and entered through the back door, just as he and Bo had done many times in the past. He saw a silver-haired man sitting at a table, drinking coffee. Ethan had met him before but couldn't remember his name.

"Mind if I join you?" Ethan said.

The silver-haired man looked up and smiled.

"Ethan Paxton. Sure, help yourself. Coffee's in the kitchen."

Ethan smiled at the man and walked back to the kitchen. He saw a heavyset woman peeling potatoes at the sink.

"Morning. Mind if I grab a cup of coffee?" he said.

The woman turned around, immediately recognizing Ethan as Bo's brother. She dropped her potato in the sink, wiped her hands on her apron, and walked over to him, giving him a big bear hug. When she released him, she put her hand on Ethan's cheek.

"Our prayers are with your brother," she said, tears forming in her eyes.

"Thank you, that means a lot," Ethan said. "JB and I are going out—"

"I know, he told me last night. Fine boy, just like his daddy."

Ethan nodded.

"Can I grab my own coffee?"

"You bet, and grab some eggs and taters over there, too."

"Oh, thanks, but Kathy just made me some—"

"Oh, my God, Kathy," she said, putting her hand to her mouth. "How's she doin'?"

Ethan poured his coffee.

"She's taking it pretty hard."

"Give her my best and tell her that anything she needs, just ask, okay?"

"Okay, thanks, uh . . . . "

"Milly. And you're Nathan, is it?"

"Ethan," he said, smiling. "Common mistake. Thanks, Milly."

Milly gave him another bear hug, almost spilling his coffee, and kissed him on the cheek before going back to her potatoes.

Ethan rubbed his cheek, checking for lipstick, as he walked back to the silver-haired man at the table. He sat down, taking a long swig of coffee. The man held out his hand to Ethan.

"Slammer," he said. "Slammer Perkins. Met you once with Bo a year or so back."

Ethan shook his hand.

"Yeah, I remember. Hard name to forget. You're a fishing guide, too, right?"

Slammer nodded.

"Not as good as your brother. He's the best in the county, maybe the state."

"How'd you get the name 'Slammer'?"

He pointed to his cap, the blue one with the white "K" on the front.

"Back in my college days, many years ago, during the time they'd outlawed the slam dunk 'cause of Lew Alcindor or whatever his name is now. I played for Kentucky and had a brain fart one night and dunked the ball. Just couldn't stop myself. The refs called me on it, took the points away, and we lost the game by those two points." He smiled at the distant memory. "So I was 'Slammer' from then on."

Ethan smiled at this.

"Were you one of the men that went out looking for Bo last night?" Ethan noticed the dark circles around the man's eyes.

"Yep. We were out on the lake for a few hours, got back 'round midnight," he said, shaking his head. "Can't see much at night, though."

"Yeah, well, thanks for doing that," Ethan said. "JB and I are going out this morning to check some of Bo's private spots."

"Good. Ol' Bo had a few hidden spots that he'd never talk about. He loves this ol' lake."

Ethan nodded, taking another swig of the hot coffee.

"Me 'n' some other fellas are goin' out again this mornin' around seven, see if we can find somethin' in the daylight," Slammer said. "There's gotta be somethin' out there. Three men can't just vanish."

Ethan felt a shudder when Slammer said "vanish."

"That Mercedes in the lot one of the coach's?"

"Yeah, guess so. Sure ain't mine. The fellas that ol' Bo took out yesterday had some shady dealin's, which means shady friends, you know what I mean?"

Ethan leaned in. "I think so. You talking about the coach that was accused of shaving points?"

"Yep. Don't think Bo knew about that, but me'n the other fellas were talkin' about it last night. Jerry Jim Wilson, or some shit."

"Jerry Joe Williams," Ethan said. "I just heard about it two nights ago, but I didn't say anything to Bo." Ethan pursed his lips. "Wish I would have, now."

"Wouldn't a mattered to Bo. He'd a taken them fellas out anyway. Nothing ever bothers ol' Bo."

Ethan smiled. *You're right. Nothing ever seems to bother Bo, but what about now?*

"Uncle Ethan, you ready?" JB said from the front of the restaurant.

Ethan turned and waved to JB.

"I'm comin', JB."

He finished his coffee and held out his hand to Slammer.

"Thanks for everything you're doing, Slammer. Give my thanks to the other fellas, will you?"

"Sure will, son. Good luck today."

Ethan nodded and headed down the hallway toward JB and the unknown.

This is getting more and more complicated, especially if some bad people are involved. It may be about time to call Jake Delgado.

22

Ethan followed JB out of the restaurant and stepped into the pontoon boat that was floating next to the dock. Ethan looked up at the eastern hills surrounding the lake and saw the sun beginning to peek out, casting welcome light onto the dark lake.

"We gonna have enough light, JB?" Ethan said, staring out at the lake.

"Oh yeah. It'll light up real quick once the sun pops over the hills, 'bout ten minutes or so."

JB put the outboard motor in gear, and they slowly began their journey out of the "no wave" zone. Once past the buoys, JB opened it up, and they moved down the middle of the lake at fifteen miles per hour.

Ethan stared at the shoreline on the right side of the lake, the one they were closest to, and looked for any movement or any flash of red, the color of Bo's bass boat. There were only a few other boats on the lake at that hour, and they were mostly on the other side. The landscape all looked the same to Ethan—cottonwood and pine trees coming down to the shoreline, with little inlets and coves every hundred yards or so.

Standing in the front of the pontoon boat, he looked back at JB, who was sitting behind the steering wheel looking straight ahead. JB reminded him of his older brother, when Bo was in his twenties, a casual confidence about him. Ethan thought about what must be running through JB's mind right then and thought again about his daughter's ordeal in Mexico. The same scenario was playing out today, not knowing what to expect. It sent a shudder through Ethan's bones.

The wind in Ethan's face felt good, healing. It was cool, almost cold at six o'clock, before the sun was fully over the lake. The surface of the lake was half in sunlight, half in darkness—an eerie gloominess and quiet, with even the birds not up and chirping yet. This was Bo's favorite time of day. This and twilight, when they were usually headed back to the dock, a full day of fishing behind them. Ethan thought about just four days ago, when he and Bo had spent the day at Copperhead Cove and Ethan caught his first smallmouth bass. He remembered the grin on Bo's face and smiled. So much had happened since that Sunday, and so much remained to be uncovered.

"Here we are, Uncle Ethan," JB said. "Keep your eyes open for anything."

Ethan nodded and peered at the shoreline as they entered the mouth of the small cove. He was beginning to know the cove fairly well, having been there five or six times with his older brother. He knew that Bo's favorite fishing spot on the cove, where Ethan had caught his smallmouth, was on the right, next to the large tree hanging out over the water and the fallen trees next to it. A smile crossed his face as he saw the spot, remembering Sunday.

JB expertly maneuvered the pontoon boat next to the big tree, slowly pulling the hull up onto the rocky shore. Ethan jumped out onto the little beach and tied the rope to a small cottonwood sapling. He turned and looked at the trees, which were just a few feet from him. He remembered what Bo had said on Sunday: *I don't go on shore much anymore.* Ethan stood still, not wanting to move until JB was next to him.

"You okay, Uncle Ethan?" JB said, jumping from the pontoon boat onto the shore.

Ethan smiled weakly.

"Your dad got bit by a copperhead right here, didn't he?"

JB laughed.

"Yeah, but that was years ago. He loves to tell that story to scare other folks away. They won't bother ya unless you step on 'em or somethin.'"

Ethan laughed nervously.

"Yeah, that's what I'm afraid of, stepping on one."

JB smiled.

"Just follow me."

JB walked around the little beach, looking for some telltale sign or clue. Ethan took a deep breath and followed him, looking around the beach, but also listening for any movement or vibration.

"They don't rattle like a rattlesnake," Bo had said. "They shake their tail, kinda like a vibration noise."

JB walked to the edge of the small beach, away from the big tree, and bent down to pick up an empty whiskey bottle.

"These guys were drinking yesterday, right?" JB said, showing the bottle to Ethan. It was a Jack Daniel's bottle.

"Yeah, and that's what they were drinking," Ethan replied.

"They were probably here in the cove," JB said.

"Your dad told me he never took clients here, only family," Ethan said.

JB glanced at his uncle.

"Let's keep lookin'." JB turned and walked toward the big tree leaning out over the lake. He looked underneath the tree and saw something that made him stand up straight.

"What is it, JB?"

JB motioned for Ethan to look down.

"Someone pulled himself underneath the tree, and he was bleedin'. See the dark area there? That's blood."

Ethan bent down and looked at the dark patches and where someone had dragged himself underneath the big tree trunk. He touched his finger to the dark patch and smelled it, then tasted it. It had the distinct salty flavor of human blood.

"That's blood, alright," he said.

JB climbed over the tree trunk and hoisted himself to the other side. Ethan shook his head and followed his young nephew.

"Whoever it was, they was hurt," JB said. "Hurt bad enough they couldn't get over the tree, so they slid underneath."

JB walked down to the water's edge, next to the submerged trees, and saw footprints in the soft sand.

"Someone was in the water here," he said, looking at Ethan.

Ethan was beginning to get an eerie feeling about the place, a feeling that something bad happened here recently. The shudder went through his bones again.

JB continued to search the surrounding area, bending down and looking at something in the bushes next to the submerged trees.

"More blood," he said, as he took another step into the brush.

"JB, you think you should be walking in there?" Ethan said, standing ramrod still.

JB continued to walk through the brush, right up to the edge of the lake. He bent down and picked something off a limb that was sticking out of the water, only a foot from the shore.

"What's that?" Ethan said, taking a tentative step forward.

JB turned around and stared at Ethan. His eyes were moist.

"My dad's fishin' cap."

The shudder turned into a full blown shiver going up his spine as Ethan stared at the baseball cap. It was the same one Bo had worn on Sunday.

"My dad was here . . . . " JB said, his mouth trembling. "And he's hurt bad."

Ethan rubbed his eyes as he thought about the possibilities.

"Time to get the police involved," Ethan said, looking at his brother's distraught son. *And time to call Jake Delgado and ask him to get his butt back here, pronto.*

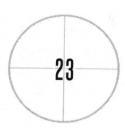

23

The slit of sunlight hit Frankie's eyes, causing him to jerk awake. He blinked, looked around the shabby motel room, and put his hand in front of his eyes. He glanced at Bo, who was still asleep on the bed. Frankie sat up in the chair, arched his aching back, yawned, and glanced at his watch. It was six forty-five. *Damn Jack Daniel's.* He rubbed his throbbing forehead, stood up and walked to the window and peered out. The sun was just rising above the forest and hills to the east. He looked around the deserted parking lot, saw nothing, and closed the curtain all the way.

It was decision time. He had to figure out what to do with the fishing guide and what to do with himself, the car, his life. It was the dawn of a new day, and he was still alive.

He walked into the bathroom and threw water on his face, looking into the mirror at his sore, red eyes. *Damn, I look like a zombie.* He had a day's growth of stubble on his chin and cheeks, and his hair looked like someone had taken a blender to it. He brushed his hair with his hand, but it did no good. He threw water on his head and took a comb to it. Some help, but not much. Then his bladder suddenly got his attention. He stood over the toilet and eliminated the yellow liquid, urine mixed with Jack Daniel's, for a solid minute.

He washed his hands, then walked to the bed and checked Bo's breathing. He was breathing steadily, rhythmically. Frankie checked the bandage, saw a slight ring of red, but otherwise it looked okay. He'd change the bandage later, after Bo woke up.

Frankie glanced at the door. He needed fresh air, but did he dare walk outside? He walked to the window and peered out one more time. It looked safe, so he unlocked the door and opened it a crack. The cool, morning air felt good, so he opened the door and walked outside. He looked up as the sun hit his face. He heard the birds singing, the world coming to life once again. He closed the door to room eleven and walked out into the empty parking lot. He knew he was taking a chance, but he had to get some exercise and sunshine. His back ached, his head hurt, and he thought once again, *What the hell?*

Frankie looked around in all directions and walked to the side of the building, next to room twelve, and checked on the Cadillac. It had early morning dew on it, which was evaporating as the sun rose in the sky. All looked well, so he walked to the back of the motel and looked down at the town of Crockett. He stood there, amazed at the view of the town and countryside. The horizon extended for miles to the west. *Damn, why is this place empty? What a beautiful view.* He looked to his right and saw twelve balconies extending from the rooms. He also saw the cobwebs on every balcony. The place had obviously been empty for a long time.

He stretched his back, did a couple of half-ass bends, and walked back to room eleven and opened the door, doing one more search of the parking lot and the woods beyond before walking in and shutting the door. He froze when he saw Bo holding the .357 Magnum in his hands, pointing directly at him.

"What the hell?" Frankie said, his eyes bulging.

Bo's eyes were open wide, bloodshot and red.

"I'm getting' out of here," he said, his voice rough and raspy.

Frankie stood still, staring at the .357. He watched as Bo tried to get out of bed, falling on the floor when his left leg gave out.

"Arrggg," Bo cried.

Frankie rushed to the man's side and took the gun from him. He saw the spot of red on Bo's bandage beginning to grow. *Shit, he opened up the wound.*

"Okay, fishing guide, let's get you to a doctor." He picked Bo up under the shoulder blades and laid him down on the bed.

"God damn, it hurts," Bo said through clenched teeth.

"I'm gonna have to change the bandage before we move you," Frankie said, reaching for the first aid kit.

Frankie took the old bandage off, seeing the blood seeping out of the wound and a hint of green puss around it. *Shit. Looks infected.* He cleaned it with a clean washcloth, some disinfectant from the first aid kit, put fresh gauze on it, and taped it up as best he could.

"Looks like the bullet went clean through, Bo," Frankie said. "That's a good thing."

"Sure as hell doesn't feel like a good thing," Bo said, his teeth clenched.

"You have a doctor in Crockett?" Frankie said, looking at Bo.

"Yeah, Doc Welby."

Frankie stopped and stared at Bo.

"Are you shitting me?"

Bo looked up, grimacing.

"No, why?"

"That's the name of that doctor from the television . . . never mind. Let's go."

He hooked his arms around Bo underneath his shoulders, and they walked slowly to the door.

"You sure you want to do this?" Bo said.

"No, but if I don't you're gonna die."

They walked out into the morning light to the silver Cadillac. Frankie laid Bo down in the back seat, being careful with his leg. He put a pillow from the room under his head and his injured calf.

"You comfortable, Bo?"

Bo nodded.

"Let's go."

Frankie went back to room eleven and grabbed the Magnum, shut and locked the door, and slid into the driver's seat of the Caddy.

"Change of plans, Bo," Frankie said. "I can't risk taking you to someone that knows you, so we're gonna drive over to Bowling Green."

Bo sat up quickly, but laid back down in agony.

"But that's over an hour away," he said, grimacing in pain.

"I know, but you've lasted this long, you'll last another hour. I just can't risk it."

Frankie started the Cadillac and backed out into the parking lot, hoping like hell he didn't pass anyone coming up the hill. He drove through the empty lot and started down the narrow road, finally reaching the main road.

Turning right would take him back into Crockett. Turning left would be the road to Bowling Green, fifty miles away. He turned left.

"Sorry, Bo, but they'll be looking for us in Crockett, and they'll be checking the hospital and doctors. Can't risk it."

Bo was quiet until they had driven several miles.

"Can I at least call my wife from Bowling Green?"

Frankie thought about this for another few miles, then turned and looked at Bo.

"They'll be looking for you as well as me, so they may go to your farm."

"Who's they?"

"The guys my boss will send to deal with us."

"Hit men?"

"Yeah, something like that."

"Is my wife, my family, in danger?"

Frankie was silent. He didn't want to make the situation worse, so he lied again. "No, they won't hurt anyone's family, unless they feel threatened." He thought about the cottonmouth at the lake. "They're kinda like that snake that bit ol' Augie. If they feel threatened, they'll strike."

Frankie turned and saw Bo staring at him, eyes wide with fear.

"I need time to think, Bo. Our lives depend on it right now."

As they drove the country highway toward Bowling Green, Frankie's mind raced. *I'll have to get rid of the Cadillac, somewhere they can't find it. And I'll have to get another car somehow, but I can't rent one, can't leave a paper trail. I'll have to buy a cheap one . . . or steal one.*

"What happens in Bowling Green? What're you gonna tell the doctor?" Bo said.

"I'll tell him you had a hunting accident," Frankie said. "Probably happens all the time in this back country, right?"

"What about names?"

"John Smith or Joe Blow, anything but our real names."

"They won't treat us without identification."

Frankie thought for several seconds. "We'll tell 'em we left it behind when I rushed you to the hospital. They gotta treat you. They just can't leave your leg like that."

"You woulda had a better chance at the regional hospital in Crockett, or with Doc Welby."

"Yeah, but they know you there."

Bo was silent.

"You're diggin' a deeper hole for yourself, mob guy," he finally said. "Why don't you trust me and my family? We'll hide you so no one will ever find you."

Frankie glanced back at Bo.

"Why would you do that?"

Bo smiled for the first time.

"Well, 'cause you took care of me . . . you and the cottonmouth, and, well, you're my new best friend."

Frankie glanced back several times, his mind racing again.

"Would this Doc Welby," he shook his head when he said the name, "be discreet? I mean, would he play dumb if someone with big muscles and a flat nose came asking questions about you and me?"

"If I asked him to, he would. He's our family doctor. Been stitching me and my kids up for years."

Frankie pulled over to the side of the road, stopped the car, and rested his head on the steering wheel. *Can I trust this yahoo fishing guide with my life?*

"Frankie, we're in this together, whether we like it or not. What happens to you happens to me, right?"

Frankie raised his head, turned in his seat, and looked at Bo.

"It's life or death, Bo. No other way this can go. Life or death."

Bo nodded, a grim smile on his face.

"Then I choose life, but you need to trust me."

Frankie nodded and started shaking his head back and forth, up and down. "What the hell?"

He turned the car around and headed back toward Crockett. *This fishing guide better be a stand-up guy, or my life isn't worth an Augie fart.*

24

Tonelli was doing his usual pacing, glancing at the clock on the wall, muttering to himself. *Goddammit! Where are those jamooks?* It was eight fifteen in the morning on Thursday, and still nothing from Augie or Frankie. Tonelli slapped his office wall as he paced.

"Mr. Tonelli," the voice on his intercom interrupted, "Mr. Goldberg is here." Tonelli hit the lit button.

"Send him in."

Tonelli stood behind his desk, watching the door. He hadn't seen Julius "Julie" Goldberg in five years, but he used to be the best damn tracker in the family. *How old is he now? He might be in a damn wheelchair.*

The door opened and a man with short-cropped, silver hair entered. He was clean shaven, tanned, and walked with confidence. He was short and fit.

"Julie, good to see you," Tonelli said, reaching out his hand.

"Howdy, Two Toes," Goldberg said, smiling broadly. "They still call you Two Toes?"

"Just the old guys, like you," Tonelli said, grinning. *Damn, the guy looks great.*

Tonelli sat in his chair and motioned for Goldberg to sit.

"What have you been doing the past five years?" Tonelli said. "You look great, Julie."

"Been down in Miami, soaking up the sun, playing some golf, screwing my brains out."

Tonelli laughed. *Damn, he missed the old gang.*

"Young ones or the old biddies with blue hair?"

"The young ones," he said. "They like old guys with money that are hung like a horse."

Tonelli laughed again. He remembered the stories about Goldberg back in the day. The guy was a legend when it came to the women.

"You been working at all?"

"Naw, not much. Every now and then I'd get a call, do some light stuff. I still got what it takes to get the job done, though." He leaned in, over Tonelli's desk. "What'd you bring me up here for?"

"Let's wait until Fanelli gets here."

Goldberg stiffened.

"Fanelli? Is he involved in this?"

"Yeah, I need you both. Why, is there a problem between you two?"

"I hate that hairy dumbass, Two Toes. He's a jamook's jamook, to use your words."

Tonelli frowned.

"Mr. T, Mr. Fanelli is here," his secretary said, popping her gum over the intercom.

That goddam gum is going up her ass today.

"Send him in, and quit popping that fucking gum!"

"Sorry, Mr. T."

"And quit calling me Mr. T, goddammit!"

Tonelli hit the end button on his phone, shaking his head.

"Can't get decent help anymore."

The door opened and a huge hulk of a man stood in the doorway. Giancarlo "Rhino" Fanelli was tall, probably six foot five, and almost as broad. He had a dark shadow on his chin, even though he probably shaved half-an-hour before. He had black hair and was the hairiest man Tonelli had ever seen. Tonelli stood up and walked to the door.

"Carlo, how are you?"

The two men shook hands as Tonelli motioned for the man to take a seat. Tonelli winced and looked at his hand, shaking it behind Rhino's back. The man was a human hand-crusher. He used Fanelli's given name of Carlo in public, but called him Rhino behind his back.

Fanelli stopped when he saw Julie Goldberg sitting in front of him.

"Please, Carlo, sit," Tonelli said.

Fanelli walked over and sat down next to Goldberg. The two men glared at each other for several seconds. *Shit, they're gonna kill each other in my office.*

"Would you two like some coffee?" Tonelli said, trying to lighten the mood.

"Black," Fanelli said, not taking his eyes off of Goldberg.

"Two creams, three sugars," Goldberg said, still glaring at Fanelli.

Tonelli punched a button on the phone.

"Maria, can you get us some coffee in here? Just bring the pot and some cream and sugar."

"Sure, Mr. T," the voice said, without a hint of gum smacking. "Uh, Mr. Tonelli."

Maybe I won't have to shove it up her ass quite yet. The jury's still out.

Tonelli looked at the two men: one short, tanned, silver-haired, and clean shaven, but the other looked like he just stepped out of the gorilla cage at the Chicago Zoo.

"Gentlemen, I brought you—"

"I'm not working with this schmuck," Goldberg said, looking at Tonelli.

"I ain't workin' with this Jew motherfucker," Fanelli said, glaring at Goldberg.

Tonelli stood up and slammed his hand on his desk, causing his new stapler to fall to the floor. The two men stared at him, eyes wide.

"I don't give a shit how you two feel about it," Tonelli said, his face red, the veins popping out of his neck. "I am the goddamned boss of this family, and you two are gonna work together. Capisci?"

Goldberg stretched his neck, glaring at Fanelli again. Fanelli stared at Tonelli.

"But, boss—"

"But boss what, you fucking Rhino?"

Fanelli hunched his shoulders and dropped his gaze.

"Nothin', boss."

Tonelli turned his face to Goldberg.

"Julie?"

Goldberg nodded, throwing his hand in the air.

"Capisco."

Tonelli, satisfied that the two men were under control, started his pacing.

"I need you to go down to some Podunk lake in Kentucky and find out what happened to Augie Stellato and my son-in-law."

Goldberg's eyes grew wide again.

"Stellato's still alive? I thought he was—"

"He's not dead, goddammit!" Tonelli slapped his desk with his palm. "Or at least he wasn't before yesterday."

Goldberg stretched his tanned neck again.

"Okay, just askin'."

"They drove down there on Tuesday to take care of some college basketball coach who took fifty large from me."

"You gonna whack somebody for fifty large?" Goldberg said.

"No, you idiot, he lost me and the family over a million."

"Jesus," Goldberg said. "What'd he do?"

"He was supposed to make sure his team didn't cover the spread in a tournament game in late March. We had a million riding on it with bookies around the country. We would've cleaned up, but his team covered the spread, and then some."

"Did Augie whack him?" Fanelli said.

Tonelli's face started to turn red again.

"I don't know, you fuckin' jamook. He never checked in, and neither did my idiot son-in-law."

Fanelli's eyes narrowed.

"Augie was one of the best in the business. How'd he—"

"I don't know. That's what you two clowns are gonna find out."

Goldberg stretched nervously in his chair.

"You don't need both of us for that, 'cause I can do it alone."

"Shut up! Listen!" Tonelli's veins were popping out again. Goldberg slumped in his chair as he stretched his chin.

"Okay, okay."

"Julie, I need you to be the brains, find out what happened—fast. Capisci?"

"Capisco."

"And Rhino, I need you to be the muscle, in case we need to whack somebody else down there. Capisci?"

"Yeah, boss. Capisco."

"Maria will give you all the info, rental car stuff, hotel they stayed at. And I want you down there today, so she's got you on a flight out of O'Hare into Nashville at eleven thirty. It's a two-hour drive from Nashville to the Podunk lake." Tonelli looked at the clock on the wall. "That gives you three hours to get packed and get to the airport."

Goldberg stretched his neck again.

"Uh, boss, I need to bring up my fee."

"Get your ass outta here. We'll talk about your fee when you get back."

The two men stood up, glared at each other, and started walking to the door.

"One more thing," Tonelli said.

"What's that?" Goldberg said, turning around.

"If you find my son-in-law alive, make sure he doesn't stay that way."

The two men stared at Tonelli.

"You wanna whack Bunny's husband?" Fanelli said.

"Yeah, and this doesn't get out to anyone, especially Bunny. Capisci?"

The two men nodded as they reached for the door.

"And make sure the two coaches and the fishing guide are dead."

They stopped cold.

"Two coaches?" Goldberg said. "I thought you said one."

"Collateral damage, same as the fishing guide. I want them all dead."

Goldberg looked at Fanelli, who was looking at him.

"I think we need to talk about my fee," Goldberg said, starting to walk back. When he saw Tonelli pick the stapler up off the floor, he turned back to the door.

Two Toes hurled it at the door as the two men rushed out. It shattered against the wall, just like the first two.

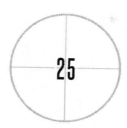

25

Ethan and JB reached the Silver Creek dock at eight thirty, after scouring Copperhead Cove for an hour for more clues. JB pulled the pontoon boat up to the dock, and Ethan jumped out, tying the rope around a dock anchor. He pulled out his cell phone and dialed the same number that had saved his daughter nearly twenty-one months ago. *Sorry, Jake. I know it's early, but get your ass out of bed.*

"Hello," a raspy voice said after four rings.

"Jake, it's Ethan."

Silence.

"Ethan? You know what time it is?"

"Yeah, and I'm sorry, Jake. But it's an emergency."

"Damn, it's always an emergency with you," Jake said. "Hold on, let me take a piss first."

To know him is to love him. Good old Jake, the cantankerous old fart.

Two minutes went by, and Ethan started getting impatient.

"Sorry, old buddy, but nature doesn't wait for anybody," Jake said.

"You drinking again, Jake?"

"I had a couple of Bushmills last night. Why you ask?"

"Just curious. I need your help, Jake."

Silence again.

"The last time you needed my help, all hell broke loose. How is Molly, by the way?"

"She's great," Ethan said. "I'm in Kentucky, Jake."

"Well, at least you're in the country. That's an improvement."

"Yeah, I guess it is. What do you having going on right now? Client-wise, that is?"

Jake laughed.

"You kidding? My life ain't improved THAT much since I saw you last."

"So you're free?"

"Depends. I have a bad feeling about where this is going, Ethan."

"I need you to fly back here. Today, if you can."

"You serious? Fly to Kentucky today? I'm not that free, old buddy."

"Jake, my brother is missing, and I need your help."

"Holy shit, Ethan. What does your family do, take lessons on getting in trouble?"

"I think he's been . . . hurt or . . . murdered." Ethan had trouble getting the words out of his mouth, just as he had when Molly had been kidnapped.

"Oh . . . damn. You have time to explain?"

"No, I don't," Ethan said. "Just trust me, and get on a plane today. I'll pay all your expenses when you get here. Can you do that?"

"Well, I just got a credit card, so guess I might as well use it."

"Good. Thanks, Jake. Fly into Nashville, and call me with your flight info. I'll come pick you up and bring you up here."

"Where's 'up here'?"

Ethan rubbed his eyes. Sometimes Jake could be a pain in the ass.

"Kentucky. Quail Hollow Lake, about two hours from Nashville."

"Okay," Jake said. "You know, it's not easy being your friend."

Ethan smiled again.

"I know, but it's keeping your career going."

Jake laughed.

"That's true. I'll book the flight and call you from the San Diego airport. Your cell, I take it?"

"Yeah, my cell. Thanks, Jake. This may take a while, so I hope you don't have any plans."

"I got a real bad feeling about this, Ethan. But I'll be there."

"Okay. Call me from the airport. Oh, and Jake?"

"Yeah?"

"Dress casual. I mean real casual." Ethan hung up and rubbed his swollen eyes again.

Ethan saw JB in the parking lot and walked over to join him.

"Your dad's Explorer, isn't it?" Ethan said.

"Yeah, it's been sittin' here since yesterday morning. Hasn't moved," JB responded.

Ethan looked at the car several spots down from the Explorer.

"You see many of those down here?" he said, pointing to the white Mercedes Benz.

JB bent down and looked at the license plate. "SONNY03. Guess we know who this belongs to."

"Sonny Daye," Ethan said. He looked inside and saw several beer cans on the floor on the passenger side. "Williams must have come with Daye."

Ethan stepped back and looked around.

"I'm surprised no one has reported them missing."

"We'll get a call today probably, on my dad's guide service phone at home. Someone has to be wondering about 'em," JB said.

"Well, we need to call your local police or sheriff, or whoever takes care of stuff like this. You know who to call?"

JB nodded.

"Sheriff Parsons, in Crockett. He has jurisdiction over public property, like the lake."

"You want me to call him?" Ethan said.

"No, I know him, so I'll do it," JB answered.

"This is going to turn into a circus real soon. That's why I called my private investigator friend in San Diego, the one who saved Molly two years ago."

"I remember you talkin' about him. Friend of yours from the Air Force, right?"

Ethan nodded.

"He's trying to catch a flight to Nashville sometime today, so I'll have to drive down and pick him up. He won't want to stay at Bo's place. Too much commotion. Is there a place I can book for him in Crockett?"

"Yeah, the only motel in town, the Riverside, but it's probably booked up for graduation."

"Nothing else around?"

"Well, there's the Ridge Motel, but nobody stays there anymore."

"Why's that?"

JB laughed.

"Everybody 'round here thinks it's haunted. Stupid jerks."

"Really? Why?"

"Some guy got killed up there about three or four years ago. Real messy. Probably a drug thing."

"Is it even open?"

"Yeah, the Riverside manages it, but there ain't nobody up there regular. Maids go up from the Riverside when they have someone stayin' there, which ain't very often."

"Sounds like a nice, quiet place. Jake may like that. He's a bit of a loner."

"Sure, it'll be quiet, but he may get a little freaked out at night. It's up on the ridge, with forest all around. My mom used to manage the restaurant up there until it closed down. It used to be the place to go for folks around here. Great ribs."

"I'll call the Riverside and make a reservation for Jake. Even ghosts won't want to mess with him."

"Okay, and I'll call Sheriff Parsons from inside the resort."

"JB, you doin' okay?" Ethan noticed him clutching his dad's fishing cap.

JB's eyes turned moist so he wiped them with his hand.

"Yeah, I'm okay. I just wanna see my dad again—alive, I hope."

Ethan put his hand on his nephew's shoulder.

"Me too, son."

JB started walking toward the resort restaurant, his shoulders slumped, his head down.

"JB," Ethan called after him. "You need to call your mom, too."

JB just nodded and continued to trudge up the gangplank to the restaurant.

Ethan yawned and shook his weary head. *Damn, it's going to be one tough day, and I haven't slept in over twenty-four hours.*

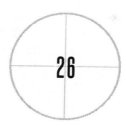

26

Frankie and Bo waited in the small parking lot until they saw a GMC Yukon pull up and park two spots over from them. A white-haired man, medium height and build, got out carrying a black bag. He glanced at the silver Cadillac as he walked up to the glass door and put his key in the lock.

"That Doc Welby?" Frankie said.

"Yeah, that's him," Bo said. "He didn't see me."

"Okay, let's give him a couple of minutes to get settled in."

Frankie looked around and saw no one else in sight. The small doctor's office was located on the east edge of Crockett, on Highway 495. It appeared to be a one-doctor office, so they would be alone with Doc Welby, unless he had an assistant or receptionist inside.

Frankie glanced at his watch.

"It's eight thirty. Is he alone inside?"

"I guess so. He unlocked the front door."

"Okay, let's go before someone else shows up," Frankie said, opening his door.

Frankie opened the rear passenger door and helped Bo out, putting his arm under his shoulders as he did before. They slowly walked to the front door and opened it. They didn't see anyone in the reception area, so they walked to the door marked "Wallace W. Welby, M.D."

"You ready?" Frankie said.

Bo nodded.

Frankie opened the door and saw the doctor sitting at his desk.

"I'm sorry, young man, but we're not—"

He stopped when he saw Bo limp in.

"Bo? What happened, son?" Doc Welby got up and walked quickly to Bo's side and helped carry him to the examination table.

"Hi, Doc," Bo said. "Had a little accident." Bo glanced at Frankie and back to Welby.

"When did this happen?" Welby said, already beginning to remove the bandage on Bo's calf.

"Yesterday, around sunset," Bo said. "I was out on the lake."

"Imagine that," Welby said, smiling. "Did you fall? Get bit by a copperhead? What happened?"

Bo looked at Frankie, his eyes widening.

"He was accidently shot," Frankie chimed in. "I was in the boat with him."

"Shot? On the lake? How?"

"Somebody on shore shooting at birds, or snakes, or something. A stray bullet, I guess," Frankie said, glancing at Bo.

Doc Welby glanced up at Frankie, his eyes narrowing.

"How in the world could he hit you in the calf, Bo?"

"Uh, I was standing up in my bass boat, pulling in a smallmouth. Guess I was just unlucky, Doc."

Doc Welby looked down at the wound and whistled.

"Who bandaged you up?" He looked at Frankie. "You do this?"

Frankie coughed.

"Uh, yeah, with a first aid kit."

Doc Welby nodded.

"Not a bad job." He turned to Bo. "Looks to be infected, number one," he said, "and the bullet went clean through, tore some muscle." He looked closely at the wound. "Appears to have missed the bone, though."

Frankie smiled, proud of himself.

"That's what I told him."

Doc Welby didn't acknowledge him.

"Must be pretty painful, I'd say."

Bo nodded his head vigorously.

"Oh yeah, it's painful, Doc."

"Well, my assistant doesn't come in until nine, but I can fix you up until you can get to a hospital."

"Hospital? Why a hospital?" Frankie said, a little too urgently.

Welby looked at the strange man, his hair disheveled, his clothes wrinkled, smelling of lake water.

"Who are you, again?"

"Frank . . . uh, Franklin. Benny Franklin."

Doc Welby squinted his eyes.

"Benny Franklin. That short for Benjamin Franklin?"

Frankie laughed nervously, glancing at Bo.

"No. No. Just Benny. My folks had a sense of humor, I guess."

"Are you one of Bo's fishing clients?"

"Yeah, came down from, uh, Indianapolis yesterday."

Doc Welby looked from Frankie to Bo, shaking his head.

"Well, both of you need to get cleaned up and put some clean clothes on." He waved his hand in front of his face. "You both smell like murky lake water, and, dare I say, whiskey."

Frankie glared at Bo with wide eyes as Doc Welby worked on the wound.

"We didn't get back in until late last night, Doc." Bo shrugged his shoulders at Frankie. "And we had a couple of drinks at Frankie's . . . uh, Benny's motel. I fell asleep and woke up this morning and, uh, here we are."

"Are you staying at the Riverside?" he said, looking at Frankie.

"Uh, yeah, the Riverside," Frankie said.

Doc Welby cleaned up the wound, removing dried blood and lake gook. He put something red on the wound, which made Bo flinch in pain.

"Sorry, Bo, but we need to try to stop this infection. I'll give you a shot or two in a minute."

"No problem, Doc. Thanks."

"You know, I'm supposed to report any gunshot wounds to the sheriff."

"Sheriff Parsons?" Bo said. "Naw, you don't have to bother him, do you?"

Welby glanced at Bo.

"I said I'm supposed to notify him. Are you saying you don't want me to?"

Bo shrugged, trying to act like it was no big deal.

"Hell, Doc, he's got other things to worry about. Let's just keep this to ourselves, okay?"

Welby began wrapping the wound.

"It's your call, Bo." He glanced at Frankie again, looking him up and down. "But if he comes around asking questions, I'm not going to lie, son."

"Thanks, Doc."

"You going home after this, Bo?" Welby said.

"Uh, yeah, right after you patch me up."

"You want me to call Kathy for you? Let her know you're on your way?"

Frankie was behind Welby, shaking his head from side to side. Welby glanced behind him and caught the last shake.

"No. No, that's okay, Doc," Bo said. "I'll be home in fifteen, twenty minutes. Don't wanna worry her, ya know?"

Welby nodded, finished taping up the wound, and walked to the cabinet across the room.

Frankie stared at Bo with bulging eyes, his shoulders hunched, his arms and hands out in front of him. *What the hell are all the questions?*

Welby came back and gave Bo a shot for the infection, rubbing his arm with alcohol, and putting a Band-Aid on the puncture wound.

"You really need to go to the hospital and have this checked in a day or two," Welby said. He glanced at Frankie again. "If that's not possible, come see me tomorrow morning so I can change the dressing and check on the infection."

"Thanks, Doc, I will."

"I'll give you a prescription for the pain, but don't use it unless you really need it, okay?"

"Okay, Doc. Thanks."

"And don't drink for a few days. You need to keep hydrated. Lots of water. No whiskey." He looked directly at Frankie when he said this. "And you, young man, need to clean yourself up and," he looked at his clothes, "get a fresh set of clothes on you." He walked away shaking his head.

"Uh, thanks," Frankie said.

"See you boys tomorrow," Welby said. "Go home, Bo."

"Sure will, Doc. Thanks again."

Frankie and Bo walked out of the room and through the reception area. Frankie glanced at his watch. It was eight fifty-five.

They walked to the Cadillac, with Bo getting into the front passenger seat this time. Frankie started up the car and began pulling out of the parking lot.

"What the hell was that?" Frankie said. "It felt like the Grand Inquisition."

"It's a small town, Frankie. Or should I call you Benny," Bo said, smiling.

Frankie shook his head. *This fishing guide is going to be the death of me yet.*

"I didn't expect so many questions from a country doctor. He took me by surprise."

Bo laughed.

"He's a good man, kind and concerned. People 'round here really look up to him."

Frankie noticed Bo staring at him.

"What?"

"Those the same clothes you wore when you went diving in the lake yesterday?" Bo said.

Frankie looked down at his wrinkled shirt and dirty slacks.

"Yeah, I didn't think about changing. I was scared shitless all night." Frankie looked at Bo. "You're not much better, fishing guide. I guess we both look like someone dragged us right out of the lake, and we smell like it, too."

"Well, you have a change of clothes at the motel. I don't." Bo continued to stare at Frankie. "We goin' back to the Ridge?"

"Yeah, for now," Frankie said. "I gotta think, dammit. Nobody will let me think."

They entered Crockett's Main Street and were passing right in front of the Riverside Motel when a sheriff's car with its lights blinking came toward them.

"Get down, Bo!"

Bo slumped in his seat as the car approached. Frankie glanced at the man driving, who was looking directly at him. *Oh, God. He saw me, saw the Cadillac, but hopefully didn't see Bo.*

Frankie looked in his rear view mirror and watched the police car continue east down Main Street. He let out a lung full of air and looked down at Bo.

"He looked right at me, Bo."

"That was Sheriff Parsons, and he hardly ever flashes his lights. Something big happened." Bo looked up at Frankie. "Bet he's going to the lake because of us. Maybe someone found the coaches in the boat."

Frankie's eyes got big, then bigger when he saw another sheriff's car approaching, lights flashing.

"Stay down, here comes another one."

Frankie looked straight ahead until the car was next to them. In his peripheral vision he saw a young woman driving the car, and she, too, was looking at him. She continued past without stopping.

"How many cops you got in this Podunk town?" Frankie said, his voice higher than normal.

"You just saw both of 'em. That was the deputy sheriff, Cheyenne Smith."

"I guess we just became public enemy number one," Frankie said. "Looks like the cat's out of the bag."

"Hey, I didn't kill anybody, mob guy. I'm the victim here, don't forget it," Bo said, sitting up.

Frankie glanced at Bo and continued on to the Ridge Motel. *We're both gonna be victims if we don't figure out what to do next.*

27

Ethan and JB were sitting in the resort restaurant having coffee, waiting for the county sheriff to arrive.

"That's Sheriff Parsons," Millie said loudly, looking out the kitchen window. "And he's got his lights flashin."

Ethan and JB gulped down the last of their coffee and headed for the parking lot.

"They made it here pretty fast," Ethan said, trying to keep up with JB.

"They don't get many calls like this one," JB said, "so I expect they're kinda excited."

The two men ran over the foot bridge and saw the flashing lights. They stood next to Bo's Explorer, waiting for the sheriff to get out of his cruiser. Sheriff Parsons, an average-sized, middle-aged man with a salt-and-pepper, well-trimmed beard got out of the car, putting on his big-brimmed sheriff's hat. He spotted JB and began walking toward them.

"Howdy, JB," he said, holding out his hand.

"Sheriff," JB said, pointing, "this here is my Uncle Ethan."

"Ethan Paxton, Bo's brother," Ethan said, shaking the sheriff's hand.

"Good to meet you, Ethan. I'm Cecil Parsons, Sheriff of Crockett County." Parsons talked with a slight regional southern accent that most of the people in Crockett County used, but had no arrogance in his voice.

Another sheriff's cruiser came down the hill, lights flashing, but no siren. It pulled up next to Sheriff Parson's cruiser and stopped, the lights turned off. Ethan saw a fairly young woman in uniform get out and put her hat on.

She was medium height, with dirty-blonde hair, and had a confident gate as she approached the three men. Ethan saw her face under the brimmed hat and noticed that she was very attractive.

"Hey, Sheriff," she said as she strode up to Sheriff Parsons.

"Deputy," he said. "You know JB, Bo's son?"

"Sure do. Howdy, JB," she said, shaking the young man's hand.

"And this is Bo's brother, Nathan."

"Ethan. Ethan Paxton." Ethan smiled, used to the name mix-up.

"Howdy, Ethan. Where you from?" the deputy said, shaking his hand.

"California."

"Didn't think you were from 'round here," she said, smiling. "You don't talk like your brother."

Ethan smiled.

"I guess I stand out a little around here."

"Is this Bo's Explorer?" Parsons said, pointing to the blue truck.

"Yep," JB said. "Hasn't moved since yesterday morning."

"And no sign of your daddy's boat?"

"Nope."

Sheriff Parsons looked around the parking lot.

"That Mercedes over there belong to anyone you know?"

"No, but we know who it belongs to," Ethan said. "Sonny Daye, coach at Southern Tennessee."

"Sonny Daye. Huh." Parsons looked at Ethan and then at JB. "He was your daddy's client yesterday?"

"Yep," JB said, "along with another coach from up north."

"What's his name?"

JB shrugged, looking at Ethan.

"Jerry Joe Williams, coach at Midwestern, in Iowa," Ethan said.

"No shit. Jerry Joe Williams. Huh."

"You know the names?" Ethan said.

"Oh, yeah. Sonny Daye's a big 'un 'round here. The other guy, not so much. But I remember seein' his name lately, somewhere."

"Probably on the news," Ethan said. "He's being investigated for points shaving."

"Yeah, points shaving. Huh." Parsons scratched his beard, staring at the Mercedes.

"You think there's a correlation there, Mr. Paxton?" the deputy said.

"Call me Ethan. I'm sorry, but I didn't get your name?" Ethan said.

"Oh, sorry. Cheyenne Smith, Deputy Sheriff."

Ethan smiled.

"To answer your question, yes, I think there is a definite correlation."

"How so?" Parsons said.

"Well," Ethan said, "Williams was being investigated for points shaving, so he had to be involved with some shady people, right?"

Parsons and Smith nodded.

"If he screwed up somehow and didn't do what he was supposed to do, and these shady people lost a lot of money, they'd be pretty pissed, right?"

Parsons and Smith looked at each other and nodded.

"Okay, so what if these shady people were really bad people—people that didn't let something like that go by?"

"What people you talkin' about?" Parsons said, his eyes narrowing.

Ethan cleared his throat.

"The mob."

Parsons and Smith looked at each other again, their eyes widening.

"Excuse me, Ethan," Smith said. "Why would you assume the mob's involved?"

Ethan shook his head.

"I'm not assuming anything, and I don't know if they're still around, but I do know that they were involved about twenty-some years ago when they had a big points-shaving scandal at Boston College. I looked it up."

Parsons and Smith nodded.

"And if they're involved here, you think that's what happened to Bo and the two coaches?"

"Pretty big coincidence," Ethan said, turning to JB. "Show 'em Bo's cap."

JB took his dad's cap out of his back pocket and held it up.

"Dad was wearin' this yesterday, when he took those two guys out."

"Where'd you find it?" Smith said.

"In a cove yonder, 'bout six miles down the lake."

"In the water, on shore . . . ?" Smith asked.

"Well, kinda both. It was on a twig stickin' up outta the water, 'bout a foot or two from shore, in some bushes."

Parsons and Smith looked at each other again.

"Tell them what else we found," Ethan said.

"Blood. Under the big tree trunk where somebody slid underneath, and in the bushes, close to where I found Dad's cap."

"Fresh blood?"

"Yes," Ethan said. "Hadn't completely dried yet."

Parsons took his hat off, scratched his head, and put it back on.

"Well, that don't exactly prove that your daddy was . . . that it was your daddy's, uh, blood," he said, looking at JB. "Coulda been an animal. And couldn't he have lost his fishin' cap while they was out in the cove, and it just floated in to shore?"

"What animal would slide under a tree, making large drag marks?" Ethan said. "And we found fresh footprints on the sand next to the water. Human footprints. And a Jack Daniel's bottle, empty."

"What's the Jack Daniel's got to do with this?"

"That's what the coaches were drinking," Ethan said.

"And my daddy would never leave his fishin' cap behind. He loves this ol' thing."

Parsons scratched his beard, glancing at Smith.

"Well, you got some good points, there, Ethan, JB. Proves they were probably in that cove anyways."

"Enough to investigate?"

Parsons turned to Smith.

"Deputy, what do you think?"

Smith stared at Bo's cap and then at JB. Then she turned to look at the blue Explorer and the white Mercedes and then turned back and looked up at Parsons.

"Bo Paxton is the best fishin' guide in the county, and he's never been in any kinda trouble, that I know of," she said, looking at JB. "It ain't like him to just up and leave or disappear, especially with clients. Somethin's real fishy here, Sheriff."

"One more thing, Sheriff," Ethan said. "About eight other fishing guides went out last night looking for Bo and his boat when he didn't come in. They checked every fishing spot that Bo ever took a client to, so this lake's been combed clean with nothing to show for it except what we just told you."

Parsons nodded and pulled Smith aside. They talked quietly for several seconds and then turned back to Ethan and JB.

Parsons nodded.

"It sounds like enough to investigate," he said, looking at Ethan. "I'm gonna need your help locating this cove, JB."

JB nodded, but remained silent.

"By the way, Sheriff," Ethan said. "I hired a private investigator from California to come take a look. He's helped me in the past and can be another set of eyes on this."

Parsons's eyes narrowed.

"Why you need a PI on this, 'specially one from so far away?"

"Well—"

"You been in trouble before, needin' a private eye?" Parsons said, leaning toward Ethan.

Ethan anticipated the question.

"My daughter was kidnapped two years ago, in Mexico. Jake, the private eye, found her and saved her from . . . well, he saved her. I'd trust him with my life."

"Still don't answer the question. Why you need a PI?"

Ethan knew he was treading on thin ice.

"It's not that I don't trust you and Deputy Smith, here," he said, "but Jake can be another pair of eyes, and he's a hell of an investigator. Won't do any harm, will it, Sheriff?"

Parsons scratched his beard.

"Well, I can't tell you not to hire a PI, but he's gotta stay out of our way."

"No problem. I'll make sure of that," Ethan said, knowing that Jake was a bull in a china shop.

Parsons stared at Ethan.

"Okay, when's he get here?"

"He's flying out from California today, so I have to go to Nashville and pick him up tonight when he gets in."

Parsons looked closely at Ethan.

"When's the last time you slept, son? Your eyes look mighty red and weary."

Ethan smiled.

"It's been a while. I drove up from Memphis last night and got here around four thirty this morning."

"Well, you be careful, son. These country roads 'round here can be dangerous at night, 'specially if you're tired."

Ethan nodded. "Thanks, I will."

Parsons turned to JB. "We'll find your daddy, JB. You tell your momma that, okay?"

JB nodded.

"Thanks."

"Sheriff, do you have anybody else on your staff, or is it just the two of you?" Ethan asked.

"Regular, it's just Cheyenne and me, my office staff, and a couple of part-timers," he said, "but we got reserves that I can call up to help. We'll have some people on this, don't you worry. Bo Paxton is a popular guy in these parts, and he's got a lot of friends. You just go back to Bo's place and get some rest. We'll take it from here."

Ethan nodded.

"Sheriff," JB said. "What about the two coaches? They are, or was, clients of my daddy's. People are gonna be callin' us to find out where they are. It could get pretty crazy 'round here when word gets out."

Parsons took off his hat and scratched his head again.

"That's a good point, son. They's pretty famous folks, 'specially Sonny Daye. We could get all kinds of outsiders down here real soon."

"Sheriff, can we keep a lid on this for at least a day?" Ethan said. "Give you a chance to investigate, and give my friend a chance to get here and look around?"

"We'll do what we can, but once these two coaches' families start askin' questions, it's gonna be all over the news. About a day is all we're gonna get, son."

Ethan pursed his lips and nodded.

"Good enough."

"You gonna be at Bo's place the rest of the day?" Parsons said.

Ethan nodded again.

"Okay. We'll be in touch. Let us know if you hear anything, 'specially from Bo."

"We will. Thanks," Ethan said.

Parsons and Smith tipped their hats and walked back to their respective cruisers. As he was opening the door, Parsons turned to Ethan and JB.

"By the way, I saw a fancy lookin' silver Cadillac drivin' down Main Street in Crockett on my way out here. Strange lookin' fella driving. Seemed pretty nervous. You two be careful, and if you see a silver Caddy, give me a call."

"Sure will, Sheriff. Thanks," Ethan said, waving.

A shiver ran down Ethan's spine as he walked to JB's pickup. *A silver Cadillac with a strange, nervous man driving?*

28

The silver Cadillac pulled into the empty Ridge Motel parking lot at nine fifteen. Frankie, still paranoid, looked around in all directions before getting out. Bo got himself out of the passenger side, limping, but on his own power.

"We can't stay here forever, Frankie," Bo said. "You thought about where you're gonna go?"

Frankie walked around the front of the Caddy to room eleven.

"I'm stayin' here until I figure it out. That's all I know." He opened the door with the room twelve key.

"How the hell did you open the door with a key to room twelve?" Bo said.

Frankie shrugged his shoulders.

"It just opened. I dunno."

"What room did you check-in to?"

"Twelve, but it only had one bed, and I wasn't about to sleep with the Hulk."

Bo chuckled.

"Can't blame you there. So these guys that you think are comin', they'll come to room twelve?"

Frankie nodded.

"Guess so."

"And we're right next door." Bo shook his head. "This is crazy, man."

The two men walked inside, Frankie closing the door and locking it.

"What about the car, smart guy?" Bo continued.

"What about it?" Frankie said.

"It sticks out like a boil on a duck's ass around here. You can't leave it parked outside if you plan on stayin' here. These guys will know what you're drivin', right?"

"Yeah, it was booked by my boss's secretary on his credit card. I have to get rid of it somehow and get something else."

"Listen, Frankie, why don't you take me to my place, and we can put you up. I have a fairly big spread, with lots of forest around the holler to hide in."

Frankie shook his head.

"I told you, they'll be comin' after you, too, and they'll find out where you live."

"We'll figure it out," Bo said, a worried look on his face. "I know this county better'n most folks. But we can't stay here. I won't stay here in this flea bag."

Frankie stared at the fishing guide, seeing the defiance in his eyes. *He's feelin' better, so now he's gonna turn on me. I knew it.*

"We have to get out of the county, out of the state—and your family, too," Frankie said. "You don't know these people. They're animals, not humans."

Frankie saw fear in Bo's eyes for the first time, and that made him even more afraid.

"Frankie, think for a minute. They know where you're stayin', so this is the first place they'll look. What are you gonna do, hide under the couch?"

Frankie put his hands up.

"I can't think right now. I have to take a shower and get out of these stinking clothes. Let me think, goddammit!"

Bo nodded.

"You go take a shower, change your clothes, but this won't go away. We're both up shit creek if we stay here."

Frankie walked into the bathroom and shut the door, took his clothes off, and turned on the water in the shower. He looked at his clothes, in a pile next to the toilet. *What a friggin' mess.* He walked into the shower and let the hot water fall over him. He saw the dirt, grime, and lake sludge slide off of him in a steady, dark stream. He saw Augie's face looking up at him in the dirty shower water. *Did I kill him? He was gonna die anyway, wasn't he?*

Frankie soaped up and washed the filth of the day before down the drain. When he turned the water off and grabbed a towel, he heard a noise from the other room. It sounded like a door closing. *Oh shit, Bo's leaving!*

He threw a towel around his waist, checking his dirty pants pocket for the car keys, and opened the bathroom door. He didn't see Bo, so he walked into the room. *Where the hell was he?* He'd left the .357 Magnum in the car, along with the other snub-nosed revolver in the glove compartment. He hurried to the window and looked out. Bo was standing next to the Cadillac, looking at the forest on the other side of the parking lot.

Frankie opened the door a crack.

"What are you doing?"

Bo turned around when he heard Frankie's voice.

"Thinkin'. Something you should be doin', too."

"Don't go anywhere."

"Don't worry, mob guy. I ain't goin' nowhere—yet."

Frankie shut the door and hurriedly put clean clothes on. He combed his hair and rushed outside, still trying to get his shoes on. Bo wasn't next to the Cadillac. Frankie couldn't see him anywhere. *Where the hell did he go?*

"Frankie, over here," he heard Bo say from around the corner.

Frankie put his shoe on, quickly walked around the building, and saw Bo staring out over the ridge at the town of Crockett.

"You know, this was a great place once," Bo said. "Kathy—my wife—used to work up here at the restaurant. Best ribs and chicken in the county back then."

"What happened?"

"A kid got killed up here couple years back. It was pretty gruesome. Some kinda torture thing, probably drug related." Bo turned to look at Frankie. "I bet you're the first person to stay here since it happened. Townsfolk won't have anything to do with the place. Even the maids don't like it. Surprised the Riverside rented you a room."

Frankie laughed.

"It's graduation week."

Bo looked at Frankie and started laughing.

"Well, son, you done graduated to a whole other level since yesterday."

Frankie tilted his head back and laughed.

"Guess I did, but you know what, fishing guide?"

"What's that?"

"You done graduated right along with me."

Bo stopped laughing.

"Yeah. Let's get the hell outta here, mob guy."

Frankie grabbed Bo's arm.

"Why are you helping me, Bo? I was one of the guys that they sent to kill you and the two coaches. You should be putting a bullet through my head."

Bo looked at him.

"First of all, I don't kill people. Second, you saved my ass on the lake, and third, I kinda feel sorry for ya."

"Really? Why do you feel sorry for me?"

"'Cause you remind me of a homeless puppy, wanderin' around the countryside with nowhere to go, with a deer-in-the-headlights look. I like puppies."

Frankie felt the tears beginning to flood his eyes, so he turned around and wiped them away.

"Let me help you, Frankie. This is my country, my people. We can protect you from these thugs, whoever they are. But you have to trust me."

Frankie wiped his eyes again. He nodded.

"Okay, fishing guide. Take this puppy home."

Bo clapped him on the shoulder.

"Let's clean that room up and get the hell outta here."

The two men grabbed everything out of room eleven and threw it into the trunk of the Cadillac. Frankie went back in, took a couple of towels from the bathroom, and wiped everything down that they might have touched.

"C'mon, Frankie. The maids won't be up here for another six months," Bo yelled from the car.

Frankie smiled as he closed the door to room eleven. *Goodbye, Motel Hell.*

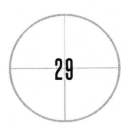

29

It was almost ten o'clock when Ethan and JB arrived back at the Paxton farm. Ethan had driven Bo's blue Explorer back from the lake, with JB driving his pickup. As they drove down the lane, approaching the house, Kathy came running out, waving her arms. *Oh shit! She saw Bo's truck and thinks it's him.* Ethan knew the waterworks would be working overtime when Kathy saw it wasn't Bo.

"Bo! Bo!" he heard her yell. Then she stopped dead when she saw that Ethan was driving the Explorer. She slumped into a sitting position on the grass, holding her face in her hands, the despair written all over her.

Damn, I wish it was Bo instead of me. Poor Kathy.

Ethan pulled up into the gravel driveway and parked in Bo's usual spot, getting out quickly and running to pick Kathy up off the lawn.

"Kathy, I'm sorry. I didn't stop to think about what you'd think when I drove Bo's truck up the lane," Ethan said, picking her up. *JB must not have called his mom from the resort.*

She crumbled into his arms, sobbing uncontrollably.

"I thought it was over, the nightmare was over." She cried in Ethan's arms until JB pulled up and rushed to them.

"Mom?" he said.

She rushed to her son, falling into his arms and sobbing a fresh bucket of tears.

Ethan wiped away a tear of his own as he watched the mother and son. He jerked when he heard his cell phone ring. He pulled it out of his pocket, dropping it on the green lawn. *Damn, it's probably Jake.* He picked it up.

"Hello?"

"Ethan, that you?" Jake said on the other end.

Ethan blew out a sigh.

"Yeah, Jake, it's me."

"You okay? You sound winded."

Ethan rubbed his tired, sore eyes.

"Yeah, I'm okay. You got your flight info?"

"Yep. I'm at the San Diego airport ready to board. They put me on standby for a ten thirty flight, connecting in Denver."

"Okay, let me go in the house and get a pen and paper," Ethan said, scrambling up the short hill to the kitchen. Once inside he grabbed a pen and pad from Bo's desk. "Shoot."

"I'm scheduled to get into Nashville at seven forty-five tonight, United Flight 593."

"Got it. I haven't slept in almost two days, and I'm running on fumes," Ethan said, rubbing his eyes once more. "Hope I don't kill us both driving back on these country roads."

"Try to get some rest this afternoon, Ethan. I'll see you . . . when I see you."

"Yeah, that's what everybody's telling me. When you get to baggage claim, look for me. I'll be the one asleep on the floor."

"Okay, bud. See you tonight."

Ethan hit the end button and put his hands to his face, the strain and lack of sleep hitting him hard. *At least I'll have someone I can trust and depend on helping with this nightmare.*

JB and Kathy walked into the kitchen. Kathy was wiping her tears, walking under her own power.

"I'm sorry, Ethan," she said, hugging him. "I . . . . " Her voice trailed off.

"No, I'm sorry, Kath. I should have called to warn you. I just didn't think."

"Me, too, Ma," JB said. "Uncle Ethan told me to call you, but the sheriff came, and I just forgot."

"It's okay, both of you. Do you have any news?"

"I'll let JB tell you while I go to the bathroom," Ethan said. *I don't want to be here when he tells her we found Bo's cap.*

Ethan climbed the steep stairs to his room and then went to the bathroom, closed the door, and sat on the toilet, fully clothed. He thought about Copperhead Cove, finding Bo's cap, the blood. *God, please let him be okay.*

After relieving himself, Ethan went back downstairs, expecting fresh waterworks from Kathy. Instead, he saw her staring at Bo's cap. No tears, no words. Ethan looked at JB, who was standing still, staring at his mother.

"Kath, you okay?" Ethan said, putting his hand on her shoulder.

She looked at him, her eyes glassy, moist with fresh tears.

"I wanted him to wear another cap, actually took this one off his head yesterday morning," she said, trembling. "Then I put it back on him. He was so happy." Then she fell apart all over again.

"JB, why don't you take your mom upstairs and let her lie down," Ethan said.

JB nodded, grabbed his mom under the arms, and guided her up the stairs.

Ethan stared at them until they were out of sight, then went to the kitchen and poured a cup of coffee, walked out onto the deck, and sat down heavily. He looked out over the small pond, staring at the ducks. Garth and Brooks walked up to him and licked his hand, their sign for Ethan to pet them. He began stroking Garth's head, scratching behind his ears. Brooks whined next to him, waiting for his turn.

Ethan's mind was racing from one thought to another, almost too fast to control. He wanted to shut it off, but, just like two years ago, he couldn't do it. Back then it was Molly. Now it was his big brother. He slumped in the deck chair, hanging his head in exhaustion. He looked up when he heard the sound of a car approaching. He stared down the lane. What he saw just about knocked him out of his chair.

A silver Cadillac broke out into the open, coming down the lane fast. *A silver Cadillac, with a strange, nervous man driving.* Ethan stood up and peered into the car. He saw a strange-looking man at the wheel. Then he looked at the passenger side. He blinked and looked again. He jumped off the deck, running down the lawn to the gravel driveway as the silver Cadillac pulled to a stop in front of him.

Ethan stared at the man in the passenger seat then shouted, "Bo!"

The ducks flew off the pond, quacking. The dogs began barking. The birds in the trees began flying around.

Ethan reached the door of the Cadillac and opened it. Bo got out and hugged him so tight that Ethan almost couldn't breathe. They stood there for what seemed like minutes, but it was only a few seconds. Then they heard the scream from the second floor of the house, chasing the ducks away for the rest of the day.

"Bo! Oh, my God! Bo!"

Ethan stood back and looked at his big brother. He was a mess—his clothes wrinkled and dirty, his hair disheveled—and he smelled like he'd slept with a family of smallmouth bass. Then Ethan saw the bandage on his left calf.

"How you doin', little brother?" Bo said. "What are you doin' back here?"

Ethan stared at his big brother, mouth open, unable to speak. He didn't have to when the freight train named Kathy came running down the lawn.

"Bo! Bo!" she cried, running up to him and almost tackling him to the ground.

Ethan caught both of them before they tumbled over. Then he looked at the driver, who was still sitting in the car. Ethan walked around the front of the car and approached the driver's door.

The man got out and stood in front of Ethan.

"Frankie," he said, holding out his hand.

Ethan looked at the strange, blond-haired man and took his hand.

"Ethan, Bo's brother."

"You look like him," Frankie said.

Ethan nodded, not smiling.

"Who are you?"

Frankie coughed, smiling nervously.

A strange, nervous man . . . .

"He's okay, Ethan," Bo said, escaping Kathy's bear hug. "I'll explain inside."

Ethan looked back at the man.

"Come on in, then, I guess."

JB had joined the group and was hugging his dad, tears rolling down his cheeks. Ethan let them enjoy the moment as he guided Frankie up the lawn to the deck.

"Have a seat. Want some coffee?" Ethan said.

"Uh, sure, thanks."

Ethan walked into the kitchen, poured two cups, knowing Bo would want one, too. Walking back out onto the deck, he saw the three Paxtons crying, laughing, and hugging. Ethan stopped and watched, fighting back his own tears.

"Here you go," Ethan said, handing the cup to Frankie. He sat down next to the man.

"Thanks, uh . . . ."

"Ethan."

"Thanks, Ethan," Frankie said, nervously putting the cup to his lips.

"Why you so nervous, Frankie?" Ethan said.

"Ethan, I'll explain," Bo said, picking up the cup that Ethan had set on the table. "Let me get some of Kath's coffee in me first." He gulped the entire cup down in seconds.

"I'll get you another cup," Kathy said, walking into the kitchen, a smile as wide as the pond on her face.

Bo sat down next to Frankie, putting his hand on the man's shoulder. JB sat across from the stranger, staring at him. The three Paxton men and the stranger sat silent for a few seconds, looking at each other, drinking their coffee.

Bo proceeded to tell them the entire story, from the time Sonny Daye caught the smallmouth, the nightmare at Copperhead Cove, and up through the visit to Doc Welby.

"And Ethan, my boat's at the bottom of Copperhead Cove, with the two coaches tied up inside."

Ethan's eyes grew large as he stared at his brother.

"What? Why?"

Bo looked at Frankie and nodded.

Frankie coughed, blinked a few times and twisted his neck, obviously extremely nervous.

"Frankie, what the hell happened?" Ethan said, leaning forward.

"I, uh." Frankie coughed again. "I didn't know what to do, so I . . . ."

"Jesus," Ethan said, when Bo was finished. He looked at Frankie with fresh eyes.

"He saved my ass, Ethan. I'd be food for the smallmouth if he hadn't pulled me outta the lake and fixed me up." Bo clapped his new friend on the shoulder. "Not sure what his motives were, but who cares, I'm here."

Ethan smiled weakly at the stranger. *Motive. What the hell was this little man's motive in saving my brother?*

"I guess we'll see what his motive was, right, Frankie?" Ethan said, staring directly into the stranger's eyes.

Frankie stared back at Ethan, his eye twitching.

A strange, nervous man.

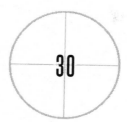

30

Julie Goldberg waved his arms in the air in disgust.

"How can it be delayed that long?"

"I'm sorry, Mr. Jones, but the thunderstorm has shut down O'Hare Airport until it passes. United has nothing to do with that."

Goldberg, alias Thomas Jones, walked away, waving his hands at the United customer service rep. He walked up to Fanelli and told him the bad news.

"Damn thunderstorm is coming in and everything's delayed," he said, not looking at the huge, hairy man.

"Shit happens," Fanelli said. "Might as well hit the bar."

Goldberg stared at him.

"It's eleven fifteen in the morning. You serious?"

Fanelli stared back.

"What the hell else is there to do at the goddamned airport?"

"Ah, screw you. Go to the bar. I don't give a shit."

Fanelli hauled his considerable bulk out of the plastic chair and began walking to the nearest airport lounge.

"Have fun, asshole."

Goldberg pulled out his cell phone, took a deep breath, and dialed Tonelli's cell phone. Not many in the family had Tonelli's private number, but Two Toes had given it to him before they left.

"Yeah," Tonelli said on the other end.

"It's Julie. We're delayed getting out of O'Hare. Goddamned thunderstorm has shut everything down."

"Shit happens," Tonelli said. "When do you expect to get out?"

"United says around three or three thirty."

"A four-hour delay?"

"Looks like it."

"What time will that get you into Nashville?" Tonelli said.

"I dunno, around six or seven, I guess."

Silence.

"Well, keep me posted. You got all the info on Augie and Frankie from Maria?"

"Yeah. We're booked into the same motel as they were. Not looking forward to this, Two Toes."

"Quit calling me that," Tonelli said. "Nobody calls me that anymore, you jamook."

"Sorry, been out of the loop for too long. What do I call you? Mister Tonelli?"

"Yes, that would be appropriate. As long as you're on this job, you work for me. Capisci?"

Fuck you and your capisci. "Yeah, okay." A pause. "Mister Tonelli."

"You friggin' Jew bastard," Tonelli said. "You get your mind around this thing and do your job, or you don't get shit. Capisci?"

Capisci this, asshole. "Yeah, sure, Mister Tonelli." Goldberg's voice dripped with sarcasm.

"Julie?"

"Yeah?"

"Find out what happened to Augie and that idiot son-in-law of mine by tomorrow."

"Okay, Mister Tonelli." Goldberg hit the end button. *I could be in Palm Beach screwing a rich, young broad right now.*

Goldberg pulled out the notes that Maria had given him. Augie and Farmer were booked into the Ridge Motel in Crockett,—goddamned Crockett!—Kentucky. *They'd better have room service.* Farmer was driving a Cadillac DeVille. The fishing guides name was Bo—friggin' Bo!—Paxton. What the hell was this shit? Andy and Barney in goddamned Mayberry? He could be thumping the thirty-something blonde from the country club right now, but here he was back in the shit. Why'd he answer that damn call from Tonelli, the friggin' wop.

Goldberg put the notes away and looked around at all the civilians. *Might as well join the big gorilla in the bar. It's going to be a long-ass day.*

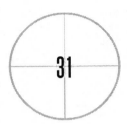

31

Ethan finished his second cup of coffee and, glancing at Frankie, motioned for Bo to join him down by the pond. The two brothers walked the short distance, Ethan helping Bo down the small hill.

"Bo, what do you know about this guy? He could be setting you up for the next hit or something?"

Bo smiled at his younger brother.

"I don't know, son. Gut feeling, I guess. He seems like a lost lamb in the wilderness. He did pull my ass outta the lake. Now why would he do that if he was gonna kill me?"

Ethan shook his head.

"I don't know. Something just doesn't feel right. You said his father-in-law is head of the family in Chicago?"

"Yep, that's what he said."

"And he said that he was sure the hit man was going to kill him after he killed the two coaches and you?"

"Yep."

"It doesn't add up, Bo. Why would he come all the way down here to save your hillbilly ass, when he and his hit man buddy were planning on killing you?"

"I asked him the same thing," Bo said. "He told me he didn't want to be a part of it. That he was a glorified gopher for the hit man."

Ethan walked down to the edge of the pond. He found a small rock and tried to skip it across the surface. It sunk on the first bounce.

"Jesus, Bo, you brought the guy into your home, into your family. You ever hear of the Trojan horse?"

"USC Trojans? Yeah, sure."

"No, not the goddamned USC Trojans, the Trojans from ancient times." Ethan sometimes wondered if they were actually related.

"I knew what you meant, little brother. Just pulling your chain. Yeah, what about it?"

"The people from Athens let the big wooden horse into their compound, thinking it was friendly. It was filled with the enemy. The people ended up dead."

Bo scratched his two-day-old beard.

"You think he's . . . ?" Bo's voice trailed off as he stared at Frankie on the deck.

"I don't know, but he could be leading the next goon right to you and your family."

Bo lowered his head and rubbed his eyes.

"I don't think so, but we'd better talk to him, I guess."

Ethan nodded.

"Let me talk to him, without you around. That okay?"

"Okay, but go easy, brother. He's a mess."

Ethan nodded again.

"The sooner the better."

The two brothers trudged back up the hill to the deck, Ethan halfway carrying Bo.

"I'm goin' inside to talk to Kathy," Bo said, disappearing into the house.

"JB, why don't you go in and talk to your mom and dad?" Ethan said.

JB caught on right away, stood up, and walked inside. Ethan sat across from Frankie.

"So Frankie, what's the deal here? Why'd you really help Bo on the lake?"

Frankie ran his hand through his hair.

"He was in trouble, that's all."

Ethan leaned over the deck table.

"But you were sent to kill him."

"No. No, sir, I wasn't. I'm not a killer. I've never killed anyone."

"But you came down here to kill Williams, the coach."

"Not me. Augie. Tonelli, my father-in-law, sent him to kill the coach, not me."

"Then why did you come?"

"I . . . I don't know. My father-in-law is not someone you say no to. I think Augie was supposed to kill me, too."

"Why?"

Frankie's hand began shaking.

"Because he hates me, thinks I'm a screw up. He didn't want me to marry his daughter. I don't know. I just knew I wasn't supposed to go home."

"Then why'd you sink Bo's boat with the coaches anchored inside? You were trying to hide it, right?"

"I panicked, man," Frankie said. "Bo had passed out, and I didn't know what to do. I was scared shitless, and when I saw the drill and bungee cords and stuff I just did it. I didn't think about it. I just did it."

"You know how that's going to look to the police, or FBI, when they get hold of it, right?"

Frankie stared at Ethan, his eyes bugging out, the fear evident.

"They gonna think I killed them coaches? I didn't kill anybody. I made goddamned sandwiches!"

Ethan saw him shaking.

"Settle down, Frankie. I just want the truth."

"That is the truth, goddamn it."

Ethan sat back and stared at the frightened man. *Maybe Bo's right. He's just a pawn.*

"What's your wife's name?" Ethan said, trying to lighten the mood.

Frankie looked up at him.

"Bunny."

Ethan's eyes widened.

"Bunny?"

"Yeah, it's an Italian thing."

"You're not Italian."

"Yeah, no shit. That's why Bunny's father hates me."

"What's your last name?"

Frankie shook his head.

"Farmer. Go ahead and laugh."

Ethan stared, a smile forming on his face.

"Frankie Farmer?"

Frankie frowned.

"Yeah, Frankie Farmer."

"And your wife is," Ethan suppressed a grin, "Bunny Farmer?"

"Yeah, ha ha. Laugh all you want. I've been livin' with that for five years."

Ethan couldn't help it and began chuckling. The chuckle turned into a laugh. Frankie stared at Ethan and cracked a smile. The smile became a chuckle, then a laugh.

"It's pretty friggin' stupid, isn't it?" Frankie said.

Ethan nodded, laughing even harder.

"Yeah, it's pretty friggin' stupid."

Bo walked out of the kitchen, hearing the laughter.

"What the hell?"

Ethan turned and looked at his brother.

"I think he's okay, Bo. For a bunny farmer."

The three men laughed so hard the dogs ran off, barking.

"Welcome to the Paxton family," Ethan said, holding his hand out to Frankie.

Frankie, tears in his eyes from laughing, shook Ethan's hand.

"Thanks. You got any bunnies you need tending to?"

After several minutes of bunny jokes, Ethan turned serious.

"You have to hide that car, get it out of sight," he said, looking at the silver Cadillac. "It stands out like—"

"Like a boil on a duck's ass," Bo said, completing the sentence. "I already told him."

Frankie nodded his head.

"I know, but where?"

Bo turned and looked all around the farm.

"Look around, Frankie. There's woods so thick around my farm, you could hide a Sherman tank. I think we can hide a little, bitty Caddy."

"We'd better do it now, before someone drives down that lane and sees it," Ethan said.

"JB, you know that old, dirt road 'bout a half mile past the oil rig?" Bo said to his son, who had just walked out from the kitchen.

"Yeah, that'd be a good spot. I'll drive it down there and throw some branches over it."

"Take all my fishin' gear out of the trunk first, son. And anything that Frankie here needs."

"I'll help you, JB," Frankie said, standing up.

JB and Frankie began unloading the Cadillac while Bo and Ethan watched.

"Sorry about your boat," Ethan said, looking at Bo.

Bo pursed his lips and shook his head.

"That boat was my life, my living," he said. "Don't know what I'm gonna do now. Already took a second on the farm to buy it."

"Is it insured?"

Bo looked at his brother and frowned.

"This is Kentucky, son. We don't spend money on insurance and such shit."

Ethan shook his head.

"Too bad, Bo. Think there's any way to salvage it if you can bring it up outta the lake?"

"Maybe the hull, but the motor and electrical stuff will be ruined, stuff like the fish finder. Won't be worth hauling up."

"Well, we've got to tell the sheriff about it. There are two dead bodies in it."

"Yeah, I suppose so." Bo looked at Ethan. "A shitstorm is on its way, little brother. Reporters, television, news folk from everywhere, they all gonna be in Crockett County within a day."

Ethan nodded.

"And don't forget the men from Chicago. Sounds like Frankie's boss is one mean, sadistic son-of-a-gun—the type of guy that would kill his own son-in-law."

Bo glanced at the silver Cadillac.

"Think it was a mistake bringin' him down here?"

Ethan nodded.

"Could be, Bo. Could be."

The two brothers heard the phone ring in the kitchen.

"That may be the first call from a concerned family member," Bo said.

"Bo," Kathy said from the kitchen window, "Doc Welby called and wants to know if you made it home okay. I told him you sure did."

Bo smiled.

"Good ol' Doc Welby. I knew he'd call."

Ethan stood up and stretched, a big yawn escaping.

"You look worse than me, little brother," Bo said. "When's the last time you slept?"

"What's today, Thursday? Tuesday night, I guess."

"Well, son, get inside and get some damn sleep. I'm home. We can handle things okay."

"Better call the sheriff first. Let him know you're home and fill him in on what's happening," Ethan said. "You got his number inside?"

"Yeah, I'll come in with you once JB and Frankie get the Caddy unloaded."

Ethan walked into the house.

"Kathy, you got Sheriff Parsons's number handy?"

"Right there on the wall, next to that damn singin' fish of Bo's."

Ethan saw the fish and punched the red button.

The tune "Don't Worry, Be Happy" came out, the fish's head and tail moving back and forth. *Good ol' Bo and his fish.*

Ethan dialed the number on the wall and waited for someone to answer.

"Crockett County Sheriff's Office. How can I help you?"

"Sheriff Parsons, please," Ethan said.

"He's out right now. Can someone else help you?"

"Is Deputy Smith in?" Ethan said.

"Sure is. Just a minute, darlin'."

Gotta love the south.

"Deputy Smith, can I help you?"

Ethan recognized Cheyenne Smith's voice.

"Cheyenne, this is Ethan Paxton."

"Well, hi there. Thought you were gonna catch up on your sleep?"

Ethan smiled.

"Didn't have time. When we got back home from the lake, guess who showed up in a silver Cadillac?"

"Oh, God. That strange, nervous-lookin' guy we saw in Crockett?"

"Yeah, but it was his passenger that got all the attention," Ethan said.

"No! Bo?" she said. "I'll be damned."

"Yep. A little worse for wear, but okay. He's got a bullet wound in his left leg and a real interesting story."

"The sheriff's still down at the lake talkin' to folks. I'll radio him and tell him to get right over to Bo's place. I'll be out shortly myself, in fifteen."

"Okay, Cheyenne. See you then."

Ethan hung up the phone and looked at Kathy.

"Well, say goodbye to your privacy for a while, Kath. The sheriff's coming."

"Ethan, can I talk to you a second?" Kathy said. "Let's go into my sewing room, outta ear shot."

Ethan followed his sister-in-law to the room off the kitchen and closed the door.

"What's up, Kath?"

"I don't like that young fella that brought Bo home," she said. "He's gonna be nothin' but trouble."

Ethan nodded.

"I agree with you, Kath. I think Bo made a big mistake bringing him here, but he's here now and the sheriff is on his way."

"Is Bo in trouble, Ethan? Tell me straight."

Ethan stared into her eyes.

"Could be, Kath. He did nothing wrong. Matter of fact, he's the victim, but he brought a guy here who's an accomplice to murder. That's not gonna sit well with the law."

"But he had no choice. He had to do it in order to get home, didn't he?"

"I guess so, but the fact remains, Kath, he, and you, are harboring a member of organized crime—a man that was sitting in the boat when the killer shot the two coaches, and a man that, on his own admission, sank Bo's boat with the two dead coaches in it. That doesn't sound good. I don't care who you are."

Ethan saw the tears well up in Kathy's eyes.

"I need to get back out there before the sheriff comes." He hugged his sister-in-law.

"Bo's gonna be okay, Kath. He didn't do anything wrong except bring a stray cat home."

I wish I could believe that myself.

Ethan walked out onto the deck and sat down next to Bo.

"Sheriff Parsons and his deputy are on their way. You ready for this?"

"Why wouldn't I be? I've known Cecil for years. Been fishin' with him several times. Good ol' boy."

"But what about Frankie? You comfortable having him around with the law asking questions?" Ethan leaned closer to Bo. "Two people were killed, Bo, in your boat. You know how that's going to sound? Plus, your boat's at the bottom of the lake now, with the two dead bodies in it."

Bo looked anxiously at his brother.

"Now that you mention it, it does sound a little screwed up, huh?"

"Yeah, it does. And with Frankie here, all buddy-buddy like, it may send the wrong signals to John Law."

"John Law? What the hell is that?" Bo said, his eyes furrowing.

"Just an expression. Anyway, do you want them questioning Frankie at this point?"

"What do you think?"

"This could snowball real fast, and you're right smack in the middle of it, Bo."

Bo and Ethan looked down at Frankie, who was carrying the last of the trunk contents to the garage.

"It's up to you, Bo, but you've got about five minutes to decide. They know that the silver Cadillac is here, and that a strange guy was driving it, but they don't know he's connected to the mob yet."

Bo stroked his two-day-old beard, the events of the last twenty-four hours starting to show in his face.

"I'm gonna tell Cecil the truth, exactly what happened, and let Frankie decide if he wants to tell 'em who he is and what he's doin' down here."

Ethan nodded and clapped his brother on the shoulder.

"Good enough, Bo."

Frankie and JB walked onto the deck just as the sheriff's cruiser pulled up into the driveway. Cecil Parsons got out and started walking up the lawn to the deck.

Frankie looked at Bo, eyes wide and questioning. Bo motioned for him to sit down.

"Morning, gents," Parsons said, climbing the two steps onto the deck.

"Morning, Cecil," Bo said, standing and holding out his hand.

"Bo, you look like somethin' the cat dragged in," the sheriff said. "We were mighty worried about you, son."

Bo smiled, stealing a glance at Ethan.

"Yeah, it's been pretty damn weird the last day or so."

"Ethan, you look a little more relaxed than you did at the lake," Parsons said, taking his big-brimmed hat off.

"Well, having my big brother back safe relieved a lot of stress, Sheriff."

"Guess you ain't got any sleep yet?"

Ethan smiled, feeling the weariness.

"No, not yet."

Parsons squinted his eyes at Frankie.

"And who's this?"

"This is the guy that pulled me outta the lake, Cecil," Bo said. "Wasn't for him, I'd be fish food right now."

"That so? Huh." Parsons held out his hand. "You a client of Bo's?"

"Uh, not exactly," Frankie said, glancing nervously at Bo. "I was, uh, close by when it happened."

Parsons continued to stare at Frankie, nodding his head.

"Close by, huh?"

Everyone turned around when they heard another car coming down the lane. The second sheriff's cruiser pulled up into the driveway, and Cheyenne Smith climbed out.

"Come on up, Cheyenne," Parsons yelled, waving his hand.

Ethan got up and offered his chair to the deputy.

"Mornin' folks," she said, climbing the steps. "Thanks, Ethan, but I'll stand."

Ethan nodded and sat back down.

"This gentleman here, Cheyenne," Parsons said, pointing at Frankie, "saved Bo on the lake yesterday. His name's, uh, what'd you say your name was, son?"

"Frankie," he said, nodding to Cheyenne.

"Frankie," Parsons said. "Frankie what?"

Frankie looked at Bo, who nodded for him to continue.

"Frankie Farmer."

Sheriff Parsons squinted again, looking from Frankie to Bo.

"Huh. Interesting name, Frankie. Where you from?"

"Up north," Frankie said, shifting in his chair.

"Up north. Big area, up north," Parsons said. "Can ya narrow it down some?"

Frankie coughed nervously.

"Chicago."

Parsons eyes widened as he glanced at Ethan and then at Cheyenne.

"Chicago, huh?"

Frankie nodded, glancing at Bo again.

"Look, Cecil," Bo said, leaning forward. "Let me explain what happened yesterday. I'll bring y'all up to speed."

"Please do, Bo. Please do."

Bo told the sheriff and his deputy the entire story, from meeting Sonny Daye and Jerry Joe Williams at the resort at six o'clock on Wednesday morning, to the events on the lake that proceeded the shootings. When he got to the Copperhead Cove part, he stopped.

"What's wrong, Bo?" Parsons said.

"Well, this next part all happened damn fast, and I was under a lot of stress, so I've gotta go slow and make sure it comes out right."

"Take your time, son," Parsons said, smiling.

Bo glanced at Frankie before continuing.

"Well, Sonny Daye had hooked his first smallmouth of the day and was pulling it in, then . . . . "

Parsons sat quietly, waiting for Bo to continue.

"And then all hell broke loose." Bo told them about the two men in the gray fishing boat pulling into the cove, the big man pulling out a rifle and shooting Daye and Williams. "He woulda got me, except I dove backward into the lake. He hit me in the left calf. Hurt like hell."

Bo pulled out his bandaged leg and showed it to Parsons and Smith.

"What'd you do then?" Smith asked, her eyes wide in anticipation.

"I swam for a clump of underwater trees that had fallen into the lake last spring. They were completely submerged, close to the shore, and I thought I could hide amongst 'em."

"Yeah? Did the shooters try to finish the job?" Parsons said.

"Shooter. There was only one guy shootin'," Bo said, glancing at Frankie. "A big fella. Knew what he was doin', too. Took the coaches out with one shot each, to the head."

Parsons looked at Frankie. He kept staring at the man even after Bo started telling the rest of the story. Frankie was shifting in his chair, nervous and uncomfortable.

"My leg was bleedin' like hell, and they would've found me 'cause of that, so I swam underwater to a spot on the other side of the trees and tied my T-shirt around my leg, trying to stop the flow of blood."

"Did it work?" Smith said.

"Yeah, it stopped the flow some."

"And did the shooter and," Parsons looked at Frankie, "his accomplice try to find you?"

Bo told them the rest of story about the big guy pointing his gun at him and how the cottonmouth struck the big guy.

"Three strikes: one to the leg, one to the arm, and the last one to the neck, right on the jugular," Bo said, with emphasis.

"Damn," Parsons said, "never heard of anyone taking three strikes. Damn moccasin must've been real pissed."

"He was, Cecil, and he had his mouth open at me after the big guy hit the water face down."

"Huh. And?"

"I pushed off the shore with my good leg and moved out into the lake a few feet. That must've removed the threat, so the cottonmouth closed up shop and slithered away."

Parsons was scratching his head, staring at Bo.

"You damn lucky, Bo."

"Yes sir, I thought I was a goner, for sure."

"And the big guy, the shooter, what happened to him?" Smith said.

"Well, he was face down in the water, his legs still on the shore. He was gurgling and thrashing some, but he had too much venom in him. He drowned within a few seconds." Bo didn't look at Frankie.

"So the snake saved your hillbilly ass," Cecil said, smiling.

"Guess so, but that's where Frankie here comes in." Bo looked at Frankie, who was looking down at his feet.

"That so?" Parsons was staring at Frankie again, watching his reaction, leaning in, his elbows on his knees. "Go on, Bo."

Bo cleared his throat.

"I was about five feet away from shore and was sinkin' fast. I had nothin' left, and my leg was dead weight. Didn't know if I could make it back, and wasn't sure I wanted to with that pissed off cottonmouth around. Then Frankie walks up and hands me, uh, a long stick and pulls me outta the lake, helps me to my feet, and half carries me to his boat."

Parsons looked from Bo to Frankie.

"Were you the second man in the boat, with the shooter?"

Frankie shifted in his chair again, glancing up at the sheriff, and then at Bo. He cleared his throat, twice.

"Simple question, son," Parsons said.

"Y–yes, sir, I was."

Parsons sat up straight, looking at Bo, Ethan, and Cheyenne, in order, and then back at Frankie.

"You understand what you're tellin' me, Mr. Farmer?"

"Yes."

"I'm gonna have to place you under arrest, Mr. Farmer, as an accomplice in the murders of Sonny Daye and Jerry Joe Williams, and the attempted murder of Bo Paxton. You understand the charges, son?"

Frankie looked at Bo, his eyes pleading.

"Cecil, he saved my life, and he took care of me when I passed out, got me to the dock, bandaged me up. I wouldn't be here if not for him." Bo was staring at Parsons, doing his own pleading.

"Well, I understand that, Bo, and that'll be taken into consideration, but my job is to uphold the law, and this man is admittedly an accomplice to two murders and one attempted murder. There's no gettin' 'round that."

Ethan had been sitting back, listening to Bo and Parsons. He finally sat up straight and leaned in to Parsons.

"Sheriff, there's another wrinkle here that you need to know about." Ethan glanced at Bo, and then at Frankie.

"Go ahead, Ethan," Parsons said.

Ethan looked at Bo, then Frankie.

"You want me to tell him or you?"

Frankie blinked and mumbled something under his breath.

"What did you say?" Ethan said, leaning forward.

"You tell 'em."

Ethan nodded and turned his gaze to the sheriff.

"When Bo passed out, Frankie here decided to sink Bo's bass boat . . . with the coaches tied up inside. It's at the bottom of Copperhead Cove."

Parsons jaw dropped and a low guttural sound came out of his mouth. He turned at glared at Frankie.

"You a damn murderer, son. Not just an accomplice, but a damn murderer. Why'd you do somethin' like that?"

Frankie's eyes were bugging out.

"I was scared, man!"

Parsons squinted his eyes as he looked at the frightened man.

"Scared, stupid, don't matter. You're in a world of shit, Mr. Farmer."

"Sheriff, there's one more thing you need to know, and this is a game-changer," Ethan said.

Parsons turned to Ethan.

"Goddamn, son, what more could there be?"

"The big man, the shooter, was a hit man with the Chicago mob."

Parsons nodded.

"I sorta figured that." He looked at Frankie again. "And this man was with the shooter, hunting down those poor coaches, and you, Bo, so what does that make him?"

"I made sandwiches," Frankie said.

Everyone turned to him, staring at the strange man.

"Say again?" Parsons said.

"I made sandwiches and drove the car. But Sheriff, I had nothing to do with those murders. I was gonna be Augie's next victim, no doubt in my mind."

Parsons laughed out loud.

"What nonsense are you spoutin', boy?"

"It ain't nonsense, Sheriff. The big guy had a whole trunkful of stuff to saw up, cut off, and shoot me and the others with. I didn't know about any of it until me and Bo were in the boat after the, uh, snake thing."

Parsons shook his head and started waving his arms.

"You were in the boat with the shooter, son, and you did nothin' to stop him from killin' two innocent men and almost killin' Bo here. I don't give a shit if the shooter was gonna kill you after or not. That don't mean diddly squat to me."

"But Cecil, he's just a pawn. He didn't know what was gonna happen," Bo said, seeing the situation going from bad to worse.

"Don't mean diddly squat, Bo. He was in the boat, with the killer, so that makes him an accomplice to murder. And burying those poor coaches at the bottom of the lake makes him as guilty as the shooter. Open and shut."

Frankie suddenly stood up, his eyes bulging.

"I ain't an accomplice, and I ain't no murderer! I was a stupid little asshole that let my father-in-law talk me into something that I knew was wrong. I ain't goin' to jail."

"Sit down, son, ain't no reason to get riled—"

"Shut up!" Frankie yelled, pulling the .357 Magnum and pointing it at the sheriff. "All of you, shut up!"

Bo put his hand out.

"Frankie, put the gun down. You're just makin' it worse."

"I trusted you, Bo. You said, 'Come to my place, and I'll protect you.' Is this protecting me? I didn't kill anybody. I made fucking sandwiches, for cryin' out loud!"

"Settle down, Frankie, ain't no need . . . . " The sheriff backed away and put his arms up when Frankie pointed the gun at him again.

"I'm getting in my Cadillac, and I'm going home," Frankie said, tears streaming down his face. "I ain't never killed anybody, but I'll sure start if someone tries to stop me. All of you, get in the house, now."

"Frankie, come on." Bo took a step toward the distraught man and stopped when Frankie pointed the gun at him.

"Bo, I like you. You were a friend to me, but I ain't going to jail." Frankie turned and pointed the gun at the sheriff. "I ain't going to jail." Frankie turned and saw Deputy Smith reaching for her gun. "Take your hand away, lady." Smith moved her hand up, away from her holster.

Suddenly, a body came from the shadows near the house and flew at Frankie, knocking him to the deck, the Magnum falling harmlessly to the lawn below.

Ethan had been watching JB in the shadows, waiting for him to move. When Bo's son flew out at Frankie, Ethan ran down and picked up the gun.

Frankie lay face down on the wooden deck, blood running from his nose. JB was still on top of him, while Sheriff Parsons clapped handcuffs on the man. The two men picked Frankie up and sat him down in the chair.

Blood was running down Frankie's T-shirt, another blood flow starting above his right eye. Bo took a napkin and wiped the blood from his face.

"Frankie . . . . " Bo shook his head, unable to say anything else.

Frankie stared up at Bo, tears streaming from his eyes, mixing with the blood.

"I'm sorry, Bo."

"Well, son, that about wraps this up," Parsons said, signaling for his deputy to take Frankie to her cruiser. "Read him his Miranda rights, Cheyenne."

"Wait," Ethan said. "I didn't get to make my point before . . . all this happened."

"Okay, Ethan, what's your point?" Parsons said, continuing to stand, sounding impatient.

"The Chicago mob made these hits. They sent a professional hit man to whack those two coaches and Bo, just because he was a witness. When they realize that two witnesses are still alive down here, what do you think they're gonna do?"

Parson's eyes grew wider as he stared at Ethan.

"They'll be sendin' someone else down to finish it."

Ethan nodded.

"You can bet on it, Sheriff."

Parsons looked at Frankie.

"You said somethin' about your father-in-law. Is he with the mob?"

Frankie looked up at Parsons.

"He is the mob."

"What the hell does that mean?"

"He's the boss of the Chicago mob," Bo said.

Parsons shook his head.

"This damn story just gets better 'n' better. What's his name, this boss?"

Frankie stood frozen, blood dripping down his face, tears from his eyes.

"Son, what is your daddy-in-law's name?" Parsons was leaning within inches of Frankie. Frankie blinked away a tear.

"Tonelli. Anthony Tonelli."

Parsons stepped back, his eyes growing wider as he stared at Frankie. "Holy shit."

"What is it, Sheriff?" Cheyenne said.

"I had some run-ins with Tonelli while I was on the Chicago PD, twenty-some years ago." Parsons took his hat and beat it on his leg, shaking his head. "He's as mean as a moccasin and just as deadly." Parsons turned his gaze on Bo. "You knew this? And you brought this man to your home?"

Bo nodded.

"He was just as afraid as I was, Cecil. They're gonna be after him, too. He's a good kid who got involved with the mob because he married the boss's daughter. That's all. He's not a threat."

"I beg to differ with you, Bo, but we got the Chicago mob boss's son-in-law in custody. He's a damn big threat, to everyone in this town—hell, in the county!"

"He's right, Bo," Ethan said. "No one's going to be safe if they send their goons down here."

"We got work to do," Parsons said to his deputy. "Let's get this man locked up, and then we have to drag Copperhead Cove for Bo's boat and hopefully the two bodies."

"Sheriff," Ethan said, "you mentioned at the lake that you can call up some more deputies if you needed to. Think this is a good time?"

Parsons nodded.

"Yeah, this is a good time. You try to get some sleep, son, because hell is coming to Crockett County."

Deputy Smith grabbed Frankie and led him down to her cruiser, reading him his Miranda rights as they walked. She put him in the backseat, handcuffing his arms to a metal bar above the door.

"Bo," Sheriff Parsons said, "I don't know what to say to you, son. Very poor judgment, bringin' that fella up here to your farm, but I know you was under a lot of stress."

"Cecil, we were holed up in the Ridge Motel. I couldn't stay there, and I didn't know what else to do."

"The Ridge, huh?" Parsons scratched his head. "That's the first place these goons are gonna check when they come ridin' into town. Maybe we should stake it out."

"That'd be a good idea, Cecil. We were stayin' in room eleven, and the big guy, the shooter, stayed in room twelve."

Parsons nodded and looked at Bo's son.

"JB, you saved the day, son. Nice work."

"Thanks, Sheriff," JB said, embarrassed.

"One more thing," Ethan said, as Parsons put on his hat. "This probably means the feds will be coming, right?"

"Yep. The murders took place on federal property, and the dead guys are a couple of high profile people. The FBI will be down here quicker'n flies on shit."

"Especially when they know the mob's involved," Ethan said.

"Yeah, that'll raise the red flag for sure. I've got a busy afternoon. Bo, get some rest. You too, Ethan. See you boys soon—very soon. Don't go anywhere, Bo. You're in some pretty deep shit, son."

"I'm gonna drive down to pick up my PI friend in a few hours. Will be back around ten o'clock tonight," Ethan said. "You got my cell phone number, Sheriff?"

"I got it from you at the lake," Parsons said. "Bo, I'm gonna send someone out this afternoon to watch out for you and your family, maybe a couple guys. You're a target, son, and, hate to say it, an accomplice, so be careful and watch everything. You're lucky I ain't haulin' your ass to jail."

"Okay, Cecil," Bo said. "Thanks."

"You got anyone you and Kathy can stay with?"

"My daughter, out on McKenzie Ridge, but it's a small place. I'd rather stay here, at home."

"Suit yourself. I'll send someone as soon as I can deputize a few folks. Might be later this afternoon. In the meantime, get some rest, son."

Bo nodded. Parsons tipped his hat to Ethan and JB and walked to his cruiser.

"Well, big brother, another fine mess you've gotten us into," Ethan said, clapping Bo on the shoulder.

Bo shook his head.

"Damn cottonmouth should of put me outta my misery when it had the chance."

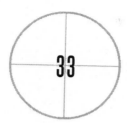

33

When Parsons and Smith were out of sight, Kathy came out of the house and ordered Bo to go upstairs, take a shower, and rest.

"You need to get some sleep, too, Ethan," she said. "Your eyes look ready to pop out of your sockets, they're so red."

Ethan smiled at his sister-in-law.

"I will, Kathy, just take care of Bo right now. He's pretty down."

She smiled back and closed the door to the kitchen. Ethan and JB were sitting on the deck alone, both quiet, contemplating what just happened.

"Nice move, JB," Ethan said. "You should've been a defensive back for the Tennessee Titans."

JB smiled for a second and then turned serious.

"I'm worried about Dad, Uncle Ethan."

"He'll be okay once he gets cleaned up and gets some rest."

"No, I'm worried about what's gonna happen in the next few days. I heard the conversation, and it scares the hell out of me."

Ethan looked at his nephew, who had deep furrows in his forehead. He was so much like Bo, but much more of a thinker, like Ethan. He was always thinking, always contemplating, and it showed in his face. He was a lot like Ethan's son, Charlie.

"Wish I could sugarcoat it, JB, but it's gonna be a wild few days, to be sure. I don't know what's going to happen, but we have to protect your dad in any way we can."

"How? We live out here in the middle of nowhere. If someone wants to sneak up on us, they have three ridges of forest to do it in. We'll never see 'em comin'."

Ethan gazed out at the pines and cottonwoods covering the ridges of the hollow in all directions. JB was right, they were sitting ducks here in the clearing.

"What about your sister's place?" Ethan said.

"Too small, and too vulnerable. We'd be better off here."

"Any other ideas?" Ethan knew JB had been thinking about the situation.

"How about we go out on the lake, on a houseboat? Dad and I know some secret coves that no one would ever find. There's hundreds of miles of woods we could get lost in. Just wait this thing out."

Ethan stared at JB and then looked out over the pond. *Not a bad idea, but how long would they have to be out there?*

"I don't know if the sheriff, and eventually the FBI, would want Bo to disappear right now. He's a material witness to double murder. You could end up having the mob *and* the FBI looking for you."

"We can't just sit here and wait for some goons from Chicago to show up."

Ethan nodded.

"You're right, we have to do something. Not just for Bo, but for your mom and for you. You're all in danger now."

JB leaned forward.

"I can get a houseboat tonight, and we could be on the lake by sundown. No one will ever find us, guaranteed."

Ethan sat back and thought about the houseboat idea. It might ease the immediate problem, but they would have to surface eventually. And the mob, from what he knew and read, had a long memory.

"I think it's a great idea for you and your mom, and probably your sister," he said. "Get you out of danger until this thing is done." Ethan looked at JB closely. "But your dad is smack dab in the middle of this mess, and there's no way he can avoid it. And I'm gonna be right there beside him, come what may."

Tears began to fill JB's eyes.

"I don't want to lose my dad."

Ethan reached over and gave him a pat on the shoulder.

"We'll figure it out, son. I have the cavalry coming in tonight, and he'll have some ideas."

Ethan looked at his watch. Twelve noon. *Jake has no idea what he's walking into, but he'll soon find out.*

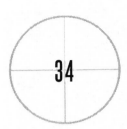

34

The United flight out of Chicago finally departed at four twenty-five in the afternoon. The thunderstorms that passed through Chicago delayed all flights by almost four hours. Goldberg was sitting in first class in an aisle seat in row two, downing his second Jim Beam on the rocks. The massive man sitting next to him was already asleep, snoring so loud Goldberg couldn't hear the announcement over the intercom.

What a friggin' animal, the hairy bastard.

Goldberg poked Fanelli in the arm.

"Wake up."

Fanelli moved his lips and mumbled something, but kept his eyes closed.

God Almighty, I'm gonna kill the damn gorilla.

The female flight attendant stopped and turned off the button above Goldberg's head.

"Can I help you, Mr. Jones?"

Julie smiled. Mr. Jones. Maria was a creative genius, the friggin' idiot. But she did a nice job on the fake driver's license.

"Another JB rocks, please," he said, holding up his empty glass.

The flight attendant, a middle-aged redhead, took the glass.

"Of course, Mr. Jones."

Goldberg settled back and closed his eyes, trying to ignore the snoring next to him. He'd been running the facts around in his head for three hours while they waited for the weather to clear in Chicago. They would rent a car in Nashville, drive the 120 miles to Crockett, Kentucky, getting in around ten o'clock, check in at the Ridge Motel, which sounded like a friggin' dump, and get a good night's sleep. Two rooms: one for the gorilla and one for him. First thing in the morning, at five o'clock, they would drive to the lake and start looking around. He had a list of things he would check on, based upon his experience as a tracker for the family. He hadn't worked for the Tonelli family in four or five years, but he knew Augie Stellato, a legend in the Chicago mob. He'd whacked more people than anyone before or since. *I thought the man was dead.*

"Here you are, sir," the flight attendant said, handing Julie his drink. "Will there be anything else?"

"Yeah, how about some heated nuts?"

She feigned a smile.

"Of course, sir, let me see what we have in the galley." She shook her head as she walked back to the front of the airplane.

"Friggin' airlines nowadays," Julie said out loud. "No friggin' respect for the customer."

Someone behind him said "Amen."

Goldberg took a swallow of the JB rocks and closed his eyes again, thinking about the next few hours. He'd check the motel's records to see if Stellato and Farmer had checked out. *Shit! He forgot to get their aliases from Maria. Gonna have to call the half-wit in Nashville.* If they hadn't checked out, he would ask for their room numbers. If something happened to them on the lake, he'd know it by looking at their rooms. You could always tell if someone was planning on coming back by the stuff they left in the bathroom and in the closet. If it was clean, it meant they made it back from the lake and were around somewhere. If it wasn't clean, it probably meant they never made it back from the lake.

"Here you are, sir," the flight attendant said, a hint of sarcasm in her voice. "Warm nuts, just for you."

"Thanks," he said, "I like my nuts hot." He smiled at her suggestively, his white teeth gleaming. The redhead frowned and walked away, shaking her head again.

"Friggin' stewardesses nowadays. Can't take a joke," he said out loud.

The same voice behind him said, "Amen, brother."

Goldberg started to turn around, but thought better of it. *Friggin' jamook, I'll whack your ass if you don't shut the hell up.*

As the Boeing 737 began to lift off, Julie finished his JB and water and drifted off to sleep, his head on Rhino's shoulder.

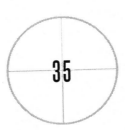

35

After over an hour on the rural roads of Kentucky and Tennessee, Ethan finally reached Interstate 40 and headed west, toward Nashville. He glanced at his watch again. It was almost seven o'clock. The sun was heavy in the western sky and was directly in his eyes. He put on his sunglasses and pulled down the visor. He'd made this drive many times, returning from visiting his older brother, but this time was different. He wasn't on holiday, and he didn't have his son and daughter with him. After picking up Jake, he'd have to turn around and make the same two hour drive back to Crockett.

Ethan rubbed his tired eyes again, feeling the strain of the past two days, the sun in his eyes, and the stress of his brother's situation. He'd slept for a couple of hours in the afternoon, but it was a restless sleep. He kept waking up with every sound outside. He'd finally given up around four o'clock and walked out onto the deck to join Bo and JB.

As he stared at the white line of the interstate, his mind went back to the conversation on the deck just a few hours earlier.

"Dad and I have been talkin', Ethan," JB said. "We think maybe the houseboat idea ain't so bad."

Ethan, rubbing his eyes for the hundredth time, shook his head.

"You can't just disappear, Bo. You're a material witness in a double murder."

"I know, little brother, but I didn't do anything. I was the damn victim," Bo said indignantly. "Why's everybody on my ass?"

Ethan put his hand on his brother's shoulder.

"It's the way the law works, Bo. You are a victim, but so were those two coaches. Nobody else knows what happened out there but you and Frankie Farmer."

"Ethan, I ain't gonna sit here and wait for some goons from Chicago to show up and kill me and my family. I ain't gonna do it, son."

"I understand, but disappearing on the lake somewhere is not the answer," Ethan said. "You'd just be digging a deeper hole for yourself. Right now you have justice on your side because you are the victim, but if you go away and hide, the matter of guilt may shift to you."

"How'd ya figure that?"

Ethan rubbed his forehead.

"You brought a guy from the Chicago mob to your home, innocently or otherwise, and that put a shadow of doubt in the law's mind. You're a witness to murder, but you also harbored an accomplice to murder. Do you understand?"

"I didn't harbor nobody," Bo said, his voice rising. "I just wanted to go home, and that was the only way he'd let me do it. Why don't you understand that?"

Ethan nodded.

"Bo, I understand, and I know the stress you were under this morning. I really do." Ethan leaned forward. "But in the sheriff's eyes, you appeared to be more than an innocent victim when you brought him to your home. That's why you can't just disappear somewhere and hope it all goes away. I guarantee you, the law, meaning the local sheriff and the FBI, won't look at you favorably if you just disappear. And the mob, that's a whole different story, Bo."

For the first time in his memory, since they were little kids growing up in Indiana, Ethan saw tears in Bo's eyes. Ethan's heart hurt when he saw this, imagining the pain that his brother was going through.

"I don't know what to do, Ethan," Bo said, the confidence gone from his voice.

"I'm going to be driving down to Nashville to pick Jake up. He was a cop for fifteen years and has seen a lot of crap in his life. Let's wait and let him help us."

"Do you trust him?" Bo said, wiping a tear from his cheek.

"He saved my daughter, my family. Yeah, I trust him as much as I can trust anybody."

Bo nodded, reaching out and grabbing Ethan's arm.

"Then I trust him."

The two brothers hugged each other without talking.

Ethan's thoughts were jolted back to the present when he had to brake for a big rig that pulled out in front of him. He blinked several times and wrestled with the steering wheel. *Damn, I've got to get some sleep.*

Ethan knew he was putting a lot of pressure on Jake Delgado, and he hadn't seen him since right after Molly's ordeal. Ethan rubbed his swollen, red eyes once again and continued down the interstate, his mind racing from Mexico to Kentucky and back.

At seven thirty, Ethan pulled into the short-term parking lot at Nashville International Airport. He found an empty slot close to the terminal and got out of his rented Buick. He stretched his tired bones before beginning the walk to the arrival terminal. It was hot and muggy, the sweat starting to run down his back.

Once in the terminal, Ethan checked the arrival board in the baggage claim area. He spotted United Flight 593 and glanced to the right, seeing "on time" next to it. He'd flown so many miles over the past fifteen years, he knew that it would take Jake fifteen to twenty minutes to deplane and walk to the baggage claim area. Enough time to get a cup of coffee.

Ethan hopped onto the escalator and rode up to the departure terminal. He spotted a Starbucks to his right and walked over and stood in line. *A little caffeine is what I need right now.*

While standing in line, he watched the arriving passengers make their way to the escalator that went down to baggage claim. He yearned for the days when his family was able to meet him at the arrival gate, but since 9/11 that didn't happen anymore. They had to meet you at baggage claim or, if it was an international flight, outside of U.S. Customs. How things had changed in the last two years since the terrorist attacks.

He approached the counter and ordered a medium black coffee. While waiting, he glanced at the arriving passengers and noticed a tanned, silver-haired man walking next to an extremely large man with dark features and hair everywhere. They looked out of place in the terminal full of families on vacation. They walked with a quick gait, staring straight ahead. Ethan watched them get onto the escalator and saw their heads disappear as the escalator took them down to baggage claim.

The mob would be sending someone to finish the job. A chill went through Ethan's body as he grabbed his coffee and headed for the escalator. He took a sip of the hot, black coffee and hopped onto the escalator, glancing at his watch. It was seven forty-five, so Jake's flight would be taxiing up to the gate. He got off the escalator and found an empty chair. He sat, sipping his coffee, glancing around the baggage area. He spotted the silver-haired man and the big man next to a revolving carousel of luggage. Ethan glanced up at the sign over the carousel, which gave the flight number and departure city for the arriving bags. *United 286 from Chicago.*

Ethan stood up and walked closer to the two men, stopping ten feet away. The silver-haired man was in casual clothes, with tan slacks and a white aloha shirt, something that someone from a warm climate would wear. He had a deep tan on his face and arms. The big man was dressed in a dark suit, with hair poking out of the sleeves near his hands and out of his collar. He had a dark complexion, like someone from Italy or the Middle East. The two men were talking to each other when suddenly the silver-haired man turned around and looked at Ethan.

Ethan froze and then turned his gaze away, checking his watch. When he looked up, the silver-haired man had turned back to the carousel. *Something in his eyes, cold and calculating.*

Ethan jerked when he felt a hand on his shoulder, spilling part of his coffee on the floor. *What the . . . ?*

"You looking for me," he heard someone say behind him.

Ethan looked to his left at the smiling face of Jake Delgado, who was dressed in his usual jeans and blue-and-white flowered aloha shirt. Ethan, who was six feet tall, had to look up at his friend.

"Jake!" Ethan said, putting his arm around Jake's shoulders. "Damn, you got here fast."

"Right on time, bud," Jake said. "You look like you've seen a ghost. Everything all right?"

Ethan turned and looked at the two men from Chicago. They grabbed their suitcases from the carousel and walked toward them, heading directly at Ethan and Jake. Ethan looked up at Jake.

"The two men walking toward us, they look suspicious to you?" Ethan said.

Ethan saw Jake glance at the silver-haired man and then at the big, hairy man as they walked past.

"Suspicious in what way? They look like a couple of goons, if that's what you mean."

"That's what I mean," Ethan said.

Ethan watched the two men walk out of the baggage claim area, toward the rental car area.

"Come on, let's follow them," Ethan said.

"Wait, what about my bag?" Jake said.

"We'll come back for it." Ethan was already walking toward the door that would lead to the rental car area.

"Jesus, Ethan, you're spookin' me, man," Jake said, following his friend.

Ethan watched the two men walk across the street into the Avis Rental Car area. He motioned for Jake to follow him and crossed the street, keeping a safe distance from the two Chicago men.

"I want to see what kind of car they're driving," he said as Jake caught up with him.

"Why? What's going on?" Jake said, peering through the shadows at the Avis counter.

"They're from Chicago," Ethan said, craning his head to look over the passing cars.

"So?"

"I'll explain later," Ethan said, not taking his eyes off the two men.

He saw them stop next to a black Lincoln Town Car, pop the trunk, and throw their bags inside. The silver-haired man got behind the wheel, and the big man climbed into the front passenger seat. The Lincoln pulled out and drove out of the Avis lot, toward Ethan and Jake.

Ethan turned toward Jake as the Lincoln approached them. As they passed by, he stared at the driver, who was staring back at him. Their eyes locked for a split second, and then the car was gone. Ethan squinted, but couldn't read the license plate number. All he saw was "Tennessee" on the plate.

"They're in a Lincoln Town Car," he said, looking at Jake, "with Tennessee plates."

Jake looked at him like he was from another planet.

"You got a lot of 'splainin' to do, Lucy," Jake said, shaking his head.

Ethan smiled up at his old friend.

"Yeah, guess I do. Damn good to see you, Jake. Now let's get your bag and get on the road."

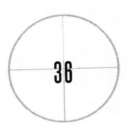

36

Jake retrieved his suitcase from baggage claim, and the two men walked to the short-term parking lot. After Jake threw his suitcase into the trunk of the Buick, they got into the car and began the two-hour journey to Crockett, Kentucky.

"You hungry?" Ethan asked Jake as they took the on-ramp onto Interstate 40.

"Nope, ate in Denver," Jake said. "But if you are . . . . "

"No, I ate something before I drove down here. It's great to see you, Jake. Or should I call you Bull?"

Jake laughed.

"No, I retired the 'Bull' crap, so to speak. That was a past life. I'm just Jake now."

Ethan smiled.

"Good. It was really confusing."

Jake returned the smile.

"Yeah, that was a confusing time, bud. How are Molly and Charlie?"

Ethan patted his friend on the arm.

"They're both doing great. Charlie's going to be a senior at UCLA this fall, and Molly's graduating from St. Elena next week. She'll be going to UC San Diego in the fall. They both ask about you all the time."

Jake's smile widened.

"They're great kids, Ethan. You should be proud."

"I am. Thanks to you, they're both around to enjoy life."

"How about the charter pilot? How's that going?" Jake said.

Ethan grinned.

"We're getting married in September, and I want you to be there."

"No shit. That's great, Ethan. She's a beauty, for sure."

Ethan smiled as he drove east on the interstate.

"That she is."

Ethan kept glancing at Jake, almost staring.

"What're you looking at?" Jake said. "You wondering about the scar?"

Ethan grinned.

"You got it fixed, didn't you?"

Jake nodded and ran his hand over his left cheek.

"Yeah, Amos talked me into getting some plastic surgery about a year ago. How's it look?"

Ethan remembered the large, purple scar on Jake's left cheek that went from his left eye to his jawbone, the result of a bar fight years ago. The same man that had kidnapped Molly during 9/11 was the one that sliced Jake's cheek five years prior to that. The scar had stood out like a warning beacon the last time Ethan had seen his friend in 2001.

"You can hardly see it now," Ethan said. "It looks like a thin line instead of that great purple . . . thing."

Jake rubbed the thin line and smiled.

"Yeah, I'm not the Frankenstein monster anymore, according to Amos."

Ethan knew that Jake was talking about Amos Stillwater, an ex-San Diego cop who helped him during Molly's kidnapping.

"How is Amos, by the way?"

Jake grinned again.

"He and I are partners now in the PI firm."

Ethan's eyes grew big.

"No shit? Hey, that's great. You guys make a great team. What's the name of the firm?"

Jake grinned.

"Well, we thought about Private Investigations of San Diego."

Ethan's eyes narrowed.

"Not bad. Sort of bland, isn't it?"

"The acronym is much more interesting."

Ethan thought for a second and then laughed.

"P.I.S.D. Very clever."

"Yeah, well, we decided to keep El Toro Investigations."

"I like P.I.S.D. much better. Has some swagger to it." Ethan laughed out loud. "Hello, PISD Investigations. Can I help you?"

Both men laughed.

Ethan's smile faded.

"How's the drinking? Still pounding Bushmills like you used to?"

"Sometimes, but Amos keeps me in line. He's a good friend. He wanted to come back here with me but was working a case."

"Yeah, he's as rock solid as they come," Ethan said. "But you're still drinking?"

"Yes, mother, I'm still drinking, just not all night like I used to."

Ethan smiled and clapped his friend on the shoulder.

"Sounds like things are looking up for you."

"Okay, enough of the kumbaya crap. What's going on?" Jake said, turning toward Ethan. "What's the deal with the goons back at the airport?"

Ethan glanced at Jake.

"The shit has hit the fan, Jake."

Jake stared at him.

"And what does Chicago have to do with it?"

Ethan told him the entire story, from the time he heard Bo was missing until that afternoon's confrontation with the sheriff and Frankie Farmer. It took nearly an hour to recount the events. When he was finished, he looked at Jake, who was sitting stone silent, staring at the dark road ahead.

"Jake?"

Jake slowly turned his head and looked at Ethan.

"We're going up against the mob?" he said.

Ethan nodded.

"Looks like it."

"Holy crap, Ethan," Jake said, shaking his head. "This is some serious shit."

Ethan nodded again, not speaking.

"So what do you want me to do?" Jake said.

Ethan looked at his friend.

"At this point, I'm not sure, Jake. Tomorrow is going to rain down hell with the press, the FBI, and probably the mob, all converging on little ol' Crockett, Kentucky."

"Holy crap," Jake said again, staring into the blackness of the Tennessee night. "What the hell did you get me into?"

"You wanna turn around and go back to San Diego?"

Jake turned and looked at Ethan.

"You know me better than that."

Ethan smiled weakly.

"Yeah, I do. Thanks, old buddy."

Jake shook his head.

"You take friendship to a whole other level."

Ethan nodded and stared at the long country road ahead.

"Yeah, I guess I do."

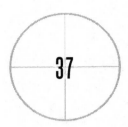

37

Goldberg and Fanelli pulled into the parking lot of the Riverside Motel at exactly ten o'clock. Just like Frankie and Augie two days before, their black Lincoln Town Car stood out against the rusted pickups and ten-year-old Chevrolets.

"That was a long-ass drive," Fanelli said, yawning. "What the hell is this?" he said, looking at the cheap motel.

"Tonelli's secretary told us to check in here," Julie said. "Don't you ever listen?"

"Fuck you."

"You friggin' idiot," Goldberg said. "Eat shit and die."

"Fuck you."

Goldberg shook his head and got out of the air-conditioned car. The heat and humidity hit him square in the face.

"Jesus Christ Almighty," he said as he walked to the motel office. He opened the door and heard the little bell tinkle. "You gotta be shittin' me," he said, looking up.

He walked up to the counter and looked around. It was empty, so he rang the little silver bell. *Unbelievable.*

A plump, young girl with a pimply face walked out, wiping something from her face.

"Can I help y'all?" she said in a heavy southern accent.

Goldberg looked at her and shook his head. *Unbelievable.*

"Yeah, I got reservations."

"We're all booked up, sir," she said. "It's graduation week."

Goldberg glared at her.

"I just said I had a reservation."

The young girl glared back.

"What's the name, sir?"

Goldberg hesitated, trying to remember his fake name.

"Jones . . . yeah, Jones."

She glanced at him and then pulled something up on the computer. "Jones . . . Jones . . . ." She looked up at him, her eyes widening. "Oh, you're booked at the Ridge."

"Yeah, the Ridge," Goldberg said. "Where is it, next door to this, uh, palace?"

She smiled nervously.

"Nooo. It's up there," she said, pointing out the door, "on the ridge."

Goldberg looked out the glass door.

"What? Where?"

"You're the second person this week with reservations at the Ridge," she said. "Nobody ever—"

"What was the other guy's name?" Goldberg said.

"Why?"

"Because I'm curious, that's why."

The girl stared at him and then looked at the computer.

"Ford."

Goldberg leaned in.

"Ford, like the car?"

The girl giggled.

"Yeah, that's what I said."

"What was his first name?"

She looked at him suspiciously.

"F."

"F?"

"Yes, F. Ford."

That friggin' Farmer. Couldn't even change the letter of his first or last name. What a schmendrik.

"Just him. Nobody else?"

"No, just Mr. Ford."

"He check out yet?"

"I can't give out that information."

"He's a colleague of mine. Just need to know if he's still in town."

The girl looked at the man, squinting.

"They didn't actually check out, but the room was clean when the maid went up there this morning."

"What room he stay in?"

"Twelve."

"Okay, give me that room and one more."

The girl giggled again.

"I have lots of rooms, mister. It's empty up there."

"Whaddaya mean, empty?"

"Empty. Like, no one else is up there."

"Why?"

"Well, 'cause, like, uh, I don't know."

"So why you renting me a room up there?"

"'Cause you booked it, and it's graduation week."

Unbelievable.

The girl slid a form in front of him.

"Please fill this out, Mr. JONES."

"Why'd you say my name like that?" Goldberg said as he filled out the registration form.

"Like what, Mr. JONES?"

"Like that, you twit."

"I'm going to need a credit card, sir," she said, staring at him.

"I'm paying cash."

"But I need a credit card."

"Listen, you pock-faced little bitch, I'm paying cash, and I ain't givin' you no friggin' credit card."

The girl's lip began to tremble.

"Okay, but you'll have to give me a deposit."

"A what?"

"A deposit, like, a hundred dollars? The guy, Ford, gave me a hundred the other day."

Goldberg glared at the girl. *That friggin' Frankie Farmer, the schmuck.*

"What's that get me, a blow job?"

The girl backed away, her jaw trembling.

"Sir, I don't think that's necessary."

Goldberg slid a hundred over the counter.

"I'm sorry. I'm tired and . . . I'm sorry. Will this cover it?"

The girl regained her courage and took a step forward.

"You booked two rooms for three nights, at forty dollars a night each, that's two hundred and forty dollars, plus tax . . . plus the deposit."

Goldberg almost reached over the counter to grab her pimply face. *What the fuck?*

"Okay. Okay. Here's four hundred, will that cover everything, miss?"

"Will you be requiring change, sir?"

Goldberg glared at her. *The brazen bitch, shaking me down in Po-dunk, Kentucky!*

"I won't require any change, miss."

The girl smiled and grabbed the money. She slid two keys to him, along with a map to the Ridge motel and a registration form.

"Fill this out. Rooms eleven and twelve, sir. Have a nice evening."

Goldberg stared at her as she disappeared behind a door.

What the hell just happened? He scribbled on the card, grabbed the keys and the map and walked out of the office, shaking his head. *I hate this friggin' state already.*

Goldberg got into the Lincoln and looked at Fanelli, who was snoring. *Unbelievable.* He turned the interior light on and looked at the map. After turning it upside down several times, he shook his head, put the car in drive, and pulled out of the parking lot.

As he turned left at the only traffic light in town, he spotted a restaurant. He pulled into the parking lot, which was nearly empty, and looked up at the sign: "Joe's Ribs and Taters." *Unbelievable.* He nudged Fanelli, but only got a grunt. Goldberg hit him harder and got a grunt and some mumbling.

"Fanelli, wake the fuck up!"

Fanelli opened his eyes and blinked.

"We there?"

"No, we ain't there. You hungry?"

Fanelli sat up and looked at the sign over the restaurant.

"Ribs and what?"

"Ribs and who gives a fuck. You hungry?"

"Yeah."

The two men got out of the Lincoln and entered the well-lit restaurant. Goldberg saw two teenagers sitting at a table in the far corner, sucking each other's faces.

"Sorry, y'all, but we're closed," a pimply-faced kid said from the kitchen.

"You still got the stove going?" Goldberg said.

"Yeah, but we're closed."

"Stove's on, then you're open." He put two twenties on the counter in front of the kid. "Okay?"

The kid looked at the twenties with wide eyes.

"Yeah, like, sure. You want menus?"

"Just give us two orders of ribs and whatever the fuck those other things are," Goldberg said. "And two beers."

"You want your taters mashed, fried, or baked?" the kid said.

"Whatever. Surprise us," Goldberg said.

"Fried it is."

The two men sat down at a table in the middle of the restaurant. It had a red and white checkered tablecloth with three kinds of barbeque sauce in the middle. A young, attractive girl came out of the kitchen with silverware and two mugs of beer.

"Here y'all go," she said. "Your food'll be out in a bit."

Goldberg looked at her fresh face, no pimples.

"What's your name, sweet cheeks?"

The girl blushed and twirled her blonde hair.

"Candy," she said.

Goldberg smiled.

"I bet you taste just as sweet as your name."

The girl smiled nervously and walked back into the kitchen.

Fanelli shook his head.

"She's a friggin' teenager, you perverted asshole."

Goldberg's smile turned to a frown.

"Fuck you, you hairy bastard."

Fanelli smiled and took a swig of his beer.

After filling themselves with ribs and taters, Goldberg and Fanelli got back into the Lincoln and drove up the same winding road that Frankie and

Augie had navigated just three days before. It was just wide enough for the large Town Car to fit, but Fanelli's eyes were wide open the entire trip up the dark, desolate road. Once they broke out into the parking lot of the Ridge Motel, Fanelli let out a pent-up sigh.

"It's empty," Fanelli said, looking around.

"No shit, it's empty," Goldberg muttered to himself as he looked at the deserted parking lot.

"Why ain't there any other cars up here?" Fanelli said, staring at the empty lot.

"'Cause we're the only ones up here."

Fanelli turned and stared at Goldberg.

"Why?"

Goldberg glanced at the large, hairy killer and laughed out loud.

"You big ox. You scared of being alone?"

Fanelli stammered.

"No . . . no . . . but why ain't there anyone else up here? Is it haunted or—"

Goldberg tilted his head back and laughed.

"'Cause it's friggin' graduation week. How the hell should I know?"

Fanelli looked at the dark forest on the other side of the parking lot and then looked at the twenty-four empty rooms of the motel.

"I ain't stayin' here."

Goldberg was still laughing as he parked the Town Car in front of room twelve.

"You chickenshit, hairy bastard. Just get out and get your friggin' bag outta the trunk." Goldberg threw him the key to room eleven. "You want me to come tuck you in later?"

Goldberg entered room twelve still chuckling as he watched the Rhino slowly approach room eleven.

"Bawk, bawk," he said, mimicking a chicken.

Goldberg opened the door to room twelve and turned the light on. The bed was made, and the room seemed clean. He walked into the bathroom, looking for anything that Augie or Frankie may have left behind. Finding nothing, he opened the closet. Still nothing. *If they were here, they left no trace behind.*

Suddenly, Goldberg heard a yell from the room next door, and in three seconds Fanelli was running into room twelve, eyes wide with fear.

"What the hell?" Goldberg said, staring at the hairy mob enforcer.

"There's blood, and the room's a mess, and … I saw something move."

"Settle down, Nancy. Jesus Christ. You look like you saw a friggin' ghost."

"There's something in there. I swear on my mother," Fanelli said. "Go look."

Goldberg shook his head and walked outside and down to room eleven. He poked his head into the room and saw an unmade bed, towels strewn on the floor, and then he heard a scratching noise. He turned to look at Fanelli, who was right behind him.

"Get your hairy ass off of me," Goldberg said.

He took two tentative steps into the room and stopped to listen. When he heard the scratching sound, he backed up a step, right into Fanelli. This made Goldberg jump as he let out a little scream.

"Goddammit, Rhino, will you get the hell back!"

Goldberg pulled his snub-nosed revolver out of his ankle holster and walked slowly to the bathroom where the scratching noise was coming from. He stopped and craned his head sideways, looking inside. He heard the sound again and pulled his head back, taking a deep breath. *Jesus Christ, maybe it is a ghost.*

Goldberg held the revolver out in front of him, cocked, reached with his left hand around the door, and turned on the bathroom light. The pistol ready to fire at anything, he jumped quickly into the doorway and yelled, "Freeze!"

He stood with bulging eyes, staring at a hairy animal that was staring back at him. Suddenly, it scampered right at him, causing Goldberg to drop his revolver on the floor. He stood rock still while the raccoon ran between his legs and out into the bedroom. Fanelli jumped up on the bed in terror. The two men stood motionless as the animal ran out the door and into the forest across the parking lot.

Goldberg, his eyes still wide with fright, glanced at the hulking Rhino standing on the bed. His whole body began to shake with laughter at the sight of the mob hit man. Rhino stared back at him with the look of a deer in the headlights, unable to move.

"Holy crap, you should see yourself," Goldberg said, laughing so hard tears began to run down his cheeks. "The big, hairy, Chicago mob enforcer, scared of a little critter." Goldberg doubled over with laughter.

Fanelli stepped down from the bed and glared at Goldberg.

"Yeah, well, who screamed and dropped his fucking gun?"

Goldberg slowly stopped laughing as he glared at Fanelli.

"Okay, this ain't gettin' out to nobody, right? It never happened. Understand?"

Fanelli smiled and nodded.

"Just between us little girls," he said.

Goldberg then looked at the bed for the first time. He saw the covers pulled back and bloodstains on the sheet.

"What the fuck?"

"I told you, asshole. There's blood everywhere."

Goldberg looked around the room at the towels, some red with blood stains, lying on the floor. He saw empty beer cans strewn around the room and an empty Jack Daniel's bottle lying on its side on the desk. He turned and looked into the bathroom, seeing more towels and a clump of clothing on the floor next to the shower. He walked in, holding his pistol in front of him, and picked up the dirty slacks.

"Somebody was staying in here," he said. "And they were hurt."

Fanelli stood in the doorway of the bathroom, nodding his head.

"You think it was Augie?"

"Or Farmer. Or both."

"Holy Jesus, they got iced," Fanelli said.

Goldberg looked up at the huge man.

"Or maybe one iced the other."

Fanelli's eyes grew wide.

"Well, I ain't stayin' in here."

"Well, you ain't stayin' with me."

Fanelli's face grew dark.

"Let's get the hell outta here."

Goldberg shook his head.

"No, we'll find another room for you tonight, even if we have to break in. Go try the room next door with your key."

"It ain't gonna work in another room, you idiot," Fanelli said.

"Well, Augie or Farmer got into this room without a key, didn't they? They only rented room twelve. Go try room ten."

Fanelli slowly walked to the door and peered out, looking in all directions for their furry friend. He almost tiptoed to the next door and put his key in the lock. It opened.

"What kind of place is this?" he said, looking back at Goldberg.

"Who knows, but at least you got a place to sleep tonight."

Goldberg gave one more look at the mess in room eleven and then closed the door.

"Get some sleep. We leave at five o'clock," he said, looking at Fanelli.

"Yeah, like I'm gonna get any friggin' sleep tonight," Fanelli said as he slowly walked into room ten.

Goldberg stood in front of room eleven, squinting at the dark forest beyond. *Where are you, Augie and Farmer?*

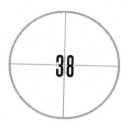

38

Ethan and Jake drove down the lane leading to Bo's house in complete darkness, except for the headlights on the rented Buick. When they turned the corner and could see the house, Ethan noticed no lights on and no one on the deck. He checked his watch, which read ten thirty-five. Surely they wouldn't all be asleep yet, knowing that he and Jake were coming.

"Nice place, but looks kind of dark," Jake said as they passed the small pond.

Ethan didn't respond, especially when he saw Bo's Explorer and JB's pickup missing. As they drove up the gravel lane, he noticed an eerie silence. The dogs normally barked at any car coming down the lane, but Ethan heard nothing. He pulled the Buick up and parked in the driveway.

"Something's wrong," he said, looking at Jake. "They have dogs that won't let anyone approach without barking up a storm. And there's always a light on somewhere, especially when they knew we were coming."

Ethan started to get out of the car, but Jake held him back.

"What's wrong?" Ethan said.

"Could be something or someone you don't want to see inside."

Ethan shuddered when the thought hit him. *Oh shit, the mob's been here!*

"Don't panic, but we better check things out first," Jake said.

They got out of the car and started walking around the house, listening for any noise. Jake had a tire iron in his hand, Ethan a baseball bat that he'd grabbed from the carport. They walked the perimeter of the house and saw and heard nothing. Ethan looked at Jake when they got back to the driveway. When he saw Jake nod, he walked up to the door just off the deck that led to the kitchen.

Ethan peered inside and saw no lights on, except for the red message light on the telephone. A cold chill ran down his spine as he tried the door. It was unlocked, as always, so he opened it and walked inside, Jake right behind him. Ethan stopped and listened for a sound, anything that would indicate someone was home. Again, nothing.

"This is freaking me out," Ethan said, turning on the light. They heard a noise in the corner as the kitchen was flooded with light. Jake held the tire iron above his head as Ethan walked slowly to the far corner of the kitchen where the noise had come from. He looked around the corner and saw Kathy's calico cat staring up at him with eyes as big as saucers. He glanced at Jake, shaking his head, and looked around the kitchen. It was neat as a pin, except for a cat food bowl filled to overflowing. He saw the note sitting on the counter. Ethan remembered the last thing JB had said before he had left for Nashville. *I can get us a houseboat tonight, and we can disappear before sunset.*

"Oh shit," Ethan said, reaching for the note, which had his name printed on the outside. He opened it and began reading it out loud.

Ethan,

We're sorry, but we had to get out of the house. We took Garth and Brooks with us, in case you are wondering. You know where we went. I will try to contact you soon when things blow over. Feel free to use the house and food, but I think you need to find another place to stay because . . . you know why. Be safe. I'm sorry.

Love you, brother.

Bo

Jake looked blankly at Ethan.

"What the hell is that about?"

Ethan had not told Jake about the conversation with Bo and JB right before he left for Nashville.

"They decided to disappear," Ethan said.

"Disappear? How do you disappear?" Jake said, shaking his head.

"They know this county and the lake better than almost anyone around. Believe me, they can disappear."

"But the sheriff," Jake said, "he isn't going to like this, is he?"

Ethan shook his head.

"No, he isn't. But they weren't worried about the sheriff."

"The mob," Jake said. "The mob scared 'em off."

Ethan nodded.

"And maybe they're better off because a small county sheriff isn't going to do much against the Chicago mob."

The phone rang, making both men jump. Ethan picked it up.

"Hello?" he said.

"Hello, Bo?"

"No, this is his brother Ethan."

"Ethan, you made it back from Nashville. This is Deputy Smith. We've been trying to reach Bo for hours. Is everything okay?"

Ethan put the phone on speaker.

"Hi, Cheyenne. I'm here with Jake Delgado, the private investigator I told you about. You're on speaker phone."

"Oh, hello, Mr. Delgado," Deputy Smith said. "Is Bo there?"

Ethan looked up at Jake, shaking his head.

"Uh, no, he isn't."

Silence.

"It's almost eleven o'clock. Where would he be at this hour?"

Ethan paused.

"I don't know, Cheyenne. Jake and I just got here. Everyone's gone." Ethan cringed when he said it.

"Gone? The whole family, or just Bo?"

"Everyone, even the dogs," Ethan said. *How the hell is he going to explain this?*

"Did they go to his daughter's house?"

Ethan paused again.

"I don't think so. She's probably with them."

Silence.

"Ethan, what's going on here?"

Ethan hit the hold button.

"What do I tell her, Jake?"

"The truth. Only the truth," Jake said.

Ethan punched the hold button again.

"Cheyenne, I think Bo took his family and decided to disappear for a while."

Silence.

"Hold on while I get Sheriff Parsons on the phone."

Several seconds went by as Jake and Ethan stared at each other.

"Ethan, this is Sheriff Parsons. What the hell is going on out there?"

"Bo took his family and disappeared, Sheriff," Ethan said. "They didn't want to stay here and wait to get whacked, I guess."

"Goddammit! I should've sent two men out there this afternoon, but I couldn't round 'em up in time. Goddammit!"

Ethan waited for the sheriff to calm down.

"Ethan?"

"Yeah, Sheriff."

"I'll be out there in fifteen minutes. You hold tight. Don't go anywhere."

"I'll be here, Sheriff."

The line went dead.

"Well, the local constabulary is real pissed," Ethan said.

Jake nodded.

"So what? At least your brother and family are safe for a while."

Ethan nodded.

"Yeah, but he left me and you holding the bag."

Jake laughed.

"Ah, hell, Ethan, we're big boys. We can handle it."

Ethan smiled. *I hope so, with a pissed-off sheriff, and hit men from the Chicago mob on their way, and probably the FBI not far behind.*

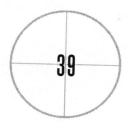

39

Ethan made a pot of coffee and took it and two cups out on the deck where Jake was sitting.

"Sorry we don't have any Bushmills, Jake, but coffee will help keep you alert."

Jake chuckled.

"I drank my share of Bushmills back then, didn't I? I've slowed down quite a lot, thanks to Amos, but I still enjoy a couple of pops in the evening."

"You look good, Jake. Lost some weight. Got your scar fixed. You seem more relaxed."

Jake nodded as they both stared out at the quiet, dark pond in the distance.

"I've got to give Amos credit for most of it. He's been a good influence on me over the past couple of years. Sure wish he was here now."

"We could use him, I think, over the next couple of days," Ethan said, taking a sip of the strong coffee. He yawned and rubbed his swollen eyes.

"Damn, Ethan, you look like shit. When you gonna get some sleep?"

"Good question. Not sure I'll be able to sleep out here, with visions of hit men dancing in my head."

Both men laughed nervously as they peered down the lane at approaching headlights.

"Here comes the sheriff," Ethan said. "Sounds like he's tearing down the lane pretty fast."

The sheriff's cruiser spit gravel everywhere as it roared up the driveway and slid to a stop behind the Buick. Parsons got out and walked quickly to the deck, his large hat already off.

"What in the Sam Hill is going on here, Ethan?" Parsons said.

"Hello to you, too, Sheriff," Ethan said, leaning back in his chair.

Parsons glanced at Jake.

"This the PI you talked about?"

"Yeah. Jake Delgado," Ethan said.

Parsons nodded to Jake and turned back to Ethan.

"You look like crap, son. You get any sleep today?"

"A little. Not much."

"Well, don't count on much any time soon. We have a shitstorm headed our way, and my primary witness is . . . somewhere out there," Parsons said, waving his hat in the direction of the lake.

Ethan pursed his lips.

"Really sorry about that, Sheriff. Bo and JB talked to me about their plan to disappear right before I left for Nashville to pick up Jake. I thought I'd talked them out of it, but guess they got too spooked."

Parsons hung his head and shook it slowly back and forth.

"Can I sit down and have a cup of that coffee?"

"Sure, I'll get you a cup," Ethan said, walking into the kitchen.

Parsons pulled out a deck chair and sat down heavily.

"Here you go, Sheriff," Ethan said, pouring the black coffee into a clean cup.

Parsons looked up at Jake and noticed the thin red line on his left cheek.

"Where'd you get that souvenir, Jake?"

Jake rubbed his left hand over his cheek.

"Got it a long time ago when I was on the police force in San Diego."

"How many years were you on the force?" Parson said, staring at the newcomer.

"Fifteen."

"Why'd you leave?"

Jake pointed to the scar.

"This had some to do with it. I got drunk one night and put three men in the hospital. Another one was shot by my ex-partner."

Parsons looked Jake up and down.

"You a big fella. Hot temper, too?"

"When I'm pushed, I guess."

Parsons nodded and turned to Ethan.

"Well, Ethan, looks like you and Jake here are left holding the bag for your brother."

"Hold on, Sheriff, we're just innocent bystanders. How do you figure we're left holding the bag, as you said?"

Parsons leaned toward Ethan, taking a swig of coffee.

"'Cause those goons the mob is gonna be sending down here will be looking for Bo and Frankie Farmer. I can protect Frankie, somewhat, but I can't protect Bo, or you and Jake, for that matter, out here."

"Then I guess it's good that Bo isn't out here," Ethan said. "You think maybe he realized he was a sitting duck out here against whomever the mob sends down?"

"I reckon he did, son. Can't blame him for protecting himself and his family, but he's gotta pop his head up some time and face the music."

Ethan nodded.

"I told him the same thing, but you know Bo."

"Those mob enforcers are gonna shoot first and ask questions later. You know that, right?"

Ethan rubbed his eyes and looked at Jake.

"Yeah, you're probably right, Sheriff."

Parsons sat back and took another swallow of coffee.

"Well, let me get you caught up on what's been happening since I saw you last." He took out his handkerchief and wiped his forehead. "Damn, it's hot tonight."

Ethan and Jake glanced at each other, both knowing something bad was coming.

"We drug the lake this afternoon, out at Copperhead Cove," the sheriff said. "Found Bo's bass boat just where he said it would be, under twenty feet of lake water."

Ethan stared at the sheriff.

"And there were two bodies tied up inside, a little worse for wear after spending a night in the lake."

Ethan sat stone still, waiting for the kicker.

"And they were identified as Sonny Daye and Jerry Joe Williams. One shot through the neck and the other through the forehead. Williams didn't have much of his face left. Both of 'em had their ID's on 'em."

Ethan slumped in his chair. Even though he'd believed his brother's story, he was hoping it wasn't true. Now the shitstorm was indeed coming.

"And we found another body, close to the shoreline. Big fella. He had cottonmouth bite marks on his neck, arm, and leg, just like Bo said."

"You identify him?" Ethan said.

"Not yet. Didn't have ID on him, but we're workin' on it. Has to be the mob fella that whacked the two coaches and clipped Bo."

Ethan nodded. The loose ends were being tied up just in time for the storm that was coming.

"You think the cause of death was the cottonmouth venom?" Jake said.

"Probably. That or being drowned. Probably both. He had a lung full of water, too. But no gunshot wounds anywhere we could find."

"Have you alerted the press yet?" Jake said.

Parsons turned to Jake.

"Well, we had to, son. Some hillbilly reserve that I swore in today couldn't keep quiet and blabbed to his buddies about two famous coaches that got pulled outta the lake. Spread like wildfire. That's why we was tryin' so hard to get hold of Bo. To warn him."

"So the press knows," Ethan said. "How about the FBI?"

"I called 'em an hour ago. They'll be here tomorrow morning, seven o'clock, sittin' on my stoop."

Ethan looked at Jake. They nodded their heads in unison.

"The storm's coming," Jake said.

"Like nothin' this little county has ever seen," Parsons said.

Ethan pulled his chair closer to Parsons.

"Have you seen any suspicious people around town today? I don't know, maybe someone like a mob hit man?"

Parsons shook his head.

"Not yet, but I'm gonna stake out the Ridge Motel in the morning, since that's where Farmer and the dead guy were stayin.'"

Jake squinted.

"How do you know they aren't up there right now?"

Parsons scratched his head.

"Well, son, I don't. But we ain't had much time to do much about it today. I'll have my deputy check it out tomorrow while I'm dealin' with the feds."

"They'll be looking for Frankie and Bo," Ethan said. "You think you can protect Frankie?"

"Hell, Ethan, I can barely protect our little town from drunk drivers, how the hell am I gonna protect a mob boss's son-in-law?"

"The FBI might have some ideas, if he makes it through the night," Ethan said.

"Which brings me to you two," Parsons said. "I can't protect you out here. You're pretty much on your own. You gonna be okay tonight?"

Ethan looked at Jake, who was looking at the dark hills surrounding Bo's farm.

"Lots of entry points all around us," Jake said. "Someone could sneak up in the middle of the night, and we'd never know about it."

"You have firearms out here?" Parsons said.

"Yeah, Bo's got some hunting rifles upstairs," Ethan answered.

Parsons took out a Glock 9 mm handgun from his holster.

"I got another one in the cruiser. You know how to use one of these, Jake? It's fully loaded."

Jake held the weapon in his huge hand.

"It's been awhile, but I'm sure it'll come back real quick."

"You want me to send someone out in a cruiser—park in the driveway just to be a deterrent?"

Ethan looked at Jake, who was shaking his head.

"I think we'll try it on our own tonight, Sheriff, but thanks," Ethan said.

Parsons stood up, throwing down the last of his coffee.

"Suit yourselves, but I'll send someone out in the morning, just to check up on ya. And if you hear from Bo, you tell me, y'hear?"

"Sure will, Sheriff, but I think Bo and family are ghosts right about now."

Parsons shook his head again.

"Never could tell ol' Bo anything."

Parsons started walking to his cruiser and turned back.

"You get some sleep, Ethan, if that's possible."

Ethan smiled and waved.

"I'll try, Sheriff."

"Good meetin' ya, Jake. Take care of this guy, will ya?"

"I'll do my best," Jake said, not smiling.

Sheriff Parsons started up the cruiser, backed up, spun gravel down the driveway, out onto the lane, and out of sight.

Jake and Ethan sat back down, Jake peering out into the darkness. Ethan knew that his friend was thinking.

"What's the plan, Jake?" Ethan said, pouring another cup of coffee.

Jake turned and looked at his friend.

"I think we need to pay a visit to the Ridge Motel tonight."

Ethan's eyes grew wide.

"Tonight?"

"Yeah, tonight. If there's anybody up there, they won't expect visitors tonight. You know how to get there?"

"Yeah, I've been there a couple times when they had the restaurant open. But it's deserted now."

"Then if Chicago mob guys are there, they'll be easy to spot."

Ethan thought about this.

"Okay. Maybe we'll see a black Lincoln Town Car in the parking lot."

Jake smiled.

"Now you're thinkin', old buddy."

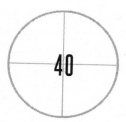

40

Ethan and Jake drove through the deserted town of Crockett at midnight, the only activity coming from the bar on Main Street. They moved slowly, looking for anything that would raise a flag. When they passed the Riverside Motel, they searched for a black Lincoln Town Car, but saw only pickups, Chevys, and Fords.

"They'd have to check in here before they could go up to the Ridge," Ethan said.

"Why's that?" Jake asked.

"The same people own both motels, and everything is run by the folks at the Riverside. At one time, the Ridge was the place to stay, with a great view of Crockett and the river valley. They had a pretty nice restaurant up there, too, with ribs and steaks. Up until a few years ago, Bo would take me and my kids up there for dinner once each trip. But they had some trouble up there about three or four years ago. Some teenager got killed. Bo's son said it had to do with drugs and was a pretty grisly murder. Since then, nobody ever goes up there anymore. Until now."

"Maybe we should check with the registration desk here at the Riverside. See if anyone checked in tonight," Jake said.

"Sure, if there's anyone at the desk this late." Ethan pulled into the full parking lot and found the only empty spot.

"Sure is busy for a small town," Jake said.

"It's graduation week," Ethan said. "Matter of fact, tonight was the high school graduation, so there might be some partying going on."

They got out of the Buick and walked to the office. It was locked, but they could see a young girl inside behind the registration counter. Ethan knocked on the glass door, causing the girl to look up. She waved her arms and mouthed the word "closed." Ethan put one finger up and mouthed "question."

The young girl let out a sigh and walked to the door, unlocking it and opening it a crack.

"We're closed," she said, starting to close the door.

"Wait," Ethan said, "we just want to ask you a question."

The girl, homely and pimply-faced, kept the door open.

"We're full, and we're closed."

Jake pulled out his private investigator license and showed it to her.

"We just want to ask you a question."

"You ain't the law. That ain't a badge," she said.

"I'm a private investigator, investigating two murders," Jake said, glancing at Ethan.

"Two murders, where? Here in Crock . . . you mean the two basketball coaches?"

Ethan grimaced. *Oh crap, it's already spread through town.*

"Yeah, the two basketball coaches," Jake said, keeping his face as serious as he could.

"Okay, come on in." She opened the door and let the two men in.

"What d'ya need to know from me?" she said, eyes wide.

"Has anyone checked into the Ridge Motel tonight?" Ethan said.

She looked at him, her eyes wide.

"I knew it! I knew that guy was bad news."

"What guy," Jake said.

"A guy with short, white hair, real tan, fancy, you know—a real jerk."

Jake glanced at Ethan and nodded.

"When did he check in?" Jake said.

"About two hours ago," she said. "Funny, ain't nobody stayed up there in over two years, but we had two guys this week, both really freaky."

"Did the guy tonight check in alone, or was somebody with him?" Jake said.

"Well, he checked in alone, but he paid for two rooms, for three nights."

Jake looked at Ethan and smiled.

"Did you see the other man?"

"No, he was in the car."

"Did you see the car?" Jake said.

"Saw 'em pass through the parking lot. A big, fancy thing."

"What color?" Ethan said.

"Black."

Ethan nodded.

"Did he fill out a registration form?"

"Yeah, sort of," she said. "He gave me a fake name. Jones or something. He weren't no Jones."

"Where was he from?" Jake said.

"Uh, just a minute, I'll see what he put down." The girl walked to the counter and pulled out the registration box, flipping through it. "New York."

Jake glanced at Ethan.

"Yeah, right, New York. What kind of accent did he have?"

"Not New York, and not from 'round here, that's for sure."

"Did he pay by credit card?" Jake said.

The girl coughed.

"No, he paid cash. Wouldn't give me no credit card."

Jake looked at Ethan again.

"Sounds like our guys."

Ethan nodded and looked back at the girl.

"You said they checked in about two hours ago, around ten o'clock?"

"Yes, sir."

"What rooms did you put them in?"

She looked at the registration card.

"He wanted room twelve, 'cause that's the same room the guy from a couple of days ago stayed in, and I gave 'em room eleven, too."

"So they knew the guy that stayed here a few days ago?" Jake said.

"Yeah, he said it was a 'colleague,' or somethin' like that."

Jake slapped Ethan on the back.

"Let's go, partner."

Ethan turned to the girl.

"You've been very helpful, uh . . . ?"

"Jamie May," she said, blushing. "Y'all are nice. Not like them other fellas. Hope you catch 'em."

"Jamie May," Ethan said, "you should close up now and go home. And stay home, okay?"

She looked at him nervously.

"Why, am I in some kinda danger?"

"We don't know, but two men were murdered on the lake. Just be careful, okay?"

"Okay, thanks. You look familiar," she said, looking at Ethan. "You from around here?"

"No, but I have a brother that lives out by the lake. Bo Paxton. You know him?"

"Bo? Oh, sure, everybody knows Bo. He's a good ol' boy," she said, gleaming. "I went to high school with his daughter and had such a crush on JB, his son. He was older'n me by a few years . . . . "

"Thanks, Jamie May," Jake said. "Lock up and go home."

Ethan and Jake opened the door and walked outside.

"Say hi to JB for me, and tell him to call me."

Jake nodded and shut the door, walking quickly to the car, Ethan following right behind. They got in and sat motionless for several seconds.

"Should we call the sheriff?" Ethan said.

Jake sat staring straight ahead.

"They haven't done anything yet, that we know of."

"Well, I don't want to wait until they do. Let's let the sheriff deal with them."

Jake turned and looked at Ethan.

"Let's drive up there and confirm it's the same car you saw at the airport. Then we'll know for sure that they're from Chicago."

"Damn, Jake. Pretty risky."

"If we can get an ID on the car and the plates, we can have the sheriff run a check with the rental car company. They had to give them a credit card. Couldn't rent a car without one."

Ethan nodded.

"Guess you're right, but I don't like it."

"There's nothing about this situation that I like," Jake said, "but we're knee-deep in it, so let's go."

41

Frankie tried to ignore the sounds in the cell next to him. A drunk, who was brought in by Deputy Smith around eleven o'clock, was yelling for his lawyer. Frankie was lying on his bunk, his arm over his eyes, wondering how he'd wound up in this Podunk jail cell.

I didn't do anything wrong. I actually saved a man. Why am I here?

"Lemme talk to m'lawyer," the man in the next cell slurred. "Go'dammit!"

Frankie took his arm off his eyes and looked up when he heard the outside door open. It was Deputy Smith.

"Sheriff Parsons wants to talk to you," she said. "Put your hands through the slot so I can handcuff you."

Frankie did as she asked. The handcuffs slapped on his wrists and locked. Smith unlocked his cell.

"Let's go."

Frankie slowly walked out of the cell, following the deputy, rubbing his bloodshot eyes.

"What about?" he said.

"You'll see," she said, as the jailer opened the outside door. "Thanks, Bobby Joe."

They walked into the sheriff's office where Deputy Smith sat him down in a chair opposite Parsons. She left the handcuffs on and sat next to him.

"How you feelin', Frankie?" Parsons said.

"I was okay until you put that drunk next to me."

"Yeah, sorry about that. Homer is a regular 'round here, and he always makes his presence known," Parsons said. "He'll pass out in an hour or so."

"Great, just great," Frankie said. "He's already puked twice."

"Got some news for you, and need to ask you some questions," Parsons said.

"What kind of news? A presidential pardon?"

Parsons chuckled.

"No, not quite. Bo Paxton has disappeared."

Frankie stared at the sheriff, unable to speak. *He's the only man that can clear me! Oh, shit. Tonelli sent someone down to whack Bo.*

"What do you mean, disappeared?"

Parsons sat up in his chair, rubbing his eyes.

"I mean, he and his family just up and disappeared. Poof."

Frankie sat in disbelief, staring at the sheriff and then at Deputy Smith.

"How's that possible?"

"'Round here, someone like Bo can make himself invisible. That lake is over six hundred miles of shoreline and has thousands of little coves and inlets. It's all forest from the shoreline up, so if Bo wants to disappear, he disappears."

That chickenshit. He throws me under the bus and then takes off.

"I need to know who your boss is sending to finish the job down here," Parsons said. "You have any ideas?"

Frankie squirmed in his chair.

"Hell, I don't know. Could be any number of goombahs. He has 'em all over the damn country."

Parsons chuckled again.

"Goombahs. Nice term for killers. You a killer, Frankie?"

Frankie stared at Parsons, shaking his head.

"Do I look like a killer? Hell, I didn't even know how to use the damn gun I pointed at you."

Parsons leaned forward.

"I know you're not a killer, otherwise you wouldn't have saved Bo out on the lake. Why'd you do that? Why'd you save someone you didn't even know?"

Frankie shrugged his shoulders.

"I don't know, just instinct. He seemed like a nice guy."

"Bullshit, Frankie. You wanted someone around that would corroborate your story—that the big guy was the shooter, and that you were a pawn. That right?"

Frankie shook his head.

"No, I didn't even think about that. I just didn't want to be a part of this thing. I didn't want those two coaches to die, especially Sonny Daye. You're right that I'm a pawn, set up by my father-in-law. He wanted me dead, so he sent me to," he looked around, "Bumfuck, Kentucky, to get iced by the real killer."

"We did some research on the killer. Augustus Stellato, alias Augie the Ax, age sixty-three. Hit man for the Tonelli crime syndicate in Chicago. He hasn't been active in quite a while, though. Why'd your boss send him instead of one of his goombahs, as you put it?"

"Sheriff, I don't know anything. I swear on my dead mother's grave. I was being punished because I'm married to his daughter and he hates my fuckin' guts."

Sheriff Parsons sat back in his chair and looked at Frankie.

"I believe you, Frankie. And I think you're a decent man who saved one of our local boys from certain death—you and the cottonmouth."

Frankie nodded, looking down at his feet.

"But, unfortunately, you're an accomplice to double murder in the eyes of the law. The killer is dead, killed by the venom of a pit viper, or by drowning, whatever."

Frankie looked up when the sheriff said drowning.

"But fact is, he's dead and can't testify or be tried. That leaves you, the only other man in the boat when Sonny Daye and Jerry Joe Williams were killed and Bo Paxton was shot. You and Bo are the only two people on this earth that were witness to those killings. And Bo has disappeared."

Frankie pleaded to the sheriff with his eyes. *I'm not a killer!*

"The FBI will be down here in the morning," the sheriff said, looking at his watch, "in about six hours. You know why they were called, right?"

"No."

"Because two high-profile coaches were killed on federal property. The lake belongs to the federal government. They'll be taking over in the morning, so I just wanted to prepare you for that."

Frankie lowered his head and shook it slowly.

"We'll protect you, as best we can. You should be safe here, until the FBI decides what to do with you." Parsons glared at him. "You have any idea who your boss is sending down here, Frankie?"

"No, none. I wasn't a part of that side of the business," he said, tears forming in his eyes. "You can't protect me, Sheriff. No one can."

"Well, that may be so, but we'll do the best we can, son. Go on back to your cell, and try to get some sleep. The feds will be here in a few hours."

The feds, the mob—I'm a dead man. A dead man walking.

42

As Ethan and Jake turned left at the only stoplight in Crockett, they saw two hot-rod cars speed by them and heard the shouts of teenagers. Ethan followed them as they entered the parking lot of Joe's Ribs and Taters. They saw four or five cars and lots of activity inside the restaurant.

"What the hell is a tater?" Jake asked.

Ethan laughed.

"They call potatoes 'taters' down here, and tomatoes 'maters.' It's a southern thing."

"Okay, so what's going on here at one o'clock in the morning?" Jake said, staring at the kids inside and listening to the loud music blaring.

"Not sure, but it's probably a graduation party."

Ethan continued on to the road that led to the Ridge Motel. It had been several years since he'd been up there with Bo and Kathy and his two kids, but he remembered the narrow, winding road well, which was even scarier at night. As they approached the top of the hill, they heard more shouts and loud music. Ethan pulled off to the side of the road and turned his headlights off.

"Oh, shit, the teenagers have brought the party up to the Ridge," Ethan said, staring at the scene spread out before them.

Four or five cars were parked in the middle of the parking lot, with their doors open and music blaring from their stereos. Several teenagers were dancing, some were making out, and all of them were drinking. Beer cans littered the parking lot.

"This is all we need," Ethan said.

"Maybe we can use it to our advantage," Jake said, smiling. "They can be our diversion while we do our investigative work."

Ethan and Jake, the 9 mm Glock in his belt at the small of his back, got out of the Buick and quietly closed their doors. They walked along the perimeter of the parking lot, staying in the woods. They watched the partying teenagers, who were oblivious to the two men. As they got to the north end of the lot, they peered across to the last two rooms of the motel—rooms eleven and twelve. Parked in front of room twelve was a black Lincoln Town Car.

"Bingo," Jake said. "Same car as we saw in Nashville, right?"

"Sure looks like it," Ethan whispered. "We have to get a closer look so we can get the license plate number."

While the music blared and the teenagers drank, Ethan and Jake walked quickly through the darkness to the side of the building, right next to room twelve. They saw a light on in the room. Jake bent down and looked at the license plate on the Lincoln.

Jake stared at the plate and the number and then stood up.

"Got it," Jake said.

Suddenly the door to room twelve opened and a silver-haired man walked out. Jake ducked behind the wall, out of sight. The man had something in his right hand, and he was walking toward the partying teenagers.

"Shit, he's got a gun," Jake said softly.

"Christ Almighty," Ethan said, whispering, "what's he gonna do, shoot them?"

They watched as the man strode up to the cars and pointed his gun at one of the teenagers.

"Get the fuck outta here, you pissants," he said.

"Who the fuck are you?" someone from one of the cars yelled.

Over the blaring music, the silver-haired man raised his gun and fired two shots in the air.

"That's who the fuck I am. Now get the fuck outta here before the next one goes into someone's pissant brain."

Suddenly, the music stopped and was replaced by screaming as the teenagers rushed to their cars and peeled out of the parking lot, headed for the winding road that led down the steep hill. As the last car disappeared out of sight, the silver-haired man looked around the parking lot, shaking his head. He turned, looked in the direction of Ethan and Jake, and took several steps toward them, but he stopped when a man came out of room ten.

"What the hell's going on, Goldberg?" the big, hairy man said, rubbing his crotch.

"Damn teenagers were having a fucking party, that's what," the man said. "Where the hell were you?"

Ethan poked his head around the corner to get a look at both men. They were the same two men he saw at the Nashville Airport, no question. Jake pulled him back quickly and glared at him.

"I had my headphones and my blinders on," the big man said. "I heard the shots, though. Was that you?"

"Yeah, that was me. It sure cleared the little pissants out quick."

"You stupid jamook. It'll probably bring the law up here, too," the big man said.

"What law? There ain't no law in this Podunk town. If there is, they're home screwin' their fat wives by now."

"Why'd the kids come up here, anyway," the big man said.

"They probably thought the place was empty," the silver-haired man said. "Don't know what they thought about the Lincoln sitting here. Dumb-ass hillbillies."

"You think we should leave?" the big man said.

"Hell no. We paid for three nights, we're stayin' here three nights, or whatever it takes to find Augie and Frankie and that redneck fishing guide."

Ethan glanced at Jake. *That's the evidence we needed.*

"Go back to bed, Rhino. We leave at five o'clock sharp."

The big man nodded and went back into his room, closing the door. The silver-haired man stood still and looked around the parking lot. He kept his gaze on the corner of the building and slowly walked toward it, holding his gun in front of him. When he got to the corner he quickly jumped out, holding his gun, ready to shoot. There was no one there.

Ethan and Jake had hidden behind a tree on the edge of the forest, just ten feet from the silver-haired man. They held their breath as the man peered in their direction. He lowered the gun and walked backward toward his room.

"Damn, glad we got the hell out of there when we did," Ethan whispered, his heart racing.

"We got what we came for, so let's go talk to the sheriff," Jake said.

The two men watched the man named Goldberg walk back into room twelve, closing the door. They skirted the edge of the parking lot, came to the Buick, and opened the doors quietly and quickly. Ethan backed down the narrow road, lights off, until he was certain their headlights wouldn't be spotted, then turned them on, backed into a turn off, and headed down the hill.

"That was too close, Jake," Ethan said. "Glad you pulled me back into the forest when you did."

"Just years of sneaking around, spying on cheating husbands," Jake said. "No use sticking around any longer."

"Sheriff Parsons has to do something now," Ethan said. "We have proof that it's the mob hit men, and they're looking for Bo and Frankie."

"What's he gonna do, send Deputy Dog to arrest two Chicago hit men? He'll wait for the FBI. Won't risk doing anything until then."

"At least he could stake the motel out or something. He can't just wait until they're gone," Ethan said.

"This is a small town, Ethan, and the sheriff is practically alone. He doesn't have the resources for this kind of thing."

Ethan thought about this.

"Then you and I will have to do it, if he can't."

"Do what? Arrest two professional killers? I don't think so. You're not paying me enough, my friend."

"Just stake them out, that's all. If they leave, we can follow them and at least know where they are."

"Christ, Ethan, you turning into a vampire or something? You haven't slept in what, three days? You need to shut your mind off for a while."

"Not now. Not while we have these guys in our sights. My brother's life is on the line, Jake."

Jake stared at Ethan.

"Damn, it's hard being your friend."

At one thirty on Friday morning, Ethan and Jake walked into the Crockett County Sheriff's Office. The small, three-cell jail was adjacent to the Sheriff's Office, connected by a walkway. Most of the lights in the office were off, except for one in the back. There was a small counter in the front area, but no one was manning it, so they walked back to where the light was coming from. The door was cracked open slightly. They peeked in and saw Deputy Sheriff Cheyenne Smith lying face down on the desk, slight snores coming from her mouth.

Jake looked at Ethan and smiled.

"Small town America," he said. "You gotta love it."

Ethan cleared his throat, and the deputy raised her head, blinking several times.

"Mr. Paxton, I wasn't expecting you."

Ethan smiled at the deputy, who was rubbing her eyes, trying to wake up.

"Sorry to bother you, Cheyenne, but we weren't expecting to be here at this hour either."

Cheyenne looked at Jake and back at Ethan.

"Is this the PI you talked about?"

Ethan nodded.

"Deputy Smith, meet Jake Delgado."

Jake leaned over and shook the woman's hand, dwarfing her small hand in his huge grip.

"Pleasure, Deputy Smith."

"Please, call me Cheyenne. We don't stand on ceremony 'round here."

"Okay, Cheyenne, call me Jake."

They smiled at each other, a little bit too long in Ethan's mind.

"So, Cheyenne, we have some pretty important news to report," Ethan said.

"That so?" She looked at the clock on the wall. "At one thirty in the morning, I hope it's pretty damn important. By the way, have you gotten any sleep yet?"

"No, he hasn't, Cheyenne. He's training to become a vampire," Jake said, grinning.

Cheyenne laughed, a little too loudly in Ethan's mind.

"Okay, ha, ha. No, I haven't slept much, but I have the rest of my life for that," Ethan said, shaking his head as he glanced at Jake. "We know where the Chicago mob guys are, which is right here in Crockett."

Cheyenne sat up straight, suddenly wide awake.

"They're in Crockett? Where?"

"At the Ridge Motel. Did you get a report of a gun being fired up there?" Ethan said.

"No. Did they fire on you?"

"No, one of the goons fired in the air to scare off some teenagers who were partying up there."

"Oh, my God," she said. "I'm surprised someone didn't call it in, but everyone 'round here has guns, so it's not that unusual."

Ethan looked at Jake.

"Well, those kids were getting pretty drunk, so they may not remember much in the morning. But we got a good look at both goons and at their car and license number. They're in a rental—a black Lincoln Town Car."

"Give it to me, and I'll run it through the Kentucky DMV."

"It was rented in Tennessee, with Tennessee plates," Jake said.

"How do you know it was rented in Tennessee?"

"Because we saw them rent it," Jake answered. "They were there when Ethan picked me up."

"That's okay. We share information. You got the plate tag?"

"J499SVW," Jake said. "Rental company was Avis, at the Nashville Airport."

"And we got two names," Ethan added. "Goldberg and Rhino."

"Rhino?" Cheyenne said, looking up.

Ethan shrugged his shoulders.

"Big, hairy guy, probably Italian. The other guy, Goldberg, definitely wasn't Italian."

"Hold on, and I'll run it through the computer. Be back in a sec." Cheyenne walked into the next room.

Ethan and Jake pulled out two chairs and sat down in front of the desk.

"Nice gal," Jake said, "and damn attractive for a cop."

Ethan chuckled.

"Yeah, I noticed you two had a moment there. Keep your mind on the job, Jake."

Jake grinned.

"Don't worry about me, old buddy, but she's a hell of a lot better to look at than you."

Ethan looked around the office, which was Sheriff Parsons's office, with plaques and citations covering the walls. He got up and looked closely at one of the citations. It was from the Mayor of Chicago to Cecil H. Parsons, dated October 25, 1983. "For bravery and dedication beyond the call of duty," it read.

"Looks like Sheriff Parsons really was on the Chicago PD twenty years ago," Ethan said.

"No shit?" Jake said. "He knows what he's doing. I could tell that right off."

"Wonder how well he knows Tonelli's mob?"

"From what he said, pretty well," Jake said. "Hope they don't have a reunion in little old Crockett, Kentucky."

Cheyenne walked back in as they were talking about Sheriff Parsons.

"They're running the plates and contacting the rental company now. We should have something within twenty minutes or so."

"Just reading the sheriff's citation from Chicago PD," Ethan said.

"Yeah, he was pretty big up there. He was injured while on duty and had to retire. He came down here around ten years ago, more as a retirement gig than anything. Not much action around here, usually."

"Well, that's all about to change," Jake said.

Cheyenne smiled weakly and nodded her head.

"He's at home trying to catch a few winks before the crap hits the fan in a few hours."

"How'd you get the night shift?" Jake said. "You'll be on duty tomorrow, too, right?"

"Yes, but I'm younger, and he needs the sleep more than I do," she said, smiling at Jake.

"So you volunteered?" Jake said.

She nodded.

"I might regret it now, with the news you just gave me."

"What do you want to do with the two goons at the Ridge?" Ethan said.

"I'm not sure. I only have one other person on duty, manning the jail next door. Bobby Joe's a reserve and can't handle things by himself."

"That's what we figured," Ethan said. "You want us to stake the Ridge out tonight? We don't have anywhere else to go. My brother's house is empty, and Jake doesn't even have a place to sleep tonight. Guess a car is as good as anything."

Cheyenne rubbed her chin.

"I don't know. What would you do if they decide to leave before we can get someone up there?"

"We'd follow 'em, I guess," Ethan said. "Jake's good at that kind of thing."

"I've been on a hundred stakeouts, but lately just following cheating husbands," Jake said.

Cheyenne looked at him.

"You were a cop. Ethan told us. How long?"

"Fifteen years on the San Diego PD. Been a PI for the last seven years," Jake said.

"You know how to handle a firearm then, I assume."

"Your boss gave me a Glock."

"Are you sure you want to do this, Ethan?" she said. "You haven't had any sleep, and it's boring as hell on stakeout. Plus, it's dangerous."

"As long as one of us stays awake, we'll be fine," Ethan said.

"I'll let him get some shut eye," Jake said. "I slept on the plane out from San Diego."

"Okay, I guess I don't have much choice," Cheyenne said. "I don't want to wake the sheriff, so I'll go ahead and let you two keep an eye on the Ridge. I'll give you a walkie-talkie so you can call me if anything happens."

"Speaking of something happening," Ethan said. "You've got the mob boss's son-in-law in your jail. How you going to protect him in this little place, with no one but yourself and an inexperienced reserve?"

"If they come before seven o'clock, I'm cooked. But after seven, we'll have plenty of manpower here, plus the FBI is coming in."

"I guess we'll have to make sure they don't come until after seven, then," Jake said, smiling at her.

"That would be much appreciated, Jake," she said, returning the smile.

Ethan looked at Jake and then at Cheyenne.

"Alrighty, then. Let's get to work, Jake."

The two men got up and shook Cheyenne's hand as she handed them a walkie-talkie.

"You want a weapon, Ethan?" she said.

"No. Wouldn't know how to use it if I had one," he said. "I'll let Jake handle that part, if it comes up."

"Give it to me," Jake said. "We may need it."

Cheyenne opened a desk drawer and pulled out another Glock 9 mm.

"I need this back."

Jake smiled at her.

"I'll deliver it personally. Thanks."

She handed him a box of nine-millimeter shells.

"Try not to kill any civilians."

Ethan and Jake nodded to Cheyenne and walked out of the office. Ethan stopped and turned back to the deputy.

"Can I talk to Frankie?" he said.

"Why?" she said with a worried look on her face.

"He might know these two goons, and any information would be useful."

"He told us he didn't know who Tonelli was sending down here."

"Maybe. But we got a good look at them, so maybe if we give him the names and description, he'll recognize them. It's a shot," Jake said.

"I guess it would be okay. Let me go over and see if he's awake."

Ethan and Jake stood in the front office area as Cheyenne unlocked the door and entered the walkway to the jail.

"You think he might know them?" Jake said.

"Maybe. Like you said, it's worth a shot. He is part of the mob, after all."

Cheyenne came back, Frankie following behind her in handcuffs.

"Hi, Frankie," Ethan said. "How you doing?"

Frankie looked tired and haggard.

"Okay, but wish the bastard next to me would quiet down." He stared at Cheyenne when he said this.

"I'll take care of it," she said, walking back into the walkway. "I'll be right back." She stopped and pointed at Jake. "You're responsible for him until I get back."

Jake nodded.

"Yes, ma'am."

"You doing okay?" Ethan said, seeing the exhaustion on Frankie's face.

"You already asked me that. How's Bo?"

Ethan glanced at Jake.

"He's, uh, disappeared."

"I heard. The chickenshit," Frankie said.

"Whoa, Frankie, that's my brother. He's anything but a chickenshit, and you know that."

"Then why'd he take off like a scared little kid?"

"You already tried to run off, didn't you?"

Frankie stared at Ethan and then turned to look at Jake.

"Who's this?"

"A friend, an ex-cop. He's helping me out."

Frankie nodded.

"He's your muscle?"

Ethan ignored the comment.

"Frankie, we need your help."

"I'm in jail, in case you hadn't noticed. How the hell can I help you?"

"Your boss, Tonelli, has sent two goons down from Chicago. They're here, in Crockett."

Frankie's eyes widened, the fear spreading over his face.

"Oh, shit. Oh, shit."

"Frankie, we know where they are, and we're going to be watching them the rest of the night. They're at the Ridge Motel."

"Holy shit," Frankie said. "Who are they?"

"That's where you can help us," Ethan said. "One has short-cropped silver hair, very tanned, and is the leader. The other one called him Goldberg. You know him?"

"No."

Jake leaned forward.

"The other one is huge, hairy, dark, looks like a gorilla, nicknamed—"

"Rhino." Frankie's eyes grew wider, the fear evident.

"Rhino. Yeah, that's what the other one called him," Ethan said. "What's that, a nickname?"

"His name's Fanelli, and he's a badass son-of-a-bitch."

"Does he work for Tonelli?" Jake said.

"Yeah, he's the main enforcer," Frankie said, his voice cracking. "He handles all the tough cases. He's a killer. The worst kind."

"You know him personally?" Jake said.

"I met him once or twice, but only from a distance. Even Tonelli was afraid of him."

"Why?" Ethan said.

"'Cause he could crush your windpipe with one hand and have a cannoli with the other. He has no conscience."

Ethan and Jake looked at each other.

"The other guy, the tanned guy, you don't know him?"

"I heard of a guy from Miami. He had a girl's name. Julie, or something like that. Real smart, but not part of the family."

"So he's a contractor, brought in for this job," Jake said.

"Yeah, sounds like it," Frankie said. "Oh, God, I'm a dead man."

Ethan walked to him and put his hand on his shoulder.

"We're going to be watching them for the next few hours, and then reinforcements are coming in, including the FBI. You'll be okay."

Frankie glared at him.

"You don't know these people. They kill for the joy of it. If they're comin' for me, I'm a dead man."

Ethan glanced back at Jake and then at Frankie.

"Hang in there, Frankie. We'll get you through this."

"I'm a dead man, and so is your brother."

44

Jake and Ethan drove up the winding hill in the thickening fog and parked off the road, their headlights off. Jake walked up the hill and peered through the fog at the motel and the black car parked in front of room twelve.

"They're still here," Jake said, shivering as he climbed back into the driver's seat, grabbing a light jacket from the back seat. "Damn, it's cold."

"There's no other way they can go except down this hill, right?" Ethan said.

"They've got to come right past us to get out."

Ethan sat nervously, staring through the darkness and fog.

"If this fog gets any thicker, we may not be able to see them until they're right on us."

"We'll hear 'em, so not a problem."

Ethan shifted in his seat and began rubbing his eyes, then pulled his jacket collar up over his neck.

"You need to get some shut-eye, Ethan. You won't be any good to me unless you get a couple hours sleep."

"Yeah, okay," Ethan said as he reclined his seat. "Wake me when something happens." He laid his head back and was asleep immediately.

Ethan felt a hand on his shoulder, shaking him.

"Wake up, partner. They're moving," Jake said in a loud whisper.

Ethan sat up straight and rubbed his red, burning eyes, peering through the fog, which had gotten thicker. He rubbed his swollen eyes again, squinting through the soup-like mist.

"I don't see anything," Ethan said quietly.

"I heard voices and a door shutting."

"Oh, shit. How long was I out?"

Jake glanced at his watch.

"About three hours. It's almost five o'clock."

Ethan shook his head, trying to loosen the cobwebs. He squinted through the heavy fog again. Jake had cracked his window open so the windows wouldn't fog up.

The two men sat silent, listening for any noise from the motel.

"Will they be able to see us when they drive by?" Ethan said, looking at Jake nervously.

"Don't think so. We're too far off the road, and they'll be looking straight ahead through this fog."

"What are we doing, Jake, following two killer goons in the middle of the night?" Ethan was now wide awake.

"We're just keeping an eye on 'em, that's all," Jake said.

Suddenly, they both sat up straight when they heard a car engine roar to life.

"Here they come," Jake said. "Scrunch down in the seat, just in case."

"I thought you said they couldn't see us."

"Just in case."

Ethan peered over the dashboard, waiting for the headlights to pierce the fog. When he saw the low beams of the black Lincoln, he scrunched a little further down in his seat. The car passed them without incident and rounded the first curve, out of sight.

"Okay, partner, let's go," Jake said, turning on the engine and headlights.

Ethan sat up and glanced backward toward the road. Jake pulled out onto the road, backed up, and pointed the car down the steep hill.

"What if we lose them?" Ethan said. "Worse yet, what if they see us?"

"We'll catch up to them at the bottom of the hill."

They rode in silence as the Buick slowly maneuvered down the windy road through the thick fog. Ethan couldn't see more than five feet in front of them and gripped the seat until his knuckles were white.

"Damn, this is some thick fog," Jake said, leaning forward and peering through the black night.

"Just go slow, Jake," Ethan said. "These are some steep hollows around here. They'd never find us if we go over."

Suddenly, Jake slowed the Buick to a stop and turned off his headlights. Ethan stared down the road and saw two faint red lights.

"They stopped for some reason," Jake whispered.

"You think they saw us?" Ethan said, glancing at Jake.

"Don't know," Jake said, putting his hand on his Glock.

They sat silent for what seemed like several minutes. Eventually, the red tail lights ahead of them grew dimmer and then disappeared.

Jake waited another thirty seconds before turning on his head lights, then slowly let gravity pull them down the hill.

"What do you think they were doing?" Ethan said, his eyes wide as he peered through the fog.

"Don't know," Jake said, leaning as far forward as he could.

They crept down the hill at five miles an hour, both men looking for any hint of red tail lights ahead of them. They finally came to the bottom of the hill and stopped at the crossroad. Jake looked in both directions before pulling out onto the highway. There was no other traffic on the road as they drove toward the town of Crockett.

"You look on the right, and I'll look left," Jake said. "Let me know if you see their car."

Ethan squinted through the fog, which was not as thick as before. He saw the lights of the all-night diner ahead and then spotted the black Lincoln.

"There it is," he said, pointing toward the diner. "They must be inside getting breakfast."

"Lucky bastards," Jake said. "My stomach's been growling for hours."

Ethan felt his own hunger pangs as they pulled into an adjoining gas station parking lot. Jake shut the engine off.

"You sure they're inside?" Jake said.

"No, but I can't see any movement inside the car."

Jake's stomach growled.

"We need food," he said looking at Ethan. "You ever been inside that diner?"

"No."

"Let's go. I need to eat something."

"Hold on, Jake, we can't just go in there and sit down next to those guys."

"Why not? We're just two travelers looking for some breakfast before we go fishin'."

"Jesus," Ethan said. "Some stakeout."

Jake chuckled.

"Yeah, let's eat," he said, as he put the Glock in his belt behind him and covered it with his aloha shirt.

"Wait. You think they'll remember us from the airport?" Ethan said, his nerves on edge.

"We'll find out. Let's go, partner."

They climbed out of the Buick and walked across the parking lot toward the diner. As they opened the door, they looked around at the mostly empty diner. The two goons were sitting in a booth by themselves. Goldberg looked up at them, stared for a couple of seconds, and then went back to his menu. The one named Rhino didn't even give them a second glance. There was no one else in the diner except a white-haired man wearing a greasy apron.

"Sit anywhere, gents," the man said. "Coffee?"

"Yeah, black," Jake said.

"Same," said Ethan, as they walked to a booth across the diner from the goons.

They sat down and pulled out two menus from the holder on the table.

"Don't look at 'em," Jake said. "Not even a glance."

Ethan nodded and looked at the menu.

"This is nuts, Jake."

Jake grinned as he looked at his menu.

"This whole thing is nuts, Ethan. Let's fill our bellies and enjoy it."

Twenty minutes went by, and as Jake and Ethan were gobbling down their eggs, bacon, and coffee, they heard the two men stand up from the booth. When Rhino belched, Goldberg waved his hand in the air.

"You friggin' pig," they heard Goldberg say.

Rhino smiled.

"You pay, big shot."

As he opened the door, he glanced back at Ethan and Jake, a slight scowl on his face, then walked out into the cool morning air.

Goldberg put a twenty dollar bill on the table and began walking toward the door, shooting a glance at Ethan and Jake. Ethan looked away when Jake nodded at the man. Goldberg frowned and headed toward them.

"Do I know you?" Goldberg said to Jake.

"Don't think so," Jake said, coolly. "Ain't from around here."

Goldberg glanced at Ethan.

"You look familiar. We met?"

Ethan shook his head, unable to speak.

"We're from California, here to do some fishing," Jake said. "How about you?"

Goldberg stared at Ethan, then at Jake.

"Fuck off," he said as he walked out of the restaurant.

"What the hell was that?" Ethan said, leaning toward Jake.

"Just being friendly, partner."

Ethan shook his head as he dug into his wallet and pulled out a twenty.

"Let's go," Ethan said.

"Hold on, Columbo," Jake said, putting his hand on Ethan's arm. "They're still outside. We don't want to raise their suspicions."

"Oh, like nodding at the guy is not going to raise their suspicions?"

"Just being friendly. Ain't that what folks around here do?"

Ethan glanced out the window and saw the two goons get into their car.

"Okay, let's go," Jake said, standing up and stretching his back.

The sun was starting to peek through the fog as they walked outside. The black Lincoln was pulling onto the highway, headed toward downtown Crockett.

Jake patted his stomach as they walked to the Buick.

"I needed that, partner."

Ethan's nerves were getting the best of him.

"We took a big chance, Jake."

Jake grinned.

"Relax, Ethan. They don't know us, and we got to fill our tummies with some grub. It's all good."

They climbed into the Buick, Ethan in the driver's seat, pulled out of the parking lot, and headed for downtown Crockett, keeping their eyes peeled for the black Lincoln.

Jake looked at his watch.

"Six o'clock. Sun's coming up. The fog's starting to lift. Now we need to be careful how close we get."

Ethan gazed straight ahead, looking for the Lincoln.

"We need to call Cheyenne on the radio."

"Good idea," Jake said as he picked up the walkie-talkie. He held the button down and said, "Deputy Smith, come in."

Several seconds went by, and then the speaker squawked.

"Deputy Smith here. Who's this?"

"Jake and Ethan. They're in Crockett, and we're tailing them."

"Where are you now?" Cheyenne's voice cracked over the radio.

"Heading up Main Street, about a block or two from your location," Jake said.

"Any idea where they're going?"

"They just ate at the diner, so … no, we have no idea."

Ethan spotted the black Lincoln as it turned right onto a side street.

"There they are."

"We have them in sight," Jake said into the walkie-talkie. "Looks like they're headed … oh, shit."

"Jake, what do you mean 'oh, shit'?"

"They're headed for you, Cheyenne. They're headed for the jail."

"Oh, shit."

"Call Sheriff Parsons now, Cheyenne, and tell him to get reinforcements down there," Jake said into the radio. "Ethan and I will be there in two minutes. Lock all your doors, and arm yourself."

"They wouldn't come in here."

"They're hit men for the mob, Cheyenne. Just do it!"

"Okay. Okay. Out."

They turned right onto the street that led to the Sheriff's Office, picking up speed on the residential street. They were two blocks from the jail.

"What do we do?" Ethan asked, staring ahead, beads of sweat forming on his forehead.

Jake reached into the glove compartment for the Glock that Cheyenne had given them.

"You may have to use this thing, Ethan."

Ethan had never used anything but a hunting rifle and an M-16 in the Air Force.

"I don't know if I can shoot anybody, Jake."

Jake glanced at him.

"It may come down to you or them, so just let your survival instincts take over."

Ethan slowed down as they approached the turn off to the jail. It was located at the end of a cul-de-sac, all by itself. He peered down the empty street, looking for the black Lincoln. The parking lot was empty, except for one police cruiser.

"Jake!" Ethan said, looking straight ahead. The black Lincoln was coming their way.

They saw the silver-haired man at the wheel of the black car as it passed them, slowly. The man was staring at them, a sinister look on his face. The hairy man was looking right, down the cul-de-sac, at the jail. The Lincoln sped up and continued down the residential street.

"What the hell are they doing?" Ethan said, looking into the rearview mirror.

"Looks like they're casing the area," Jake said. "We may have spooked them off, for now."

They turned left onto the cul-de-sac and headed for the jail. They pulled into the parking lot and scrambled out of the car.

"Cheyenne," Jake said into the walkie-talkie, "we're outside. Let us in."

The radio squawked.

"On my way."

Ethan glanced back down the dead end street, looking for the black Lincoln.

"I think we scared them off, Jake."

"You don't scare mob enforcers off, Ethan."

As they stood in front of the door to the Sheriff's Office, they heard the lock snick. Cheyenne opened the door, a semi-automatic rifle in her hands.

"Ethan, keep looking down the cul-de-sac, and let me know if you see 'em," Jake said. "Cheyenne, did you call Sheriff Parsons?"

"Yes, but it'll be fifteen minutes or more before he can get here. We can't scramble enough reinforcements to matter much."

"Where's Frankie?" Jake said.

"In his cell."

"Go get him. We're getting the hell away from here."

"I can't let my prisoner leave the jail," Cheyenne said.

"If you don't, he's dead, and so are you. Go get him," Jake said. "Oh, and it would look more realistic if you had someone in the back seat."

"The only people here are Bobby Joe and a drunk passed out in a cell."

"They'll do. Just a couple of bodies is all we need."

Cheyenne shook her head and scrambled back inside.

"Any sign of 'em, Ethan?" Jake said.

"Not yet."

"Okay, get in the car, driver's seat, and point it toward the cul-de-sac. You're gonna drive us out of here."

Ethan nodded, walked quickly to the Buick, got in, and backed it up. He had the Glock sitting next to him and hoped he wouldn't shoot himself in the leg.

Cheyenne and Frankie walked out of the Sheriff's Office, Frankie still in cuffs, a frantic look on his face. They were followed by a young guy in uniform, half carrying a middle-aged man who was barely able to walk. Cheyenne turned and locked the door.

"Cheyenne, I want you to drive the cruiser out of here with your siren blasting and lights flashing. We're taking Frankie with us," Jake said.

"I can't let you take the prisoner," Cheyenne said, glaring at Jake. "He's my responsibility."

"They'll follow you, not us," Jake said. "We'll have Frankie lying down in the back seat."

"And what happens if they follow us? Then what?"

"Just do a loop around town or something, until they see that you don't have Frankie. By then we'll be long gone."

"Jake, I can't do that."

"Now, Cheyenne, before they come back," Jake said, glaring back at the deputy. "If you don't, we're all dead."

Cheyenne walked quickly to the police cruiser, helped Bobby Joe get the drunk into the back seat, then got in and waited for Jake's signal.

"Frankie, get in the back seat of the Buick and lie down," Jake said.

Frankie was shaking with fear as he crawled into the Buick, his hands cuffed in front of him. Jake got in on the passenger side and signaled Cheyenne to start the siren and flashing lights.

"Follow Cheyenne out of the cul-de-sac, Ethan, and then turn the opposite way she does when we hit Main Street. Stay back. Don't get too close."

Ethan put the Buick in gear and followed Cheyenne's flashing cruiser out of the parking lot. They turned right onto the residential street leading to Main Street, with no sign of the black Lincoln.

"Stay down, Frankie, and don't pop your head up," Jake said, not looking back. "Got it?"

"Y–yes," Frankie said weakly.

The flashing cruiser reached Main Street and turned left, heading out of town.

Squawk. "Jake, you know what you're doing?" Cheyenne said through the walkie-talkie.

"We're going the opposite direction, Cheyenne. Lead them away from us, and make sure you let Sheriff Parsons know what's going on."

"Roger that. Take care of my prisoner, Jake."

Ethan turned right onto Main Street, toward the center of town.

"Slow down, Ethan. Go the speed limit through town," Jake said.

Ethan nodded and took his foot off the accelerator, all the time looking for signs of the black Lincoln.

"What now, Jake?"

"We get the hell out of Dodge," Jake said, "and hopefully with no damn Lincoln behind us."

They drove through the small town, past the Riverside Motel, and reached the turn off that led to the lake, with no sign of the black Lincoln.

"Should I go straight or turn right, toward the lake?" Ethan said.

"Turn right and head for the lake," Jake said. "At a normal speed."

Ethan took a deep breath and blew it out.

"Sure hope this works, Jake."

Jake looked behind them to see if anyone was following them. He took his own deep breath when he saw an empty highway.

"I think we're clear," he said. "Frankie, stay down until I tell you to sit up."

Frankie was shaking in the back seat, nodding his head.

Ethan drove toward the Quail Hollow Lake turn off, glancing in the rearview mirror every few seconds.

Squawk. "Jake, are they following you?"

"No, you see any sign of them, Cheyenne?"

"Negative. I'm all alone out here, and the drunk is about ready to throw up. I'm shutting down the sound and light show."

Jake felt tightness in his stomach.

"Roger that. Where the hell are those guys?"

"Jake, I let Sheriff Parsons know to be on the lookout for a black Lincoln Town Car. And he's not happy about you two taking the prisoner."

"We'll take care of him," Jake said. "We're headed for the lake."

"What are you going to do at the lake?"

"I don't know. We'll figure it out when we get there. We'll take good care of Frankie."

"You'd better. I'm headed back to the Sheriff's Office."

"Be careful, Cheyenne, and wait for the Sheriff before you turn in to the lot. They may have circled back and could be waiting for you."

"Roger that. Out."

Jake looked at Ethan and then back at Frankie.

"Well, we're safe for now, boys."

Ethan blew out another breath.

"For now."

"But our cover is blown," Jake said, a solemn look on his face. "Where the hell are they?"

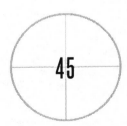

45

Julie Goldberg watched from the parking lot of the Riverside Motel as the police cruiser, sirens blasting and lights flashing, turned left on Main Street and headed out of town. The woman police officer was driving, with another officer in the front and someone in the back. Then he watched as the Buick approached Main Street and turned right in the opposite direction. He was parked behind a big rig, out of sight, but caught a glimpse of the two men from the all-night diner as they passed slowly by the motel.

"Think he's still in the jail?" Rhino said, watching the Buick pass.

"What do you think?" Goldberg answered. "Those two guys from the diner are connected somehow. I think he's in the backseat of one of those cars, lying down like the scared little asshole he is. Question is, which one?"

Rhino scratched his head.

"I dunno."

Goldberg waited, deciding what to do.

"The police cruiser was a diversion, the friggin' siren blasting and the lights all lit up. They wanted us to follow it. He's in the second car, the Buick."

"You think?"

Goldberg shook his head as he put the Lincoln in gear and drove slowly through the parking lot, stopping before turning onto Main Street.

"They're headed out of town," he said.

"Well, hell, you don't have to be Einstein to know that," Rhino said. "This shitty little town ain't much bigger than a fart in a blizzard."

Goldberg ignored him and waited. He knew Frankie Farmer was in the backseat of the Buick, all curled up like a scared dog.

"Why aren't you following them?" Rhino said.

"They need to think they aren't being followed. Once they do, they'll show their hand," Goldberg said.

"Don't lose 'em, asshole. They could hole up in any little shithole they want, and we'd never find 'em."

Goldberg looked at Rhino with disgust.

"You're an idiot."

Rhino raised his left hand and gave Goldberg the finger.

"That's right, show your IQ," Goldberg said, shaking his head again.

"One of these days, you spray-tan son-of-a-bitch, you're gonna go too far," Rhino growled.

Goldberg smiled, knowing he'd gotten to the hairy bastard.

"Yeah, you let me know when that happens, caveman."

Goldberg slowly pulled out onto Main Street, headed in the same direction as the Buick.

"Who are those two guys?" Goldberg said, mostly to himself.

"Cops? Friends of the fishing guide?" Rhino said. "Maybe one of 'em *is* the fishing guide."

Goldberg remained silent, thinking.

"No, I saw them at the Nashville airport, both of 'em. They're from out of town, but why'd they come to a shithole like this?"

Rhino sat up.

"You saw those two guys, the ones in the diner? How come you didn't tell me?"

"I just did, you idiot. If you used your brain as often as you scratch those hairy balls, you'd know shit."

Rhino's face began to turn red.

"So all this time you knew they were watching us?"

Goldberg glanced at the big man.

"No, I didn't know until the friggin' big redhead nodded at me in the diner. He was too smug, too confident, not a local yahoo."

Rhino looked up the road, peering through the early morning mist.

"Who the hell are those guys?"

"Doesn't matter, 'cause they'll be leading us to Frankie and the fishing guide."

"Yeah, but how we gonna know where they went?"

Goldberg saw the sign up ahead that read "Highway 495—Quail Hollow Lake."

"They're going to the lake," he said.

"How the hell do you know?"

"The sign, you schmuck. Quail Hollow Lake. Tonelli told me that's where he sent Augie and Farmer."

Goldberg turned right onto Highway 495, making sure there were no cars within sight ahead of them.

"Why would they go to the lake? Maybe they're goin' somewhere else," Rhino said.

"They're going to the lake. And I'll tell you who they are—they're dead men," Goldberg said, a smile on his tanned face. "We got a friend who's been telling us every move they make."

"What the hell you talkin' about?"

Goldberg grinned at Fanelli.

"You'll see. My ace in the hole."

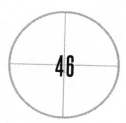

46

Bo sat on the deck of the houseboat, drinking his coffee and gazing out at the sunrise. JB sat in the lounge chair next to him, scratching his beard. Kathy was in the galley making grits and eggs, the smell wafting out to the deck. The sun was just over the horizon, warming Bo's face against the cold morning air.

"Smells mighty good, mother," Bo said over his shoulder.

Bo turned back around and continued to stare out at the lake, the fog beginning to lift off the surface.

"Dad, what're you thinkin'?" JB said, taking a swig of coffee.

Bo sat silent, taking another gulp of coffee.

"Dad?"

Bo slowly turned to his son, his eyes glistening.

"What's wrong, Dad?"

"We gotta go back, JB," Bo said.

JB stared at his father.

"It's a death sentence, Dad. You know that."

Bo turned and stared out at the eastern shore of Quail Hollow Lake. They had left the Silver Creek Resort dock at dusk the night before after fueling up the houseboat and filling it with food and supplies for a week. Around nine thirty they had pulled into a remote cove on the Tennessee side, one that only a few local fishermen knew about. It was invisible from the main lake, covered by trees and brush, the perfect hiding place. They had docked close to shore and tied up for the night.

"I can't hide out here like a coward," Bo said. "Not while my brother is tryin' to save my sorry butt. I gotta go back and face the music."

JB shook his head.

"What can we do against the mob?"

"Probably nothin', but it ain't just us. Ethan's back there, along with this private eye friend of his, and Sheriff Parsons, and Cheyenne."

"And professional killers, just waitin' for you to show your face," JB said, his voice rising.

Kathy was standing in the doorway, listening.

"Your dad's right, JB," she said, drying her hands with a dish towel. "It's the right thing to do."

Bo turned to look at his wife, her red hair glistening in the early morning sunlight. He smiled at her and raised his coffee cup.

"A little more coffee, mother?"

Kathy stepped back inside and came back out with the coffee pot, filling up Bo and JB's cups. Bo patted her on the fanny.

"Momma knows best," he said.

JB stared at his parents, shaking his head.

"You're both loony as a rabid dog."

"Well, son, I think sittin' out here with our tail between our legs is a little bit loony, don't you?"

Kathy smacked him with the dish towel.

"Speak for yourself, Bo. I ain't got no tail!"

Bo smiled widely and stood up.

"Let's get this big, old tub rumbling and get back home." He looked at JB. "You with us, son?"

JB stood up, hesitated, and then walked over and hugged his father.

"Yeah, let's go home."

Bo took another gulp of coffee and stared out at the lake, which was turning gold from the morning sunlight.

"I wish I knew what was ahead of us when we get back."

"Dad, didn't Sheriff Parsons say the FBI would be in Crockett this morning," JB said.

Bo looked at the clock in the galley. Seven o'clock.

"Yeah, he did. They should be pullin' in to the Sheriff's Office right about now."

"You're a witness to two murders, Dad. They're gonna want to talk to you when we get back."

"Yeah, I know, son. Everybody's gonna want a piece of ol' Bo when we hit the dock."

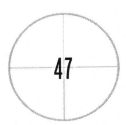

47

Sheriff Parsons was sitting in his office, a white porcelain mug of hot coffee on his desk. Deputy Smith sat in one of the two chairs facing him. Parsons glanced up at the clock.

"Seven o'clock," he said. "The feds will be here any minute."

Cheyenne shifted in her chair, looking at the clock.

"So one more time, Deputy, what are we gonna tell the FBI when they get here, about how we let a mobster go this morning?"

Cheyenne brushed the hair from the front of her face, wiping moisture from her forehead at the same time.

"Sheriff, I'm sorry."

Parsons waved her off when he saw the door open. He got up and walked around his desk to the front of the little police station. Cheyenne followed. Standing in the doorway were two serious-looking men in black suits.

"Morning, gentlemen," Parsons said, holding out his hand. "The FBI, I presume."

"Yes, sir," the older man with short, salt-and-pepper hair said. "I'm Special Agent Whitman and this is Special Agent Torres." The two men showed the sheriff their badges.

Parsons leaned down to look at the IDs.

"Sheriff Cecil Parsons of Crockett County, and this here's Deputy Smith," he said, pointing to Cheyenne.

The two agents nodded their heads at Cheyenne.

"We understand you've had a double murder down here involving two well-known sports figures," Agent Whitman said, looking at Parsons.

"Well, yeah, we have."

"And that you have one of the suspects, a member of the Chicago mob, behind bars," Agent Whitman continued.

"Well, uh, I—"

"And a second witness, a Mr. Bo Paxton."

Sheriff Parsons glanced at Cheyenne, the smile gone from his face.

"There have been some developments," he said.

The FBI men stood motionless, staring at the sheriff.

"The, uh, suspect, Frankie Farmer, has, uh, vanished, and so has the other witness."

Whitman's eyes widened, but he showed no other sign of surprise.

"Say again?"

"The suspect, Frankie Farmer, is gone."

"The witness, what happened to him?"

"We don't know but think that he got scared and took his family and … vanished."

Whitman turned slowly and looked at Agent Torres, who remained ramrod straight, his face as solid as stone, looking like it would explode from the inside out.

"Would you gentlemen like to step into my office, and we can discuss these, uh, developments," Parsons said, waving his arm toward his office.

Whitman and Torres walked quickly into the sheriff's office and continued to stand while the sheriff sat in his oversized chair.

"Please, have a seat," Parsons said.

"We'll stand," Whitman said.

Parsons cleared his throat.

"Suit yourselves. Coffee?"

The two agents shook their heads.

"Where is the suspect, Sheriff Parsons?" Whitman said.

Parsons took a swig of his lukewarm coffee.

"Cheyenne, can you heat this up for me?"

While Cheyenne walked out of the office with the sheriff's mug, Whitman leaned forward and put his hands on the sheriff's desk.

"Where is the suspect, Sheriff?"

Cheyenne came back and placed the full mug on the sheriff's desk.

"I think I can answer that," she said, standing in front of the two FBI agents.

Whitman and Torres slowly shifted their gaze to Deputy Smith.

"There are two mob enforcers in Crockett right now," Cheyenne said, clearing her throat. "And they came by the police station this morning. Or, I should say, they drove by the police station this morning. And," she stopped, took a drink from the sheriff's coffee mug, and cleared her throat again. "And, uh, I gave the suspect to two men who were, uh, here."

Whitman squinted at Cheyenne, shaking his head slowly.

"I don't follow."

"The fishing guide, Bo Paxton, the witness that vanished," she said, taking another swig of coffee, "well, his brother and a private investigator that he'd hired, Jake something or other, well…"

Whitman slammed his open palm on the sheriff's desk.

"Where . . . the hell . . . is the suspect!" His nostrils were flaring, his eyes wide open now.

Cheyenne flinched, jerking her head backward.

"He's gone, with them."

"Who?"

"The fishing guide's brother and the, uh, PI."

"And where are they?" Whitman said, his voice lowered to almost a whisper.

Cheyenne glanced at Parsons.

"I don't know, maybe to the lake."

"The lake. The lake where the murders happened?" Whitman said, his voice rising.

Cheyenne coughed.

"Uh, yes, Quail Hollow Lake."

Whitman just stared at Cheyenne and then turned his gaze toward Sheriff Parsons.

"Do you know the hail storm that is about to fall on your heads?"

Sheriff Parsons stood up, putting his hands out, palms down.

"Okay, let's calm down here."

Whitman stepped forward and put his face two inches from Parsons's face.

"The storm to end all storms, Sheriff Cecil Parsons of Crockett County."

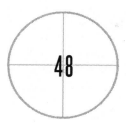

48

Ethan drove down the familiar steep incline toward Quail Hollow Lake. He'd been down this road many times with Bo, but never under these circumstances. The sun was cresting over the eastern hills, shining directly into his eyes. He grabbed his sunglasses, but before he put them on he glanced in the rearview mirror and checked on Frankie, who was lying still, a slight whimper coming from his mouth.

"You okay, Frankie?" he said. Ethan glanced at Jake, who was looking straight ahead at the approaching lake, a look of concern on his face. "*You okay, Jake?*"

"My . . . my wrists hurt," Frankie said, looking sideways at Ethan's reflection in the mirror.

Jake turned around and helped Frankie into a sitting position.

"Shit, we forgot to get the handcuff keys from Cheyenne," he said, looking at Ethan. "Sorry, Frankie, but you'll have to suck it up."

Frankie shifted his wrists around, trying to loosen the cuffs.

Ethan saw genuine concern in Jake's eyes. *Was the big lug a softy after all, or was it something else.*

"We'll figure something out. Just sit back and try to relax," Jake said, patting Frankie on the arm.

"What's eating at you?" Ethan said, as he pulled into the familiar Quail Hollow Resort parking lot, empty except for one old Ford pickup and a red Toyota Celica. He thought about how many times Bo and he, and sometimes his own two kids, Charlie and Molly, had pulled into this lot with a day of fishing, swimming, and fun ahead of them. He glanced at the clock on the dash of the white Buick. Seven fifteen.

"We need to hide the car," Jake said. "The goons will be here, sooner or later."

Ethan remembered a spot up on the hill opposite the parking lot, tucked in behind some trees. He turned the Buick right and headed up the steep hill, maneuvering it around a stand of trees and parking in a secluded spot.

"This okay?" he said, looking at Jake.

Jake nodded as he looked down on the lake and the dock.

"Yeah, this'll do."

"Sheriff Parsons and Cheyenne are probably going through hell right now," Ethan said.

"Why?" Jake asked.

"The FBI was scheduled to be at the police station at seven."

"Oh, shit," Jake said. "And we have the suspect."

"Exactly," Ethan said. "Poor Cheyenne, she'll take the blame."

Jake pursed his lips.

"We did what we had to do to protect him and Cheyenne. Damn it."

Ethan turned off the engine.

"Now what?"

Jake looked at him and hunched his shoulders.

"Hell, I don't know."

Ethan's mouth fell open.

"What do you mean you don't know? You're the one that said to drive to the lake!"

"Well," Jake said, shaking his head, "we had to go somewhere."

Ethan glanced at Frankie, who was wide-eyed and shaking again.

"Okay. Okay. Let's think a minute. I know a few people here. Maybe we can get a boat and take Frankie out on the lake, and—"

"And what?" Frankie said from the backseat. "Throw me overboard?"

Jake looked at Ethan, a slight smile on his face.

"There's an idea."

"What?" Frankie said, his voice two octaves higher.

Jake turned and looked at the frightened man.

"Relax, mob guy, we didn't bring you out here to get rid of you. You're a witness for Bo, just as he's a witness for you. Got it?"

Frankie shook his head up and down.

"Yeah, I got it."

Ethan couldn't help but chuckle.

"'Course, throwing you overboard would get rid of our problem."

"What?" Frankie was big-eyed again.

"Frankie, relax, man, we're pullin' your chain," Jake said, glancing at Ethan. "Aren't we?"

Ethan burst out laughing, Jake right behind him.

Frankie sat in the backseat staring at the two men.

"What?"

"Okay, let's go down to the dock before too many people get here," Ethan said. "If we're lucky, I'll know someone that will give us a boat. Where the hell we're gonna go, I have no damn idea."

"It's a big lake, so we'll get lost for a while," Jake said. "Until we can figure something out."

Ethan nodded and opened his door. He opened Frankie's door and helped him slide out.

"What about Frankie's cuffs?" Ethan said, looking at Jake.

Jake stopped and thought a moment.

"He'll have to stay in the car until we get a boat."

Ethan looked at Frankie.

"Sorry, man, back in the car."

"What?"

"I'll stay with him," Jake said. "Take your Glock, Ethan, just in case."

Ethan glanced nervously at Jake.

"Hell, I'll probably end up shooting my foot off, or my ass," he said as he shoved the gun into his belt behind his back.

"If I hear a shot, I'll get Frankie and me out of here," Jake said with a smirk.

"What?"

This time it was Ethan.

49

The black Lincoln drove slowly along the narrow country road. They hadn't seen the white Buick, but had passed several signs for Quail Hollow Lake. Suddenly the road started down a steep decline and the car picked up speed.

"Holy crap, Goldberg, slow the hell down," Rhino said, grabbing the dashboard with both hands.

Goldberg slammed on his brakes, causing both men to jerk forward and then back again.

"Asshole," Rhino said, seething.

"Damn, this is one steep mother of a hill," Goldberg said, eyes wide and staring at the remaining decline straight ahead.

"Just don't run us into the lake, asshole."

Goldberg glanced at Rhino in disgust.

"Friggin' caveman."

He eased the Town Car slowly down the steep hill, keeping his foot on the brake the entire way. He glanced in the rearview mirror to make sure no one was following them. They finally reached the bottom of the hill where the road took a sharp right turn and leveled out. Goldberg blew out a nervous breath, and Rhino finally took his hands off the dashboard. The lake was right next to them, on the left.

"That lake sure came out of nowhere," Rhino said.

Goldberg eased the Town Car down the road until he spotted a clearing ahead.

"This must be the resort Tonelli talked about," Goldberg said as he approached the parking lot. He looked around and didn't see a white Buick.

"Shit, they're not here."

"I told you, you friggin' moron," Rhino said, shaking his head.

"Doesn't mean they won't show up, though. I need to hide this damn car so they don't see it."

"Where, in the lake?"

Goldberg ignored him and saw that the road continued on past the parking lot, up a slight incline, and turned right into the woods.

"Up the road."

He guided the black Town Car slowly past the parking lot, looking at the Quail Hollow Resort on his left. He didn't see much activity, but smoke was coming out of the kitchen chimney. He drove up the small hill and turned right, into the wooded area. He saw a cabin about one hundred yards up the road so gradually pulled the Town Car into a stand of trees off the road.

"This should do it," Goldberg said. "Nobody can see us unless they drive up this way, and even then we're far enough off the road where they shouldn't notice."

"Now what?" Rhino said, looking at the woods all around them. "I don't like these places. Too many furry critters."

Goldberg chuckled.

"Yeah, you don't like them little varmints do you, Nancy?"

Rhino glared at him but kept silent.

"We'll take turns watching the resort. If they show up, we'll follow 'em. I know they got Frankie with them," Goldberg said. "I'll take the first watch, you just sit back and watch the woods for any little furry critters."

Goldberg climbed out of the Town Car, checking for his pistol in his ankle holster. He walked down the dirt lane until he got to the paved road and peeked out at the parking lot and resort below. Still no white Buick anywhere in sight. He found a large boulder off to the left that gave him a good vantage point and sat down, watching and waiting.

Doubt started to creep into Goldberg's mind. *What if they didn't come to the lake after all? I'll be screwed.*

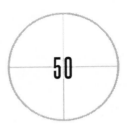

50

"Jake, look!" Frankie was pointing down at the resort parking lot.

Jake followed Frankie's finger and saw the black Town Car slowly crossing in front of the parking lot and continuing up the road on the opposite hill. Then it was out of sight.

"Jake, that's them, right?"

"Yeah, that's them, but what are they doing?"

"Hiding, just like us," Frankie said, his voice becoming shrill.

"Shit, I gotta warn Ethan," Jake said. "If they're up on that hill looking down at the parking lot, Ethan will lead them straight to us."

"What are you gonna do, Jake?" Frankie was shaking as he watched the road.

Jake looked in the back seat and saw a green cap with a fish on the front.

"Hand me that cap," he said to Frankie.

Frankie handed him the cap.

"That's it? You're just gonna wear a friggin' fishing cap? That's your disguise?"

"You're a nervous little man, you know that Frankie?" Jake said, seeing a blanket on the floor in the backseat. He reached down and picked it up. "Gotta be carrying something."

"You're not leaving me here, are you?"

"Afraid I have to, Frankie. Now, you've got two choices. Stay in the car, out of sight, and don't move, make a sound, even fart."

"What's the other choice?"

"You get out of the car, try to escape, and you get killed by those mob guys up the road, or by me. Your choice."

Frankie took a gulp of air.

"I'm staying put."

"Good choice. Lie down on the seat, and lock the doors when I get out. We'll come get you when it's safe."

"When's it gonna be safe?"

Jake stared at him.

"Very good question."

Jake opened his door slowly and got out, the green fishing cap on his head, the blanket under his arm, his Glock tucked away inside the blanket. He closed the door quietly and motioned for Frankie to lock it. He took off his jacket and reversed it, knowing that the mobsters had seen it in the all-night café. He put it back on and began walking quickly and quietly down the hill, out of the stand of trees into the clear. He pulled the cap down over his face and pulled his jacket collar up over his neck, covering his red hair.

He sauntered into the parking lot in front of the resort and began whistling. He didn't look around, but kept his gaze on the bridge that went from the parking lot to the dock. He fought the urge to look back and kept walking until he reached the door to the resort. As he opened it, he glanced back up the road quickly. Seeing no movement, he walked into the warm building.

"Ethan, you in here?" he said, not seeing anyone around but smelling the coffee.

"Back here," he heard Ethan say.

Jake followed the voice back to the restaurant where he saw Ethan sitting at a table with two men, a cup of coffee in front of him.

"Taking it easy, I see," Jake said.

Ethan smiled as he looked at the big redhead.

"You going fishing, Jake?"

"More like I'm the bait, old buddy. We got company up the road."

Ethan's smile faded.

"They're here?"

Jake nodded, looking at the two men.

"Who are you guys?"

A tall, silver-haired man stood up. He was nearly as tall as Jake.

"Slammer Perkins. I'm a friend of Ethan's brother, Bo. And you are?"

"Jake. Jake Delgado. A friend of Ethan's."

"Howdy, I'm Ronnie Bass," a short man with a full, brown beard said, holding out his hand. "Bo's a friend of mine, too."

Jake shook his hand then reached out and shook Slammer's hand.

"A fisherman named Bass?"

Ronnie nodded and smiled.

"They call me 'Largemouth' around here."

Jake tilted his head.

"Why?"

"Never mind. Jake's not a fisherman," said Ethan, staring at Jake. "Where the hell is, you know?"

"Safe, for now."

Ethan glanced around nervously.

"Ronnie's going to take us out onto the lake in his boat."

"When?" Jake said, looking at the two men. "And how?"

"Whenever you're ready," Slammer said. "I hear you have a special 'friend' you want to go along."

Jake stared at Ethan.

"Yeah, just some acquaintance of Bo's," Jake said.

"I told them about Frankie," Ethan said. "They're okay with it if it helps Bo."

Jake nodded at the two men.

"Well, we have a problem, gents. Two mob hit men are up the road looking down on us right now. They want to kill Frankie, and probably us, and definitely Bo. And if you help us, they'll want to kill you, too."

"They gotta find us first," Slammer said, smiling. "First thing, we gotta get your friend down here without them goons seein' him."

"Yeah, I know. But how?" Ethan said.

"You got the keys to your car?" Slammer said.

"Yes, why?" Ethan said.

"I'll drive my pickup up the hill to where your car is, put your friend in the bed, under a tarp, drive back down to the dock, load up my boat with fishin' gear and beer and the 'special cargo,' all under the watchful eyes of our gooney-bird friends up yonder. Meanwhile, Ronnie will take you two on his boat the back way, out of sight, and I'll meet you a few miles down the lake."

"Sounds like a plan, but what if they follow you?" Jake said.

"Then I lose 'em on the lake. There's a thousand little coves to get lost in. I'll contact Ronnie to let him know where I am. You two have to stay out of sight, even on the lake."

"Okay, let's do it," Ethan said. "Jake, you okay with this?"

Jake hesitated. Ethan knew he was thinking through all the variables.

"Jake?"

"Why don't you bring the 'special cargo' around back here so he can go with us?" Jake said.

Slammer shook his head.

"No way to get him across the foot bridge without the goons seeing us."

"You going to put him in your boat, right? Why can't you bring him around back and put him in the pontoon boat with us, then take off up the lake? If they're watching, they'll follow you, not us."

Slammer looked at Ronnie Bass and nodded.

"That'll work."

"Okay, let's go for it," Jake said, a slight smile on his face. "The sooner the better."

Slammer gulped down the rest of his coffee and tipped his cap.

"See y'all on the lake."

"Hold on. Wear this cap and jacket," Jake said, taking them off and handing them to Slammer. "You and I are about the same size, so they'll think you're the same guy that just walked down the hill. Less suspicious."

After putting on Jake's jacket and cap, Slammer sauntered out of the restaurant, whistling while he walked down the ramp to the parking lot as Jake and Ethan watched from the restaurant.

"Let's go, fellas," Ronnie Bass said, taking one last gulp of coffee. "Time to boogie."

Jake and Ethan followed the man out the back of the restaurant to a rental pontoon boat from the resort with "Quail Hollow Lake Resort" painted on the side

"Hop on, gents," Ronnie said.

Jake and Ethan stepped quickly onto the boat, as Ronnie untied it from its mooring, jumped on board, and started the outboard motor.

"Take those two blankets on the bench, lie down, and put them over you. Don't move or make a sound until we're out of the 'no wave' zone. Got it?"

Jake and Ethan nodded and laid down on the floor of the pontoon boat, pulling the blankets up over them. Jake took the Glock from the blanket and put it in his front belt, ready for anything.

Jake felt the boat begin to move forward, slowly at first, then a little faster.

"Ethan, you got the gun that Cheyenne gave us?" Jake said in a whisper.

"Yeah, it's here beside me. Jake, what the hell are we doing?" Ethan whispered, as he fingered the weapon.

"Saving the poor bastard's life, I hope," Jake whispered back. "And ours, too."

51

Goldberg peered down at the man walking across the parking lot. He looked like the same guy that had walked into the resort a few minutes earlier. Squinting through the morning sunshine, he saw the same cap and jacket and decided it was the same guy. Still, there was something different about him, something about his gait, his swagger. He watched as the man climbed into a big, red pickup, started it up, and backed out of the parking lot. He drove up the hill opposite the parking lot and disappeared behind a stand of trees.

What's up in those trees?

Goldberg kept his eyes glued to the trees on the other side of the road, trying to see any movement, listening for any sounds. He heard the truck engine idling. *What the hell is going on over there?*

Several minutes later he saw the red truck emerge from the trees and head down the hill to the edge of the lake next to the parking lot. It backed up to the lake, close to a blue fishing boat anchored in the water. The big man in the cap got out and began loading fishing gear into the boat. Goldberg couldn't see very well, the pickup blocking his view, so he moved to a better vantage point where he could see the boat more clearly. He saw a large, tan tarp covering half of the floor of the boat, fishing gear on top of it.

Just another yahoo fisherman headed out for the day.

Goldberg watched as the man pushed the loaded boat off the shore and into the lake, stepping into the boat and starting up the outboard motor, slowly heading out onto the lake. Goldberg got a rush of adrenalin when the man looked up in his direction and tipped his cap, then made a left turn and disappeared behind the resort, out of sight. Goldberg watched, ready to hop into the Town Car and drive down to the dock, but the blue boat emerged within two minutes from behind the resort and proceeded up the lake.

Goldberg kept watching the trees and the resort, waiting for the Buick to show up, and out of the corner of his eye saw a pontoon boat slowly heading out from the back of the resort toward the main body of the lake. It passed in front of the many houseboats docked on the lake, about one hundred yards from the dock. A man was driving the boat, but no one else was visible. He continued to watch the two boats head out to the main body of the lake, the sun directly in his eyes. Goldberg diverted his gaze back to the parking lot where another pickup was pulling in and parking. Then he glanced back up at the stand of trees.

What the hell is up there?

Goldberg walked to the black Lincoln, got in, and started it up. Rhino was asleep in the passenger seat. He woke up when the Lincoln pulled out onto the road and headed down the hill.

"Wha's up?" Rhino said, yawning.

"Nothing, just checking on something," Goldberg said. "Go back to sleep."

Goldberg guided the Lincoln down the hill, across the parking lot, and headed up the steep hill toward the stand of trees. As he made the right turn, he saw the white Buick hidden behind the trees.

"Holy shit!"

"What . . . what the . . . ? " Rhino was sitting up straight, staring at Goldberg.

"They were here. They got the little shit into the goddamn boat right under my friggin' nose," Goldberg said as he got out and checked inside the Buick.

"What the hell are you talkin' about?" Rhino said, turning his gaze to the white Buick. "Holy shit!"

Goldberg reached into the glove compartment of the Buick and pulled out a rental agreement. He read the name, Ethan Paxton.

"I'll be goddamned," he said, mostly to himself.

"What is it?"

"What's the name of the fishing guide we're lookin' for?" Goldberg said.

"Bo."

"Bo what? His last name?"

Rhino pulled out a slip of paper from his pocket.

"Bo Paxton. Why?"

"It's his goddamned brother. They're on the lake. Goddamn it!" Goldberg said as he got back into the Lincoln. He began pounding the steering wheel. "We gotta get to the boat."

"What boat?"

Goldberg ignored Fanelli as he guided the Lincoln back down the hill to the parking lot. He saw a man loading up an outboard fishing boat that was idling next to the dock. They made eye contact.

"Come on, Rhino," he said, walking quickly across the bridge to the dock.

Rhino lumbered out of the Lincoln and nervously followed Goldberg across the swaying bridge.

The man loading the boat nodded at Goldberg and went inside the resort, leaving the boat alone, idling.

"C'mon," he said, waving to Rhino.

Goldberg climbed into the boat, with Rhino climbing in gingerly after him, rocking the boat side to side.

"Sit down, and shut up," Goldberg said, untying the rope that anchored the boat to the dock. He put the motor in gear and turned the throttle. The boat slowly pulled away from the dock.

"How'd they move Frankie without you seein' them," Rhino said, holding on to both sides of the boat.

"I said shut up," Goldberg said, looking back at the dock. No sign of anyone, so he turned around, twisting the throttle and picking up speed, heading out to the main body of the lake. He peered into the distance and didn't see any other boats on the lake in front of them. He passed the "no wave" sign and opened up the outboard motor to full speed. They sped down the lake, leaving a large wake behind them.

"I didn't know you knew how to operate one of these things," Rhino said, a slight hint of respect in his voice.

"I live in Florida, you idiot."

"Oh," Rhino said, scratching his balls.

The sun was fully over the eastern hills, so Goldberg grabbed some sunglasses that were sitting on a cooler next to him and put them on. He saw the walkie-talkie next to the cooler and smiled. *My ace in the hole.* In front of the cooler were three rifle cases, as promised.

"How we gonna find them?" Rhino said, suddenly noticing the rifle cases. "Where'd those come from?"

Goldberg grinned at Rhino as he felt the cool air on his face.

"Don't worry about it. I got it covered."

52

They had been grilling her for nearly an hour, with Whitman on his cell phone half the time. Cheyenne was exhausted and spent and rubbed her already-red eyes.

"Like I said, they either went to Bo Paxton's place or to the lake," she said. "They were headed out of town in that direction."

"How far is the lake from the fishing guide's place?" Whitman said.

"Two miles, if that," Sheriff Parsons said, glancing at Cheyenne. "It's on the way to the lake."

Special Agent Torres walked into the office.

"They're here," he said.

Whitman stood up and pointed toward the door.

"Time to go."

As Cheyenne walked out into the bright sunshine, her mouth fell open. There were at least a dozen men and women in the parking lot, all wearing dark-blue jackets with "FBI" emblazoned on the back. Several dark-blue Crown Victoria sedans were parked in the normally empty lot.

"Listen up!" Whitman said, scanning the crowd of men and women. "Our suspect is with two civilians. One is the brother of the witness, who has," he glanced at Cheyenne, "vanished. They're driving a late model white Buick Regal with Tennessee plates. Two other suspects, armed and dangerous and suspected to be part of the Chicago mob, are driving a late model black Lincoln Town Car, Tennessee plates. They may be headed for Quail Hollow Lake, about twelve miles southwest of Crockett, on Highway 495. Two units stay here in case any of the suspects or witnesses return. The other four units follow Special Agent Torres and me. Communicate, people! And stay alert and ready. Move out!"

Cheyenne watched the dozen men and women scramble to their respective cruisers as they followed Agents Whitman and Torres to one of the blue cruisers.

"In the back," Whitman said to them. "You're our eyes and ears today."

The caravan of five dark sedans left the parking lot, with Whitman and Torres leading them. Two cruisers remained at the police station. The caravan turned right at Main Street and headed through downtown Crockett, at the speed limit.

"You have boats at the lake, I assume?" Whitman said to Sheriff Parsons.

"Yeah, we keep a speedboat docked at Quail Hollow Resort," Parsons replied.

"You have people who can drive it available?"

"Yeah, they work at the dock."

"They aren't on your force?"

"Volunteers. Deputy Smith and I are the only full-time officers," Parsons said.

Whitman glanced at Torres, who was looking straight ahead, as always.

"Small town America. Got to love it."

"Aren't you going to check Paxton's place?" said Cheyenne.

"We'll swing by there, but I don't expect them to be that stupid," Whitman said. "They're on the lake, and they're looking for the brother, the fishing guide."

Cheyenne saw Parsons nod in agreement.

"It's a mighty big lake, Agent Whitman," she said.

"If they're on the lake, we'll find them," he said. "And you two had better hope we do."

Cheyenne watched as Agent Whitman dialed a number on his cell phone.

"This is SAIC Whitman," he said into the phone. "I need four Bureau speedboats at Quail Hollow Lake Resort, outside of Crockett, Kentucky, gassed and ready to go, in forty-five minutes."

Cheyenne glanced at Sheriff Parsons, her eyebrows raised.

"I don't give a Goddamn, just have them there," Whitman yelled into the phone.

Cheyenne glanced again at Parsons, who just shrugged his shoulders. They were now merely passengers in the escalating and widening FBI net. *I hope Ethan and Jake are at the resort and not out on the lake,* she thought. *Don't get into a battle with the FBI. Forget Frankie, and give him up.*

Sheriff Parsons told them to turn left onto a dirt road.

"Bo's place is about a mile down this road," he said.

When they got to the clearing and saw Bo's house, it looked empty. No dogs came barking to meet them, which was strange. No cars in the driveway. No sign of anyone around.

Whitman radioed to another cruiser to check the house while the other Agents waited outside next to their cars, guns drawn and at the ready. A man and a woman approached the house, one peering through the kitchen window while the other knocked on the door.

"FBI. Open up!" the male agent said loudly.

No answer. No movement.

"FBI. Open up!"

The man looked down at Whitman for the go ahead and then kicked the door open, the female agent right behind him, guns pointed in front of them. After less than two minutes, the two agents came out of the house.

"Empty," he yelled to Whitman.

Agent Whitman looked around the eighty-acre property, not seeing any signs of life, except for a few ducks on the pond.

"They have dogs?" he said to Sheriff Parsons.

"Yeah, two or three, and they're usually pretty loud."

"Well, he must have taken them with him. Should make him easier to find."

Cheyenne saw the smile on the sheriff's face.

"What are you smiling about, Sheriff?"

He leaned closer to Cheyenne.

"They won't find Bo unless he wants to be found."

Cheyenne nodded, her own smile cracking her nervous face.

"And where does that leave us?"

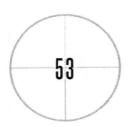

53

"Okay, you guys can get up now," Ronnie Bass said as they lumbered down the lake in the slow pontoon boat. They had been on the lake for thirty minutes.

Jake and Ethan threw the blankets off and stood up, stretching and looking back.

"Any sign of your friend?" Jake said.

"Yeah, I caught sight of him right before we rounded that last bend," Ronnie said. "He knows where to meet us."

Ethan reached down and took the blanket off Frankie, who was shaking.

"You okay, Frankie?"

Frankie stared up at Ethan.

"These handcuffs are killing me."

The pontoon boat slowed and turned right into a small cove that was covered by dozens of cottonwood trees.

"Hey, I know this cove," Ethan said, suddenly nervous. "What the hell?"

"What's wrong?" Jake said, glancing at Ethan.

"Ronnie, why you bringing us here?" Ethan said.

"This is where Slammer and I agreed to meet," the bearded man said. "It's secluded from the main lake, so nobody can see us."

Ethan looked at Jake.

"This is where it all happened."

"All what happened?" Jake said, tilting his head at Ethan. "Oh, hell no."

Ethan nodded at him.

"Ronnie, did you know this is where Bo and those coaches were shot?"

"No shit? I never heard," he said, glancing back at Ethan. "This is a favorite fishing spot of Bo's. I knew that."

The boat slowed again, making another right turn into the main body of the cove. Ethan saw the tree hanging out over the lake where he had caught his smallmouth bass just a couple of days before. They sidled up next to the tree and gently eased up onto the sandy beach, where Ronnie Bass cut the engine.

"We'll tie up here and wait for Slammer," he said, as he hopped onto the shore and tied the boat to a small cottonwood tree.

Ethan looked at the shore with the small, sand beach and cottonwoods and brush everywhere. Then he looked down at the water.

"Bo said the coaches both died right here in this cove."

Frankie stood up, visibly shaken. He pointed behind them.

"Right over there is where I sunk his bass boat, with the two coaches tied up inside."

Ethan glanced at Jake, who squinted as he looked around the secluded cove.

"Why'd he bring us here?" Jake said quietly, looking at Ethan.

Ethan jerked his head up when he heard the sound of an outboard motor. Looking through the cottonwoods, he saw the blue bass boat coming through the mouth of the cove.

"Is that Slammer?" Ethan said.

"Sure is," Ronnie said. "Told ya he'd find us."

Ethan and Jake stared at the blue boat as it chugged into the quiet cove, sidling up next to the pontoon boat.

"Morning, gents," Slammer said, throwing a rope to Ronnie, who tied it around the same small tree. "Everybody doin' okay?"

Ethan and Jake nodded at the big man.

"Why'd you bring us here, Slammer?" Ethan said.

Slammer was already on the shore, standing next to Ronnie Bass.

Frankie stared at the shore, toward the brush next to the fallen tree. He started shaking.

"Get me outta here!"

Ethan put his arms around the shaking man.

"Frankie, it's okay."

Jake stood motionless on the pontoon boat, looking around the cove.

Ron Parham

"Why'd you bring us to this death trap, Slammer?" Jake said. "Why here, of all the coves on this damn lake?"

When Ethan turned to look at Slammer and Ronnie Bass, the two men were standing, smiling, rifles pointed at him and the other two men on the pontoon boat. Ethan glanced at Jake and saw him move his right hand behind his back, gripping his Glock.

"Jake?" Ethan whispered.

"Be ready to move fast," Jake said.

244

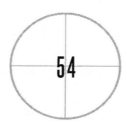

54

Bo held his cup out so Kathy could fill it up with coffee again. He smiled up at her from his seat at the wheel of the houseboat. She patted his cheek, a tear beginning to form in her eye.

"You're a good man, Bo Paxton," Kathy said. "We'll make it through this, with God's help."

Bo grabbed her hand and kissed it softly.

"Thanks, Kath. Let's go find Ethan and that friend of his."

Bo put the big, lumbering houseboat in gear and headed out of the cove where they had spent the night. He maneuvered the boat into the main channel and headed for the Kentucky border. He glanced at the clock on the dashboard. It was eight o'clock. He figured it would take them almost an hour to get back to the Silver Creek dock.

"What are you thinkin', Dad?" JB said, sitting just behind him. "You gonna turn yourself in to Sheriff Parsons right away?"

Bo glanced back at his son and smiled.

"Something tells me I won't have to go lookin' for him. He and the feds will be at the dock, lookin' for me."

"You sure you want to do this?" JB said, the worry on his face evident. "We still have time to just disappear. Hell, nobody would find us up in the hollers."

Bo had thought about that all night, about just getting lost in the Kentucky hills with his wife and son. But he still had his daughter and granddaughter back in Crockett and his brother, who was fighting his battles for him. He knew he wouldn't last a week with those thoughts running through his head.

"Can't do it, son. Besides, I'm the only witness to two murders and the death of the killer—besides Frankie, who may be dead by now."

"If he's dead, then the killers will be lookin' for you next," JB said.

Bo stared straight ahead, thinking about what might lie ahead of them.

"Sometimes a man has to do what he has to do, son. Just ain't no gettin' around it." He looked up at his son. "I've never been a quitter, and I don't plan to start now."

"Well, I'm gettin' the twelve-gauge and the .30-06 ready, just in case," JB said.

Bo felt a shiver up his spine when he heard his son talk about the guns. He was putting his family in danger, and this gave him pause. *What am I doing?*

The two dogs, Garth and Brooks, sidled up to Bo, waiting for a pat on the head. Garth nudged Bo's hand, waiting for a rub. Bo looked down at the brownish-gray Weimaraner and smiled.

"I'm countin' on you and Brooks to let us know if anyone's around," Bo said, patting Garth on the head. "I need all the help I can get, old buddy."

Bo heard the familiar sound of a bolt action as JB got the guns ready. He glanced back at his son, who was looking down the barrel of the Remington 700 .30-06. Bo shut his eyes for a second, wondering how this day would end.

The green houseboat slowly plowed through the swift river channel in the widest part of the lake and crossed back into Kentucky. Bo heard a distant clap of thunder, causing him to look to the east.

"Looks like a storm's comin'," he said, realizing the dual meaning of his statement.

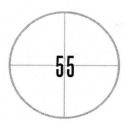

55

"Put your hands out front where I can see 'em, big man," Slammer said, pointing the rifle at Jake.

Jake gripped the Glock tighter, wondering if he could put the two hillbillies down before they could get a shot off. He glanced over at Ethan and saw the fear in his eyes. He relaxed his grip. He slid his right hand off the weapon and put it out in front of him, palm down.

"Smart move," Slammer said, waving the gun toward the three men. "Now all of you, off the boat."

Jake helped Frankie as they slowly walked to the end of the pontoon boat, jumping onto the shore, Ethan right behind. *Sorry, Ethan. Not sure how we're going to get out of this one.*

Slammer took two steps toward them.

"Stand over there next to the tree."

Jake helped Frankie as the three men slowly walked to the fallen tree. Slammer pointed the rifle at Jake.

"Reach behind you, big man, and take out the pistol and throw it in the water. Two fingers. Slowly."

Jake stared at Slammer. *Shit.*

"Now, you red-haired bastard!" Slammer raised the rifle and aimed it at Jake's head.

Jake slowly reached behind him and took the Glock out of his belt, holding it up with two fingers so Slammer could see it.

"Out in the lake," Slammer said.

Jake tossed the gun into the lake and watched it sink.

"Any other weapons on you or the brother?" Slammer said, glancing at Ethan.

"I don't have anything on me," Ethan said, turning around and picking his shirt up so they could see his belt. He glanced at Jake, nodding toward the pontoon boat.

Jake stared at Ethan and then remembered the second Glock that he had left under the tarp on the pontoon boat. *Good man, Ethan.*

"Okay, mob guy, get your ass over here, now."

Frankie took a tentative step forward and stumbled, falling face first into the sand. A moan escaped from his bloody lips. Ethan reached out and helped him up. Frankie's face was smeared with blood and sand.

"You okay, Frankie?" Ethan said.

Frankie stared at him, wiping his mouth with his sleeve, his hands still handcuffed together.

"I told you I was a dead man," he said to Ethan.

Ronnie Bass grabbed him and forced him to his knees.

"What now, Slammer," Jake said. "You gonna kill him and then us? Are you a killer now?"

Slammer laughed, tilting his head back.

"Hell no, I ain't no killer. But we got a couple of bad sons-of-bitches on the way that can do the job."

Jake glanced out at the mouth of the cove, watching for another boat.

"How do they know where to find us?" Jake said.

Slammer reached behind him and pulled out a walkie-talkie.

"They should be in range right about now."

"How much they pay you, Slammer?" Jake said, staring at the radio.

"Enough to retire on and get the hell off this damn lake," Slammer said.

"How about you, Ronnie? They payin' you, too?"

"Hell, yeah. I'm finally gonna get outta this sinkhole and do some real livin'," he said.

"What makes you think they won't kill you, too?" Jake said. "The mob doesn't leave anyone alive that can be a witness. Don't you know that?"

Ronnie glanced nervously at Slammer, waiting for him to answer. Slammer frowned at Ronnie.

"He's just jabberin'. Nothing to it. Keep your mind on what you're gettin' paid to do."

"You didn't get the name 'Slammer' because of a basketball game, did you?" Jake said, staring at Slammer. "You were in the joint, maybe made some mob contacts. That right, big man?"

Slammer smiled.

"You're a pretty smart fella, for a PI. Yeah, I was in the slammer, long time ago."

"What'd you do?" Jake said, trying to keep the conversation going and Slammer's fingers off the walkie-talkie.

"Well, since you won't be around to repeat it, I shaved points for the mob back in my college days, 'bout twenty-some years ago."

Ethan stared at the silver-haired man.

"You play for Boston College?"

Slammer's smile faded.

"How'd you know that?"

"I read it on the internet. Big points-shaving scandal back in the late seventies."

"Huh, two smart guys. Yeah, I was into the mob for a bundle, so they had me by the balls. Thought I was through with them until I got a call a few days ago tellin' me they needed my help."

"Who called you?" Jake said, watching the walkie-talkie. *Keep talking, you hillbilly.*

"Shit, I don't know. Some goon from Chicago. Told me they needed me to get a couple boats, load 'em up with stuff, and have 'em ready. That's all."

"Looks like you're a long way from just getting a couple of boats, Slammer. You're pointing a gun at innocent civilians. How much they say they'd pay you?" Jake said.

"Enough talk. Shut the hell up." Slammer looked at the radio and pressed the "talk" button.

"Anyone hear this?" he said, taking his hand off the talk button.

"Yeah, where are you?" The scratchy voice said.

Slammer stared at Jake and then at Ethan.

"Right side of the lake, just before the state line. Big rock with a red 'X' painted on it. Take a right into the cove just after the rock."

"Okay, should be there in a few minutes. You got 'em?"

"Yeah, we got 'em. The target plus two civilians."

"Good. Out."

Slammer put the walkie-talkie into his back pocket.

"Sorry about the two of you," he said, looking at Jake and Ethan. "Collateral damage, as they say."

Frankie was kneeling on the small beach, mumbling to himself. Suddenly, he stopped shaking, glanced at Ethan, stood up, and whipped his arms around, hitting Ronnie Bass square in the face, the hillbilly's rifle dropping harmlessly to the ground. Frankie screamed as he ran into the bushes.

"What the . . . ?" Slammer stammered, pointing his weapon at Frankie.

Jake quickly bolted, running and jumping onto the pontoon boat, pulling himself up in one swift motion. He ducked down just as he heard the blast from Slammer's rifle. He crawled across the bottom of the pontoon boat toward the tarp. He heard yelling on the shore, and another shot rang out, but not in his direction. Jake listened for a cry, but none came. He reached under the tarp and felt for the Glock. He felt something metal and grabbed it.

"Hey, big man, get your ass down here!" he heard Slammer yell, the voice close.

Jake rolled onto his back just as Slammer jumped up onto the pontoon boat and raised his rifle at Jake. Jake rolled over onto his back, pointed, and fired, all in one motion, hitting the big man in the chest. Slammer fell backward off the boat, the rifle flying into the air. His body hit the beach with a thud.

Jake scrambled up and ran to the end of the boat, his gun pointed at the beach. He saw Ronnie Bass running through the bushes after Frankie, a rifle in his hands. With both hands, Jake pointed the Glock at the bearded man and fired. He heard a scream and watched the man fall face first into the brush. A second later, he saw Frankie fall forward. *What the hell just happened?*

Jake looked down at the beach next to the pontoon boat and saw Slammer lying motionless, blood covering his chest. Jake jumped down and glanced over at Ethan, who was lying on his back.

"Ethan, you get hit?" Jake yelled.

Ethan raised himself up on his elbows and looked at Jake.

"No, but hit my head pretty good on this damn tree when I fell backward. I'm okay. He just missed me."

Jake turned and looked up at the bushes. Seeing no movement, he reached down and felt Slammer's neck for a heartbeat. He was dead. He grabbed Slammer's rifle and jumped into the blue bass boat, laying the rifle on the bottom of the boat, under a tarp.

"We gotta get outta here, before the goons arrive," Jake said. "You know how to drive one of these things?"

Ethan got up slowly, feeling the back of his head for blood.

"Yeah, I can drive it. What about Frankie?"

"I think he's dead, but I'll go look for him," Jake said. "Get this thing ready."

Ethan started up the outboard motor as Jake jumped off the boat and ran toward the brush. Suddenly, he heard a scream and saw Frankie running up the hill.

"Frankie!" Jake yelled, running through the thick brush.

Jake ran through the bushes toward Frankie, who was about twenty feet away, but stumbled over something and fell forward. He put his hands out in front of him, breaking his fall, but the Glock fell into the bushes. Looking down he saw Ronnie Bass, lying face down, motionless, blood covering his back. He felt his neck for a pulse and noticed two red marks. *Jesus, something bit him good.*

Jake glanced around in the bushes for the Glock but stood up quickly when he heard the sound of another boat at the mouth of the cove. Peering through the trees, he saw two men in a fishing boat entering the cove— one with short-cropped silver hair, the other one taking up half the boat. *Goldberg and Rhino!*

"Ethan, get out of the boat and run up here—fast! And grab the rifle."

Jake watched the approaching boat as Ethan stumbled out of the blue boat and ran up the beach into the bushes toward Jake, without the rifle. Jake bent down and grabbed Ronnie Bass's rifle a few feet away. Ethan ran up next to him, panting.

Jake peered out into the cove and saw the two mob enforcers coming toward them through the water, now only fifty yards away.

"C'mon," Jake said, "we have to get lost, fast."

The two men scrambled up the hill through thick brush. When they reached the top, they saw Frankie lying face up.

"I—I can't run," Frankie said breathlessly.

Jake picked him up and carried him, looking for a hiding place. They dropped down behind a stand of cottonwood trees.

Jake looked back at Copperhead Cove, where the two hit men were pulling up next to the blue bass boat.

"Holy crap, Jake," said Ethan, kneeling down next to Frankie, out of breath.

Jake stared down at the cove.

"Yeah, holy crap."

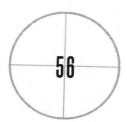

56

Julie Goldberg pulled the boat up alongside the blue bass boat, looking at the shore for any signs of life. He saw the big hillbilly immediately, lying on the sandy beach, not moving. He glanced inside the blue boat and noticed the outboard motor idling. His gaze turned to the bushes beyond the sandy beach.

"Shit, something went wrong here," he said, mostly to himself.

"Where are they?" Rhino said, looking in all directions. "I thought they—"

"Shut up," Goldberg said. "Load your weapon, and keep your eyes peeled on the shore."

"Fuck you, you Jew son-of-a-bitch. I'm tired of you telling me what to do."

Goldberg turned to Rhino and clenched his teeth.

"Listen, you hairy bastard. The two yahoos that were supposed to be watching our mark fucked up. One of them is lying over there, dead. You want to argue, or do you want to end up like him?"

Rhino looked to where Goldberg was pointing and saw the lifeless body. He turned his gaze to the shore, searching the trees and bushes for movement.

"Where the hell could they go?" he said.

"They're somewhere in those bushes, or in the lake beyond," Goldberg said. "And they're probably armed with this asshole's weapon." He glanced at the dead body and spit. "Friggin' hillbilly son-of-a-bitch."

The two men got out of the boat slowly, keeping their eyes on the thick brush, looking for any movement. They took a few steps onto the sandy beach and stopped.

"Where's the second guy?" said Rhino.

Goldberg walked cautiously up the small beach to the edge of the bushes, listening for any sound, watching for any movement.

"Check the pontoon boat, and keep your eyes and ears open," Goldberg said. "And cover me."

He stepped into the knee-high, green brush, watching every step. He saw the body of the bearded man and stopped cold. He held his right hand up, his hand balled into a fist—the sign to stop, look, and listen. He saw something glistening in the bushes a few feet from the dead body. Moving slowly, he started to bend down to pick up the Glock 9 mm but stopped when he heard the vibrating sound. He looked all around him at the brush, not knowing which way to go. He slowly stepped backward, retracing his steps, listening for the vibration. He heard something behind him, a rustling sound, something coming through the brush. He turned and saw Rhino trudging up the hill. Goldberg frantically waved him back, staring down at the brush around him, panic setting in.

Rhino reached his side, breathing heavily.

"They killed both of them hillbillies?"

Goldberg darted a look at the big man and shook his head.

"Go back, slowly!" He said it through gritted teeth.

"Why, what's . . . ? " Rhino stopped when he heard the sound. "Is that a . . . snake?"

Goldberg's eyes grew big when he looked down and saw the coiled snake three feet in front of them, shaking its tail. It was poised to strike if they came any closer.

"Back away, slow. Real slow," Goldberg whispered.

Rhino took one step backward and then turned and began running through the brush toward the beach.

"You friggin' asshole," Goldberg said as he turned and bolted after the big man, glancing backward with each step.

57

Jake and Ethan watched the two men from fifty feet away, hidden behind the cottonwoods. They saw the men stop, hearing the vibration of the snake's tail.

"It's a copperhead," Ethan whispered.

"How the hell do you know that?" Jake said, looking at Ethan.

"Bo told me what they look like and sound like. He got bit by one."

"No shit?" Jake said.

They watched the two men run back to the boats, Jake stifling a laugh.

"They're not so tough," he said.

Ethan wasn't smiling.

"Those damn snakes are everywhere. That's why Bo calls it Copperhead Cove."

Jake began checking the area around where they were kneeling.

"No shit?"

"It's the big, long, black ones you have to watch out for, though," Ethan said, glancing around in all directions. "That's what killed the first hit man that shot the coaches and tried to get Bo."

"What the hell is the big, black one?" Jake said, staring at Ethan.

"A cottonmouth. A mean son-of-a-bitch, and it packs a wallop."

They heard a moan come from Frankie, who was lying on the ground beside them. Ethan reached down and touched his forehead.

"He's burning up."

"He get shot?" Jake said.

Frankie opened his eyes and looked at Ethan.

"Snake."

Ethan backed away, again looking at the ground around them.

"What? Where?"

"Bit me when you shot the . . . . " Frankie's voice trailed off as he passed out again.

Ethan reached down and pulled Frankie's pant leg up. Two red marks were just above the ankle, blood slowly seeping from each mark.

Jake and Ethan looked at each other and then peered down at the small beach, seeing the two mob enforcers safely in their boat.

"Enemies all around us," Jake said. "We're in deep shit, old buddy."

Ethan forced a weak smile.

"No kidding . . . . Uh oh."

Jake glanced at Ethan.

"What?"

"Look."

Jake looked back down at the two men. Goldberg was in one of the boats, maneuvering it out of the cove. Rhino was on the pontoon boat, his rifle pointed at the brush, searching. Jake glanced behind him, seeing the lake only fifty feet away, with only a few cottonwoods and small brush to hide behind. They were completely exposed to anyone on the lake.

"Damn!" Jake said. "They're going to get us in a crossfire."

Ethan gave him a blank stare.

"The little guy is going to circle around behind us, putting us in between them. A crossfire."

Ethan glanced behind them at the shimmering lake.

"Now what?"

Jake glanced back at the cove, watching the big man scan the brush with his rifle. He looked to his right and saw a steep rock cropping, too steep to climb, and no way around. To the left was heavy brush, too thick to pass through, and probably full of the damn snakes.

"We've got to move somewhere, or they'll pick us off, one by one," Jake said.

They both jumped when they heard the first clap of thunder. The flash of lightning followed a few seconds later.

"A storms coming," Ethan said. "Maybe that will save us."

"It sounds a long way off," said Jake, returning his gaze to the cove.

"They pass through in a hurry around here," Ethan said. "Let's hope it gets here before the little goon does."

58

Bo heard the thunder and looked toward the eastern sky again, which lit up when the lightning flashed.

"Looks like we're in for a good one," JB said, standing at the railing looking up at the sky. "Dark clouds are coming in fast."

"We've got to find a cove and ride it out," Bo said, smelling the moisture in the air already. The dogs began barking when the thunder clapped.

"Garth, Brooks, enough!" Bo said loudly. The two dogs stopped barking and slid down next to Bo's feet.

Kathy came out of the galley and looked up into the sky.

"Haven't had one of these in a while," she said, closing her eyes. "Cool air feels good."

Bo smiled, never missing a chance to look at her. She was life itself to him, and he would do anything to protect her.

"We're gonna dock somewhere and try to ride it out," Bo said, already guiding the big houseboat to the left side of the lake.

"Okay, Bo." Kathy bent down and gave him a peck on his unshaven cheek. "You need a shave."

Bo's smile faded as he thought about what he was about to do, and the tightness in his gut returned. *Sure wish I could talk to Ethan before we get to the dock. Be nice to know what we're facing.*

Another long clap of thunder, this time much closer.

"It's comin' in fast, Dad," JB said, waiting for the lightning to light up the sky. "Better find a place soon."

Bo opened the throttle wide while searching the shore for a safe haven. "If nothing else, we can make Copperhead Cove and ride it out," Bo said. JB looked at his Dad like he was crazy.

"Stay away from the cove, Dad."

59

Jake checked the detachable clip of the bolt-action rifle, the only weapon they had now, and saw one cartridge. He turned to Ethan just as the second thunder clap shook the sky.

"Damn, it's coming in fast," Ethan said, looking skyward, waiting for the flash of light.

"We have one bullet left," Jake said, peering down at the big man on the pontoon boat. "Our only hope is to drop him and get to that boat. It may give us a fighting chance."

Ethan shifted his gaze to the cove again.

"Think you can do it?"

Jake shrugged his shoulders, stood up, and leaned against a cottonwood for balance. He positioned the rifle on a small limb and began to sight his target through the scope. *Thank God they had a scope on this thing.* He saw the big man scanning the bushes from right to left. *I have to drop him before he sees me.*

"You see the other boat, Ethan?" Jake said, keeping his eyes on the big man in the cove.

Ethan looked at the mouth of the cove.

"Yeah, he's just about through the mouth, so we don't have much—"

Ethan heard the explosion of the rifle.

"What the . . .? Did you get him?"

Jake continued to look through the scope.

"Yeah, but it didn't drop him. Got him in the left shoulder. Shit."

"Now what?" Ethan said.

"He dropped his rifle in the water, so we rush him," Jake said. "Let's go."

"What about Frankie . . . ?"

"We'll come back for him. We gotta go now—fast!" Jake started running down the slope through the brush, hoping he didn't step on any snakes.

Ethan followed him, dodging the snapping limbs and brush as Jake rumbled through the heavy bushes. They reached the small beach just as the big man was climbing off the pontoon boat, leaning down to grab the rifle from the beach.

Jake ran directly at him and tackled him in full flight, sending both men into the green water. Blood was seeping out of the big man's shoulder when he hit the water. When they surfaced, standing in knee-deep water, they were holding each other, trying to get each other's arms pinned.

Ethan got to the shore, picked up Jake's rifle and stepped back, pointing it at the two men.

Jake head-butted Rhino in the nose, hoping that would make him loosen his grip. The man had Jake in a vice grip around his waist, pinning Jake's arms to his sides. Jake head-butted him again, sending blood, his own and the big man's, flying in all directions.

The big man loosened his grip slightly, but enough for Jake to slip his right arm free and punch the man's bleeding shoulder. This made the man wince and break his hold. Jake backed away and took a deep breath, then threw himself at him, landing a left and right jab on the man's face.

Rhino stepped back, holding his nose, which was spewing bright-red blood. Jake stopped and coughed up water, and just as he did, the big man body slammed him back into the water. The two men were underwater for several seconds before they emerged. Rhino took a big gulp of air, which gave Jake the opportunity he needed. A right uppercut to the jaw sent the big man flying backward, submerging him again.

"Jake, step aside!" Ethan yelled, the rifle pointed at the spot where the big man went underwater.

Jake took a step to his right and bent down as the big man lunged out of the water. He heard the click from the rifle. *I told you it was empty, Ethan!*

Rhino slammed into Jake with tremendous force, sending Jake backward onto the sandy beach. Jake tried to catch his breath as he saw the big man standing over him, ready to land the final blow. Out of the corner of his eye,

Jake saw Ethan run to the pontoon boat and reach for the rifle Rhino had dropped. Jake moved his head to the right just before the big man slammed his huge, hairy fist into him. It glanced off Jake's head and hit the sand. Jake rolled to his right and tried to stand up, but Rhino grabbed him from behind in a bear hug, pinning Jake's arms to his side again.

This time Jake was out of breath and couldn't break the hold. He felt the air leaving his lungs as the big man squeezed harder. Suddenly, Jake heard a rifle shot and felt Rhino's grip loosen. Jake grabbed the man's fingers and pried them apart, turning around, ready to slam him with a right cross. He blinked as Rhino stumbled toward the lake, finally falling face-first into the green water. Jake looked up and saw Ethan holding the big man's rifle, terror in his eyes.

"I think you did it," Jake said. "Nice shot, Ethan."

Ethan was shaking as he stared at the man in the water. He dropped to his knees, dropping the rifle.

Jake picked up the rifle and patted his friend on the shoulder.

"No time to worry about it. We gotta get out of here before the other goon comes back."

Jake picked Ethan up under the armpits and halfway carried him to the blue bass boat that was still idling. He helped Ethan into the boat and climbed in after him, scanning the mouth of the cove for any sign of the silver-haired man.

"You got to get us out of here, Ethan—now!"

Ethan nodded his head, ready to put it in gear.

"Untie us."

Jake climbed out of the boat and fumbled with the knot on the small tree. He finally got it loose when he heard the sound of a speeding boat. He looked up and saw Goldberg heading through the mouth of the cove.

"Shit!" Jake said. "We'll be sitting ducks for him out on the cove."

Ethan looked at the pontoon boat and then noticed the fallen trees on the other side and remembered what Bo had told him, about swimming under the trees to hide from the killers.

"Jake, we need to get under those trees in the water," Ethan said, scrambling out of the boat. "He won't be able to find us."

A loud clap of thunder drowned out Jake's response. It felt like it was right on top of them. Jake felt the first raindrops, then the rain began coming down in buckets.

Ethan was on the shore, climbing over the big tree that hung out over the lake—the same one that Bo had slid under the day he was shot. He turned and looked at Jake.

"Come on, Jake!"

Jake stopped, checked the chamber in the rifle, and saw that it was empty. He threw it on the beach and suddenly remembered the rifle that he hid under the tarp in the blue bass boat. Turning around, he saw the boat drifting out into the cove, at least twenty feet from the shore.

"Jake, come on, before he gets back," Ethan yelled.

Jake hesitated, trying to decide whether to make the swim to the blue boat. Not enough time. He glanced up the hill where he had dropped his Glock. Too far. Looking all around the war zone that was the beach, his heart sank. *All these weapons, either waterlogged or empty—none of them worth a damn.* He climbed over the tree.

"Get in the water, Ethan."

Ethan slid into the murky, green water next to the fallen trees and swam out ten feet, waiting for Jake, who was right behind him. They both looked out and saw the boat turning in to the cove.

"Let's go," Ethan said as he took a big breath and dove beneath the fallen trees.

Jake inhaled as much air as he could and sank beneath the water, following Ethan around the trees. The water was dark and murky, made even murkier by the rain disturbing the surface. They swam underwater until they reached the other side of the trees and then slowly surfaced, only far enough to take a breath and look around. They heard the muffled sound of an outboard on the other side of the pontoon boat. The downpour muffled all sounds, making it difficult to hear anything.

"I think he's on the beach," Jake whispered to Ethan. "He can't see us over here—can he?"

Ethan, standing on a tree limb under the water, tried to look through the fallen trees and brush and rain, but everything was a blur.

"I don't think so."

The rain came down even harder, and another loud thunder clap was deafening. Jake and Ethan kept their eyes just above the water line, staring at the area around the pontoon boat, every now and then taking another breath of air. The rain was creating a mist on the water, which made it even more difficult to see anything. They stood on the underwater branch, their heads halfway out of the water, and waited.

"What's that?" Jake said.

"What?"

"That noise, from the cove mouth. It sounds like another boat."

Ethan turned his head to look toward the mouth of the cove and saw a large, dark object moving slowly through the mist and the rain.

"It's big. Maybe a houseboat trying to get off the lake," Ethan said. "I can't tell."

Jake grabbed Ethan's arm.

"There he is."

Ethan turned back, peered through the mist, and saw Goldberg standing in front of the pontoon boat, a rifle in his hands. It was difficult to make him out, just a shadow through the mist and rain, but he was moving in their direction.

The sound of the houseboat got closer, and as it did the man on the shore stopped.

"Someone picked the wrong damn cove to park in," Jake said.

Ethan suddenly squinted, staring at the top of the hill in the bushes. He wiped his eyes and peered through the mist.

"Oh, shit. Look."

Jake followed Ethan's eyes to the top of the hill. After wiping his eyes, he saw someone standing on top of the hill, leaning against a tree.

Ethan turned and looked at Jake.

"Frankie."

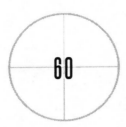

60

Goldberg first heard, then saw the houseboat through the rain and mist and stepped slowly back to the pontoon boat, keeping his eyes on the brush for any movement. He heard a sound behind him, in the water. He turned and pointed his rifle toward the sound. He looked down at the lifeless body of the big hillbilly, kicking him to make sure he was dead. Then he heard the sound again, coming from the other side of the pontoon boat. He inched forward, the rifle cocked and ready.

"Who's there?" Goldberg said, ready to blast whoever or whatever it was if he didn't answer.

"It's me, asshole."

Goldberg recognized Rhino's voice and lowered the gun. He slowly walked through the downpour toward the voice and was shocked to see Rhino lying on the beach, breathing heavily.

"Damn, I thought you were dead," Goldberg said.

"Help me up, asshole."

Goldberg reached down and helped the big man to his feet. He saw the blood seeping through his shirt in two spots—his left shoulder and upper back. Rhino was wheezing, trying to catch his breath.

"Damn, you got hit twice, and you're still standing?"

"Second one hit a rib. I think it's broke," Rhino said in obvious pain.

Goldberg helped him lean against the pontoon boat. Rhino was having trouble breathing.

"We've got company," Goldberg said. "You able to operate?"

"Give me a weapon."

Goldberg stepped back and stared at the wounded man.

"Don't know if you can help me. You look pretty fucked up."

"I'll be okay. Give me a weapon."

Goldberg reached into the fishing boat and picked up his 12 gauge shotgun, grabbing a wet box of shells at the same time. Handing them to Rhino, he said, "We got a boat coming into the cove. Not sure who or what they are. Stay here, and keep your eyes and ears open."

Rhino nodded, wiping his eyes and face with his wet shirt sleeve.

"You know where they went?"

"Who?"

"The assholes who did this to me, you friggin' . . . . "

"No, but they couldn't go far without a boat. They're here somewhere."

They both heard the houseboat approaching and crouched down behind the pontoon. The big, lumbering boat stopped about fifty feet from the beach, idling in the middle of the cove. Goldberg peered through the rain at the large boat, looking for any movement. He saw nothing.

"Who the hell is that?" he said out loud.

"Probably . . . probably just somebody trying to get out of the storm," Rhino said, his breath coming in gasps.

"Keep an eye on them while I look for those two yahoos," Goldberg said. "They have to be close by. Keep your damn head up and your eyes and ears open."

Rhino nodded, holding his chest, taking short, shallow breaths.

"Be careful of the big redhead. He's a tough son-of-a-bitch."

Goldberg slowly started walking toward the brush, wiping the rain out of his eyes and glancing down at the ground, listening for any vibration sound. *Damn, Tonelli, you're gonna pay big for this shit.*

61

JB held the binoculars steady, peering through the rain and mist at the shoreline. Bo was at the wheel of the idling houseboat.

"What do you see?" Bo said.

"A blue bass boat is floating about twenty feet from the shore, and another fishing boat and a pontoon are tied up on the beach."

"See any people around?"

"I see some movement around the pontoon, but it's hard to make out through this rain and mist," JB said.

Bo stood up and peered at the shore, but the heavy rain made it impossible to make anything out.

"We're okay here until the storm passes, no need to go in to shore."

"Wait. Dad, the man has a rifle or shotgun," JB said, the binoculars pointing at the shore. "He's looking out at us, I think."

A cold chill ran down Bo's back as he remembered just two days earlier. He put the houseboat in gear and began turning it around.

"Where you goin'?" JB said.

"We ain't stayin' here," Bo replied. "Storm or no storm."

The houseboat began moving slowly back toward the mouth of the cove, Bo glancing back at the shore every few seconds.

"Dad! Wait!" JB shouted.

Bo put the engine in idle.

"What?"

"I think someone's waving at us." JB kept the binoculars steady on the shoreline. "From the water."

Bo froze. *From the water? Why . . . ?*

"Oh shit," JB said, waving to his dad to join him.

Bo walked quickly across the deck and stood next to his son.

"What is it, JB?"

"There's another man on shore, walking toward the two guys waving at us."

Bo grabbed the binoculars and peered through the mist and rain. What he saw almost knocked him off his feet. Two men in the water next to the fallen trees, submerged up to their necks, exactly where he had been two days earlier, staring out at them, waving their arms frantically. A big man with a rifle was walking through the brush directly toward them. Bo froze when he recognized one of the men. *Ethan!*

"JB, get your .30-06, now," Bo said.

Bo kept the binoculars on the scene on shore. *Quit waving, you idiots!*

JB stood next to him, the rifle butt on his shoulder. He closed his left eye and looked through the scope.

"What do you see?" Bo said. "I think it's Ethan out there."

"Damn rain," JB said, wiping the end of the scope with his sleeve. He looked through the scope again.

"The two men stopped waving. They're going underwater."

"What about the man with the gun?" Bo said, his heart beating out of his chest.

JB kept the scope trained on the man on shore, who was now ten feet or less from the shoreline where the two men had been.

"He's standing still, looking down at the water next to the fallen trees."

Bo blinked his eyes, rubbing the moisture away.

"Dad, get down," JB said suddenly.

"Why?"

"The other guy on the pontoon boat has his rifle pointed at us."

62

Jake clung to a small, underwater branch, holding his breath until he couldn't hold it anymore. He slowly rose to the surface and poked his head out of the water, taking in a deep breath. He was in the middle of the fallen trees, about ten feet from shore. He couldn't see the man on shore because of all the debris. He felt a hand on his shoulder and heard Ethan break the surface.

After taking a deep gulp of air, Ethan whispered, "Where is he?"

"I don't know," Jake said, "I can't see through these trees."

"That means he can't see us either, then," Ethan said, panting heavily.

"But he might be able to hear us," Jake said, putting his finger to his lips.

Jake turned slowly and looked out at the middle of the cove. The houseboat was still idling, a dark shadow through the heavy rain and mist. *I wonder if they saw us waving? Who are they, and why don't they get the hell out of here?*

Ethan poked Jake in the shoulder.

"There he is."

Jake turned back around and saw Goldberg with the rifle. He had moved closer to the shoreline and was looking right, then left, searching the shoreline for them.

"It's just a matter of time before he figures we're in this clump of trees," Jake said softly.

Jake felt Ethan shaking, either from the cold or from fear. He was starting to create waves on the surface.

"Ethan, you gotta stop shaking. He'll see us."

"I . . . I can't, I'm cold. I n–need to get out of this water," Ethan said, his teeth beginning to chatter.

Jake looked back at the man on shore. He was looking in their direction, pointing the gun toward them.

"We need to go under and swim to the other side of the trees. Let's go," Jake said, waiting for Ethan to submerge.

"I don't think I can do it," Ethan said. "I can't catch my breath."

"You have to, Ethan, or we're dead men." Jake saw sudden terror in Ethan's eyes and turned around to see the man only a few feet away, bending over to peer through the fallen trees. *Damn, it's too late, he's seen us.*

"Get your ass out of the water," Goldberg said, "or I'll blast you where you are."

Jake looked at Ethan as they both took a last big breath and slowly sunk beneath the surface. Jake heard the muffled sound of a rifle shot, then saw the bullet fly past him in the water, a trail of bubbles in its wake. Another shot, another bullet. This one closer. They swam underwater, past the last fallen tree, and out into the lake. Jake grabbed Ethan's arm and dragged him toward a large object. He reached out and grabbed hold of something on the large object, pulling himself and Ethan above the surface of the green water.

Jake took several gulps of air before looking around. He heard Ethan gasping for air next to him. Jake blinked his eyes and finally was able to focus. They were holding onto the end of the pontoon boat. He looked left and then right but didn't see any movement. Out of the corner of his eye he spotted something blue floating about ten yards away. *The blue bass boat! The rifle!*

Ethan was breathing hard and was shivering, causing the water to ripple. Suddenly, they heard a voice above them on the pontoon boat.

"Game's over," the deep, gravelly voice said. "Get out of the water, now."

Jake looked up and saw Rhino standing above them, his shotgun pointed at their heads. *Damn, we shot him twice.*

"Ethan, get under the boat," Jake said, gently pushing his friend under the pontoon boat.

"Where are you going?" Ethan said, treading water.

"I'm going to swim out to the blue boat and get the rifle." His breathing was short and shallow.

Just then they heard a shot ring out. Both men ducked beneath the water. When they surfaced, they heard something directly above them. Jake glanced up and saw the big man slowly falling off the pontoon boat.

"Move!" Jake said, pushing Ethan further under the boat.

The splash was less than a foot from where Jake had been. He turned and watched the man sink below the surface. He heard footsteps on the pontoon boat. It had to be Goldberg. As they treaded water underneath the pontoon boat, Jake stared out through the green water and suddenly jerked his head back, hitting it against the bottom of the boat. Floating in front of him, eyes and mouth wide open, was the lifeless face of Rhino.

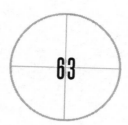

63

Bo squinted as he stared through the scope at the shore and watched the big man fall from the pontoon boat into the green water.

"I got him, JB," he said.

JB trained the binoculars on the other man, who was now on the pontoon boat. Turning the binoculars back to where the big man had splashed into the water, he saw two heads bobbing in the water underneath the boat between the pontoons. *Ethan's alive!*

"It's Ethan," JB said, keeping the binoculars trained on the two men underneath the boat. "And another man. Probably his friend."

Bo peered through the rifle scope, trying to zoom in on the two men in the water, and caught a movement from the other man on the pontoon boat.

"JB, get down!" Bo said, grabbing his son's arm and pulling him down.

The bullet grazed the wooden railing of the houseboat, just inches from JB's head, sending splinters flying through the air. Bo and JB hid behind the solid wood railing, staring at each other.

"Kathy!" Bo screamed. "Get on the floor, and don't come out!"

"That was close," JB said, breathing heavily.

Bo took a deep breath and raised his head as another shot rang out. This one bore through the side of the railing, sending splinters everywhere.

"Ahhh," JB screamed, dropping the binoculars and grabbing his shoulder.

Bo glanced at JB, then stuck his head up long enough to see the man on the pontoon boat, who was peering over the side, looking down at the water below him. He raised the binoculars and searched the water for Ethan and his friend. When he trained them back on the man on the pontoon boat, the gun was pointed directly at him. He ducked down just as a third shot whistled past his ear, slamming into the wall of the houseboat.

"Kathy, are you okay?" Bo yelled, frantic.

"Yes," he heard his wife scream. "I'm okay. Garth and Brooks are with me."

"Stay inside, and keep down!" Bo yelled, glancing over at JB. "JB, you okay?"

JB was holding his right shoulder, sitting with his legs spread out in front of him. Blood was oozing out between his fingers.

"He didn't get the bone, just flesh," JB said. "I think I'm okay."

Bo scrambled across the deck of the houseboat, keeping his head as low as possible, and grabbed a towel. He handed it to JB.

"Wrap this around the wound, and keep pressure on it," Bo said, grabbing the rifle. "Lie down on the deck. Make less of a target."

"Dad, stay down," JB said, grunting in pain.

Bo took another deep breath and slowly raised his head enough to look through the rain at the shore. The man was not on the pontoon boat, so Bo raised the binoculars and scanned the shoreline. He froze when he saw the silver-haired man standing next to the pontoon boat, peering underneath the pontoons. Bo dropped the binoculars and picked up the rifle, lining up the sight.

"Damn rain," he said, wiping the lens of the scope with his shirt.

Suddenly another shot rang out from the shore. He put the scope back to his right eye and trained it on where he had seen the silver-haired man, but he was gone. He scanned the area through the scope.

"Ethan!" he yelled, scanning the water for any movement, knowing his brother couldn't hear him through the downpour.

"Dad, get down, he'll—" JB's voice was drowned out by another shot.

Bo instinctively ducked down below the railing, waiting for the thud of the bullet, but none came. He quickly stood up and put the .30-06 back to his shoulder and peered through the scope. The sight on the shore made him freeze. The silver-haired man was holding onto the side of the pontoon boat, clutching at his throat. Then Bo saw movement in the brush on the hill behind the beach. He squinted, trying to make out what or who it was. The image slowly came into focus. It was Frankie, holding a pistol.

Bo trained the sight on the pontoon boat again and saw the silver-haired man slipping into the water, still clutching at his throat. Within a few seconds the man slipped beneath the surface of the water.

"I think the guy's dead, JB," Bo said, looking at the hillside for Frankie, but he was gone.

JB grunted through his pain and shook his head.

"I'm taking us in," Bo said, scrambling to the head of the boat and climbing into the captain's seat.

The houseboat churned slowly toward the shoreline, pulling up onto the sand next to the other boats. Bo cut the engine and walked quickly back to JB, who was trying to stand up.

"Can you hold the .30-06?" Bo said, looking into his son's eyes.

JB nodded and grabbed the gun.

"I'm going on shore, so keep the gun pointed at the pontoon boat."

"Okay, Dad," JB said. "Be careful."

Kathy came out of the cabin carrying a medical first aid kit.

"Let me see your arm," she said to JB. "And you be careful!" she said sternly to Bo.

Bo smiled at her as he walked quickly to the front of the houseboat, climbing over the railing and jumping to the sand below. He quickly tied the rope from the houseboat to a small sapling, glancing toward the pontoon boat.

"Ethan?" he yelled, searching for his brother. "Ethan!"

Bo heard a moan and water splashing. He ran to the pontoon boat and saw Ethan standing in waist-high water, shivering, but smiling. A big redheaded man was standing next to him, holding Ethan up. They both stared at Bo as though he were a ghost.

"B-B-Bo," Ethan said, teeth chattering. "G-g-good to see y-y-you."

Bo grinned broadly as he walked into the water, grabbing Ethan by the arm.

"Good to see you, little brother." Bo glanced at the redhead. "You must be Jake."

"T-that I am," Jake said. "A-a-and you must be B-B-Bo."

They each took an arm and walked Ethan toward the shore. They stopped when they saw the lifeless body of the silver-haired man lying face down in the green, murky water. They continued to the shore and fell to the sand once they were out of the cold water. The rain had stopped, but the mist was still rising over the water.

"I'll get some blankets," Bo said, running back to the houseboat.

Bo stopped and looked back at his brother.

"Ethan, were you shot?"

Ethan glanced at Bo, his teeth chattering.

"No, b-b-but I'll sh-sh-shoot you if y-y-you don't g-g-get me a b-b-blanket!"

Bo grinned as only Bo could. He came back with two wool blankets and draped them over the two men's shoulders, rubbing his brother's arms to get the circulation back.

"Y-you got any c-c-coffee on that thing?" Jake said, pointing to the houseboat, his teeth not chattering quite as much as before.

"Mother's bringing some out now," Bo said, still grinning like the Cheshire cat.

"Mother?" Jake said, eyebrows rising.

"He m-m-means Kathy," Ethan said, smiling weakly. "H-his wife."

The three men watched as Kathy walked through the sand with two coffee mugs in her hand.

"H-hi, Kath," Ethan said, reaching up for the steaming brew.

Jake grabbed the other mug, smiling at the attractive, redheaded woman.

"Ethan, you look like one of Bo's dogs after he's gone into the lake after a critter," Kathy said, grinning.

"H-ha ha," Ethan said. "W-wish I could shake the water off like Garth does."

They all laughed just as Garth ran up and began licking Ethan's face.

"Bo, d-did you shoot the g-guy in the water?" Ethan said.

"I shot the big guy on the pontoon boat, but we didn't get the other one." Bo glanced at the bushes. "It was Frankie."

Ethan's eyes widened.

"Frankie? Where is he?"

"Up there somewhere," Bo said, pointing at the brush. "I'm goin' up to look for him."

Suddenly they heard what sounded like an armada of boats entering the mouth of the cove. Bo stood up and peered over at the cove entrance, which was still covered in mist.

"Holy Mary, Mother of Jesus!" he said. "Here comes the cavalry."

Ethan and Jake stood up shakily and stared at the sight at the mouth of Copperhead Cove. At least five boats were entering the cove at a high speed, with a brown outboard with "Crockett County Sheriff" emblazoned on the side leading the small armada.

Ethan looked back at Bo.

"You r-ready for this, b-bro?"

Bo pursed his lips.

"Time to face the music, little brother."

The boats entered the cove and headed for the shoreline.

Kathy glanced down at the water's edge and saw two men lying face down in the water. She drew back with a shiver.

"Who are they?"

"They're the bad guys, and one more is floating somewhere near the bottom of the pontoon boat," Jake said, the chattering gone.

"Goodness gracious, it looks like a war went on here," Kathy said, shaking her head.

The boats pulled up onto the sandy shore one by one, led by the sheriff's brown boat. Bo saw Sheriff Parsons climb out of the boat, followed by Cheyenne Smith. They stood on the shore, staring at the strange mixture of people before them.

"Bo, that you?" Sheriff Parsons shouted.

"In the flesh," Bo said, the grin beginning to fade from his face.

When all five boats were safely on the sandy shore, a small army of men and women in dark-blue jackets climbed out and stood on the sandy beach.

"You bring enough backup, Cecil?" Bo yelled.

The army of FBI men and women began walking toward the motley group on the beach, with Sheriff Parsons and Deputy Smith leading the pack. Parsons stopped when he saw the two bodies floating in the water.

"Looks like you've been doin' some huntin' here, Bo," Parsons said.

Bo glanced at Ethan and Jake and then back at the sheriff.

"I think we were the hunted, Cecil, not them."

Bo saw a man in a blue jacket approach and stand next to Sheriff Parsons.

"Are you Bo Paxton?" he said.

Bo nodded.

"I am."

"You're under arrest for aiding and abetting, unlawful flight, harboring a criminal, and . . . shall I go on?"

Bo held his arms behind his back, waiting for the handcuffs to be slapped onto his wrists.

"Let's get this over with."

A tall, serious-looking man stepped forward and put handcuffs on Bo's wrists. Bo turned, smiled at Kathy, and nodded his head, indicating everything was all right.

"I'm Special Agent Whitman, and this is Special Agent Torres," the first blue jacket said. "We're with the FBI."

Bo nodded again.

"I noticed."

Special Agent Whitman glanced at the men in the water.

"And who are they?"

Sheriff Parsons smiled at Bo.

"I think those are the real bad guys, Agent Whitman."

Suddenly a muffled sound came from halfway up the bush-covered hill behind them. Twenty guns were quickly taken out of their holsters and pointed in the direction of the noise. Everyone's eyes were riveted on the brush. The sound, like something crawling, got closer.

"Two men go up there and find out what that is," Agent Whitman said, eyes squinting through the clearing mist.

"I'd be careful, agent," Bo said. "They don't call this Copperhead Cove for nothin'."

Agent Whitman stared at Bo.

"Snakes?"

Bo smiled and nodded.

"Too big for a snake, Bo," Sheriff Parsons said. "There somebody else up there we should know about?"

Jake and Ethan glanced at each other.

"Frankie," they said in unison.

"Frankie? Frankie Farmer?" Parsons said, eyes wide. "He's alive?"

Jake and Ethan shrugged their shoulders.

"He shot the guy over there floating near the shore," Bo said, shaking his head. "He's a tough little guy."

Whitman pointed to the brush and ordered two men to investigate. Turning to Sheriff Parsons, he said, "Frankie Farmer, the suspect you lost?"

Parsons shrugged.

"Yep. Looks like it."

The two, blue-jacketed FBI men went twenty yards up the hill, through the thick brush, and stopped, pointing their guns at something.

"What is it?" Whitman yelled.

"A dead man, lying face down," one of the FBI men yelled back. "And another man next to him, not moving, but looks like he's breathing. He has a gun in his hand. And his wrists are handcuffed."

Whitman looked at Bo and then Sheriff Parsons.

"How many dead men we got out here?"

"Four that we know of, but don't know about Frankie," Ethan said. "He was bit by a copperhead."

Suddenly, Jake stumbled forward, catching himself before he fell.

Bo looked at Jake and saw a bright red splotch on his aloha shirt, near his left shoulder.

"Jake, you get shot?"

Jake looked down at the blood, putting his hand up to feel it.

"Yeah, he nicked me," he said, looking at the blood on his hand as he fell to his knees. "But I think the gorilla broke my rib."

"Jake!" Ethan said, reaching for his friend.

Whitman looked at Jake and then at Bo.

"What the hell is this place, for Christ's sake?"

Bo continued to stare at Jake and Ethan.

"It's Copperhead Cove."

64

On Saturday morning, Anthony Tonelli was sitting at his desk in his sixty-second floor office on Michigan Avenue when he heard the commotion outside. He punched the button on the phone.

"Maria, what the hell is going on out there?" he said.

Suddenly, the door opened, and three men in dark suits walked in, holding badges.

"Anthony Tonelli?" one of them said.

"Who the hell are you?" Tonelli said, standing up.

"Special Agent Whitman of the FBI. Are you Anthony Tonelli?"

Tonelli's shoulders sagged.

"Yeah, I'm Tonelli."

"You're under arrest for murder, attempted murder, illegal gambling, fraud ... shall I go on?"

Tonelli stared at the man and raised his sagging shoulders in defiance.

"Fuck you."

The other two FBI agents handcuffed Tonelli as Maria walked in.

"Lots of people died because of you, Tonelli. Most of them your own goons," Whitman said.

Tonelli glared at the FBI agent.

"You win some, you lose some."

Whitman smiled.

"Looks like you lose this one, thanks to Frankie Farmer."

"What, I thought he was—"

"Dead?" Whitman said. "He killed two of your goons. He's a hero."

Tonelli stared at Whitman, his shoulders sagging again.

"I'll be damned."

Maria walked up to Tonelli.

"Mr. Tonelli?" she said, smacking her gum in his face.

"Maria, shove that damn gum up your damn ass," Tonelli said in a final act of irritation and arrogance.

Maria smiled.

"Mr. Tonelli, can I go home early?"

Special Agent Whitman chuckled as he led the mob boss out of the office. Tonelli tried to grab the black stapler on his desk, but it fell to the floor.

"I guess that's a yes," Maria said, smacking her gum one last time, a huge grin on her face.

Special Agent Whitman laughed as he led Tonelli out of the office.

"You can go home after we take your statement, Maria. He's not going to need you for a while."

65

"You make the best coffee in the county, Kathy," Sheriff Parsons said, wiping his lips on a paper napkin.

"Thank you, Sheriff," Kathy said, standing next to Bo, rubbing his shoulder.

They were sitting on Bo's deck, along with Deputy Cheyenne Smith, JB, Ethan, and Jake. It was nine o'clock Sunday morning, June ninth. Garth and Brooks were out running after rabbits, the ducks were on the pond, and life was good in the Paxton holler.

"Hey, Bo, it was a week ago today when I caught my smallmouth. Seems like months ago, doesn't it?" Ethan said, smiling at his brother.

"It was a nice size one, too, little brother, and good eatin'." Bo had a big grin on his face.

Jake poked Ethan in the ribs.

"I didn't know you were a fisherman."

"He's not, Jake. Just got lucky. The smallmouth thought it was my hook," Bo said, laughing.

Ethan threw a piece of toast at his brother.

"Little did we know we'd be back in Copperhead Cove so soon."

Everyone at the table grew quiet, remembering the last few days. Finally, Deputy Smith broke the silence.

"Bo, why'd you come back? You never told us," Cheyenne said. "You could have been lost forever out in those woods."

Bo looked at Cheyenne and then at Ethan.

"Guess I couldn't let my little brother fight my battles for me. And I couldn't get Frankie outta my head. He saved my life."

"And mine, and Jake's," Ethan said. "One tough little dude, surviving two copperhead bites."

"What's gonna happen to him, Cecil?" Bo said, turning to the sheriff.

Parsons took another swig of coffee and raised his mug so Kathy could fill it up.

"Well, he's an accomplice to murder, so he's got to face that. But the fact that he turned on Tonelli will work in his favor, as will saving your butt, Bo, and your brother's and Jake here. Not sure what turning on Tonelli is gonna do for his marriage, though."

Everyone laughed.

"How about witness protection?" Jake said.

"That's up to the feds," Parsons answered. "But he'll need protection, now that he squealed on his boss."

"The poor guy just wanted to fit in," Bo said. "He never wanted to hurt nobody, even them coaches."

"Speaking of the coaches, which one shaved points?" Jake said. "Or were both of them guilty?"

Ethan leaned forward.

"Sonny Daye was a good coach, a good man, from what I've read. He was just in the wrong place at the wrong time. The other one, Jerry Joe Williams, was the bad seed."

"Frankie said Williams cost the mob over a million bucks," Bo said. "Guess they don't take kindly to that kind of thing."

Everyone got quiet.

"You're a damn lucky man, Bo, you know that?" Parsons said.

"Why's that, Sheriff?"

"Those feds wanted to hang your hillbilly ass, but Deputy Smith and I talked 'em out of it. They was ready to haul your ass away."

"Bo was the victim. He didn't do anything," Ethan said.

"Nothin' except harbor a suspected murderer and then vanish the scene, like a scared little boy."

Bo's face turned red.

"Damn right I was scared, Cecil. Wouldn't you be if those goons were lookin' to kill you and your family?"

Parsons shook his head up and down, rubbing his beard.

"Yep, I probably woulda done the same thing, Bo. That's why we talked the feds outta haulin' you away. You're a good man, with a solid reputation around here. That's what we told 'em. And what you and your son did to help save Jake and Ethan here, that set well with those FBI boys." Parsons took a swig of coffee and put the cup down. "But it ain't over yet, though. You got a lot of explainin' to do, son."

Bo smiled weakly.

"Yeah, guess I do, Cecil."

Parsons rubbed his eyes.

"I got some explainin' to do myself, me and Cheyenne here. Like, why'd we let our suspect go with two civilians." He looked up at Cheyenne and smiled. "And why we didn't put someone out here at Bo's place to protect him and watch him. And why we didn't have police tape around the beach at Copperhead Cove."

Jake glanced at Ethan.

"I was wondering that myself, Sheriff, about the tape."

"Manpower and time, son. Not enough of neither," Parsons said. "Planned on puttin' the tape up on Saturday, but all this hell broke loose before we could get to it." He shook his head. "As for lettin' a murder suspect out of our jail and handin' him over to you two civilians," he said, looking at Jake and Ethan, "well, under the circumstances, it was a damn good move, and the feds agreed."

Cheyenne smiled at Jake, then Ethan.

"I'll second that."

"But I shoulda had someone out here lookin' after Bo," Parsons said. "That's on my head, and sure glad it turned out all right."

"Like you said, Sheriff, not enough manpower and not enough time. A small town sheriff can't be expected to do everything a big city PD can do," Jake said. "You did okay in my book."

Parsons smiled.

"Thank you, son." He cleared his throat and took another swig of coffee. "You know, this thing may not be over with the mob boys, much as I hate to say it. Those boys don't forget too easy. They lost three of their top enforcers down here, and the big boss, Tonelli, is goin' away for a long time. I dealt with them boys up in Chicago while on the PD up there, and they have memories like elephants. Y'all might want to sleep with one eye open for a spell."

"Hell, Sheriff, you think they want to mess with us hillbillies anymore?" JB said.

This got a roar from everyone. Garth and Brooks began barking, and the ducks flew off the pond once again.

"You got a point there, JB," Parsons said. "But I'd still be lookin' over my shoulder for a while."

"Point taken, Cecil," Bo said. "How about you? You gonna retire like everyone says?"

Parsons sat back and smiled.

"I got myself a damn good deputy here," he said, patting Cheyenne on the shoulder. "Probably time she took over Crockett County, if the voters know what's good for 'em."

"I'd vote for her," Jake said, smiling and wincing from the pain in his side. "She's a keeper."

"How's the broken rib doin'?" Bo said. "And the shoulder?"

"It's painful, not gonna lie," Jake said. "That big gorilla squeezed the hell out of me."

"When did you get shot, anyway," Parsons said.

"Right before Frankie nailed the silver-haired bastard, excuse my French. He got a shot off at me and Ethan."

"Jake took a bullet for me," Ethan said. "He jumped right in front of me, or I would've been a goner."

"Well, damn glad you were here, Jake. Ethan's got a good friend, and a tough one," Bo said.

Jake smiled, raising his coffee mug at Bo.

"It's not easy being your brother's friend."

Ethan glanced at Jake and then at Bo, a big smile creasing his face. He sat back, watching and listening to the banter. He'd been through two life-threatening events in the past couple of years and was ready for a breather. He began to think about Molly and Charlie, back in California. He missed them and wanted to go home. After a few minutes, he stood up and began walking toward the small pond.

"Where you goin' little brother?" Bo said.

Ethan turned around.

"You know me, Bo, I need some time to contemplate life, as my daughter would say. Plus, I have to get back for Molly's graduation on Thursday."

"You mean it's graduation week?" Jake said, laughing.

Ethan grinned, nodding his head.

"Plus, I have a wedding in three months."

Everyone clapped and offered congratulations.

Bo nodded his head.

"Yeah, you're the thinker in the family, but don't contemplate too long, little brother. We got a date with some bass this afternoon. Once more before you go home."

Ethan smiled.

"Sounds good. Where we headed, Bo?"

Bo grinned as only Bo could.

"Copperhead Cove, of course."

Everyone roared, "No!"

The ducks flew away for the rest of the afternoon.

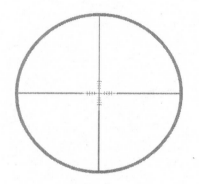

ACKNOWLEDGEMENTS

I want to express my gratitude to a few people for their support, knowledge, expertise, and encouragement in the writing of this novel. First and foremost is my older brother, Roger, who was the embodiment of Bo Paxton and provided the inspiration for the world of southern Kentucky that is the real hero in this novel. Roger and his family left California in 1980 and moved to Burkesville, Kentucky, building a home on eighty acres of wooded land in a holler near Dale Hollow Lake—from scratch. This story would not be possible or even considered were it not for Roger, Cassie, Juli, and Justin, and the life they lived in the hills and hollers of Kentucky. Next would be J.B. Hogan, who provided peer editorial support and encouragement throughout the writing of *Copperhead Cove*. Hogie, a prolific author of novels and short stories who lives in Fayetteville, Arkansas, gave me his undying support during those inevitable days and weeks of self-doubt. He is a true friend, as well as a fabulous editor and writer. My son and daughter, Jonathan and Kelli, who never failed to pump me up when I was low, who encouraged me when I wanted to quit, who loved me unconditionally when my younger brother died in my home—they are the reason I keep writing, keep creating stories, and keep on keeping on. Duke Pennell, who used "tough love" in the editing process, helping me to see my mistakes, and insisting that this be the very best story I could write. Also, I want to acknowledge my publishers, Duke and Kimberly Pennell, who gave a rookie writer a chance to be heard and provided the publishing support that helped make this novel a reality. And finally, thank you to the people of southern Kentucky who inspired this story, who live off the land, and live their lives simply, honestly, and happily.

ABOUT THE AUTHOR

After thirty years in the global logistics and high-tech industries, Ron Parham retired on his birthday in 2011 and immediately began penning his first novel, *Molly's Moon*, published in 2013. He hasn't looked back, and *Copperhead Cove* is his second thriller. His novels incorporate his many *unusual* experiences while traveling around the world on business. He writes in the seaside town of Carlsbad, CA.